VICE AND VERITY

The Valmenessian Chronicles
Book Three

Rebecca Camm

Find me at: www.rebeccacamm.com
Instagram: @readingwritingdaydreaming
TikTok: @readingwritingdaydream
Facebook: @readingwritingdaydreaming

Printed in Australia.

Paperback ISBN: 978-1-7635277-2-0

Special thanks and acknowledgements to:
Editor; Emily Morrison – emilymorrisoneditorial.com
Cover Design; Story Wrappers – storywrappers.com
Formatter; Rebecca Camm – rebeccacamm.com

This book is written in British English

THE VALMENESSIAN CHRONICLES

Alta: A Valmenessian Novella

Liars and Light

Rise and Reverence

Maker: A Valmenessian Novella

Vice and Verity

Content Notes
Vice and Verity is an adult fantasy novel. It contains cursing,
sexual references, violence, assault, and other adult themes.
A full list can be found on my website, rebeccacamm.com
or by scanning the QR code below.

For Zoe

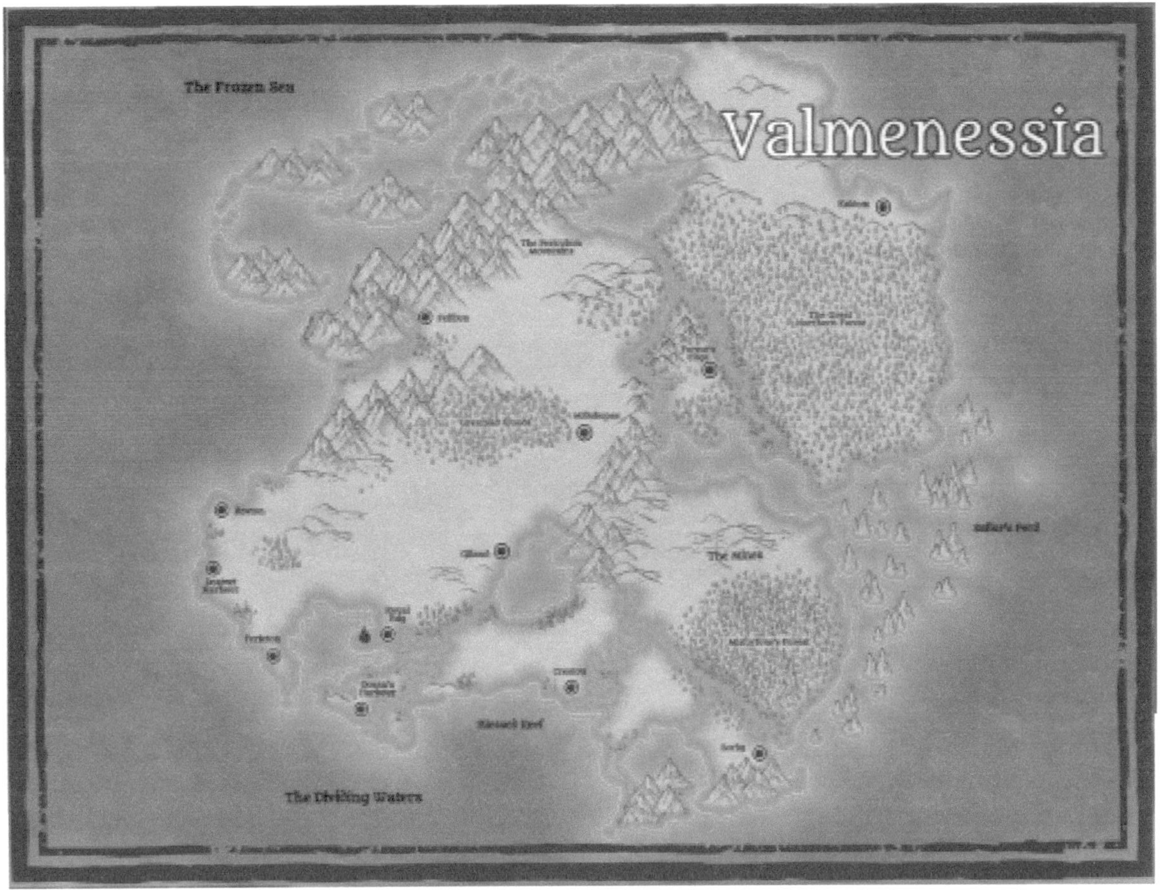

Valmenessia

The Frozen Sea

The Dividing Waters

PROLOGUE

Evelyn

12 Years Ago

The Forest's Edge Manor had so many spaces for Evelyn to tuck herself away, and being the smallest of the three children in the family, she had an advantage in the game of hide and seek. Jasmine was counting in the dining room, but Evelyn could no longer hear her after she'd fled as fast as her feet could carry her in search of a hiding place. Her cousin, Theodore, had shot her a mischievous grin before his departure, darting in the opposite direction on silent feet to find somewhere else to hide. Despite being a few years older than Jasmine, he would still play games with them, no matter if the games were for little kids or not. It was one of the reasons Evelyn loved her cousin so much; he always had time for her.

One day, Theodore would take over from his mother, Evelyn's aunt, as ruler of Forest's Edge, and Evelyn would be the lead Healer like her father before her. They would work together and take care of all those who lived in the tree-filled city.

Footsteps sounded outside the room Evelyn had hidden herself away in. She pulled her knees to her chest, making herself as small as possible in the gap between the armchair and the wall. It was a good spot in the corner of the room where, as long as she kept very still and tried not to make a sound, no one would find her.

Jasmine was clever but even this spot would have her sister fooled. Evelyn was sure of it. Unlike Evelyn, Jasmine was not a Lys Alv. She had no magic, but that didn't seem to bother her. Jasmine had dreams of travelling the world and eating tarts in every flavour possible. Evelyn wanted to go with her, but magical people couldn't leave Valmenessia. She just hoped Jasmine wouldn't leave for too long and would bring treats home when she returned.

Evelyn lay curled on her side with her legs cradled to her chest and her cheek pressed on the cool wooden floorboards. She could see the entire room beneath the chair, from between the chair legs, so when footsteps sounded, she had a clear view of her aunt, father and a strange man entering the room.

Her aunt was the lady of Forest's Edge. She ruled the city and everyone in it, and the citizens liked her a lot. Evelyn thought it was because when her aunt smiled her whole face lit up and made everyone feel all warm and gooey inside because that was the feeling Evelyn got when her aunt did it. The lady of Forest's Edge sat on the sofa, crossing one leg over the other and clasping her hands in her lap. Her back was straight, her posture regal and when she did the smile, Evelyn found herself grinning from where she lay in her hiding place.

Evelyn's father moved to sit beside her aunt. His curly black hair was a little messy, which her mother always said was because her father was constantly running his hands through it, searching for answers. Evelyn was unsure of what answers he'd find in the strands but there must have been some if he kept doing it. The bright amber sun pin of the Healers sparkled in the daylight from where it was attached to the breast of his grey coat, his butter yellow shirt visible beneath.

She chewed her lip. One day Evelyn would wear the grey and yellow uniform as well as have her own sun pin. It was supposed to be a good thing. Everyone was happy when they talked about it, but the thought had a pit gradually growing in her stomach.

The strange man with her aunt and father did not sit. Instead, he placed his hands behind his back, his long fingers intertwining as he faced them. Evelyn couldn't help but wonder where he was from. She'd been learning the histories of the cities of Valmenessia with her tutor recently and was curious to know which city he'd been living in before coming to Forest's Edge. He wasn't from her city; she was sure of it by the way he dressed.

Perhaps he was from Giland or Fellbun? Maybe even Royal Bay where the king lived with his two sons. Royal Bay always made her think of how Queen Helen died before Evelyn was born, killed by a Mors Alv. Evelyn's parents said they weren't entirely sure that was true but not to contradict the tutor. It wasn't a popular opinion to have. The queen's death had made King Dominic really mad and because of what happened now there were no more Mors Alvs.

Evelyn had heard stories about the Mors Alvs being really scary, but again, her parents told her not to believe everything she heard. Though, apparently that didn't apply to Healer training or the stuff *they* told her.

Adults had weird rules that Evelyn didn't really understand.

"Thank you for meeting with me," the man said with an incline of his head, drawing Evelyn's attention away from thoughts of the confusing things her parents told her. "Lady Royd and Mr Royd."

"You're welcome," her aunt replied, once more showing off that warm smile Evelyn loved. "Please tell us why you're here."

"I would like a position within your library to study magic," he said. His tone held no warmth, though it wasn't unkind either. If he were a book, he wouldn't be an adventure, more like a set of instructions to build something ordinary, kind of like a plain wooden box.

"Conjuring?" her father asked, shifting forward. Her father was a Conjurer so there was no wonder he found the idea of another looking to become one interesting.

The man shook his head. "Not quite. I want to investigate the properties of magic and the possibilities of harnessing it beyond those born to wield it."

"Sounds an awful lot like conjuring to me." Her father looked at her aunt with a raised brow as he sat back in his seat once more.

"I can see where you might believe that," the man continued with a wave of his hand. "But conjuring still uses magic as a learnt skill, much like a born ability, creating objects and potions. What I propose is using magic as a tool. Take magic from one object and put it in another. Imagine the possibilities of what we could achieve if we could transfer power."

Her aunt held her chin. "Transfer magic between objects or people?"

"Both," the man said. "Think, for example, of those tied to this country. With what I am proposing they needn't be. The magical population would be free to leave."

"But not without cost," her father pointed out. He didn't look too happy about the man's words. Her father loved magic; he thought it was the most wonderful thing in the world.

"Nothing is free."

"What you're suggesting, whilst intriguing, sounds impossible and open to many issues," her aunt said. "What has set you on this path?"

"A fascination and desire to see, as you say, the impossible become a reality."

"I dare say; I am sceptical."

"It is normal to be unsure of new ideas, but I hope you won't disregard my petition," the man said. "Imagine the possibilities if every single person, regardless of birth, could wield magic without restriction on creativity. Instead of only Elementum being able to summon flames, all could light fires to warm their homes. Lys Alvs would not be relied upon to provide and bear all healing, which would save countless more lives. And therein also highlights the elimination of the cost. Magic as a tool would not tire the wielder. Lys Alvs would not endure pain to heal another. Individuals would be given a choice over their fates."

Evelyn's golden eyes widened at the man's words. She had only started her Healer training and had already had to use her magic to heal another. It was painful, taking on the injuries of others and then healing herself. She was unable to hide her hurt like the older Lys Alvs. She was still learning, but maybe she wouldn't have to…

Perhaps this man could find a way for her to avoid being a Healer at all.

Nora

Nora had lost track of time or perhaps it had lost track of her.

Days blurred. Grief threatened to be her undoing whilst the emergency unfolding around her was all that held Nora together. She moved between orders, determined to focus on the task at hand and not the hole in her heart that had forged the moment Florence died.

The victory of winning back Midskopas had been short-lived for the Northern Alliance, thanks to a curse no one had seen coming. Blackened roots erupted from the cemetery ground, tearing up the earth as they grew unnaturally and raced towards the main city with horrifying speed. The curse had sprouted from the bodies of those murdered and marked with the Makers' symbol. The Alliance had received reports of the same thing happening all over.

Valmenessia had been in chaos ever since.

The Makers' Curse sought out magic with those caught in

its grasp quickly succumbing to it. Their skin turned grey with black lines that appeared like the web of a spider inked to their skin, much like the Alta tattoos, only beholden to another master. Some died quickly, whilst others' deaths were drawn out and painful.

No one knew why some survived longer than others. The only certainty was that death would take them all. The longest any had lasted once the curse took hold was a few days. The death of its host caused it to spread more aggressively, breaking through ribs and flesh, tearing apart the body it had once fed upon before unleashing itself on its next magical victim.

There was no cure. No way of fighting the Makers' Curse.

"What the fuck happened?!"

Nora spread her arms and legs, bending at the knee and bracing herself as the ground shook beneath her. They had been sent on a simple task; check in with the Healing Centre and report back. At least it was supposed to be simple.

"Run!" Aren shouted, hurtling himself through the nearby door and onto the street, ushering others out with him. His brown eyes were wide and a panicked look spread across his face as he rushed towards her. A loud rumble filled the air. He grabbed Nora's pale hand in a firm grip as he spun her around and forced her to follow.

Once, he'd been known to her as Felix, a member of the Alta who she and August had been sent to find what felt like a lifetime ago. Now, she knew him by his true name, Aren, the God of the Anima.

Looking behind her as they ran, she saw the black roots of the Makers' Curse burst through the doorway Aren had just come from. It tore up the ground and the building began crumbling as it grew and forced itself through the dirt and dark stone. The curse clawed at the path in search of its prey, moving at a frightening pace as it took over what had been a temporary safe haven. Smaller blackened roots whipped through the air and crashed into the stone buildings around it, like tentacles whirling about, forever looking for magic to satiate its hunger.

Nora's feet pounded on the ground and her heart galloped in her chest as she kept pace with Aren, his long legs propelling him down the street, fleeing what used to be one of the makeshift Healing Centres in Midskopas. The building had collapsed, the curse not only destroying it but consuming all within. Nora didn't want to think about how many victims now belonged to a very long list of the lost.

"Not that I don't like running for my life," Nora shouted over the sound of the surrounding buildings falling to rubble behind them. She sped up, releasing Aren and letting her hands flex at her side, eager to unleash her Elementum magic. She didn't though, keeping it at bay instead. There would be no use throwing magic at the curse; it would only feed it. "But do you mind filling me in on what the fuck just happened?"

"It's gotten stronger," Aren replied between breaths as he ran at her side. Other survivors fled the carnage around them, running frantically in any direction away from the curse. Dust filled the air, threatening to cloud their vision, and he coughed before continuing. "Everything was fine and then suddenly many died at once, unleashing it. Like it was waiting to strike ... Like an ambush."

Suddenly, he pulled her into a side alley, and she took the moment to catch her breath in the somewhat clearer air as Aren shifted into his eagle form. It was a beautiful sight, the feathers of his giant bird a vibrant brown tinged with gold. Aren lowered a wing and Nora wasted no time climbing onto the God's back.

"We just got the city back from the king," Nora said once she was seated. She gripped his feathers and held on tight as he took off into the sky; a sadness settled in her chest. "I'm too stubborn to let the curse take it from us."

If there was one thing Nora hated, it was losing.

Aren stayed low at first, scooping up those in their path who were fleeing the chaos, carrying them in his claws and lifting them into the air. Then once above the city, Nora was able to see the latest destruction the curse had wrought upon the Midskopas. Thick black roots curled around the buildings, strangling them before they gave in and crumbled to the ground in a tremendously loud and dusty mess. The sound reverberated through the city and made its way into the sky, rattling Nora. Most of the city was already uninhabitable to those with magic, and now with the loss of the Healing Centre, they were running out of safe places to hide and tend to the sick.

Hope was in short supply, but the Northern Alliance was clinging to whatever chance they had. They weren't going to give up.

After being freed from King Dominic's command, Nora had thought her world couldn't twist on its axis again, shifting her reality so completely. She had been so wrong. Reclaiming Midskopas was supposed to be a statement of hope for those who wished for a free life. For those like Nora. But her world came crashing down around her for the second and third time in less than a year. First, Florence had died before her eyes and then not long after the Makers' Curse had arisen.

They had been supposed to be watching each other's backs. They were supposed to keep each other alive. But Nora failed her friend. Florence had been killed on Nora's watch. A fact Nora would never let herself forget.

Nora rubbed her chest with her palm, yet the pain didn't go away. The loss of Florence was a constant ache that refused to subside, and she had a feeling it never would. She would simply get used to the pain. It had been a long time since she had felt grief like this; not only was it a fresh despair but a reminder of what she had lost so long ago as a child.

She shook her head, not letting her mind drift to her mother and brother. That was a trap of memories that were best left untouched. She already had enough sorrow to drown herself in without adding to it now.

Instead, Nora thought of the world she was now living in. It wasn't a much happier distraction, but it was better than delving down the road of the immense sadness she refused to let herself feel right now. The lesser of two heartaches.

People were getting sick at every turn and dropping dead not long after, sometimes in only a matter of hours. The reports from allied cities had stated much the same, describing the curse as a plague spreading over the land, scaling walls and forcing its way through barricades as its roots grasped at everything and everyone in its path.

Nora couldn't help but think they should have paid more attention to the radicals murdering innocents and leaving the Makers' mark. Maybe if they had they could have stopped it. At the time, it hadn't been the more pressing issue. They had focused on the blatant threat that the king openly presented rather than the one lurking in the shadows. They couldn't have known. But now they were paying the price of that ignorance.

Nora shuddered at an image in her mind, remembering the countless bodies that had been subjected to the curse. She was no stranger to death, but in all her years as an Alta, she'd never seen anything quite so disturbing as the husks left in the curse's wake. The curse was insatiable and in the last few weeks, it had consumed half of the city they thought they'd saved.

Nora dropped her gaze to where her hands gripped Aren. "We need to be doing more. Fleeing every time the curse grows isn't working."

"The Northern Alliance is working on a cure and a way to fight the Makers' Curse," Aren replied. The wind rippled through his feathers and whipped at the strands of deep brown hair that had come loose from Nora's ponytail. "That isn't nothing."

"It is insufferably slow and the curse isn't the only threat now, is it?" Nora sighed heavily. It was hard not to feel defeated. There had been so much loss. "King Dominic's guard is still patrolling the non-allied cities, though instead of simply imprisoning Anima, they're executing them thanks to his new laws. I overheard Carl say some are claiming the Anima are the ones spreading the curse and those accusing them are taking it upon themselves to act as executioners with no penalties from the king's guard."

"Overheard or eavesdropping?" Aren said, leaning to the side to make their descent.

"I just happened to be in the same room. Not that how I got the information is important," Nora replied. "As I was saying, not only is King Dominic still up to no fucking good, his precious King's Guild have executed the Anima amongst their own ranks, 'purifying' the guild for him. You'd think the curse would slow him down, but it's only made him worse."

"Some individuals thrive on destruction and pain."

"Ugh," Nora grimaced. "Everything has royally gone to shit."

"There's still hope. Hold on," Aren said.

Nora tightened her grip. She brought her body closer to his as he lowered them to the ground. He'd taken her flying on his back several times now, but she still found the landing the hardest part. Aren let out a high-pitched whistle, announcing their arrival before lowering those in his claws to the ground gently. Then he glided to a halt and swiftly shifted back into his human form. Nora found herself suddenly curled on his muscular back.

"I hate when you do that," Nora grumbled, sliding to the ground.

"You're not much of a hugger so I take them when I can," Aren grinned, turning to face Nora.

She stuck out her tongue and he laughed; his eyes sparkling. Their little friendship had developed since the reclaiming of the city. Aren seemed to think they were to be great friends with their history drawing them together. Nora didn't want to admit that maybe he was right.

"What happened?" Carl asked, stepping out from their improvised headquarters with Chester emerging at his side. It wasn't a fancy building, nor was it very big, but they couldn't be fussy with the limited space they had. The curse encroached on them every hour of every day. "We heard the commotion in the east. Please tell me it's not what I think it is."

Carl's role had grown significantly since taking Midskopas. Not only was he in charge of the Northern Wolf Pack, both in the city and back home in the Great Northern Forest, but he was now working with Gemma as head of Midskopas too. Word was that his pack continued to steadily grow in number as Anima fled the cities to a leader who could care for and protect them.

Nora offered Chester a smile but all she received was a nod of acknowledgement in return. Florence's brother hadn't been the same since her death. His red hair lost its fire, his smiles had all but disappeared and his shoulders seemed perpetually slumped. Part of her feared that he thought Florence's death was her fault and frankly she didn't blame him. She'd failed them both.

Seeing the visible effects the loss of Florence had on Chester had Nora thinking of her only family left, August. She missed him. She missed having her best friend by her side. The thought of leaving Midskopas and going north to find him had crossed her mind more than once. It had been so tempting, especially with the new threat of the curse, yet she'd stayed with the Northern Alliance.

Leaving would be selfish and she was trying to do better, be better—make up for all the wrong she caused. And that meant helping the Alliance in Midskopas, because it wasn't just the curse that threatened their lives, but King Dominic too.

"Unfortunately, I think it might be exactly what you're afraid of. The Eastern Healing Centre is gone. I was on my way out after receiving the reports from the Healers when the curse sprouted from several patients at once," Aren replied with a frown, dust flecked all over his brown skin. Nora could only imagine how she must have looked. "It grew rapidly, the rest of the curse burst through walls and ground as if summoned by a call. There was nothing we could do but run."

"The patients and Healers?"

"Most were too far for me to reach in time. The curse moved rapidly, and many were crushed by the building collapsing around them. Nora and I, and a few others, are lucky that we got out of there at all. I looked for survivors once I took to the sky and gathered who I could."

"Fuck," Carl growled, running a hand through his chestnut-coloured hair. "There has to be some way to end it. It can't be unstoppable."

"I agree, but whatever can stop the curse, we don't have access to it," Chester said with a grim expression. "We have no weapon to fight it."

"So what do we do?" Nora asked. "How do we keep all these people safe and, at the same time, stop the king's impending retaliation?"

Word had come that King Dominic's forces were marching north. They were still a way off, yet they were coming all the same.

"We remain here. We cannot abandon the citizens of Midskopas," he said, turning to face Chester. "Set up a guard to stop anyone from heading to the eastern side of the city. The curse may be taking land, but I'm not ready to cede the city to it just yet. We'll need to refine our protocols too. I'll meet with the remaining Healers. Perhaps we need to restrict access to communal areas sooner than we had anticipated, lest the curse evolve and be drawn by their magic, not just their use of it."

Chester nodded to his husband. "I'll get one of the pack to gather the Healers for you before I set up the guard."

"Thanks," Carl replied then added before Chester could leave. "If you see our scouts, send them my way too. The last thing we need is for the king to surprise us right now."

Chester kissed Carl on his stubbled cheek before striding down the street to relay the orders. Chester may have been Carl's husband but he was his second too, a role he took seriously.

"I overheard the latest about the king," Nora said, chewing her bottom lip.

Carl raised a brow.

"Eavesdropping," Aren smirked, nudging Nora in the side.

"Old habits apparently die hard," Nora shrugged. "What are our plans for King Dominic?"

"I've received a reply from Jasmine," Carl said, scratching his chin. "And we are waiting for her to arrive before we make any new plans. Within the cities, the Factions have lost numbers and whilst we're still receiving information, we can't expect those in the thick of it to do more than survive right now. The curse has made things beyond difficult and extremely dangerous. Until Jasmine arrives, we will focus our efforts on the army marching this way."

"I agree, we should prepare for his attack," Aren said. "It may be a while before his army is on our doorstep but we should use that time to ensure he cannot take back Midskopas or get passed our borders further north."

"Gemma came to me this morning sharing a similar sentiment," Carl replied. "She's called a meeting in the theatre."

"When?"

"Now," Carl said. "I would be there, but I have other matters to attend. Gemma is more than capable of running the meeting."

Nora could only imagine the myriad of things Carl was doing. He had a lot on his shoulders being the leader of the Northern Wolf Pack *and* co-leader of the Northern Alliance too.

"Probably a riveting meeting. The most riveting one in centuries. Bards will be singing all about it for an eternity, for sure. We better hurry up, wouldn't want to miss it, would we?" Nora drawled, nudging Aren's side.

The two left Carl to his other matters and headed towards

the theatre.

"You already knew about the meeting," Aren stated as they walked through the city.

This section wasn't as run down as the rest. Sure it had been affected by the fight, but the curse had not made a visit and so much of the streets and surrounding buildings had been repaired. Mostly. If only the potholes in the ground would stay fixed. They were popping up everywhere; holes that they assumed were caused by the curse destabilising the foundations. They posed no threat beyond someone tripping or falling into one of the larger ones.

Aren raised a brow. "Psychic?"

"Obviously."

He chuckled.

"Gemma came to see me last night," Nora admitted. "Asked, or should I say ordered, me to help train the Midskopas citizens who wanted to join the fight."

Aren pulled open the door to the theatre, holding it wide for Nora to slip in first. Gemma was already on the stage, giving a speech.

Most who'd come from Forest's Edge had stayed in the theatre, either sleeping on the benches that sat before the stage or on the stage itself. She'd been sharing the old dressing room with Aren. It wasn't a big space, but thanks to all the costumes, she'd been able to sleep somewhat comfortably. Now, there was no sign of anyone sleeping. Everyone in the theatre gave Gemma their full attention.

The Lys Alv was in command of the Forest's Edge faction of the Northern Alliance until Jasmine arrived in the coming days. Nora walked down the aisle, passing familiar faces as she went, and then found a seat near the front. Aren dropped into the one beside her as Gemma shot them a glare.

The Lys Alv wore her favoured forest green jacket, along with trousers and brown boots. Her white, blonde hair was tied at the base of her neck with the strands around her face tucked behind her pointed ears. A band was wrapped around her upper arm bearing the symbol of the Northern Alliance stitched onto it—five squares all on their points to represent each race and the equality they were fighting for.

"Glad you two could make it," Aeolus said, standing at the end of the aisle with his arms folded over his chest. Gemma's second and a grumpy man to boot.

"Wouldn't miss it for the world," Nora replied with a grin.

She took in his appearance. On the outside, he looked like the brutal warrior he was in leathers and with weapons strapped to him ready for battle. The band around his arm depicting the symbol of the Northern Alliance stood out in its bright red. Aeolus stood tall, his shoulders back and he wore a determined expression on his face. However, Nora knew he was feeling much like the rest of them. The loss of so many, the encroaching curse on Midskopas and King Dominic's army marching towards them. It would be odd for him not to feel the weight of all these things.

"As I was saying. Thank you all for joining me here today," Gemma continued. Her golden gaze dragged over those gathered and captured Nora's attention. They weren't as many as they were when they'd left Forest's Edge. The recapture of Midskopas had cost lives, but not as many as the curse since. "I wanted to speak with you all about our next steps, but first I want to say thank you for all that you have done.

"In coming to Midskopas, you have all sacrificed a lot to bring freedom here and to the Northern Alliance as well. Now, you are faced with not only the king's forces but the Makers' Curse too and yet you have continued to show that you will not back down easily. When I look at all your faces, I know that neither enemy stands a chance against the power of those before me. You all have a strength and determination that they cannot match.

"The king continues to inflict his tyranny upon the populace, his guard now executing and encouraging civil executions of Anima. They are being blamed for this awful curse. Which we know isn't true, yet the king once again uses fear to drive action. We know his methods and must continue to stand against them.

"Our allied cities continue to fight him within their walls and we will do the same here as his army marches towards us. Right now it might be hard to see the end, but we have been knocked down before. We have been pushed to the ground yet what sets us apart is that we continue to rise up. Let us once again do just that. Let's send them a big fuck you and show them that we will not surrender!"

Those gathered in the theatre cheered and Nora found herself rising from her seat to clap along with them. Gemma was right. She would not let this stifle her spirit, or her need to right the wrongs she'd been forced to do on the king's behalf. Nora found herself feeling rejuvenated as she sat back down. After the morning she and Aren had had, Gemma's speech was just what she needed to hear.

On stage, Gemma explained their plans and divided those gathered into teams. Nora was set to head the training of anyone who wanted instruction.

"Seat's taken," Nora quipped, sighing dramatically as Aeolus sat on her other side. He didn't look her way or at Aren, instead, his eyes were focused on Gemma.

"Thoughts?" Aeolus asked, ignoring her.

"Her speech was good," Aren replied. "Very motivational. Even got Nora out of her seat."

Nora shot him a glare. "You were standing right next to me."

"I never said I wasn't," he grinned.

"Nora?" Aeolus urged, waiting for her to answer his question.

"The reviews said it would be terrible," Nora replied. "But I think Gemma put on a great performance."

Aeolus turned, narrowing his gaze at her.

"What?" Nora asked innocently then shrugged her shoulders and looked around at those gathered. "Okay, fine. Honestly, it's a long shot but the Alliance has passion and a whole lot of spirit. I've been spending time with Aren, some might say too much, and I've learnt that skill isn't everything."

Aren huffed a laugh.

"So, who knows? We might just be able to pull it off."

2

August

The air was icy cold and the city of Fellbun was coated in snow, though it wasn't the weather that kept its civilians hidden away.

August crept forward, pulling his cloak tight around him and followed the sound of stricken sobbing and intermittent yelps of pain. Part of him knew he should ignore it, yet he couldn't help himself. Now, August didn't have to stand by and ignore another's distress. He was no longer tied to King Dominic and his time with Jord, and the other Mors Alvs had taught him to embrace his magic, to control it.

August was free to do as he wished and if there was a chance this person's pain wasn't caused by the Makers' Curse, then it was worth the risk.

Fellbun was covered in the blackened veins that pulsed like some eerie ticking of a clock as though it was letting everyone know of their limited time left as it searched for those with magic.

Despite the risk of the curse, August couldn't ignore the

calls for help. It felt wrong to walk away from someone in need. Ever since the king's tattoos had faded from his wrists, he'd felt things he never had before. In particular, a connection to people. Many may have still been wary of him, but despite that, August couldn't hide from the feeling that he was linked to everyone in some way. Be it the commonality of hopes and dreams, of location or social circles, or simply the fact that most people were just trying to live a happy life and be part of something.

One of the reasons lying to Nora had been so hard was not only his betrayal of her trust, or that he had to pretend to be an Alta, but he'd had to stand by and hide his true feelings about what they were doing. How their actions were affecting others, and not in a good way.

These feelings spurred him on. In truth, August shouldn't have been in the area at all. It had been closed off that morning to prevent the spread of the curse. But he'd gone for a walk to clear his head and organise his thoughts and had accidentally ventured into the prohibited zone. When he'd realised where he was he'd made to leave which is when he heard the cry for help. It was almost like fate had brought him there.

Rounding the corner, he spotted a man bent over on the frosty street. He was curled in on himself, clutching his stomach with one hand whilst his other shook violently as he held himself from crumbling completely onto the ground. His clothes were far from suitable for the cold weather Fellbun was renowned for, his thin shirt and loose slacks beneath his coat did nothing to keep out the chill.

August tentatively approached, crouching a few steps away. "Are you injured?"

It was a stupid question; one filled with a strange sort of hope because an injury could be healed. An injury didn't mean certain death.

"Help me." The man looked up at August to reveal grey skin taut against his skull like he'd climbed out of a grave. "Please."

He cried out and collapsed on the ground. The man's body spasmed as he coughed blood onto the ground. The red was a stark contrast to the white snow.

"Please don't leave me," the man begged through a ragged breath, lifting his head. His eyes were glassy, his lips cracked and speckled with blood. "I don't want to be alone."

August reached out as the man dropped his head once more and shook violently. Drawing back his hand, August quickly stuffed it into his pocket as the man went still. He had the curse.

August was already risking too much being so close and there was nothing he could do. August closed his eyes, bracing himself for the decision that never got easier to make. It went beyond nature to leave someone in need. August slowly rose only to fall back on his ass, startled by the man's sudden horrific gasp.

A bony hand wrapped around his ankle. "Ple—"

The sentence was never finished. The man's entire body curled back on itself, the frail fingers releasing August as the man's eyes rolled into the back of his head. As if he were a puppet whose strings were severed, the man crumpled and August froze, staring at the sight before him. His gaze ran over the man, searching for any signs of life. Lingering, even for a second, had been a mistake.

The curse burst from the man, blackened veinlike tendrils sprouting from the man's back, and dove for August.

August scurried backwards, narrowly avoiding the curse as he tore off his jacket and threw it at the dead man. It was a pathetic attempt to buy time, but there was nothing else he could do. The curse had no cure, no weapon capable of fighting it.

"Fuck!" August swore, his breath coming in quick succession as he jumped to his feet and ran from the scene. His heart pounded like a drum in his chest, strong beats that reverberated into his mind. Each thump matched his steps.

He'd fucked up. He only hoped he wouldn't pay for it.

Two days later, August leant his head back against the wall outside Lord Havilor's office, his eyes closed as he waited to meet with the ruler of the northern city of Fellbun. He'd been summoned that morning, though why the lord had wanted to see him was a mystery.

Lord Havilor was currently in a meeting with all the powerful individuals from around the icy city nestled south of the Periculum Mountains. From what he could tell, they were discussing the current state of affairs in regards to the Makers' Curse and King Dominic. Despite their efforts and promising ideas, the curse continued to grow with no successful attempts at slowing it down.

The conversation hummed through the walls and August's Mors Alv hearing gave him clear access to the meeting. He tried not to listen in, but he was finding it increasingly difficult to ignore.

"Word from Kaldom and Forest's Edge will be coming in much slower from now on," Lord Havilor told those gathered in the room. "The curse has spread far between us, meaning it is too risky to ask even avian Anima to travel unless messages are urgent. We'll become increasingly reliant on our human kin to help us, growing the list of duties we are now reliant upon them for."

Humans were not affected by the curse. It was only drawn to those with magic. There had been so much death. The mood in Fellbun was bleak, and August struggled to find hope like many others.

"We still have contact with Midskopas, though the city has become a dangerous place. There were many casualties and injuries after the Northern Alliance took it back from King

Dominic's hold. Lots of wounded magical people for the curse to feed on," the lord continued.

"As well as the curse, the king is an ever-present threat, his desires are unchanged, only on how they are being pursued. Decrees continue to be sent to the King's Guard who are still enforcing rules in the cities not under the Alliance's control, and reports have come in that he has forces marching north towards Midskopas in retaliation for the Alliance taking the city. He has sent trained soldiers with the desire to squash the resistance in one fell swoop. Regardless of the terrible outlook, last I heard, they are determined to hold the city."

"The country is in turmoil and he continues to add kindling to the fire," a woman hissed. "I heard his favoured cities are not faring well either, yet he persists with his abhorrent plans. Nothing will dissuade him from what he has set his sights on."

"How are we supposed to continue fighting on two fronts?" Another member of the group asked; a male voice this time.

It felt like an impossible task; fight a tyrannical king while holding back a terrible curse.

August did his best to ignore the rest of the conversation. There was only so much more he could hear. He hadn't needed to be privy to special meetings to know that with the death toll, the number of displaced and the work being done in an attempt to halt the Makers' Curse; the news would be far from good. Even beyond Fellbun, the cities within the Northern Alliance were all attempting to save lives whilst the curse continued to spread. Some were moved to what they believed were safe areas only for the curse to find them, reaching their doors and taking their lives.

He and the other Mors Alvs in his travelling party had arrived in the city weeks ago. They had left the safety of the Periculum Mountains and the hidden home that the Mors Alv Goddess, Jord, had created for their race. What should have been an assassination and rescue mission, to finally take down the king and bring Evelyn back, August had instead led the Mors

Alvs into the path of a curse determined to take the lives of every magical being it touched.

The Maker's Curse had spread quickly in Fellbun, taking over the once-famous Thyra's Firefall. Instead of rushing water, the curse now pulsed within the river's bed, causing landslides that continued to cut off the city from the south. Hence August was stuck in Fellbun. It was simply too dangerous to attempt to leave.

He'd wanted to continue with his journey but there had been no way out other than the northern trail, back to the Temple of the Faithful. The Mors Alvs he'd travelled with returned to the Periculum Mountains, to the safety that Jord had established for them, thinking she could protect them from the curse.

All except his friend, Tyler, who remained by August's side, that is.

Lord Havilor had put him and Tyler to work, undertaking many different tasks; relocating those who lost homes, helping distribute supplies and guarding restricted areas. August appreciated the work. He didn't care to sit around idly while the curse devoured innocent lives.

But the curse wasn't the only threat Valmenessia faced and August was becoming more and more frustrated with being trapped there.

The door to Lord Havilor's study opened, drawing August back to the present. He stood tall as nobles and business owners strode from the room and he caught sight of a few familiar faces. The owner of one of Fellbun's most popular taverns was one, with her many connections, her knowledge and influence would be critical in any plans that the group made. Another was a young man with a Healer's pin on his shirt and a grim expression on his freckled face, the second in command at the city's Healing Centre.

"Still hoping to leave?" Lord Havilor asked and August glanced over at the man standing on the threshold.

Lord Havilor looked at him expectantly. The lord was tired, the curse taking a toll on the Lys Alv. His golden eyes lacked their usual vibrance and his tall thin frame was trimmer than usual, his face drawn. August couldn't help but wonder if the lord had eaten or slept since the curse descended upon them or whether he was relying solely on his magic to keep him alive.

"Yes," August replied, striding into the study. "The sooner the better. I have delayed my journey for long enough. I may just have to take my chances with the avalanches."

"I've acquired some help on the matter, a few Elementum who are willing to aid your exit," the lord said. "It is a great risk for them to use so much magic so close to the curse, but I have told them of your intent and they wish to help."

Relief filled August's chest. "Really? When do I leave?"

"Tomorrow," Lord Havilor said. He placed a hand on one of August's broad shoulders and squeezed. "Though this is good news for you, it's not the time for foolish optimism. On top of everything going on in the world, I've lost contact with Jord. Our only ally we had access to. Fellbun is officially isolated."

"It is a difficult trek to Jord."

"It isn't the journey that's the issue," the lord said. He strode towards the window and looked out to the cursed river, and August caught the man's grimace in the reflection of the glass. "The last messenger I sent up there returned to tell me that the place was empty. There is no one residing in the Temple of the Faithful."

"Where have they gone?"

Lord Havilor shrugged. "I haven't a clue. I had hoped you or your friend would know. But I see this is just as surprising for you as it is for me."

August was speechless. Jord had been determined to remain and now she was gone? The other Mors Alvs with her? He ran a hand through his newly cut dirty blond hair and sighed heavily. Everything had turned on its head and it had really been a mess to begin with. It was hard to push on, wake up and keep going with the day. Yet he had to.

Both the king and the curse were still terrorising the citizens of Valmenessia. August didn't know how to stop the curse, but he could do something about the king.

And Evelyn … He could save her from it all too.

"You better go pack," Lord Havilor said dismissing him and breaking the silence between them. "Good luck. We're counting on you."

August left, striding down the manor's hallways and back towards his room. There he sat on his bed, torn by his eagerness to continue with his plans and the guilt of leaving Fellbun.

There wasn't much he could do for the latter when it came to the curse, however by leaving and going to Royal Bay, he'd be able to free not just Evelyn but the entire country from the king's wrath.

Last August heard of Evelyn, she had been engaged to Prince Kylan, the youngest of King Dominic's sons. August remembered the prince from his time in Royal Bay as part of the Alta. Or should he say, his brother?

Unlike Nora, August hadn't been stationed with the Royal Guard for Alta training, his Mors Alv heritage confining him to the shadows and the Alta quarters below ground. However, the times when he was privy to the goings on above ground, he'd caught glimpses of the princes from his hiding spots.

From what he'd gathered from his spying and from Nora's gossip, Prince Kylan was a dutiful son, though King Dominic was far from impressed. The man was simply ignored for the most part, left to his studies and the duties that being a second prince entailed.

August took comfort in that knowledge; that perhaps the reason why King Dominic was displeased with his son would be the reason Evelyn was safe with Prince Kylan. That perhaps the prince was kind.

Either that or the alternative; that Prince Kylan would be unfathomably cruel in order to gain his father's praise. August tried not to entertain that possibility. At least she wouldn't have to endure either outcome much longer. Tomorrow he was going south and he would bring her home.

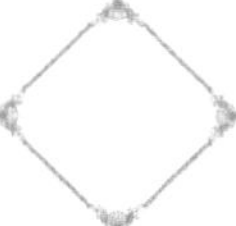

The following day, August awoke with renewed purpose. He prepared the horse Lord Havilor had gifted him, adjusting the saddle before running a gloved hand over the animal's mane.

"Leaving without me?" Tyler asked, swaggering towards him in the stable. He had his hands stuffed into his pockets, the cloak swallowing his lean build, as his brown hair fluttered in the wind. August was reminded of when he'd wanted to leave Forest's Edge without Aren, and his lips quirked to the side. Would he and Tyler tussle too?

"You should remain here," August replied, picking up his bag. "It's not safe to come with me."

"I hardly joined you on this little mission of yours because I thought it would be safe," Tyler said, his green and black eyes sparkling as he grinned. "You were planning to kill the king and save a girl, and I decided to join you. Danger was kind of implied."

"The curse." August gave him a pointed look.

Tyler shrugged. "Well, let's not let it catch us."

"You really want to come?" August asked, his tone laced with disbelief. "After everything?"

"Yeah," Tyler said with a grin. "Usurping a throne sounds fun. Even if the journey has a few extra challenges now."

August rolled his dark blue and black eyes. "We aren't usurping a throne."

"But you would make a great king," he replied earnestly,

despite the mischief dancing in his dark gaze. "And your mother was the queen after all."

"I'm not becoming king."

"Fine," Tyler sighed, his shoulders drooping exaggeratedly. "Let's be boring and just kill the one we have then. Selfish. Denying me all those lovely advantages of being friends with a king."

"You're ridiculous." August smiled at his friend. The company would be nice. "Alright, hurry up and get a horse. We are leaving in five minutes."

"Not going to put up more of a fight?" Tyler asked, raising a brow.

"No point with you. So just move your ass already."

Tyler barked a laugh and gave a mock bow. "Yes, Dark Prince."

He jogged away and August checked his pack, hoping his supplies were enough to last the journey. The letter he'd written to Nora was tucked within, nestled beside his sketchpad.

He hadn't contracted the curse from that man he'd found only days earlier. Symptoms typically showed by now. However, that had been pure luck. It would only be a matter of time before he did get infected by it, become a host to it. A sadness settled in his gut, but he did his best to dismiss the feeling. Now was not the time to lose hope. Taking precautions wasn't giving up.

Evelyn and the king weren't his only concerns. August was worried for Nora, about how she would be fairing with the curse in Forest's Edge. Lord Havilor had told him that they were experiencing much the same as them in Fellbun, but knowing that only made him more fearful. Nora was beyond stubborn and he hated to think what kind of predicaments she would be getting herself into because of it.

He hoped he'd see her again soon.

Outside the stable, snow fell, coating the ground, yet the dark root-like mounds of the curse in the distance were ever-present. They spread along the ground, like claws grasping at prey.

After they managed the difficult task of leaving the city, with the help of an Elementum, there would be other difficulties ahead. The curse would no doubt be in their way along with other threats, like the King's Guild. Who knew when they would reach Royal Bay? Time was a luxury they didn't have. Not when all that mattered was stopping the king from hurting anyone else and rescuing Evelyn once and for all.

3

Evelyn

"What's portal magic?" Evelyn asked, watching as Sloane worked. The Conjurer was busy drawing a swirling pattern onto the floor with her silver-ringed and tattooed fingers, each swirl and loop linked to create a circle in the centre.

One of the men present was quick to give Evelyn a verbal lashing yet Sloane tsked, sounding far older than she appeared and scolded the man. She couldn't have been much older than Evelyn, judging by her smooth complexion and youthful features. "Portal magic moves objects or people from one place to another within seconds."

Evelyn shuffled on her feet. "How far? Like from here to Forest's Edge?"

"Precisely," Sloane nodded, violet hair swaying with the movement as she finished her drawing with an elegant swish and then moved on to another design. "You can go as far as you like."

The memory went fuzzy around the edges and then vanished like it was blown away in a gust of wind before being replaced by another.

"I bet this is where we'll witness the beginning of the end," Louise said, her dark brown eyes alight with anticipation. The maid looked almost giddy with the possibility. "Valmenessia will be made anew."

Kylan said something, but Evelyn was too busy with her surroundings to hear the prince's words.

Vines crawled up the pillars of the brick pavilion, the lush garden visible between each gap between pillars. Vibrant green grass and the richly coloured petals in the flower beds added to the beauty of the place, whilst the sound of cascading water filled the air.

The sun shone brightly, streaming in through the hole at the centre of the pavilion's roof and onto a pit where dark red stained the cream-coloured bricks.

"The last sacrifice will take place and—"

Evelyn gasped, terror filling her. "Sacrifice?"

Louise nodded. "A sacrifice to the Makers."

Evelyn's vision blurred once more, the memory shifting.

Two men flanked Sloane. Elliot Maker, a lean man with short black hair who also happened to be Sloane's grandson, smiled wide at her, a knowing glint in his brown eyes.

"For centuries, Thyra, Jord, Nyssa, and Aren have clashed over this country and I won't stand for it any longer," Frode said, his voice unwavering, standing on Sloane's other side. He was imposing, tall with broad shoulders, like a strong wall, unyielding, and his blond hair was tousled, matching the stubble on his jaw. Disdain coated his tone. "I'm sick of their power-hungry ways."

The Human God may have had no magic, but he was no less impressive than the other Gods and Goddesses. No less intimidating.

"It is time to end my siblings' rivalry."

Sloane left their sides and moved to stand in the pit. Her chanting filled the air as she tipped her head back, face to the bright sky above. The Conjurer didn't flinch as Louise fell at her feet, nor when blood filled the ground where she stood. Sloane's chanting grew louder and Evelyn held back her sob as her friend took her last breath, the misguided hope in Louise's eyes before her death, a sight that would forever haunt Evelyn.

Tears streamed down Evelyn's cheeks as she watched as Louise's body cracked open at her chest, darkness creeping from her ribcage. Blackened limbs, like the roots of a tree, crawled from within her and spread out in the pit.

"You wanted a new world?" Frode boomed as a golden circle appeared around the pit. The blackened roots pressed themselves against the barrier that now held them. "You're going to get one."

The memory disappeared like the others, though this time there was nothing left to replace it.

First, there was an unending void.

No light, no sense, no thought or feeling.

Nothing.

Then it all came crashing in at once.

Heart racing, terror consumed Evelyn. Dread overflowed in a tirade against her senses. She thrashed in desperation against the complete and utter darkness that consumed her, but she couldn't see, nor fight against the shadows, her body remained immobile despite her efforts. Her eyes were firmly closed, her limbs motionless at her sides despite the fear that coursed through her and screamed for her to move.

Run!

Run!

Run!

Gut clenching, her breathing quickened as time stretched on and her fear grew to a terrifying panic. She could not protect herself from what preyed in the shadows, only lay motionless and wait as whatever it was drew nearer. Hungry for her blood.

Run!

The shadows merged into a creature that was now, slinking towards her, a figure made of the darkness itself. Its facial features were unrecognisable yet perhaps that added to the terror that spiked within her. Smoke in humanoid form, looming over her, the lack of a face making its intentions unclear.

Run!

The smoky figure lifted a hand with elongated fingers towards Evelyn, a sense of doom rising in her chest. Fear grew, filling her to the very tips of her fingers and toes. She would have trembled if it were possible.

Her time had run out.

As if someone had turned a key in a lock, Evelyn's eyes flew open. Her body jolted forward as she sat up, gasping for breath. She swung an arm over her eyes as the sudden light assaulted her senses. It was a blinding contrast to the terrifying darkness she had just been imprisoned by. Her free hand trembled as she raised it to her chest and found her clothing soaked through with sweat. Evelyn felt the strong thumping of her heart beneath her ribs.

There was no creature in the darkness, nothing to fear after all.

It was simply a dream.

Evelyn rubbed her eyes, attempting to clear her vision even though the incessant light continued to burn them. She tried with all her might to take in her surroundings and gain some sort of composure. Taking deep breaths, she counted each of her heartbeats until both her breathing and the thumping in her chest slowed to steady rhythms.

Where was she?

The space was bright with floral blue curtains pulled back to reveal wide windows taking up most of the opposite wall. They gave Evelyn a view of a field beyond and allowed the midday sunshine to light up the sofa and armchair in the sitting area. Nestled on the sofa were cushions embroidered with cottage scenes and beneath was a green rug on the wooden floor. A table for two was close by with a pitcher of water and a vase holding a fresh bunch of yellow daisies.

Cosy, pleasant even, and unrecognisable.

The room was unfamiliar, yet it wasn't the only thing that felt unknown to her. Evelyn's body felt odd, as though it weren't her own. As if her mind had been placed inside another's. Her skin tingled and her muscles ached like it was still trying to become accustomed to her presence.

A stranger.

A house guest.

Evelyn tried to remember what had happened to her before waking up in this strange place, in this unfamiliar body, but she was met with nothing to answer her questions. Her mind was simply blank; or at least like a foggy morning. She could remember the darkness and waking up, yet anything further back and she was met with a cloudy haze.

Chewing her lip, Evelyn was determined to remember something. She scrunched her brow in concentration, trying harder to push her mind to see beyond the fog only to cry out and clutch her head. Pain radiated through her skull, sharp and hot. Evelyn dropped back onto the bed and curled up, tucking her legs to her chest and hoping the pain would go away.

Cold sweat coated her skin and tears filled her eyes. It was like her mind was trying to protect itself from her intrusion, as though it didn't even trust her.

Why was her body fighting her?

Panic filled her once more. It was her body? Wasn't it?

Evelyn glanced at her hand, relief filling her as she recognised the fingers as her own. Light brown, free of any scars, with her standard short nails, though why this detail was standard she couldn't recall. It was her body, those were her hands, yet for some reason it wasn't happy with her.

Suddenly, a woman rushed in, her violet hair flowing behind her in her haste, closely followed by another. A maid, judging by the simple brown dress, shoes and apron she wore. The first woman sat on the bed and reached out for Evelyn's hand, only for Evelyn to recoil before she was touched.

"I won't hurt you," the woman said as though trying to calm a child. She busied her tattooed hands by running them down her cream-coloured skirts then clasped them in her lap. Evelyn couldn't help but eye the patterns inked into the woman's skin. Loops and stars of varying design. "I promise."

"Who are you?" Evelyn asked, sitting up and shuffling back on the bed until her back was pressed to the wall. She quickly wiped her eyes, hoping her tears weren't noticed.

The woman's brows rose. "You don't know?"

Evelyn shook her head, though instantly regretted it as the pain from trying to access her memories still lingered.

The woman watched Evelyn intently, her gaze searching then she smiled broadly to reveal perfect teeth and a glint in her blue eyes. "My name is Sloane, I'm a Healer."

Evelyn nodded, slowly dropping her shoulders and forcing herself to relax. Healers could be trusted; they took care of others. "Sorry, I can't remember much."

"That's okay," Sloane replied. Her voice was soft and had a calming effect on Evelyn. "We will help you remember. Won't we?" She turned to the maid standing by the door, who nodded at Evelyn. "This is Verida. I don't suppose you remember her?"

"No," Evelyn said, giving Verida an apologetic look. "Sorry."

"Don't be," Sloane replied with a wave of her hand. "You

can't help it if you can't remember, though I wonder how extensive your memory loss is." She tapped a finger to her pursed lips. "Let's start with some basics; your name."

"Evelyn."

"Evelyn … who?"

Evelyn scrunched her nose. "I don't know."

"Family?"

"I don't know—"

"Occupation?"

Evelyn shook her head; dread filled her once more.

"Where do you live?"

Shoulders sagging, Evelyn sighed, her voice cracking. "I don't know."

"Hmm, interesting," Sloane said. "But never fear, as I said, we are here to help. First, Lord Maker's trusted advisory is on his way. Verida was watching you this morning and she came to me immediately when she noticed you stirring. I sent word to Mr Walker immediately."

"Why does he want to see me? Do I know him?"

"In a way," Sloane said. "He is eager to hear of your wellbeing. You see, you work here at the lord's estate as a maid, and you were carrying some linens up the stairs when you fell and hit your head, which explains your memory loss now that I think of it. You've been out for a few weeks, but it looks like you've healed up nicely and are good as new."

"What about my memories? Will they come back?"

"I'm not sure whether they will return. Only time will tell, though we will have regular visits together to monitor progress," Sloane said, her eyes drifting to the doorway just as a man strode in.

He was an imposing figure; tall and broad-shouldered, his grey jacket open at the front almost as if it would be a strain on the fabric should he attempt to button it up. His blond hair was combed to the side, with not a strand out of place, and the stubble on his jaw was much the same, neat and uniform. It was as though he was cut from stone like a statue of a God.

The maid dropped to a curtsey at his presence. He ignored her completely, moving swiftly towards the end of Evelyn's bed and looked at her with scrutinising eyes.

"She's awake," he stated. His voice was deep and his tone firm. The man held power, what sort, Evelyn didn't know, but she felt it all the same.

"Which is clearly evident," Sloane replied, waving a hand in Evelyn's direction. The woman's attitude towards the man surprised her and she looked between the Healer and the man, questions filling her mind. She didn't get a chance to ask a single one as Sloane gripped her chin gently and turned her head this way and that. "As you can see, her brown eyes are nice and clear, and—" she pushed away the hair near Evelyn's ear causing the man's eyes to widen. "The injury is completely healed."

"Very good." He turned to leave, but Sloane's words halted him on the spot.

"She is suffering from memory loss."

"How bad is it?" he asked without facing them, though his body had stiffened, his voice strained.

"So far, all she remembers is her name."

"Monitor the situation," he replied sternly then strode from the room.

Evelyn looked to Sloane who was glaring at the door, grumbling to herself beneath her breath.

"You don't like him," Evelyn stated.

"Whether I like him is not important," Sloane replied. She reached around Evelyn's neck, removing a necklace Evelyn hadn't realised was there. Sloane quickly pocketed it, but not fast enough that Evelyn didn't get a glimpse at the pink pendant encased in gold that hung from the chain. "You won't be needing that anymore; it's done its job. Now, before I leave, how do you feel?"

"Tired," Evelyn said, her hands fidgeting before her. "Confused, frustrated."

"Take the rest of the day," Sloane replied, rising to her feet. "Tomorrow you can return to your room and duties. Verida will direct you."

"Thank you," Evelyn said, feeling completely disorientated. "Any chance before you leave, you could tell me where I am? You said Lord Maker's estate but where?"

"We are in Sorby."

"Sorby?" Evelyn chewed her lip; the name was familiar to her ears and knowledge of the place came instantly to her mind.

Sorby was the human-only city in Valmenessia; the city sat at the very southernmost point of Valmenessia in a secluded spot, which was chosen for that very reason. To the north over the river was Misfortune's Forest; much smaller than the Great Northern Forest, but still large enough to cover a lot of land. It was home to many in the Southern Wolf Pack.

To the east the lower edge of Sailor's Peril protected Sorby from anyone approaching by sea, to the south were mountains that offered the same safety and to the west, where Evelyn could see out her window, were the fields.

So there were some things she was still able to recall…

Those who lived in Sorby wanted nothing to do with the magic of the rest of the country. Evelyn's shoulders slumped. Was she included in that? She didn't feel opposed to magic though she didn't feel opposed to much right now.

"I live here?" Evelyn asked. She could have sworn she'd never set foot in Sorby though when she thought of the other cities of Valmenessia she had no recollections of being in those places either … Surely being able to recall so many details about the city meant she must have lived there.

"You do," the woman nodded slowly. "Is there a memory surfacing?"

Evelyn paused, hesitant to try delving into her mind, but after a moment she tried to explore once more. Her head immediately attempted to split itself open and she cried out, holding her head between her hands.

"Talk to me," the woman commanded. "What is happening?"

"It hurts when I try to remember," Evelyn said through gritted teeth. "At least, remember anything to do with me personally other than my name. I remember general things though, like what Sorby is though I don't recall living here. Or anywhere else for that matter."

"Don't push yourself," the woman said softly. "The memories will come back. Is there anything else before I go?"

Evelyn paused, unsure of whether her question was ridiculous or not. It felt ridiculous, she was in Sorby after all, yet she needed to know for certain. The subject seemed important. Significant somehow.

"What race am I?"

Sloane smiled broadly. "You're human, Evelyn. A healthy human."

Nora

Nora was directing her team through a set of movements, instructing them on how to attack and defend against a group as well as a single opponent. The king's army would be well trained, and not only that, they often moved in perfect synchronisation. Nora was determined to make sure that her team was able to overcome being outnumbered or cornered. There may have been fewer fighters in the Alliance but that wouldn't stop them from having a significant impact.

If they could successfully execute what Nora was teaching them that is.

"They're looking good," Aren said, coming to stand by her side. They stood outside the northern wall of Midskopas where Nora's team were training in the fields just beyond the city.

"They would be doing even better if the other trainers were doing their jobs," she rebuked, folding her arms over her chest and watching those around her go through the movements. "I know I'm fantastic, but this is ridiculous. I wasn't the only one Aeolus named as an instructor and yet here I am with the majority of the Northern Alliance, as well as some of the citizens of Midskopas, and no one seems to care they weren't assigned to me. I don't even know if I'm supposed to be teaching all of these people hand-to-hand combat. And I have a feeling the younger ones over there were assigned ranged weapons instead, where they wouldn't be in the thick of it when the time comes."

Aren looked at the three teenagers barely into puberty then grinned at her. "They want a *good* teacher."

"Your flattery isn't going to work," Nora groaned. She watched a woman who'd lost her husband to the curse conduct a perfect parry after barely being able to hold up a sword only a few days ago. "Also, I'm better than *good*. Great, amazing, phenomenal, extraordinary…"

"Wouldn't go that far," he replied, bumping her with his hip. "But they did leave their teams to join yours. Just take the compliment."

"But what if all the praise goes to my head like it did to you?" She asked in mock concern, a teasing glint in her brown eyes.

"Do you ever get tired of taunting others?"

"Nope," she grinned, though it was short-lived. She breathed a heavy sigh. "Seriously, though. I can't do a thorough job when there's so many of them."

"Do your best."

"Obviously," Nora grumbled under her breath. Changing the subject, she asked, "How'd the strategy meeting go?"

Aren shrugged. "They take my advice with a grain of salt, at least those who are not Anima. Carl is inclined to side with me; however, the others are more sceptical of my words. You'd think my hundreds of years of expertise would be more welcomed."

"Expertise in being worshipped isn't exactly going to help right now."

"Ha ha, very funny. I have seen more wars than they have

in their combined lifetimes. Just never like this. Never with this king or curse in the mix. Maybe if you'd been there to back me up, it might have helped. Given your history as an Alta, they view you more as an expert in these matters than myself."

"They may trust me to a degree, but I have no more control over what they do than you. They're scared and doing what they think is best for their people," she replied, frowning at a man's uncentred stance. She moved to adjust his posture and offered advice before returning to stand with Aren. "Also I wasn't at the meeting because I was here, busy training. You're a God, Aren, make them listen to you."

"I refuse to force my will on others," he said, shaking his head. "There was a time when I did that; believed I was right and was above everyone else. It didn't serve me well in the end."

"You mean all those centuries ruling over cities and fighting with your siblings?"

"Yeah," he replied, frowning. "I've made some terrible choices in my long life. Perhaps that is why they're not inclined to listen to me. Unfortunate, considering I'm hoping to make amends for my past mistakes."

"That sounds familiar," Nora groaned then looked up at him. "Aren, if the Makers … your parents … if the curse comes from them, is there nothing you can do to stop it? Can't you counteract their magic? Maybe if you and your siblings worked together?"

"Nora…"

"I'll go with you to find them if that is what's stopping you. I know Thyra is working with King Dominic, but the others aren't. At least, I assume they aren't. Surely you could all get over whatever little grudge you have against one another and do something right for the greater good. At least one or two of them could tip the scale and do the right thing and help us, couldn't they?"

"There is no point asking for their help. There is nothing they can do."

"But—"

"Jord will never leave her frozen mountains, Nyssa put herself under a deep sleeping spell that I have no idea how to break, and Frode … Frode has washed his hands of all Valmenessia's affairs. There is only one thing he wants and none of us can give it to him. They want no part in this world anymore."

"Wonderful. Just you and Thyra are left to manipulate the masses and fight like bratty little children. I've been called stubborn but you lot take the award for that particular character trait."

"That's not fair," he said. "I—"

"You are doing what exactly? Hmmm?" Nora raised a brow.

"I'm helping here."

She glanced around, raising a hand to shield her eyes and leaned forward for emphasis. "I can't see them."

"Who?"

"Those who give a shit about your help," Nora snapped. "The Alliance have you doing little tasks while ignoring your advice. They want you for your name alone."

"Ouch."

"Your talents are wasted here. Unless being a glorified morale booster is your intention? Should we get you one of those hats with bells?"

"What would you have me do then?"

"Fly to Royal Bay and assassinate King Dominic?"

Aren shook his head. "I wish it were that simple, but Thyra is with him. There is no way she would let me get close enough."

"She can't kill you, though."

"She can."

"I thought you were immortal?"

"To a degree," he said. "If she lights me on fire, it's going to be hard to come back from the ashes."

"Hmmm," Nora pouted. "So what you're telling me is I'm right, which usually I love being, but in this case, it's a little bittersweet. You can't kill King Dominic and you have no way of stopping the curse. So what use are you?"

"Hey," he gasped. "I'm helping in other ways."

"Yeah, a morale booster brought out on special occasions to make everyone feel better and blessed or whatever."

Aren winced, but Nora didn't care. Her words were the truth. What was the point of having a God on their side if he didn't improve their chances?

"Did your parents leave any information behind before they died?" She asked, an idea forming in her mind. "Ancient scrolls or something? Or can we contact them? I know they're dead, but as parents of Gods and Goddesses they're not like *dead* dead, are they? If the curse is being raised in their names then maybe they are aware and can assist?"

"Nora," Aren began, his shoulders dropping. He sighed, looking frustrated with himself. "I should have explained it all when I first revealed who I was. We aren't Gods and Goddesses."

Nora jolted. "What?"

"Valmenessia is a prison and the Makers—"

"Help! Beasts! Help!" Shouts rang out from the wall, halting Aren's words. "Help! Beasts in the city!"

"You'll explain later," Nora stated, fixing Aren with a firm look before she bolted towards the city. She used her wind to propel her as she ran to the gate. Behind her, she heard the distinctive rustle of Aren's shift followed by a shadow that flew over her.

"What are you waiting for? You've been training for this!" Nora called back to the guerilla trainees. "Move!" The pounding of boots followed, and she adjusted her speed so that she ran with them close at her back towards the threat. Despite the shouting ahead, her mind reeled from Aren's words.

Valmenessia is a prison.

What the fuck did he mean by that?

She didn't have a chance to contemplate it. Turning down a

street towards the commotion, Nora came face to face with the giant beast everyone was shouting about. Its body was slate grey with big black eyes and fanged teeth that lunged threateningly at everything in reach. The thing hissed and pushed its long snakelike body out of a deep hole in the ground, sliding its enormous body further onto the street.

"Fuck," Nora breathed then moved into action, grabbing her sword and pointing it towards the beast. "Surround it!" she shouted, not taking her eyes from the thing or its teeth. She could hear the movement of the others, and see them falling into position from her peripherals, but she didn't dare turn away from the beast.

It was a good thing too because the next minute the beast rushed forward on its long leathery body. Its tail swung menacingly behind it, and Nora saw the point was as sharp as its teeth. It wasted no time before it attacked, lunging for Nora with its teeth. But she wasn't going down without a fight. She ducked, dodging its attack, and sliced with her sword to cut a gash in its side. Purple blood splattered all over the place. The warm liquid ran down Nora's side, flecking onto her cheeks as it gushed from the wound.

The beast shrieked.

Whilst others launched their own attacks, Nora summoned her magic, hoping to kill the thing before it could do any more harm. Her fire magic rose to the surface ready to pounce and she let it loose on the beast only to see it had absolutely no effect. It was immune to her fire.

"Not good," she hissed.

She tried again, with an air attack that sliced uselessly at the creature before dissipating. The beast's skin gleamed, her magic unable to breach its hide, as though some sort of shield protected it.

"Well, isn't that just shit," she grumbled, darting out of the way as it attacked again. "Looks like you're going to have to spend more time with my blade, then."

The man whose stance she'd adjusted earlier stepped in as Nora moved and sliced at the beast once more, creating another deep gash that spilled purple blood from its abdomen. The beast snarled, whipping around in a frenzy. Its rage was palpable as its tail swung back and forth, crumbling the walls of the surrounding buildings. Nora couldn't help feeling a little unnerved knowing that her sword was her only form of defence.

"It's immune to magic!" Nora shouted as another man shot jets of water at the beast.

It pushed through the water as though it were a mere annoyance and lunged for the man, picking him up in its front pincers. The man screamed as he was lifted in the air, his arms and legs waving around in a panic. His terror didn't last long as his shouts were quickly silenced by the beast's sharp teeth. Its jaws closed around him, biting him in half. The pieces of his corpse fell to the ground as it opened its mouth once more and the beast slid over them, unconcerned and focused on its next victim.

Nora looked to the sky, wondering where the hell Aren was only to spot him fighting further down the street. Carl in his wolf form and Chester in his fox fought with him as they fended off another of the snake-like things.

How many of the fucking beasts were there?

Focusing on her own serpent problem, Nora moved as one with the remaining members of her team. She lunged at its body and her sword hit its mark seamlessly, a little too seamlessly as she quickly realised the blade was stuck in its flesh. An ear-piercing screech sounded and the beast rounded on Nora, swiping its teeth at her.

Nora hissed as sharp teeth cut through her clothing, drawing blood as it sliced through her arm. She lunged again, aiming to grab the hilt of her sword still protruding from its side. Stupidly, she left herself open with the attempt. The beast's fangs clamped down again, narrowly missing her head, but she was caught between two teeth. It bit down hard on her already injured arm, wedging it into a gap.

Nora cried out. The pain was excruciating and its hold was firm. She had no idea how she was going to get it to release her without dislocating her arm. Sweat beaded on her forehead as she reached out for her sword with her free hand. The beast's teeth ground together, tightening its grip further on her flesh. Her fingers were a breath away from grasping the sword's hilt when she was suddenly dragged out of its reach.

Black dots flashed in her vision, and she let out a raspy scream as pain tore through her arm. Nora's body was pulled down hard and then, to her surprise and fucking relief, the beast's jaw released her. She clutched at her arm as she lay on the ground, tears filling her eyes before she looked at the beast to see why it had released her. An arrow had pierced its eye, blood seeping from the wound.

Nora rolled her head to the other side and saw a woman standing atop rubble in the street holding a bow. Nora mouthed a thank you and the woman nodded, pointing at the beast with a flick of her chin. Nora followed her directions to see a man straddled atop it, his hands clasped around a blade's handle that protruded from the beast's head. He grinned broadly before removing the blade a little awkwardly and sliding off, welcoming the praise from the others in their guerilla team.

Nora couldn't help but smile, despite the pain. Maybe it was the adrenaline or blood loss that made her delusional, nevertheless, hope bubbled in her chest. They were Valmenessia's last chance, and Nora couldn't help but think that their odds were better than she had originally thought.

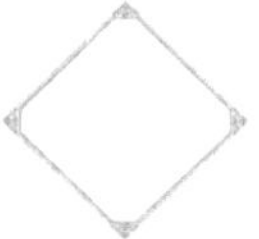

"We are evacuating the human population out of the city."

"You just can't leave it unprotected," a stocky middle-aged man said from across the table. He had been a business owner in the city once, though now represented the citizens who lived here. A voted stand-in lord of sorts. "King Dominic's army is coming to take back this city. Did so many die defending it just to give it up? What was the point? Will you really leave us exposed to invasion, not to mention any of the King's Guild that decides to come our way in the meantime?"

"The situation has changed," Nora said, sitting back in her seat and propping her boots on the table. "The increased damage to the city has rendered most buildings as just as unsafe as any other threat intent on killing us. By the time the king's army arrives, the humans will all be dead. As for the guild, they aren't as scary as they'd like everyone to believe."

"Staying is too risky," Carl stated. He stood at the head of the table, his fists on the wood as he leaned over it. Before him, a map of the city was laid out, tokens marking out the places of note. "First the king's men, then the curse, now those beasts."

"But we defeated them," the stand-in lord, whose name Nora didn't bother to learn, said. "They are no longer a problem."

"For now," Gemma said with her shoulders back and chin high. Her posture brokering no argument. "Who knows how many more dwell beneath the ground? Or what else is yet to reveal itself? It's foolish to risk so many lives to so many threats."

"The beasts in the Periculum Mountains have also awoken," Aren said. "And now these creatures. We need to stand together; divided we have no chance. There could be even more that have awakened and we need to move to a more defendable position."

"More? More of those creatures?" Carl asked, brows raising.

"Yes. Whilst many old tales are embellishments on truth or at times entirely contrived fantasies," Aren replied, glancing at Nora. "The stories of the mythical beasts' existence are not made up, more exaggerated yes, but only where the brave warriors who slew them are concerned."

If what he said was true, Nora couldn't help but think of at least one tale that had to be a lie. One that left so many questions running through her head. *Valmenessia is a prison*, and from what he seemed to be about to say next she guessed the Gods and Goddesses were not as they seemed. She hadn't had a chance to ask Aren more about what he'd said though. They'd been so busy since the attack yesterday, healing, tending to the wounded and organising the city occupants' departure, or evacuation as Carl and Gemma had put it.

"We are not abandoning the city, Harry. But I will not sacrifice the lives of so many to a vengeful curse and these beasts. The Alliance will regroup at the appointed location and the citizens of Midskopas need to leave as well. You put too much value on the city rather than its people. The relocation point isn't far and once the rest of the Northern Alliance arrives we will have a formidable army of our own to halt the king in his tracks."

"An army?" Chester asked. It was no secret that he wanted to return to the Northern Wolf Pack and Nora didn't blame him. She'd heard him in passing conversation about going home now that the fight for the city was over. From his reaction, those plans to return home had changed and Chester hadn't been told.

"Yes," Carl said, looking back at his husband, his features softening. "Notify everyone the city is no longer safe, more so than before. Everyone is expected to gather what supplies they can and journey to the relocation point. This is a tactical retreat, not a surrender of the city. Anyone who chooses to stay will be left behind. No aid will be given to those who do not come with us. We cannot afford to."

Nora hated feeling like she was giving up. But Carl and Gemma were right. The longer they stayed here, the more they would lose, and for what? Everyone would die for nothing.

"You're dooming us," Harry grumbled, pushing back his chair and storming from the room. "Abandoning those of us in need."

Gemma breathed out a heavy sigh. "Some people are too short-sighted; they cannot see past their immediate concern."

"The immediate concern should be the safety of those he is leading, not which faction possesses the city. If not the beasts, starvation will kill them if they stay. He's a fool if he can't see that," Aren said, rising to his feet. He stretched his arms over his head and yawned. "I'll help rally everyone."

The rest of the leaders left not long after and Nora was left alone with Aeolus. He hadn't said much during the discussion, instead, he stood with his back against a wall watching the interactions of the parties involved. Nora had planned on staying back and taking a moment to herself, but…

"Not that I don't like your company," Nora said tapping her finger to her chin. "Oh wait, I don't. So I guess there's no reason for me to stay."

She dropped her feet from the table and rose from her seat. The chair audibly scraped along the ground.

"Jasmine is coming with an army; no doubt Sage and Will will be with it. How do you feel about that?" He said.

The question seemed to come from nowhere. Why did he care? "Fine. Dandy even," Nora replied, fidgeting with the buttons on her coat. It was a half-truth. She was excited to see Sage and Will, but seeing them also meant facing what happened to Florence, and how was she supposed to do that? How would she face Will?

"I don't believe you," he said, moving to stand before her. He looked down at Nora, trying to read her expression.

Nora huffed a laugh. "Goddess forbid I don't have the faith of the high and mighty Aeolus. Whatever shall I do?"

"Enough with the smart mouth. You and I both know that defending this city or meeting the king's army on another field isn't going to put an end to this. More and more threats creep up on us with each passing day. Staying is far too dangerous and I, for one, cannot kill King Dominic if I die here."

"Maybe you're not trying hard enough." She didn't understand what this was about. Hadn't they just decided to leave the city?

Aeolus ground his teeth. "Same goes for you."

"Oh? Planning on killing the king *and* me?" Nora asked, folding her arms over her chest and raising a brow. "Quite the busy schedule."

"I don't want to kill you," he blew out a breath. "I'm going to Royal Bay and you're coming with me."

Nora barked a laugh. "Domineering and delusional? Did you get hit in the head during the last battle?"

"There are countless other people I'd rather spend my time with, but you are the best choice to get me where I need to be."

"*Best* choice? So you have other options? Good. Ask them."

His jaw clenched. "You are the *only* choice."

"You've been talking to Aren, haven't you?" Nora ran her gaze over his face then waved a hand dismissively. "But as I said to him, flattery is not going to work with me."

"You are extremely annoying, you know that?" He said. "Look, the reason I'm even asking is that I trust you will do what's best for you. The king's head being detached from his body is in your best interests."

"And here I was thinking you'd come to ask so we could be best buddies, sharing meals and stories and maybe a bed on our travels," she drawled, a smirk tugging at her lips. "Not cake, though. I never share my cake."

"That. The sarcasm," he said. "I hate."

"You better get used to it if we're going on a little vacation together," she replied. "Though, I have to ask, why now? Why not before we took Midskopas, or even after that?"

"It's time to end this." Aeolus stepped back, his gaze venturing towards the window where children could be seen playing in the street. "We are of no use here against a curse we can't fight."

"And his army?"

"Is just one wave in an ocean storm. Laws, guild members, armies … they'll keep coming if we don't sever the head of the beast. Once the relocation is complete, you and I are going south."

She wouldn't voice it aloud, but Aeolus was right. They were just putting off the inevitable here. King Dominic had to be stopped and she wanted a hand in his death. She owed the king that much in the very least.

Nora poured as much sarcasm into her voice as she could, despite the tightness squeezing inside her chest. "I can't wait."

August

The roads since leaving Fellbun were eerily quiet and kept August on edge. Usually, merchants and the like journeyed the tracks, moving between the northern cities, yet the travellers he and Tyler passed were few and far between, keeping to themselves and appearing wary of strangers. The actions of the king now compounded by the Makers' Curse had caused fear to settle over the land. Though the curse's telltale blackened veins were currently nowhere in sight, their lack of presence did very little to soothe anyone.

The grip the curse had on the cities where the Maker's Murders had taken place was proof of its strength. It was only a matter of time before it spread out from those cities and covered all of Valmenessia. How much longer did they have? August didn't want to think about it. Instead, he set his mind on the task at hand—reaching Royal Bay and rescuing Evelyn from King Dominic.

"Should we make camp for the night?" Tyler asked, slowing

his horse. In the distance, the sun was beginning to set. At the same time, the wind was picking up and its icy tendrils swirled and whistled through the air, adding further to the eeriness of the land. "We've made a lot of progress today and it looks like there is a cabin over there with our names on it. Let's just hope whoever is inside, if they haven't fled yet, agrees."

"I vote you knock," August replied with a yawn. He was eager to travel but he also knew when rest was needed. He was tired and tumbling off his horse because he fell asleep wouldn't be good, especially if the wind got any stronger and succeeded in its seeming attempts to push him off itself. "People seem to like you more," he added.

"It's because you've got this whole brooding thing going on, Dark Prince," Tyler said with a grin. "You can try to blame it on being a Mors Alv, but as you can see," he waved a gloved hand at his puffed-up chest. "We aren't all grumps."

August chuckled. After getting to know Tyler over the last few months, he was used to the man's teasing. Even being called 'Dark Prince' no longer bothered him. August may have been the son of a queen but that didn't make him royalty. King Dominic wasn't his father, and he was glad for it.

Drawing closer, they dismounted near a stone fence and August stayed back to hold the reins as Tyler went to see who, if anyone, still lived in the cabin. The small residence was nestled between a stable and a cluster of leafless trees, their branches sticking out at all angles. From where he stood, the trees reminded August of the curse and he grimaced at the thought. An icy breeze blew, and he lowered his head and shoulders in an attempt to protect his exposed face. The weather was miserable. August hoped they would have shelter for the night. He'd grown accustomed to always being comfortable whatever the weather was, having spent most of his life with Nora who would light a flame whenever it got too cold or summon a cool breeze if it grew too hot. She'd spoiled him.

"No one's home!" Tyler called and August looked up to see the man opening the door to the darkened cabin to stick his head inside. "Put the horses in the stable like a good boy and I'll light a fire!"

August huffed a laugh at the command but did what Tyler said anyway. He walked the horses to the shelter and made sure they were warm and comfortable before heading inside the cabin. He shut the creaking wooden door against the cold and was glad to see that Tyler had been successful. A modest fire burned in the hearth, the sound of the crackling already making August feel warmer as he sat opposite on a well-worn sofa.

"I wonder who lived here," August said, slipping his boots off to warm his feet and stretching himself out comfortably. Dust floated through the air from disturbing the abandoned house and he noticed cobwebs hung in the corners of the room. It had clearly been some time since they had left their home. The stale smell of neglect disappeared as the smoky scent of the fire filled the cabin.

"Who knows," Tyler shrugged, dropping into his own seat. "Their loss is our gain."

"There's no sign of the curse here."

"One of King Dominic's laws may have forced them to move on," Tyler replied. "Or maybe they simply decided to move on. The weather is pretty shit, I don't blame them."

August rolled his eyes as the wind whirled outside. The entire cabin groaned as if it were an effort to stand against the weather. He stretched his arms over his head, relaxing back, and the temptation to fall asleep was one he wasn't sure he could stop himself from giving in to.

With Tyler around he was safe. They hadn't seen anyone for hours and there had been no tracks in the snow. There was no reason to stay on guard or awake, so he gave in. Shutting his eyes, he leaned his head back and breathed out deeply, letting himself truly relax. Or at least as best he could give the sound of the wind assaulting the cabin.

His mind drifted to a memory of when he had been in Ferieton. The city was known for not only its high Lys Alv population but also for its navy. Like Ocean's Harbour, Ferieton sat at the opening to the Royal Bay and so the two cities had ships to protect the castle island and the monarchs who sat on the throne there.

August and Nora had been sent to the city when he was fifteen to assassinate someone the king had deemed a traitor. The plan had been simple. Nora was to befriend the daughter of the man in question and August was to drift in the shadows keeping watch. It was their usual method and one that proved successful more times than August would have liked to count.

One night in particular occupied his thoughts. It was a cold evening, though nothing like what he was experiencing now. In the south, cold was simply sweater weather, it never snowed. On this particular night, when he and Nora had crept onboard one of the ships in the harbour, it had creaked much like the cabin did and they had sat on the deck, sharing a slice of chocolate cake, looking out at the sea and telling stories of what lay beyond.

Their tales were ridiculously farfetched, but it had been a break from their reality and the inevitable murder they were to commit.

August tried to remember some of their silly stories. One story had been of countries beyond the sea being ruled by kings and queens no taller than a finger. The memory made him smile, which quickly evaporated when his foot was knocked, jostling him awake.

"What?" August grumbled, opening his eyes. "I'm trying to sleep."

"Someone's coming," Tyler said, standing by the fire.

August's Alta training kicked in as his senses honed in on the sounds around him. The creaking of the cabin, the crackling of the fire and there, the distant sound of murmured voices. He looked out the window next to the front door and saw a dim light drawing near.

"King's Guild?"

"Not sure. Could just be that the house has owners after all. Or some passerbys noticed a cabin with a cosy fire and wanted to join in," Tyler mused. He appeared at ease, though August knew the man was anything but. Tyler's tell being the lack of his usual grin and roll of his wrist.

August shoved his feet back into his boots and rose just as the door swung open. Three men strode into the cabin, smelling as though they hadn't bathed in years. They wore thick patched coats and the lower half of their faces were protected from the cold thanks to their thick beards. The three men stood side by side, eyeing down the intruders.

"Who do we have here?" one of them asked, his voice husky as he looked from August to Tyler. "Mors Alvs?"

"Spirits come back from the dead!" the man to his left said. His eyes were wide as he took a step back, only for the first man to grab him by the front of his coat and stop him from running away.

"Away with you!" the man on his right said, tugging a strange-looking weapon from a makeshift strap around his waist to wave in Tyler's direction. It wasn't a sword or any kind of blade from what August could see.

"To think we'd been told the Mors Alvs were all dead," the first man said, his voice turning to steel as he straightened his back. He appeared to have absorbed his initial shock, unlike his companions who were twitching nervously.

"The king likes to lie," Tyler said with a shrug. "We're hoping to stay for the night. We didn't realise the cabin would be occupied. Apologies for intruding, we will be on our way."

"I don't think so," the man replied, stepping forward. "You see, times are changing. Whether you have come back to life or not. The time of magic is over, and my friends and I are more than happy to help speed up the process."

"We don't want any trouble," August said, raising his hands before him. "As Tyler said, we are sorry for intruding."

"You will be," the man barked and suddenly all three men pushed forward, drawing more unusual weapons.

August gasped, his stomach turning in disgust as their weapons became clear. Body parts. They were wielding body parts.

One man swung a greyish arm at Tyler whilst the other sliced a leg through the air, a boot still on the foot. August jumped back, avoiding the boot. At the same time, he was forced to dart out of the way as the first man narrowly missed hitting him with a severed arm. The fingers were as black as the night sky from frost-bite and darker veins stood out against the pallid lifeless skin of the rest of it. A chill ran up August's spine; he knew exactly what had caused the flesh to turn that way.

"The curse!" August shouted, dodging another attack as he tried to move around the men and get to the exit. "They're carrying infected limbs!"

"Fuck!" Tyler cursed, thwarting an attack and darting away from the third man. "This is some messed up shit!"

"You're telling me!" August called back, hitting a wall in an effort to avoid a cursed arm touching him and knocked a painting off the wall. The attacker came at him again and he raised his hand, swatting the diseased limb away.

Tingles ran through his fingers, the brief contact making his stomach sink. It was unlike when the sick man had grasped his ankle in Fellbun. Then, he'd felt nothing but the man's touch, now it was as though spiders crept along his hand. Dread pooled in his chest, but August shoved the feeling away. He'd deal with it later.

"Let us leave," August told the man closest to him. "I don't want to hurt you."

"Hurt us?" the man laughed, swinging the arm at August

again. "You're about to die."

"I warned you," August replied, ducking out of the way before summoning his magic. They'd left him no other option.

August let his magic flow from him, though unlike those few months after the king's binding magic had disappeared from his skin, he now had control of it. Jord had taught him how to wield his power, harness the magic, and make it do his bidding. Now, he was its master.

He directed his attack, sending his magic out towards the three men. Their eyes went wide and each of them gasped. August didn't let up, not after they dropped their weapons to clutch their chests or when they fell to their knees. His magic fed on them, drawing strength and health from them until they each crumpled to the floor unmoving.

August didn't hate his magic. It was part of him and there were good things he could do with it. Yet, it was hard to see the positives at times like this. When he had to take a life, his magic was much like the curse. A parasite.

That part had never sat right with him. He stared down at the three men who were now unconscious on the floor. Using his magic had been necessary; it was either August and Tyler or them. The decision was easy. Anyone else would have done the same.

"More are coming!" Tyler shouted from the door, drawing August from his thoughts. Tyler's dark eyes were wide as he looked out at several torches glowing in the distance against the snow and wind. "We need to get out of here now!"

August raced after Tyler, leaving the cabin and rushing into the stables for their horses. His body moved swiftly, using the extra energy he'd gained from the three men. Panicked cries sounded from outside and August hurried to re-saddle his horse.

He wasn't quick enough.

More attackers stormed into the stable, brandishing flaming torches and more of the blackened limbs, shouting as they ran towards August and Tyler. August's gaze scanned the area for another exit, finding no other way out. They were trapped.

One or more of the attackers had apparently pressed their torches to the walls and now fire licked its way up the old wooden structure, hungry and desperate despite the cold. Smoke filled the air as the blaze roared to life and August quickly grabbed his horse's reins.

August braced to let his magic loose once more and his heart beat rapidly as he raised his hands. He was strong, but there were so many foes, he didn't know whether his magic would be able to stop them all. Or if his conscience would ever let him forgive himself for what he was about to do.

Just as August was about to summon his magic, Tyler stepped before him and let his flow through the stable. The attackers fell like saplings facing a strong wind, each one dropping to the stable's dirt floor before they could reach the two Mors Alvs.

Unlike August's magic, Tyler's worked quickly, removing the threat without time for them to suffer.

"Tyler! We have to go now!" August shouted before covering his mouth and nose with his arm against the smoke.

He urged his horse out of the stable, shielding its nose with his body as best he could. The horse needed no encouragement and followed August out of the burning stable into the cold night. Once clear, he made to mount, only to be ambushed by more attackers. Dead legs and arms swung at him from every direction as frantic cries filled the air.

Where the fuck had these people come from?

August drew his sword, hoping to dissuade the attack and give himself and his horse enough room to get free. He swung his blade to keep them back, but they used their makeshift weapons of cursed flesh to retaliate and press forward.

They wanted him dead.

August was hit from behind. His sword fell from his grasp as he stumbled forward. But he managed to keep his footing as the attackers closed in and summoned his magic once more. He hated using his magic on people and hated taking lives, but those assaulting him hadn't given him any other option.

He let his magic move over those around him, taking their lives as quickly as he could. It wasn't quick enough, their cries of pain filling his ears before they finally collapsed to the ground around him. But August wasted no time thinking about his actions as he felt their life energy fill his being. He quickly mounted his horse and looked back to the stable where he caught Tyler's gaze where he sat atop his own horse. More bodies littered the ground around him.

Tyler nodded and the two Morse Alvs spurred their horses into a canter away from the scene. With one look at the death they left behind, August silently made peace with his actions. What he'd done had been necessary.

He was no stranger to death and violence, but these seemingly ordinary people had given him a rude awakening, one he'd never forget. August had become complacent, thinking King Dominic and the Makers' Curse were the only real threats in this world. He'd forgotten that there were opportunistic beings all around, always looking for an advantage. They were quick to believe what they were told, falling prey to indoctrination, misinformation and mob mentalities. These humans had likely viewed the curse as some kind of reparation against those with magic. It was likely they viewed magic users as the reason for any bad fortune in their lives and the curse was just the planet's way of restoring balance.

Whatever the reasons, they would need to be more careful from now on. There were more players in this game than anyone realised.

Unfortunately for August, his time playing was destined to be cut short.

6

Evelyn

A human.

Sloane's words rang like a bell in her head, tolling as though trying to convince her of their truth.

Human.

She was human. Her appearance proved exactly that, yet why did it feel so foreign to her? Like it didn't fit; a pair of shoes a size too big or too small. If only she had her memories. Yet each time she attempted to access them, she was faced with a wall of pain that blocked her from delving down the path of her history. So she instead spent her days trying to memorise instructions and hoping not to get lost as she completed each task set out for her.

The estate may as well have been a maze for Evelyn. Verida, the maid who'd been there when Evelyn woke up, said she'd worked there for years, though nothing felt familiar. Another so-called fact that didn't sit right with her. Memories or not, Evelyn went along with the life she was told was hers. She was pretty sure she'd read or maybe heard somewhere, she couldn't be sure, that familiar places sparked memories. Whether that notion was accurate, she also didn't know, but at least it was better than sitting around and doing nothing.

The Healer, Sloane, had yet to seek Evelyn out or request her presence since that first day, and the lord's advisor, Mr Walker, too hadn't expressed any interest in seeing her again either. For two people who had apparently been so invested in her well-being whilst unconscious, she was surprised it had been days since she'd laid eyes on either of them. Not to mention she hadn't even seen the lord of the estate either. Odd considering she had spent all her days moving from room to room in his home.

The more she thought about it all, the more there was that didn't add up.

And then there was the large stack of letters from Royal Bay she'd seen on the table that morning, all from King Dominic and looking very important. Evelyn didn't know what they contained, yet her stomach twisted at the mere thought of the king. She didn't remember why she wouldn't like the king. Her gut was simply adamant that she didn't.

Why didn't anything make sense?

Evelyn checked the door on her left, sighing with relief when she saw the sitting room she'd been searching for. Hurrying inside, she began the task Verida had set for her; dusting. The estate housed a multitude of possessions, all of which seemed to attract so much dust. The job wasn't hard, but the constant sneezing was a nuisance, as well as the frustration that came from trying to recall anything as familiar. When she wasn't attempting to spark recognition, her mind would wander, much to her dismay. A wandering mind searching for memories meant headaches that did her no good.

Breaking down the wall hiding her memories was an impossible task and she had no weapons to aid her. She gripped her dust cloth tightly as the frustration at not knowing her past and so much of who she was remained beyond irritating.

She carefully ran her cloth over the surface of a blown glass ornament, admiring the colours and patterns as she held it in the light. Apart from thinking it was beautiful, she felt nothing towards the ornament. Odd, but not unusual considering her reactions to everything else she'd picked up. There were so many pretty things in the estate, a wide collection that must have taken decades if not centuries to collect. That's what most rich and powerful families did if she recalled correctly. She probably didn't, but there was no point dwelling on it.

The Maker family would have been like every other wealthy family and passed everything down over the years. Evelyn scrunched her lips; she couldn't recall Lord Maker or the Maker family. Considering they had the same name as the parents of the Gods and Goddesses, she thought she ought to. Surely that would have made them stand out? But then again, she couldn't recall the names of the other lords and ladies who ruled over cities across Valmenessia either.

Evelyn sighed. She was so sick of not understanding, of feeling like the pieces she was being given didn't fit the puzzle.

Movement caught Evelyn's eye and she spotted a man walking by the window. He stopped in the garden outside, placing his hands behind his back as he inspected the red roses. Evelyn couldn't help but feel that there was something familiar about him. There was a dull thud in her head where pain usually sat that made her confidence grow in that assumption.

The man looked as though he was beyond tired. There were bags beneath his blue eyes, yes, but his posture was deflated as well. He wore a hat that concealed most of his hair, though she could see that the strands peaking from under it were almost white. He wore a simple brown shirt and trousers in a darker shade of the same colour and carried a large tomb beneath one arm; nothing fancy nor remarkable in any way.

Powerful Crystals: A Beginners Guide to the Precious

Stones of Valmenessia, Evelyn read once the man placed the book on the ground, her curiosity piquing. The subject sounded fascinating and she tried to recall anything she knew about it. The dull thud turned into a sharp pain that made her wince. Apparently whatever she knew about crystals was locked behind that wall in her head.

Evelyn rubbed her temples in response to the new wave of pain and watched as the man slipped a blade from his pocket and used it to cut one of the flower stems. Almost tenderly, he retrieved a luscious rose from the bush and held it to his nose. The man sniffed the flower before abruptly dropping his hand, his head snapping to one side. His pale cheeks flushed and he quickly retrieved his book and departed from Evelyn's view urgently.

Curiosity burst beneath her skin as she fumbled to place the ornament down without breaking it and rushed to the window, ignoring the lingering pain in her head. He was the first person since she'd awoken who felt familiar and that had to mean something.

Evelyn raced from the room and rushed down the hallway towards the garden, hoping she could catch up to him. She suddenly reached a dead end and quickly retraced her steps to take another avenue, scolding herself for not knowing her way. She finally made it to the garden and swung her head left and right, scanning the area for any sight of him. But the man was gone.

Disappointment filled her, yet the feeling wasn't alone. Swirling in her gut and trying to drown the hope that was attempting to bloom amongst it all was something else. It was only small, but she held onto that seed of hope.

Whether she could recall anything beyond familiarity or not, the man was proof of one thing, her memories weren't completely lost to her. She just needed to find a way to break down that wall and set them free.

As if Sloane had been reading her mind concerning the sudden lack of interest in her wellbeing, Evelyn was called to meet with the Healer in the estate's apothecary later that day. Evelyn walked up a gravel path that was lined with neatly trimmed hedges and approached the stone apothecary building. It appeared much like a cottage on the outside, yet when she stepped inside Evelyn found nothing resembling a home.

A large cauldron sat in the centre of the room over a fire, the liquid within bubbling as steam swirled in the air. A bed was positioned in the far corner with shelves lining the walls all around the room. Each shelf was filled with all manner of what Evelyn could only assume were jars of healing remedies, bottled ingredients and medicinal tomes.

"You're late," Sloane said, appearing from behind the steaming cauldron. She blew a stray strand of violet hair from her face.

"I got lost doing my tasks and had to stop for directions," Evelyn explained, with her hands behind her back. "I'm sorry. It won't happen again."

"Sit," Sloane clicked her fingers at the bed. "How have you been feeling since I last saw you?"

The Healer resumed her ministrations with the cauldron, emptying a vial into the concoction before collecting another from a nearby shelf.

"Health-wise, I feel fine," Evelyn answered with a smile. "The headaches come and go whenever I try to recall something about my past, but other than that I'm completely normal."

"Your memories haven't returned?"

"No, they are still evading me."

Sloane tsked, sprinkling powder over the bubbling liquid.

"What are you making?" Evelyn asked, sitting up and straightening her shoulders, her curiosity getting the better of her. "A tonic?"

"Of sorts," Sloane muttered. "Tell me about your day. How are you finding the work?"

"It's slow relearning everything so it can be frustrating as nothing and no one is familiar. At least until earlier…"

"Explain."

"I saw a man," Evelyn said, recalling the one from the garden. "There was something familiar about him but I'm not sure what it was. The headaches came when I tried to recall him, so that has to mean something, doesn't it? And it wasn't just him. He had a book about crystals and when I tried to think about them, my headaches got worse."

"This man," Sloane began, looking at Evelyn with a raised brow. "What did he look like?"

"He wore a hat, but I'm sure he had white hair beneath it. He also had blue eyes and was an older man."

"Ahh," Sloane replied on an exhale. "I know who you are talking about. His name is Phillip. He used to work with your family, which may be why he is familiar to you."

"My family?" Evelyn's eyes widened as hope filled her chest. "He knows about my family?"

Sloane nodded. "He does; however, you shouldn't ask him about it. Your family passed when you were only young. It was tragic and he has terrible memories of it."

Evelyn felt a cool chill run down her spine as her shoulders drooped. Sloane had so casually mentioned her family's death as though it were simply a fact and not something that would affect Evelyn. However, it did, immensely. Evelyn may not have remembered them, but hearing of their deaths was like a hard blow to the chest. She felt herself gasp and clutched her stomach at the reality so matter-of-factly placed before her.

She was alone.

"I'm sorry," Sloane said, kneeling before Evelyn. "I didn't mean to tell you like that, it sort of slipped out. I should have known better."

Evelyn's chest heaved and she dropped her head between her knees. Sloane rubbed soothing circles on her back with her and. It was strange to feel such a loss for parents she couldn't remember even existing. Though her mind refused to let her remember them, there was something deep inside her that did. Something that felt the grief so deeply.

She didn't know how long she stayed like that when she finally became aware of Sloane walking back around her cauldron once more. Evelyn was curled up on her side, clutching her hands to her chest as she watched Sloane continue brewing her tonic from the bed. There was an almost familiar scent in the air, a cinnamony one that Evelyn breathed in and was reminded of pastries that had her feeling warm inside.

Comfort.

"We're not all that different," Sloane said. She placed her hands on her hips, as she looked down to where Evelyn lay. "Sorby, the rest of Valmenessia, and those across the seas. Human, Anima, Lys Alv, even those Mors Alv when they were still alive, we're no different when it comes down to it—magic aside that is," she smirked at Evelyn. "But everyone has the same hopes, dreams, losses and downfalls. Losing our family is part of the natural order. The lived experience isn't overly unique."

"Is this supposed to make me feel better about having no family?" Evelyn asked, sitting up. "Because thinking about others also losing those they love doesn't make me feel any happier."

"No, I was only trying to give you some perspective," Sloane scolded though there was a playfulness to her tone. "Losing loved ones from illness, accidents … it's awful, yes. But it's nothing new. Like wars for example. Each time a war begins everyone thinks it's the first and worst one. But there are conflicts wherever you go, all the time. Valmenessia isn't unusual in this. Even beyond Valmenessia, there are rulers obsessed with power, waging even worse fighting and division among their people. There's always someone who wants more power and takes it from others. Though when everyone has power, does anyone have it?" She tapped her temple. "Think about it."

"How do you know so much about the countries beyond Valmenessia?" Evelyn asked, tilting her head to one side. Sloane seemed incredibly wise in her manner and words, though she couldn't have been much older than Evelyn. She was so young and fresh-faced, and yet Evelyn couldn't help but feel the other woman had decades on her.

"Before moving to Valmenessia, I lived in a place called Devotion," Sloane said.

So the Healer wasn't from Valmenessia originally. Evelyn was intrigued by the world beyond their waters a glad for a change in topic. Those with magic were unable to leave the country and the new knowledge of someone willingly entering, who could leave at any time, was fascinating.

"Have I ever left the country?"

"No," Sloane replied with a shake of her head. "But I hope one day you will. There is so much to see outside of Valmenessia."

"We should go together," Evelyn said, thinking of what lands lay across the sea. "You can show me Devotion where you're from. I'd love to see it."

Sloane's gaze focused on Evelyn as though weighing up what to say. Finally, she nodded. "I'd like that."

Evelyn smiled, pushing on with her questions. Sloane seemed to enjoy being asked about herself and Evelyn felt there was more to the woman than just being a Healer. Something far more interesting. Talking about Sloane was a good distraction from the new knowledge that her family was gone. "What was Devotion like?"

"My family owned an apothecary," Sloane said. "It was the

only one in the city and customers would come from all over to buy healing remedies and other useful creations of ours."

"Your family were Healers too?"

"Not exactly," Sloane replied with a small shake of her head. "We had Healers in Devotion, not Lys Alvs obviously, but those who knew how to tend to others."

"Like yourself."

"Sort of." Sloane nodded, returning to her tonic. "My family's business was there to help those with conditions that didn't require a Healer or were looking for long-term maintenance of ailments."

"Sounds like your family were Conjurers of sorts," Evelyn said. "Are you...?"

Sloane stiffened, her shoulders tense.

"I'm sorry, I—" Evelyn stammered, wishing she hadn't asked. It was a stupid question. They were in Sorby. There was no way Sloane would be a Conjurer. And if she were ... Evelyn didn't want to think about what would happen to the woman if someone suspected her of using magic.

Sloane crushed a bunch of dried leaves in her hand, scattering them into the cauldron and a mint-infused steam filled the room accompanied by the sound of sizzling pops. The woman was making a tonic, Evelyn told herself, not conjuring. That's what Healers do.

"I came to Valmenessia and that's that," Sloane said finally as though Evelyn hadn't mentioned conjuring at all.

"Alone?" Evelyn asked a little more hesitantly. She was curious but also didn't want to put her foot in it again. "Do you miss your family?"

"There is no one left there to miss. They all died a long time ago."

Evelyn frowned, understanding why she had seemed so matter-of-fact about the deaths of Evelyn's family. She'd already experienced it herself. "We're both alone then."

"Alone together."

7

Nora

Nora looked out towards the new settlement where flags bearing the mark of the Northern Alliance, the familiar five squares on their points, waved in the wind. Evacuating Midskopas had been a blow and morale was so low it was practically buried along with their dead.

Nora sat atop the city wall as a cool breeze caressed her face and wished the sun would warm her. It wasn't so long ago that she'd been attacking guards along these very walls, eager to make a change. To do good.

How the world had so quickly changed. They won the city and lost it almost instantly to the Makers' Curse and beasts that dwelled beneath the ground. They'd been foolish to think the king was the only threat. In some ways, they had been just like King Dominic, blinded by their goals. At least she had been … and Florence had paid the price.

Bile rose in Nora's throat. Her grief was inescapable, trailing her like an assassin in the shadows, waiting to strike her down.

She felt the weight of its presence yet could not defend herself from the sudden blows that often snuck up on her out of nowhere. It was often the moments she had something she wanted to share with Florence, when something reminded Nora of her friend, or simply the repeated realisation that Florence was gone. The latter came without warning when Nora least expected it.

Florence had been one of the first people to forgive her and Nora was going to spend the rest of her life earning that faith her friend had put in her, even if Florence wasn't around to witness it.

But Florence wasn't the only person's death she'd had a hand in. Others rose to the surface to plague her. Criminals and innocents she'd sent to their graves. Yes, her actions were by command of the king, but that didn't absolve her. Nora was finally able to feel what she had forced onto so many others while tied to the king. An unending loss that would never be forgotten.

Nora glanced back to where Aren stood behind her, relaxing his side against the stone.

"Ready to go on Aeolus' big adventure?"

Aren chuckled. "Trust you to put it like that."

He stepped forward, shoving his hand into his pocket, and pulled out a gold necklace. On the end of the chain hung a shimmering brown stone that looked almost like it had been carved into something but the carver gave up.

"Is that charm supposed to be a stick?" Nora asked, tilting head to one side to get a better look at it.

"It's an eagle," he huffed playfully, lifting it to his eye level. "Okay, was an eagle. It's very old. My guardian gave it to me."

"Guardian?"

"I believe they are called mentors now amongst the Anima," he said. "Nevertheless, I was gifted it by someone very important to me and now I want you to have it."

"Are you asking me to be your mentee? Mentoree?" Nora scrunched her nose. "Mental?"

"You're mental."

Nora beamed up at him. "Why thank you for noticing."

"I want you to have it as a token of our friendship but also as my way of showing you that I believe in you even when you may doubt yourself. Just know I'm always on your side."

"Aim right for the heart, why don't you," she teased, despite the tears that crept into her eyes. She quickly wiped them away and accepted the necklace offered to her. She held it in her palm, seeing how the stone had indeed been an eagle once upon a time. "Thanks."

Aren beamed at her and she decided that the conversation was becoming far too heavy for her liking. Too full of feelings that she was still not able to deal with completely. Nora coughed, stuffing the necklace into her pack and changing the topic. "What did you mean the other day when you said Valmenessia is a prison?" she asked.

His shoulders stiffened immediately at her abrupt question, his smile falling.

"Is it because anyone with magic can't leave?"

"In a way," he replied, his voice holding none of the teasing she was used to. He sounded old, ancient. "Long ago magic was everywhere, it wasn't just trapped here but spread out on all the lands."

"What happened to make it only exist here?"

"What else but a war?"

"A war against magic? I'm assuming you lost."

Aren nodded. "We were trapped here with others that had the same beliefs as us."

"You mean the Makers."

"No, they were the ones who did the trapping."

Nora barked a laugh. "Did your parents put you in the naughty corner?"

"They were never our parents. That's just a story Nyssa and Jord made up a few centuries ago to control the narrative and maintain power. Along with us being Gods and Goddesses. It's just more stories."

"Huh," Nora replied, eyebrows raised. "So who are the Makers, then?"

"We call them Conjurers now. They confined us to this continent and made me and my siblings immortal."

"And they saw that as a punishment?" Nora asked, folding her arms over her chest. "Not the worst sentence, is it?"

"Try watching everyone you've gotten close to, everyone you've loved, everyone you've ever known die. Over and over again."

Nora could barely handle the loss of one friend right now. All of them would probably destroy her. "Okay, maybe it's not that great," Nora ceded. "So why doesn't everyone know about this? How is it not common knowledge?"

"The Makers' made it so everyone forgot, and time helps," Aren said. "Also I doubt the immortality was intentional on their part."

"How were they so strong? Conjurers have never been able to wield magic like that, as far as I know at least."

"Before Valmenessia was a prison, before we were trapped here, the Makers were an exclusive group. Back then it was more common for relationships to be limited to single races and the Makers were the strictest of all. Their magic wasn't restricted to a single form of expression, like healing or growing plants. Makers could wield their magic however they deemed fit and thus were considered a sixth race, unlike today where they are part of the human race. The Makers were the most powerful race to walk the land and whilst they didn't interfere with the kings and queens of old, they saw it as their duty to step when they believed things were not as they should be."

"Like parents punishing their children."

Aren barked a sad laugh. "Exactly."

Nora looked at him, trying to really see him for the first

time. Not as a God, but as a man who must have done something so terrible to warrant such an extreme punishment. "What did you do to be trapped here?"

"Things that I regret, some that I don't," he said, waving a hand dismissively. "It doesn't matter anymore. It can't be changed."

"But—"

"Would you like to discuss every horrible thing you have done?" He cut her off. His eyes glowed and his jaw was tense as he stared her down.

She hated being spoken to that way. His tone reminded her of King Dominic. "No need to be an asshole," she said, drawing out her words and averting her gaze so that she now looked north once more.

"I'm sorry," Aren breathed, stepping closer. "I…" He didn't finish his sentence. Instead, he moved from where he had been standing to sit at her side and faced Midskopas. "Even after all this time, it isn't easy."

"I get it," she nodded. Her lips tugged up at one side and a glint formed in her brown eyes. "Though I haven't done anything so diabolical to get imprisoned in a country for eternity."

"Yet," he teased. "You've still got time."

Nora shoved him and when Aren laughed she did it again only harder, pushing him over the edge. Aren fell. She stood, cupping her hands around her mouth and shouted "Asshole!"

Aren's laugh echoed around her as his Anima form rose in the sky. He looped in the air before coming to perch on the stone wall where his large eagle form cast her in shadow.

"I want to say I can't believe you pushed me," Aren said, angling his sharp beak towards her. "But that would be a lie."

Nora grinned wickedly, her smile faltering when she spotted Aeolus approaching behind Aren. He once again had weapons strapped to every inch of him, yet she knew his true weapon was invisible to the eye. His Elementum water magic was far stronger than any blade he owned.

The relocation had gone smoothly and the Alliance was fortifying their defences. She knew the only reason he would actively seek him out. Skipping over the pleasantries, Nora folded her arms over her chest and asked, "When do we leave?"

"Now," he replied.

"You know," she said. "It might have been smart to have more than just the three of us undertake this little task of yours."

"Three is plenty," Aeolus smirked. "Or are you afraid?"

"No."

"I am," Aren admitted.

"I thought you were an eagle, not a chicken," Nora smirked at Aren.

"Fear is healthy," Aren replied, tilting his head to one side. His eagle eyes looked at her pointedly. She found it a little unnerving if she was being honest with herself. "Keeps the senses alert. Are you telling me you're not even a little afraid? Should Aeolus and I stay here while you go alone?"

"Nope, you should come," Nora replied, climbing onto his back to avoid his gaze. She used her wind magic to help lift her. "But only because having you around as a distraction or backup doesn't hurt. The king is heavily guarded after all."

"Lucky you know the castle like the back of your hand then, isn't it?" Aeolus said, climbing to sit behind her.

Nora grumbled a curse as his hands gripped hard over her hips. "Loosen the iron grip." She slapped his hand. "You sure are putting a lot of faith in me, for someone who can't stand me."

"I may not like you very much, but I'm not an idiot," he replied, his hold softening. "And if it's a choice to take anyone on a suicide mission I wouldn't exactly choose someone I care about now, would I?"

"You have a point," she mused.

It didn't bother her that Aeolus had asked her to go or if he had chosen her because he was okay with her dying. At least he was upfront about it. In truth, she didn't like him all that much either.

"I thought you liked me?" Aren said, feigning offence.

"Apparently not," Nora chuckled. "We could start a club; I reckon there would be a lot of people that could join. Aeolus is full of righteous judgment. I doubt many reach his likability expectations."

Aeolus groaned irritably. "Enough. Let's go."

Aren laughed beneath them, the sensation as well as the sound was strange coming from a giant eagle. "It's going to be a lot of fun travelling with you two."

Nora rolled her eyes as they took off into the sky. Back when she was an Alta, she had had very little to do with Aren, or Felix as he was then. He'd always been a stuck-up ass, which he still kind of was. However, he'd grown on her over the past few weeks. They spent most of their days together, even shared the dressing room in the theatre as sleeping quarters, and she was begrudgingly coming to like him.

Only a little bit of course.

Now, after what he'd shared about his history, she felt like she understood him more. Understand his actions and the humour he used as a deflection from forming real bonds better. His revelations were a lot to take in, but she didn't doubt his truth. If anything, his words had given her some semblance of hope. If a Conjurer created this mess, then maybe a Conjurer could undo it. They just needed to find one and convince them. But first, dealing with the known threat took priority. The king needed to die and then they would find a way to lift the curse.

Nora frowned as they flew south high over Midskopas. The roots of the curse entwined in nearly every crevice of the city. There were very few people on the street, some appeared to be leaving, and others didn't appear to be moving at all. Midskopas hadn't been in the best condition when she'd been there with August, but now it was mostly in ruin. They soared overhead nearing the wall that bordered the south side of the city. Here the curse was thicker and from the sky, she could see the way it pulsed. She grimaced at the sight.

"Fuck."

Aeolus' tone was grim. "Couldn't have put it better myself."

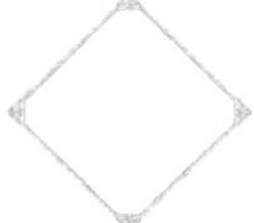

Nora's anxiety grew the closer they drew to Giland and her mind ventured to memories she did not want to dwell on. Her butt was sore from sitting on Aren's eagle back for the last few hours and the discomfort was no longer able to distract her. Memories kept forcing their way in despite her best efforts to keep them out. Images of smoke and fire burning through her childhood home, the sound of screaming, and the pain of searing burns. She was finding it more than she could bear.

Travelling by giant eagle was much quicker than Nora anticipated, and it wasn't long before Giland came into view.

Nora squashed the uneasiness as it attempted to rise in her gut. The last time she had been to Giland she'd been under the king's command. Now, she was vulnerable to all her emotions and Nora wasn't eager to find out the extent seeing the city would affect them. She had too much bad history in that place.

The city came into view and Nora sat atop her Aren in disbelief, staring at the destruction below them. The Makers' Curse had taken over the city of Giland entirely. Where giant blackened roots had plagued Midskopas in scattered eruptions, here the curse was spread out over red-bricked buildings and what was once lush green land, like a dark all-encasing web. There was no sound beyond the rustling of the wind, no scent of the orchids that used to grow around the main city, no firelight in the windows or smoke in the chimneys to ward off the winter weather.

Everything was grey. A muted, dismal version of a once vibrant place. Its life sucked completely dry.

"Fuck," Nora breathed, looking at the place that had brought her nothing but bad memories and feeling a new kind of sadness fall over her. She may have hated stepping foot in the city, but it had still been her home. Giland had been a prosperous city, with a huge population, most of which were Elementum. They wouldn't have stood a chance against the curse.

Aren flew around the city, avoiding flying directly over it. The dreadful sight of the curse was never far from her left as he continued on. The dark lines in the corner of her eye were a reminder of the power and indiscrimination of the Makers' Curse. All it wanted was magic and it wouldn't let anything stop it from getting what it desired.

"It's worse than I had imagined," Aren said. His wings beat at his side, propelling them through the air. "All those—"

Aren didn't get to finish as a blackened root shot up as quick as a lightning strike to slam into his chest. He cried out, spinning in the air as he was thrown off course and towards the centre of the city. Nora swore, clinging on tightly to Aren's feathers as Aeolus' wrapped his arms around her waist and Aren tumbled through the air.

"Brace yourselves!" Aren shouted, flapping his giant wings to right them. He picked up his pace, darting through the air and around the curse's attempts to strike him. It continued to pulse beneath them as more roots shot up. Nora's stomach performed somersaults as Aren swerved left and then right, missing the curse by a hair's width, and raced to the city's edge.

A jet of water slammed into a root at their left.

"Don't!" Nora shouted at Aeolus. "You'll only make it stronger!"

"Fuck," Aeolus hissed, watching as the cursed root absorbed his magic, feeding on it, and became even more determined to catch its prey.

Another root shot up, hitting Aren's wing, and he let out a cry of pain as he rolled again. Air rushed passed them as they plummeted toward the ground to where the curse hungrily awaited them. Noar's grip tightened on Aren's feathers. She was not ready to die.

"Hold on!" Nora shouted as she summoned her wind magic. Giant whirlwinds appeared around them as she used her magic to lift Aren and push them through the sky.

Or at least that's what she had intended.

Nora and Aeolus instead went flying from Aren's back and she lost sight of both companions as she was swept up in her whirlwind. She couldn't see where she was going as she tumbled around, all she knew was she was falling. Nora hoped they would all survive this.

The curse flailed around, like the tentacles of an octopus her panic making her lose control of her magic. The three hurtled around through the air at a rapid pace. Heart hammering in her chest, the magical wind finally released Nora, and she was now falling towards the ground. Luck, or at least a sadistic relation, was on her side as she realised she was falling beyond the cursed city. Nora let out a laugh as she flew through the sky, the ground coming up quickly to meet her. She quickly called forth her wind magic again to slow her down before summoning water to catch her. She landed in what only could be described as a pillow of water before dropping to her feet on solid ground. She smiled at her triumph before panic replaced the feeling. Aren and Aeolus.

Where were they?

Sudden shouts from above made her look up and she spotted Aeolus falling overhead. She summoned her wind magic once more and tried to slow him down. He must have seen what she was doing as he too called his magic, though he only had water. He created a waterfall and used it to slide to the ground, not as gracefully as she had but safe, nonetheless.

"Where's Aren?" she demanded, rushing over to him.

"I lost him when you used your wind magic," he replied, rising to his feet.

"I didn't know what else to do," she said, waving a hand and using her fire and wind magic to dry them. "We needed to get out of there and my whirlwinds were the best thing I could think of."

"It was good thinking."

Nora stopped, stunned. "Really? Did you just compliment me?"

"Yes," he muttered. "Come on, let's find Aren."

The two set off at a jog in the direction of Giland. They had travelled considerably far thanks to Nora's whirlwind and could still see the city in the distance. The curse's roots waved frantically in the sky whilst others pulsed on the ground as though feasting on the land itself.

Aeolus put out a hand, stopping Nora, and pointed. "There."

Still in his eagle form, Aren was entangled in the grasp of a giant black root. His body appeared limp, and his head sat at an unnatural angle. His brown feathers looked increasingly dishevelled as the curse constricted him, consuming his magic. Nora fell to her knees as tears fell down her cheeks. She had lost someone else and there was nothing she could do.

Aeolus placed a hand on her shoulder. "Not even the Gods are safe from the Makers' Curse."

But they had no time to mourn. A loud rumble shook the ground as the curse's roots pulsed and grew exponentially, spreading out further after consuming so much more magic. And what a feast it had had. The magic of a God would have been quite the meal.

"Run!" Aeolus shouted.

Nora didn't need to be told twice. She got to her feet and ran as fast as she could south towards Royal Bay. The sound of the curse tearing up the land in pursuit of them spurred her on. Her heart pounded in her chest as she pushed forward with tears in her eyes. She chanced a look behind her and saw tiny roots, like new black branches, sprout behind her, lapping at her heels.

"Run faster!" Aeolus shouted.

Nora urged her feet to push faster, summoning her wind magic at both their backs to push them forward. She glanced back again to see that the curse was still moving fast, gaining on them, even with her magic helping them.

"Hold on! This is probably going to hurt!" She called and waved her hands, throwing another gust of wind.

Nora's feet left the ground as she hurtled through the air rapidly and the world blurred around her. She felt like an arrow being shot from its bow and hoped it would be enough to save her and Aeolus. Satisfied they had enough distance between them and the curse, she flexed her fingers to summon her water magic to form a cushioned landing. Instead, what looked like a floating river of water appeared before her. She braced herself, colliding with the water and holding her breath, as she was pulled down its current before sliding onto the ground. Nora sat up coughing and spluttering and turned to see how far they had come from Giland. The city was now far in the distance, and the curse no longer pursued them.

Aeolus stood beside her and wiped a hand over his face. "That was close."

Nora dropped back onto the muddy ground, shaking uncontrollably. She lay back and threw an arm over her eyes, giving in to the feeling that demanded to overwhelm her. Tears fell over her cheeks and down the side of her face as what just happened sank in. Sobs wracked her body, her chest heaving as she gasped and choked on her grief.

Aren was gone.

Another friend had been taken from her. Another friend she couldn't save. First Florence and now Aren Was this some sort of punishment the world was forcing upon her for all the terrible things she'd done?

Nora didn't care that Aeolus was watching her cry. She

didn't care about privacy or embarrassment. She didn't deserve them. This was her punishment. And like a witness ensuring the sentence for her crimes was carried out, he stood silently as he watched her fall apart.

Her heart was torn. She could do nothing as Aren's face filled her mind. His incessant teasing and smiles were gone … Nora would never see him again.

8

Evelyn

Evelyn took Sloane's advice and didn't approach the older man she had seen in the garden. Phillip. Instead, she took note of his movements whenever she caught sight of him and hoped that she could devise an 'accidental meeting' of sorts. The only problem was, the more she saw of him, the more her courage dwindled. The man was far from approachable and, judging by the way he spoke to the other workers, would probably yell at her if she did attempt to speak to him.

Her curiosity was piqued, his knowledge of her family like a tempting carrot in front of a bunny, yet his unpleasant manner was the fence keeping her at bay.

In the meantime, she continued working on the tasks set by Verida. Ten servants worked in the estate, not including the kitchen or garden workers, and the jobs were allocated each morning before sunrise. Evelyn was beginning to fall into a rhythm and was even making friends, too. Or perhaps remaking, she wasn't entirely sure and no one had said a word to let her know either way. Her favourite place she got to visit was the kitchens. There was something comforting about the place, especially when the cooks prepared sweets. She often wondered if she spent much time there before losing her memories.

Evelyn carried linens from the line while thinking of the best way to broker a conversation with Phillip—one that wouldn't result in her having her head chewed off. Her thoughts were interrupted when she stubbed her toe on a large stone in the path and stumbled forward. She yelped as sheets went flying through the air, landing all around her as she hit the ground. Her knee smarted on impact and she groaned.

"Ouch." She hissed from the pain of hitting both her toe and knee. Then she looked at the now dirty sheets scattered on the ground and grimaced. Just wonderful.

"Are you alright?" A smooth voice asked.

Evelyn looked up to see a man with cropped black hair and brown eyes that twinkled in the sunlight. He reached for a sheet with one hand, the other placed against his lower back as though he were bowing. He wore a deep blue button shirt beneath a brown vest that matched the colour of his trousers. His shoes were polished to a glossy black and Evelyn wondered whether the shiny golden buttons on his vest had received the same level of care.

"I'm fine. Thank you," Evelyn replied, hurrying to her feet. "And please don't worry yourself. I'll pick those up."

"Nonsense. I'm happy to help," the man smiled broadly, flashing his very white teeth. He exuded confidence from every inch. The cut of his attire and direct mannerisms only accentuated what had to come naturally.

"I appreciate it," she said. She put her full weight on her leg and found it sent a shot of pain through her knee. Hoping he didn't notice, she quickly limped to collect the other sheets, bundling them unceremoniously into her arms. "I better get these to the laundry room to be cleaned again."

The man held out the last bedsheet with his gaze running over her, and she couldn't help but drop her eyes to the ground as she accepted the sheet.

"You don't remember me," he stated, curiously.

Evelyn shook her head, glancing up at him through her lashes. "I'm sorry. Do we know each other?"

He looked at her intently and for some reason reminded her of Sloane. "Huh," he clicked his tongue. "Interesting."

"What is?"

"You. Everything," he said, walking backwards. "What isn't interesting?"

And with that he turned, leaving Evelyn feeling both confused and curious.

The rest of the afternoon was a whirlwind as Evelyn became caught up in preparations for the Lord Maker's guests. Verida had found her in the laundry and, rather than scold her for the dirty sheets, recited tasks for Evelyn to complete.

The list had been long.

And so, Evelyn had set to work by helping to tidy rooms for the guests to stay in before preparing the spaces in which the Lord Maker would entertain. Her feet hurt by the time the sun had set.

She flexed her toes and stretched her knee while waiting outside the kitchen to receive the meals for the guests. She wore a plain black dress and white apron, her attire matching that of the other maids, and the manservants wore black suits with crisp white shirts and black bowties.

"I hope this night goes fast," one of the women sighed beside her as she fixed her long black hair. Maggie was constantly adjusting her hair or dress as though her appearance had altered in the seconds between now and the last time she checked. "Scratch that, I hope the entire month does."

"Nothing worse than a house full of entitled egos," Verida said with a huff.

"Here, here," a man agreed, straightening his coat.

"Is it that bad?" Evelyn asked, taking a tray from the table. The smell of roast vegetables filled her nose and her stomach grumbled.

"You'll see, new girl," Maggie winked then a bell chimed, and they were off before Evelyn could question what she meant by 'new'. Was it a joke because she'd lost her memory?

They moved in single file with backs straight and polite smiles on their faces towards the dining room. Enthusiastic conversation reverberated through the halls, along with bouts of burly laughter and the occasional cheer. Whoever was visiting the lord was in a good mood. A flicker of nervous excitement moved through her as she realised this would be the first time seeing the lord of the manor's face since losing her memory.

Doors opened and Evelyn followed behind the others, finding herself moving around a table filled with nobles in the most glamorous attire she'd ever seen. Sparkling gems, silk fabrics mixed with feathers and furs, all of varying colours were worn by the guests, who did their best to ignore the waitstaff beyond nodding or shaking their heads at the food offered.

They were engrossed in their lively conversations and the wine flowed freely as they celebrated. Lord Maker stood from his seat at the head of the table and Evelyn's eyes widened in recognition of his confident and captivating presence.

"Thank you, dear friends, for coming from far and wide to my home. Without you, we would not be in the fruitful position we have found ourselves. So, I say; to us!" he called, holding out his glass of wine. The man was the same who'd offered to help her with the sheets and the Lord Maker. Evelyn realised that was how he knew her. "To our future endeavours and all that we have earned from our patience."

"To us!" the room called in answer to the lord's toast.

Feeling a little heady from the recent and surprising revelation, Evelyn followed the line from the room with her half-empty tray in hand. Once in the hall, she whispered to Maggie beside her. "Who are all those nobles dining with Lord Maker?"

"Haven't you been paying attention? Lord Maker has been expecting his guests for weeks, why do you think we've been working so hard to get the place looking so clean?" Maggie asked with an eyebrow raised. "They are the lords, ladies and other wealthy people from across the seas."

"And they've come to Valmenessia for business?"

"And to take the land," Maggie said. "Most of the land in Valmenessia is owned by magic users. But that's all going to change. They have made a deal that once Valmenessia is ready, Lord Maker and his allies in that room will each get a city. A new patch of land for them to grow their wealth and influence."

"They plan on stealing land?"

"That's one way to put it."

"Invade Valmenessia?"

"Yes." Maggie rolled her eyes. "The rich and powerful don't become that way from being kind. They are vultures, Evelyn."

"And we are to accept it?"

"Yes, because that's the way things are," Maggie replied.

They reached the kitchen where Verida was waiting for them. She took the tray from Evelyn's hands and then handed her another with a sad looking meal on it. "Take this to the prisoner in the dungeon."

"Dungeon?"

"Yes," Verida replied. "Prisoners have to eat too."

Dismissed, Evelyn left the kitchen, following Verida's directions to the dungeons. She hadn't even noticed there was a dungeon on the grounds. But now she couldn't help but imagine the kind of person who would be locked up in one. Each step was more hesitant than the last, but she pushed on despite her nerves.

She passed the guards stationed at the stone door and took a deep breath, drawing back her shoulders. Bringing a meal to a prisoner was nothing to worry about. They were behind bars or chained, or maybe even sleeping and wouldn't be able to harm her. At least that's what she tried to tell herself.

Evelyn shivered as she descended the stairs into the cool dungeons, not from the temperature but the eerie darkness that filled the place. Despair lingered in the narrow hallway, seeping out between the bars of the cells on either side of her.

Her eyes darted this way and that, trying to glimpse inside the cells to see which held the prisoner. None were inhabited as far as she could tell in the dim light, yet there would be one that held a captive. That was the whole reason she was down there. Counting along, Evelyn slowed as she reached cell 34.

As she crept forward, she saw the cell was surprisingly well lit. Not only from the torches on the walls but also from a stream of bright moonlight. A body sat hunched against the wall, their pale wrists rested on bent knees, with their hands dangling lax as if lifeless. Whoever it was seemed focused on the ground, or something beyond it and didn't bother to look up as she stepped closer to the bars. The sound of her feet scuffing nervously on the ground was painfully loud in the silence.

"Your food," she said, her voice coming out strained as she placed the tray on the ground before the cell.

The prisoner's head jerked upright and his startling blue eyes fixed on her before he got up in one swift movement. Within seconds he was standing before her, one hand gripping the metal bars, the other outstretched to her.

Evelyn jumped back before he could touch her, eyes wide as her back pressed against the cell bars behind her.

The prisoner was handsome, even beneath the dishevelled look of someone who had been held here for a long time. His clothes were filthy, yet underneath the filth she could see they were of fine make. Stubble lined the man's jaw, and his dark hair was a chaotic mess, sticking up at all angles. A black band stood out against his pale neck; a collar.

Pain crawled up towards her temple and she winced as her heart raced, her hands becoming clammy as her fingers entwined before her.

"Evelyn," the man breathed as though her name were a prayer.

"How … how…" she stuttered. Swallowing, she asked, "You know me?"

The man frowned. Of course, he did. As soon as she'd voiced the question she'd known the answer. "I could never forget you."

Evelyn's chest tightened at his words. There was something familiar, but she couldn't… "Who are you?"

"You don't remember?" he asked, uncertainty filling his gaze. "I'm Kylan."

Evelyn tried to think, tried to recall the name from her past but all it did was make the pain in her head deepen. Unlike Phillip, this man's name was painful to even think. She clutched her head and stumbled forward before she doubled over, groaning as the pain didn't seem to subside.

Kylan took the opportunity to grasp her wrist and pull her closer. "Evelyn." she gasped, mildly aware of his proximity. His face contorted as his gaze ran over her face. The closeness gave her a better view of his features and she gritted her teeth against the sharp pain that felt like claws against her skull. "What did they do to you?"

"Nobody has done anything to me," she panted, snatching her wrist away and rubbing it as she backed away again. She closed her eyes, praying for the headache to go away.

"Your eyes," he snapped. "They're no longer gold."

Evelyn squinted at him with her fingers pressed to her forehead. "Ridiculous. Why would they be gold?"

"Because you're a Lys Alv."

Evelyn shook her head, the movement aggravating the ache and she instantly regretted it. "No, I'm human."

"Lies," he growled through the bars. "You're no more human than a dove. No matter what they tell you or change your appearance to look like. You are a Lys Alv, Evelyn. You don't belong here. Neither of us do."

"I am human. I am a human maid at this very estate."

"You are not," he stated firmly, his tone brokering no argument. "You are Evelyn Royd, Lys Alv Healer, second in line to the Ladyship of Forest's Edge, and soon to be a princess of Valmenessia."

Evelyn gaped at him. He couldn't be serious, and yet, the way her head ached had her questioning the reality she'd been led to believe.

Kylan's knuckles were white from holding onto the bars with an iron grip. Evelyn couldn't help but wonder what he would do if the bars weren't between them. "Evelyn … You may not recognise me, but surely you remember my father, King Dominic," he said. "You are my fiancé, Evelyn. Please, I don't know what they did to you, but that doesn't change facts."

"Those aren't facts," she said, though her words sounded more like a plea. "They are delusions. Lady of Forest's Edge? And a Princess? Utterly absurd. Not to mention that I don't even know you so how could we be engaged? I'm a maid and you have lost your mind."

"Evelyn—"

"Stop saying my name. You don't know me."

"I'm telling you the truth, please believe me," he begged, gripping the bars more tightly. "When I get out of here, I am going to make them pay for what they've done to you and then I am going to take you far from here. Back to your family in Forest's Edge and I will keep you safe and love you for the rest of our lives."

"No," she said, backing away from the delusional man. Her

eyes watered, not just from the ache in her mind, but from the forcefulness of his words. How he was so adamant about who she was overwhelmed her. "I won't go anywhere with you because you're the one who is lying. I'm a human and a maid. I'm from Sorby and my family is dead."

"That's not true!" Kylan reached for her, pressing himself into the bars. "Evelyn..."

"Don't!" She shouted and the tears she'd been trying to hold back fell on her cheeks. He didn't know her. This was a trick. Or the ravings of a delusional lunatic. She spun on her heel and ran back up the hallway to the stairs where she took two at a time until she reached the ground floor, all the while hearing Kylan desperately calling her name.

She didn't stop when the guards called after her, shocked by her dramatic exit. She ran all the way to the servant's quarters. When Evelyn reached the room she shared with three other maids, her hands were still shaking and when she looked in the mirror her face was streaked with tears. Kylan had completely undone her.

He was so angry, so furious, at what he believed happened to her. But he had to be wrong. Evelyn stared at her reflection, pushing back her dark hair to look at her ears. There was no denying the round tips.

She was human. Her brown eyes and her rounded ears were proof of that. Not to mention a lack of strong hearing, speed and of course healing magic.

She was not a Lys Alv, and she had no idea why the sight of him and the weight of his words had had such an effect on her. Seeing Phillip hadn't hurt like that and she didn't know what to make of it.

Kylan was undoubtedly familiar. Evelyn was just unsure whether she knew him for a good reason or a bad one.

Straightening her dress, she wiped her face and took a few deep breaths.

Verida pushed open the door, her gaze falling on Evelyn, concern creasing on her brow. "I saw you rushing this way. Everything okay?"

"I'm fine," Evelyn replied, straightening. "Just a hiccup. I'm not sure I should go back down to the dungeons again."

"No?"

Evelyn frowned at Verida. "Did you send me down there on purpose?"

"There are things they do not want you to see." Verida reached out and placed a hand on Evelyn's shoulder. "Don't trust anyone, Evelyn, not even me. Everyone has their own ambitions and without your memories you're more vulnerable than anyone, they will manipulate you in whatever way they can."

"And was sending me to see the prisoner your way of manipulating me?" Evelyn asked. She couldn't say his name for fear that voicing it aloud would bring on another stabbing headache.

"Manipulate you into accessing your memories? Possibly," the maid replied. Her eyes fell on Evelyn's cheeks. "I'd say you felt something at least. More than you have trying to remember anything else. But remember you cannot trust anyone. I don't want you to be paranoid, however, you need to be cautious."

Evelyn swallowed hard. "You want to warn me not to trust anyone and yet you want me to trust your word right now? You don't make any sense."

Verida just watched her with lips pressed into a thin line. Nothing was ever easy in this place.

Eventually, Evelyn broke eye contact and sighed heavily, wiping her face. "Anyone in particular I should watch out for, then?"

"Everyone."

9

August

Much to August's disgust, the humans that attacked them were not the only ones to threaten him and Tyler with cursed body parts as weapons. What had originally shocked and revolted him, August now expected every time they spotted someone travelling along the road. Not that every person they saw attempted an attack on them. A few had tarnished his view of the general population and had made the journey increasingly harder. They were even more wary of strangers than they usually were as Mors Alvs, now they constantly watched each other's backs, alert and ready for any threat.

Before, they could have gone relatively unnoticed by just covering their faces and Mors Alv features, which wouldn't look out of the ordinary in winter. But with fanatics attacking anyone they suspected of having magic, their chances of slipping by unnoticed were practically zero. The humans were likely touching everyone they came across with an infected limb just to be safe. If the person was also human, the curse didn't affect them so no harm done. But if they had magic they would fall victim to the curse, problem solved. It was a win-win for the human fanatics either way.

August hated feeling so separated from people again. It was like going back in time to when he was an Alta, avoiding any contact with anyone outside the king's secret soldiers. It was exhausting and stirred memories of his past.

As an Alta, he'd been given the choice to carry any weapon from an extensive collection of finely crafted swords, daggers, bows, axes and anything else one could imagine to inflict pain and death. He had chosen none of the weapons offered. Instead, Rana had a sword forged especially for him. Something that the other Alta had resented and did not to hide the fact. Not Nora though, who had simply rolled her eyes and said Rana had always favoured him so why would this be any different? August had the scars to show the other's envy. They were some of the few scars that weren't linked to terrible memories.

Sure, the pain of receiving the scars of their envy had been awful, but the reason for their jealousy made it worth it. Rana had been the closest thing he had to a real parent and the sword she gifted him was one way she could show her affection whilst under King Dominic's command.

But he'd lost his sword. And August felt its loss more deeply than he would have thought. It wasn't so much the sword itself, but what it had represented that stung now that it was gone. No longer having it in his possession had him feeling as though something crucial was missing. Now, he'd lost one of the only things she'd ever given him.

Of all the things to be upset about at present, losing his sword wasn't exactly the most crucial. Yet he couldn't stop thinking about it. August looked down to where the skin of his hand was turning grey and small black lines, like a spider's web, decorated the centre of his palm. He'd caught the Makers' Curse.

"Something's up ahead," Tyler said, bringing August back

to the present.

He put his glove back on and looked up to see Tyler pointing to where dark smoke billowed in the distance. Multiple dark plumes of smoke cut through the pale sky. It was difficult to tell if they rose from chimneys, or something worse. Judging by everything else that had happened of late, it was most likely the latter.

"Do you want to risk it?" August asked. For all they knew it was a town filled with humans who brandished dead limbs as weapons, eager to attack them. But then what did that matter to him anymore? So long as they didn't kill him, the weapon choice was now a moot point.

"I know what you're thinking, but let's scope it out," Tyler replied. "If they are fanatics we can always go around before they have the chance to throw blackened legs at us."

"I feel like the chances of that are high if our past experience is anything to go by."

"True, but call me an optimist," Tyler grinned. "I'm hoping they are more of the friendly variety, less body parts and maybe a hot meal."

"Unlikely. Though, who am I to squash your fantasies," August replied sarcastically. Then he gestured with his gloved hand for Tyler to continue on. The movement was uncomfortable, most likely sore from the position of holding the reins for so long. At least that's what he told himself. "Lead the way."

Scoping out what the smoke was coming from was the smart move, even though August doubted they would find what Tyler was looking for. It was far better than being caught unawares at least.

Drawing closer to the plumes of smoke, they slowed their horses to a group of trees where they saw what they had presumed was a village was actually a travelling party. There wasn't much coverage near this part of the main road, so they kept their distance, remaining in the tree line in case they needed to make a run for it. Tyler and August observed the tents and wagons scattered around the clearing in clusters and the people moving between them.

"Thoughts?" August asked, his gaze running across the group and trying to see if they were in any danger.

"They don't look like opportunistic murderers to me," Tyler replied.

"I agree," August said, reaching out with his magic just in case. He could sense every race within the camp, yet knowing they were most likely not wielding dead body parts only slightly lessened his apprehension. "Though, I don't think it's the best idea to stop and chat. They might still attack us just for being Mors Alvs. Let's keep moving."

A howl sounded suddenly, echoed by the answer of more wolves. The pounding of many feet grew louder and the next thing August knew, they were surrounded. Wolves circled them, their teeth on display as they leaned back on their haunches, ready to pounce should August or Tyler prove a threat.

August's horse kicked up, unsettled by the arrival of predators. He tried to soothe the beast with a hand on its neck.

"Well this isn't good," Tyler said, stating the obvious.

A mouse darted down the back of one of the wolves and once on the ground shifted into a man with curly dark hair and well-worn boots. He took long two strides, closing the gap between them, and placed his hand on the head of August's horse. The horse calmed immediately under the man's touch.

"Who are you?" the man asked, his gaze focused on the horse as he ran his hand up and down its nose.

"My name is August, and this is my friend, Tyler," August said. "We are only passing by on our way south. We mean you no harm."

"Drop your hoods," the man commanded, finally looking at them.

August hesitated, but when Tyler lowered his hood

immediately, he sighed and followed suit. His magic rose to the surface in anticipation of an attack from the Anima. Their leader would likely command the wolves to strike once he saw they were Mors Alvs. He braced himself, only to be surprised as the man showed no fear or shock as to what they were. Instead of the usual response, his face looked almost intrigued.

"Mors Alvs," the man said, raising a thick brow. "You're travelling south?"

"Yes," August replied. "We came from Lord Havilor in Fellbun and are friends with Lady Jasmine Royd."

"Some very important individuals."

"They are," August nodded. "Lady Royd's younger sister, Evelyn is a friend of mine."

Friend. The word didn't feel quite right … quite strong enough.

"Evelyn?" the man repeated, the name seemingly familiar on his tongue.

"Yeah, I'm also acquainted with Florence, Omari, Will, Sage and Nora from Forest's Edge. Do you know them?"

The man pursed his thin lips. "And who did you say you were again?"

"August."

The wolves around them seemed to immediately relax, hiding their sharp teeth and moving into sitting positions. The leader nodded, a smile creeping onto his face, then turned and pointed at two wolves. They dropped their heads in a bow and took off back towards their camp, howling as they went.

"I'm Lou," the man said, looking between August and Tyler. "Come with me."

He looked to Tyler. There was a possibility that this was a trap, and these people were leading them to their deaths. Historically speaking Mors Alvs weren't exactly welcomed or well-liked after the king decreed them dangerous and traitors. The humans they'd come across had been nothing but hostile, and this was the first time since leaving Fellbun that they'd had any semblance of a conversation with someone. Perhaps it was Lou's ease at discovering him and Tyler were Mors Alvs, or maybe it was that he was an Anima who seemed to recognise August's name, that had August follow him. Either way, a group of Anima was the safer bet than a group of humans at the moment.

"How do you know me?" August asked.

"Mutual friends, it seems," Lou replied. "I'm a member of the Northern Wolf Pack. You might have heard of us joining the Northern Alliance."

"I have," August said, his shoulders relaxing.

"Are you coming or what?" Lou shifted, a mouse appearing again before their eyes. Then he ran up the leg of the nearest wolf who raced to the camp with the rest of the pack close on their tail.

"Do you trust them?" Tyler said with a grin once they were alone.

"Yeah," August sighed, running a hand through his hair and turning to watch the wolves moving around their camp spiritedly.

"Alright then. Race you," Tyler winked, flicking his horse's reins and urging the animal forward before August could react. "What are you waiting for?"

They reined their horses with those travelling with Lou's party, where someone said they would feed and water them. Then the two Mors Alvs followed Lou in his human form through the camp as he checked in with those they passed by, travellers setting up tents, cooking and gathering around fires.

August moved to draw his hood, but Tyler reached out and stopped him. "Let them see who we are. The world needs to get used to the idea of Mors Alvs again and see that we are not what the king made us out to be. These are our allies, right? We don't have to worry about them sending word to the king about two Mors Alvs heading in his direction."

The last time August had been with those from Forest's Edge, Jasmine insisted he not hide his identity either. But he hadn't really had a chance then, spending all his time in the Manor before leaving with Aren. Both Jasmine and Tyler were right. It was time to stop hiding.

He looked around and saw that even though some turned away from him and Tyler, many were not afraid. Some even smiled in their direction, which August found himself returning.

"Doesn't everyone here freeze to death at night?" Tyler asked, grimacing at the tents' flimsy fabric.

"We still have several Elementum keeping the population warm when needed," Lou replied, pointing to one who summoned a ball of flame to hover by a group plucking berries off branches. "The further south you go means there's no snow in Winter like in Fellbun. Just a lingering icy breeze. It's easier to keep warm and dry."

"Excellent," Tyler grinned, rubbing his hands together. August realised he'd probably never seen a Frost Season that wasn't white. "I can already feel myself warming up as we speak."

Lou approached a large tent and drew back the flaps to reveal Omari inside, standing with his hands on his hips and his head almost reaching the roof of the tent. The man turned at their unexpected arrival. "August," he said in surprise, his brown eyes running over him and Tyler. He stepped back, gesturing with a dark hand for them to enter. "What brings you here?"

"We were on our way south," August replied, once inside. Logs sat in a circle around a blanket, a map of the country spread out on top. The rest of the tent was occupied by weapons, more blankets and other supplies scattered throughout the space. "There is a king still warming a throne who shouldn't be."

August didn't mention his plan to rescue Evelyn. He knew he could trust Omari, but he felt it was better to keep that part to himself. The tent flaps opened again and two people August didn't recognise entered, carrying bowls and a basket.

"Come and sit," Lou said, gesturing to a log on his left. "You must be hungry."

August didn't take much convincing. The smell of the food made him more agreeable to orders and he sat down happily. A bowl of hot stew was handed to him and the basket that carried fresh bread was placed near his feet. The sight of bread caused his stomach to grumble loudly.

"I'm surprised to find you here, Omari. I'd have thought you'd be in Forest's Edge," August said.

"I'm assuming you know about the curse. I doubt there's anyone who hasn't at least heard of it by now. Jasmine asked me to go to Midskopas after the curse took Forest's Edge. It spread like wildfire through the Manor Grounds and absorbed so much magic that it continued to take over the rest of the city in no time."

"Nora?"

"She's in Midskopas. Travelled with Gemma to free the city from the king's occupation," he replied. "Last I heard she's alive and well."

Good. Nora was alive. He should never have thought otherwise. The woman was a fighter after all. Relief flooded August, twirling with anticipation at the thought that he'd see her further south. They would have to travel via Midskopas and then he'd be reunited with his best friend. There's no way she wouldn't join him on his mission. August and Nora had been separated for far too long.

"How many did you lose?" August asked.

"Too many," Omari said, sadness filling his gaze. "Jasmine's mother, for one, as well as countless citizens, magical and human. We lost just as many humans to the sudden crumbling of buildings as those vines sprouted from the dead. Many Healers who'd been trying to help, and the Anima we'd been trying to free after the king enslaved them as well. Daphne and some other humans chose to stay in Forest's Edge just in case, but most have fled along with the Elementum, Lys Alvs and Anima."

"Fuck," August breathed.

"An understatement," Omari said bitterly. "What news from Fellbun? We haven't heard from Lord Havilor in a while."

"The curse has them trapped within the city," August replied between mouthfuls of his food. He paused, frowning. "They have enough supplies to see them through for the next six months, or more if they keep losing people. There has been a lot of death, yet the lord is still eager to fight. His silence isn't abandonment."

"I'm glad to hear it. Lord Havilor is one of our closest allies."

"He is a good man."

"That he is." Omari nodded. "If I could be even a fraction like him one day, I'd be happy."

"You're already a great leader," August said earnestly. Omari had taken on a lot since Jasmine's father died. Not only supporting the lady of Forest's Edge, but also in his own role as a leader of the city.

"So great that I didn't care to pay more attention to the murders," Omari said, pacing back and forth, his muscular shoulders taut. "I failed. I failed my people and it is a regret I will take with me to the grave when the curse finally kills me too. I'm worried it will take us all."

"It will have to get in line. King Dominic is still vying for our heads and we passed a couple of opportunistic groups on the way here," Tyler said, stuffing a piece of bread into his mouth. "Fanatical humans brandishing cursed limbs as weapons, so you can add them to the list of threats we face."

"They would really go that far? Shit," Lou hissed. "What the fuck has this world come to? The curse isn't killing us fast enough?"

August nodded. "They brandish blackened arms and legs helping the curse rid the land of magic. I have a theory that some see the curse as a chance for humans to take control. Humans have been at a disadvantage in Valmenessia for centuries and some could deem this as their chance to change that."

Lou growled before jumping to his feet and storming from the tent.

"He'll be notifying his scouts to be on alert," Omari explained, hands on his hips and brows taut. "I know you're eager to go murder King Dominic, but you should think about staying with us for a few nights. Jasmine is on her way as we speak. You'll be safe with us, and we can travel south together."

"You're going south as well?"

"The king's army marches toward Midskopas," Omari replied. "We will march our own in answer."

"We have an army now? Seems a lot has happened since I left."

"Yes, and I would ask that you both consider joining. I know you have another task, but your presence would be invaluable," he said, offering August a friendly smile, dimples appearing on his cheeks. "Think about it. Stay here until Jasmine arrives. Rest, eat."

"Thank you," August said appreciatively. "We'll think about it."

"That's all I ask."

Tyler dragged a piece of bread through his bowl, gathering every last drop of the stew. "Putting an end to his army would be a sizable blow to his hold on the country."

"True," August agreed with a nod. "But there will be more where they came from eventually. Killing him would be a bigger strike."

"Yes, fine, but we've been travelling with very little rest since Fellbun and I'm tired so let's take a break and recoup. Wait for Lady Royd to arrive and discuss your plans with her. *All* of them."

August sighed, noting Tyler's meaning; the plan that involved Evelyn that he'd not mentioned to Omari. Tyler was right.

"If we stay," August said finally to Omari, and Tyler let out a whispered 'thank the Goddess.' "It will be only until Jasmine arrives. I'd like to speak to her and I also want to see what kind of army the Alliance has before I decide whether I go to the king or join you."

"Whatever army we have, it will have to be enough," Omari replied. He looked towards the tent flap, a frown creasing his lips. "We are running out of time and things are only going to get worse."

"Speaking of time," August began. He looked at his friend before returning his attention to Omari. "There's something you need to know, both of you, that may make you rescind your offer."

10

Nora

Aren's death was a blow to an already wounded heart. She had let him in, warmed to his friendship, enjoyed his jokes and company, only for him to be cruelly taken away. Maybe the grief was worse because it confirmed what Aren had told her. Something she hadn't truly believed until now. The Gods and Goddesses could be killed.

Aren, God of Anima, would no longer walk the land or soar through the skies. If the stories about him were true, which she had a feeling most were, then he'd spent his long life fighting. With his siblings, monsters, in mortal wars, avoiding death at every turn, only to be taken by surprise by the Makers' Curse.

One would think Gods and Goddesses would meet their deaths in epic battles or acts of bravery and sacrifice, some legendary moment that would have the entire world pause in shock. But that's not how the real world worked, and Aren said they had never been Gods or Goddesses, just prisoners trapped in Valmenessia to pay for their crimes.

Aren had been taken in what felt like a split second with only Nora and Aeolus to witness his downfall. Those surrounding Giland would not have known to look to the skies. But Nora had and it was something she would never forget.

"I grew up in Kaldom," Aeolus said, breaking the silence and drawing Nora's thoughts to the present. He strode beside her on the main road that ran the length of the country from the north all the way south to Royal Bay. They had been travelling during the day and resting at night, but their determination to get to Royal Bay and end the king once and for all pushed them on at a gruelling pace.

Nora raised a brow. The citizens of Kaldom were notoriously hard like the environment they lived in. "That explains your warm countenance and charming personality."

"It's a hard life in the northern city," he continued, ignoring her sarcastic comment. "Nothing comes easy. No matter how much magic or coin you have, everything requires hard work and a high price. Not everyone is made for that harsh life. Kaldom hardens its inhabitants or it rejects them. For this reason, the population is small and very close-knit because many end up leaving one way or another. Either they reach a certain age and travel south or they simply … die. Far too many die. Growing up, I lost a lot of friends and family I cared about and even though loss was almost a way of life, it never got easier. To this day, I still feel it. The emptiness of the space that each person filled."

It was the most Nora had ever heard him speak. He ran a hand over his face, sighing heavily. "What I'm trying to say, is that you will never stop feeling it. The people who leave this world never leave you." He tapped his temple. "They will be in there forever, reminding you that they existed and that they meant something to you."

Nora's eyes burned with unshed tears. She sniffed as Aeolus' words hit her harder than expected. She'd cried so much after Aren died that she wasn't even sure there were any tears left inside her, but the feeling didn't lessen just because her tears were spent.

"Remembering them will get easier."

She looked at her feet and clenched her hands inside her coat pockets. "Why are you telling me this?"

"Because I need you to get past this. To know it gets easier. I need your head to be clear for what comes next. You don't have any experience dealing with your emotions. But we don't have time for you to grieve or let this get the better of you. You need to get out of your head," Aeolus said. "You can't afford to be distracted by your thoughts. Aren's death was a tragedy, but we have a job to do."

"I'm not distracted," Nora lied. Well, it was a partial lie at least. "I'm aware of what needs to be done."

Despite her grief, they were making good time. When she travelled north with August they had stayed clear of the main roads for the most part, not wanting to draw attention to themselves. August being a Mors Alv had always been something they had to hide. No matter what they did to his appearance he didn't exactly blend in, and his mere presence demanded attention despite his desire to go unnoticed. Aeolus and Nora didn't have that problem.

They appeared human and if someone pressed them on their race, they were both Elementum; the favoured race of King Dominic. The only thing they really had to hide was being part of the Northern Alliance, which was easily done. They had no markings or objects connecting them to the group, having removed their armbands before they left Midskopas. So they walked freely, something Nora had never done before. If she wasn't forced into taking indirect routes with August, then she was moving on orders of the king, connected to him. She may have still held more freedom than most, more freedom than August ever had, but right now she moved because it was her choice and she didn't have to hide. But freedom meant something different to her than to the average person in Valmenessia. Her chains had been magical and literal, their chains took the form of unjust laws, racial propaganda and corrupt politics.

That was all going to change. That was what the Northern Alliance was fighting for.

As Aeolus and Nora journeyed, there were far fewer travellers along the road than there had been all those months ago with August. Those they did see were few and far between, with less than a handful of wagons that passed by. Which was probably why the one ahead in particular stood out to Nora.

"Really? You're not distracted?" Aeolus asked, giving her a doubtful look. "Because this is not the first time I've tried to talk to you. But it is the first time you've responded."

"Maybe it's because I'm busy watching our asses," Nora said reaching out to grab his wrist and pull him to a stop. "And everything you've said up until now has been boring. If I don't ignore you then I'll fall asleep, and if that happens my eyes aren't open to see anything suspicious."

"There's no threat," he replied stiffly, snatching his arm back.

Nora chuckled though it didn't hold its usual cockiness. She summoned her wind magic and threw it out to her side. The sound of a woman shrieking directed their attention in time to see her land on her ass on the side of the road. A bow and quiver of arrows clattered beside her.

"Then explain this?" Nora said, as the woman fumbled to her feet and snatched up her bow. "Because she doesn't look very friendly, and she's been following us for a while too."

"You did just use your magic on her," Aeolus grunted as they strode towards the woman. "Maybe that's why she is pissed off?"

The woman in question looked up, her golden eyes wide, and started to back up only to stand on an arrow and lose her footing again. "Don't come any closer," she stammered on the ground. She shuffled back and searched for an arrow with her hand while keeping her eyes on the pair. She found one and frantically nocked it, the arrow aimed at them.

"We need you to settle something," Nora said, ignoring the woman and moving closer. She embraced the distraction from her grief, the possibility of a reprieve, even if only for a short time. "This guy, in his completely arrogant obliviousness—"

Aeolus swore beneath his breath, shooting her an evil look.

"What? It's an accurate description of you," Nora replied before looking back to the woman. "Anyway he seems to think you *aren't* a threat, but he obviously didn't see you following us for the last few hours. Men. Am I right?"

The woman scrunched her brow at Nora. She was very pretty. Long curly red hair fell below her shoulders and freckles sat along her petite nose and flushed cheeks.

"So," Nora said, waving her hand for the woman to answer. "Were you following us?"

"Not you," she replied, lifting her chin. "Him."

"Hmmm," Nora said, giving Aeolus a shit-eating grin. "Lookey here, I *was* right after all."

"Who sent you?" Aeolus asked, crossing his arms over his broad chest and ignoring Nora's blatant smugness.

"Nobody sent me," the woman replied with a grimace as though the suggestion of being under anyone's command was abhorrent.

"Fine," Aeolus said, rubbing his forehead. "Why are you following me?"

The woman didn't answer, and Nora barked a laugh. "Stubborn. I like her."

Aeolus shot Nora a glare, then turned his stern face on the woman who was still sitting on the ground with her arrow aimed at him. "Last chance to answer me," he said.

The woman pressed her lips together and stared Aeolus down. That was probably not her brightest idea.

"Fuck this," Aeolus hissed and stormed forward, grabbing

her by the upper arm before she could loose the arrow. Her weapon fell to the ground almost immediately as he dragged her away from the road and through the tall grass that bordered it.

A few curious onlookers peered in their direction, but didn't approach. Everyone was evidently too busy going about their business of getting from one cursed place to another to care. The woman struggled against Aeolus' hold, spitting curses at him, and despite Nora and Aeolus being on the same side, Nora felt anxiety rising within her. The scene felt like it was heading into uncomfortably familiar territory. Something Nora didn't want to relive.

"Wait," Nora said, snatching up the woman's weapon and following them into a group of trees.

Aeolus dropped the woman next to a trunk then stepped back, his gaze narrowed on his captive. He raised his hands; a stance Nora knew well, and she couldn't help herself. She stepped between Aeolus and his target and stared him down despite the uneasiness in her chest.

"No," Nora said, her voice not as strong as she'd liked. "Find another way to get the information you want."

"I would have thought you were all for it," he snapped, his fingers flexing in his eagerness to use his water magic. "Don't try and pretend that you wouldn't do the same."

Nora shook her head. "Not anymore. I'm not the king's puppet doing his dirty work for him and last time I checked you think he's an evil man. Might want to take a moment to reflect on the fact you're about to do something he orders done without a second thought."

Aeolus sneered but lowered his hands, nonetheless.

"You work for the king?"

Nora turned to the woman. "Work*ed*, not anymore. Though I think it would be more appropriate to call it enslaved."

The woman's brows shot up though her eyes glistened with something that looked too much like sympathy for Nora's liking.

She immediately regretted clarifying.

"I'm with the Northern Alliance now. So all good," Nora said. "Now, let's try this again. What's your name?"

"Charlie."

"Okay, Charlie. What's your issue with him?" Nora asked, angling her head at Aeolus. "I know he's a stick in the mud, but his moral compass isn't that off-kilter."

"You just stopped him from, I assume, torturing me," Charlie said pointedly.

"I did," Nora replied. "But look, I've been on the receiving end of that and it sucks. But he only does it with good reason. "

"So, you admit it," Aeolus stated with a slight grin.

Nora scrunched her nose at him. "Hate to quote you, but 'I'm not an idiot'."

"You are if you think that he is a morally good person," Charlie said, rising to her feet. "He's fooled you."

Nora turned back to Charlie. "Oh really?"

"Yes," Charlie said. "And I'm not the only one who thinks so. Others recognised him and notified me he was in the area. He killed my father and before you start defending him, there was nothing to warrant my father's death. No 'good reason'."

Aeolus stilled. "Your father? Who—"

"Edmund Wallis."

Silence settled as Nora looked at Aeolus and tried to read his expression. She'd never heard of the man but that wasn't of any relevance. Aeolus' face was blank which in and of itself was telling. No one was expressionless, especially when being accused of murder.

"Take your bow," Aeolus said, breaking the silence. "And go home."

He turned his back on them and strode towards the road.

"Please, you have to help me," Charlie said, pleading to Nora. "He's a murderer."

Nora braced herself, stiffening her shoulders. She'd been too kind, too protective of this woman she'd just met and it had only encouraged Charlie to think she cared. It had been a mistake.

"I've killed far more than Aeolus," Nora stated, stepping towards Charlie. "There would be a line down the street to the next town of pissed-off relatives if they ever came looking for me. You think I'm a sympathetic ear? Your father must have been involved in something awful to warrant Aeolus being involved in his death. But me? I never needed a reason beyond my victim being an inconvenience. Killing is as menial for me as taking a bath." Nora halted a step before reaching Charlie, folding her arms over her chest and narrowing her gaze on the Lys Alv. "Stop following him. We wouldn't want you to inconvenience me."

"No." Charlie jutted out her chin. "My father was a good man. I won't stop until I punish his murderer."

Nora sighed. "Don't make this more difficult than it has to be. I'm trying to turn over a new leaf and you being a pain in my ass is going to ruin all my hard work."

"If everything you've said is true," Charlie said. "You deserve to be punished, just like him."

"Fate's taking care of that for me," Nora said, dropping Charlie's bow to the ground. "This is the last time I'll tell you. Don't follow him, it won't work out well for you. Go spend the time you have with what family you have left while you can."

Nora left Charlie sitting in the dirt and jogged to catch up with Aeolus once she hit the road, surprised when he slowed for her.

"I'm not discussing this with you."

"We all have our secrets," she replied, stuffing her hands into her coat pockets. "And yours are apparently far juicier than I had originally thought."

Aeolus didn't respond to her baiting. He went back to his quiet brooding and they walked in silence, neither looking back for Charlie. Nora was in no place to judge Aeolus' behaviour; she'd tortured and killed far too many to be shocked or even critical of him. Plus, Aeolus was insufferably self-righteous. Charlie had to be mistaken about her father. If Aeolus had killed him, then her father had to have been up to no good. Poor girl just didn't know about it. She wouldn't be the first in the dark about her father's true nature…

Nora kept her questions to herself and pushed aside thoughts of her own father, letting her recent grief settle back onto her shoulders, weighing her down and grounding her once more.

Nora

Night fell and with it the air turned crisp as Nora veered from the road. She strode through the grass to a small, cleared patch that showed frequent use by others who had travelled through before them.

"It's not completely dark yet," Aeolus grumbled behind her.

She didn't bother to look back at him or justify making camp early. Instead, she conjured a fire and sat down, sighing in relief at no longer being on her feet. Nora looked up and spotted a familiar constellation of stars, bright against the black sky. "By all means, keep going. I'm staying here."

Aeolus swore, then stomped over to the welcoming warmth of the fire, and she grinned at her little victory. The win only felt sweeter when another group decided to join them, much to Aeolus' dismay. A middle-aged couple sought the safety of numbers during the night and were completely non-threatening as far as Nora could tell and were friendly enough, despite Aeolus' rudeness. He didn't hide his feelings on sharing the campsite and

Nora had somewhat agreed with him, at least until the couple offered to share with her their food. She could have kissed the man who had presented her with a piece of cake.

"Where are you travelling to?" Nora asked them, her mood instantly elevated thanks to the food. Aeolus was not as easily pleased. He sat beside her, looking as grumpy as ever and refused the offer of food. "Heading south?"

"There's nothing for us there," the woman with long brown braids said. She sat on a fallen log on the opposite side of the fire, the flames dancing between them. "We're going west to Rovton to be with family. We should never have left in the first place."

"Oh?" Nora said. "Why's that? Did things not pan out as well as you thought?"

"It was a mistake," the woman replied with a solemn nod. "We had gone to Giland for a holiday when…" She looked at her husband.

"There was an incident," he said. "A misunderstanding. However, Lord Gudrid had already made up his mind and would not hear any explanation."

"After the incident, we were stationed in the kitchens at the mines, cooking for the guards," the woman finished.

Nora thought of the mines and how the prisoners sent there were mostly Anima sentenced to hard labour that would no doubt end in their deaths for petty crimes or unjust laws.

The man frowned. "All those prisoners."

Aeolus' gaze narrowed and fixed on something in the distance. He was forever monitoring their surroundings. Since Charlie had snuck up on him, he'd been extra cautious. Neither he nor Nora commented, despite their outward sympathy for the prisoners in the mines. The risk of showing their disdain for the king was far too high.

"They're gone now. All of them," the woman across from Nora said. "May Jord protect them."

"Were they killed?" Nora asked, leaning closer to the fire

and lifting her palms to the heat. Her heart stuttered in her chest at what the woman implied. Something terrible had to have happened to the prisoners if the woman was praying to the Goddess of Truth and Passing. Perhaps it was like everywhere else and the curse had spread through the mines, killing everyone inside.

"King Dominic ordered the mines closed. The guards rounded up all the prisoners and forced them into wagons. They were taken south where they were offered to the lake," the woman replied, her delicate features dropping into a frown, and she shook her head. "Awful."

"Anyone not executed has been reallocated to join the forces heading north."

"Did they have any markings? Tattoos around their necks or wrists?" Nora asked, thinking of the Anima who'd attacked Forest's Edge.

"Not that I'm aware," the man said. He shook his head and his long unkempt, golden hair swayed with the movement.

King Dominic must not have bound them to him before sending them to the mines. Nora couldn't help but wonder whether there were now those amongst the king's army that would change sides when given the opportunity. Hope swelled in her chest at the thought. "All able bodies were being sent to join the attack on the rebellion. My wife and I want no part in that. We have been participants in his evil deeds for far too long," the man continued. "We ran in the night and now we're going home."

"You should be careful who you speak so freely with," Aeolus said.

The man's face paled. "I—we—" he stammered, clutching his wife's hand, her eyes wide as she looked between Nora and Aeolus.

"You are safe with us," Aeolus assured them. "But please, do not be so forthcoming from now on. The world is not what it was and it is not safe."

The couple nodded and for a moment, the only sound was the crackling of the fire. Nora's mind, however, was busy toying over something the woman had said.

"Wait. You said something about a lake?" Nora asked, breaking the silence. "Why did they give the prisoners to the lake?"

"A creature dwells in there," the woman explained, her words softer after Aeolus' warning. "I wouldn't have believed the stories if I hadn't seen it with my own eyes. They made us go with them, to feed the guards taking the prisoners."

Nora raised a brow at Aeolus, who frowned in reply—which could have meant anything because the guy spent most of his time grimacing.

"What kind of creature?" Nora asked, thinking of the beasts in Midskopas and those Aren had mentioned as well.

"A monster that belongs only in nightmares," the woman replied with a shudder. "Only the guild remains there now, last we saw. A fitting place for such a terrible group."

Her husband placed an arm over her shoulders, drawing her close. "These people don't need to hear such tales before bed. Not when I'm sure they have other worries with the curse consuming everyone with magic. We heard it is especially bad up north. But it is hard to tell what is propaganda and what is fact anymore. Besides, it's getting late."

"You're right," the woman nodded. She rose to her feet and the couple wished them goodnight before settling in their blankets just out of the fire's light.

"Thoughts?" Nora asked in a low voice, wiping the cake crumbs from her lap.

"On the creature in the lake bunking with the guild, the prisoners used as feed, or the forces heading north being filled with the unwilling conscripted?" Aeolus replied, turning to face her so that his side was directed at the fire.

"All of it."

"We knew the king was marching north, so his soldiers had to come from somewhere," Aeolus said. "As for the prisoners, King Dominic has ordered the execution of Anima because he needs someone to blame for the curse. It makes sense he ordered his guards to drop the prisoners in the lake if something like what we saw in Midskopas has awakened there as a means to appease it. And the guild—"

"The King's Guild is full of psychopaths." Nora grimaced. "Of course, they would be attracted to an area where a monster is."

"Exactly. I've heard stories of creatures that live in the lakes," Aeolus said. He stared into the fire, the reflection of the flames in his hazel eyes. "Huge beasts that would eat fishermen and unwitting swimmers. But I thought they'd all died out centuries ago."

"I think it's best if we don't presume anything anymore," Nora groaned, flopping back onto the grass. She draped an arm over her eyes. "Feels like Valmenessia is pissed off and doing her best to punish us. Angry bitch is trying to kill us all." It was hard not to feel doomed.

Aeolus chuckled, the sound surprising Nora and she moved her arm to uncover one sceptical eye at him. "What?" he asked, brows raised.

"Are we getting along?" she asked, a playfulness in her eyes.

Aeolus sighed heavily. "Don't make this weird."

"I'm not doing anything of a sort. Tell me something about you," Nora said. "Anything at all."

He was quiet for a moment, watching the stars above them. "When I first met Gemma she hated me."

"Nope, I don't believe it."

Aeolus chuckled again. The sound was low, starting in his chest and finishing huskily on his breath. "Whether you believe it or not, it's true. She didn't like me one bit and, looking back, I don't blame her."

"Wait," Nora raised a hand. "Are you trying to get me to believe that she didn't like your winning personality? Because I just can't comprehend that. You are the most endearing person I have ever met."

"Can you be serious for five seconds?"

"Why? What would the point be in that?"

"You're insufferable."

"Apparently Gemma thought you were too," Nora quipped. "So how did you win her over and become her second?"

"I gained her trust by showing I could be relied on, that I cared for the same things she does."

"That's a boring answer. I was hoping for something scandalous or a heroic story, like a rescue or something."

Aeolus sighed heavily and Nora grinned, enjoying that she could get under his skin so easily. "It was nothing so entertaining. There is no easy fix, as you know. Everything worthwhile takes time and hard work."

"Way to kill the mood."

"I've had enough of this conversation," he declared, rising to his feet and stretching his arms over his head. "You can take the first watch."

"Sweet dreams," Nora sang, as he found somewhere close by to sleep.

Aeolus and she may never be friends exactly, but something had shifted between them. Her subconscious fear had disappeared and what was left was an understanding. They needed each other.

Aeolus and Nora took turns on watch as usual throughout the night and as the sun began to rise over the horizon they once again continued on their way. The couple were nowhere in sight, having scurried away sometime during Aeolus' watch, likely a little paranoid after his warning.

Nora hadn't slept well, her thoughts continuously drifting to Aren and Florence, with her mother and brother joining them in the end as well. She'd awoken multiple times to find Aeolus's eyes on her and a frown creasing his brow, though he said nothing, something for which she was glad. Seeing her break down and cry had been enough, not to mention his attempt at a sympathetic conversation after. She couldn't help what she did or said in her sleep, and didn't need him to voice his pity. She could already see it in his eyes.

By the time they reached the next town south of Giland, Nora was exhausted and her entire body ached. She made sure to let Aeolus know of her complaints, of course, filling the air with her groans and colourful swearing.

"Mother fu—"

"Shhh," Aeolus hissed, pressing a finger to his lips. "The whole village knows we have arrived, thanks to you."

"You're welcome," Nora grumbled though she kept her displeasure to herself from then onwards.

They made their way through the quiet streets in search of an inn to rest for the night. Rows of cottages sat on either side of the street with smoke billowing from the chimneys and warm light filling the windows. From what Nora could see, there was no sign of the Makers' Curse here. The telltale blackened tree roots were thankfully nowhere to be seen.

The sun had almost set when they reached the centre of the town where multiple businesses were still open, all looking filled to the brim with customers mingling outside. Aeolus chose one at random, at least Nora had thought that was the case until she saw the rusted sign hung above the door. A symbol made of five squares standing on their points sat beneath the inn's name and almost passed as decoration if she hadn't known what they truly meant.

The front door opened and a man stumbled through only to fall on his face. Laughter echoed from inside the inn though no one rushed out to help him. Nora stepped over the man and detected the strong smell of alcohol filling the air around him.

"Bit early to be this wasted," she said, walking into the inn.

Aeolus grunted behind her and the two made their way through the packed room towards the bar. "We only need one room," he said. "You can sleep on the floor."

Nora shot him a glare which only made the man smile. *Asshole.*

"Good evening," he said to the bartender. "My wife and I are looking for a room for the night."

Nora startled at his words, though quickly smoothed her features. She'd keep her mouth shut but if he thought she'd play along any more than that he was dreaming. She'd lied more times than she could count, but that had been with August and there was no way she'd be pretending marriage duties with Aeolus. She'd rather sleep outside in the cold. The bartender ran his gaze over them, assessing them. Nora hated it. She hated any time someone tried to know what kind of person she was.

"Where are you from?" the man asked at last.

"Forest's Edge," Aeolus replied, dropping coins onto the bar top. "Saw your sign out front and knew you were a reputable establishment.

"You would be correct." The bartender nodded, taking the money with one quick swipe and replacing the coins with a brass key. "Upstairs, second door on the right."

They followed his directions, with Nora dragging her feet behind Aeolus, and found their room easily. In the fading light, Nora was able to see a small bed, if it could even be called that, and a single table with a candle atop it. Nora eyed the worn stained blankets.

"You wanted the bed so badly, you can have it," she stated, her lip curling at the sight. She flickered he wrist, lighting the candle. "You'll catch something worse than the Makers' Curse in there."

"Charming," Aeolus huffed, sneering at the bed as though it personally offended him.

They dropped their packs and Nora took her blanket out to lay on the floor where she would sleep for the night. "So I was thinking," Nora said, sitting on the floor and resting her back against the wall. "We should find a Conjurer."

"Why?" Aeolus asked. He sat on the bed and the mattress groaned under his weight as though in pain.

"Aren gave me a little history lesson. He said that the Makers are not actually the parents of the Gods and Goddesses, but instead Conjurers who cursed Aren and the others with immortality. Apparently, way back in history, Conjurers were known as Makers."

Aeolus raised a brow.

"Before you get all sceptical, let me finish," Nora huffed, untying the laces on her boots. Something caught her eye and she glanced at the window for a moment before returning to taking off her shoes. "The Gods and Goddesses aren't actually deities, rather they were powerful people who did something bad and the Conjurers—Makers—imprisoned them in Valmenessia as punishment and apparently accidentally cursed them with immortality in the process. He didn't tell me what they'd done, only that this was their punishment. They are prisoners in Valmenessia. Which I guess also makes the rest of us with magic prisoners too, since we also can't leave. So, I was thinking, if the Makers' Murders was just some sort of conjuring, not scary deity magic, then perhaps all we need is a Conjurer to undo what they did. Undo the Makers' Curse."

He stared at her, his expression blank.

"Struggling to keep up? Want me to explain again?"

"Why didn't you tell me this earlier?" he asked, pinching the top of his nose between two fingers and closing his eyes.

Nora shrugged, wiggling her freed feet. "Aren told me just before he died and then, I don't know, I wasn't really thinking about the contents of the conversation until now. I've had other things on my mind … like the person I had the conversation with.”

Aeolus pressed his lips together and then let out a heavy sigh, his shoulders relaxing. “In the last correspondence Gemma received from Jasmine, she said they had a Conjurer working to fight the curse.”

“Really?”

“No.” He rolled his eyes. “Yes, really. We have people working to get rid of the curse. Gemma, Jasmine, Lord Havilor in Fellbun, hell everyone is searching for some way to get rid of it. We, on the other hand, have a different job to do. We don’t have time to find a Conjurer. The king is our priority.”

“Alright, alright,” Nora pouted. “Leave it up to the others, but…”

“But…?” Aeolus groaned.

“If a Conjurer presents themself to us, we don’t let the opportunity slip through our fingers.”

“Fine,” he replied. “But the others have it under control and I have our job under control. All you need to do is follow orders.”

Nora smiled smugly at him. “Sure.”

“You’re not going to fight me on it? Or say something sarcastic? Be a smart ass?”

“Nope.” She shook her head.

“Really?”

“You won’t get any smart assiness from me,” she said, drawing a cross on her chest with a finger. “And I definitely won’t say anything sarcastic about Charlie spying on us through the window. Nope, nuh-uh, you won’t hear anything from me.”

“Charlie?” Aeolus’ head snapped towards the window. “Fuck!”

He prowled towards the window, wrenching it open and shoving a hand through. Someone squealed and the next thing Nora knew, Charlie was pulled inside.

“Let go of me!” Charlie cried, slapping at Aeolus’ grip. “Let me go!”

He did just that, shoving her towards the bed and forcing her to sit, a strong hand pushing her shoulders down before releasing her.

"What do you think you are doing?" Aeolus growled, prowling back and forth in front of her.

"Flying outside our window," Nora answered for Charlie. "Isn't it obvious?"

"There's a ledge," Charlie said, jutting out her chin. "I can't fly."

"You can't?" Nora teased, a hand to her chest in mock surprise.

"Nora," Aeolus warned. He ran a hand through his hair and focused back on Charlie. "What are you doing spying on us?"

"I followed you," Charlie said. "As I told you, I'm—"

"Going to kill him," Nora finished for Charlie. She had no idea why Charlie had thought it was a promising idea to follow them, especially after Aeolus had told her to go home and Nora had made it clear they weren't to be messed with. The woman was evidently determined on revenge if she hadn't given up her ridiculous plan. "Yeah, yeah, we know. It's still not the best idea you've ever had. Not to mention that your execution is appalling."

"I'm not exactly a trained professional," Charlie said. "As long as he ends up dead that's all I care about."

"I didn't kill your father," Aeolus snapped.

Charlie jumped to her feet, pointing a finger at his chest. "I saw you!"

"You saw what we wanted you to see. The blade was a trick. It never sliced him. We used pig's blood and rehearsed the entire pretence for you."

"Liar! You killed him!"

Aeolus shook his head. "What you saw was a show. As far as I know, your father is still alive."

"No," Charlie rubbed her hands absently up her arms as though warming herself from the cold. "He wouldn't have abandoned me. He was all I had. My mother died when I was young and I have no one else. They sent me to a children's home when he died ... There is no way he'd have done that to me. We were all each other had."

Nora's insides twisted. She could feel the turmoil within the other woman. The man who'd pretended to be Nora's father had abandoned her too, sold her to King Dominic like she were a loaf of bread.

"I'm sorry," Aeolus replied. "But he did."

The room fell silent except for Charlie's steps as she stood and paced the small space. Nora looked at Aeolus, a brow raised in question. His lips pressed into a thin line in response. He was telling the truth. Nora's heart ached for Charlie, for the truth she refused to accept. Finding out your father was really alive and left you by choice in the same night would be hard for anyone to simply accept.

"Prove it," Charlie demanded, halting her steps and glaring at him. There was fire in her golden eyes.

"I don't have the fucking time, nor the desire to do so," Aeolus growled.

"Then tell me where to find him."

He looked her up and down then sighed heavily. "He's with the King's Guild. That's the last place I saw him."

"Then that's where I'll go," Charlie said, striding towards the door.

"Wait!" Nora called, following Charlie as the woman headed down the hallway. "You can't go alone!" She gripped the door frame, turning back to Aeolus. "This is fucking stupid. They'll kill her."

Nora wasn't sure why she cared what happened to Charlie, only that she did. Maybe it was her emotions were growing more and more since her tattoos had been removed and she was just a sympathetic sob or maybe it was the loss of Florence and Aren that had her wanting to prevent unnecessary death. Whatever it was, she couldn't let Charlie die for no reason.

"She's a big girl," he replied, sitting on the bed.

Nora hurried down the hallway in her socks. "Come back! He was joking! Don't do this!"

Charlie didn't bother turning around, ignoring Nora completely as she picked up her pace and ran down the stairs.

Nora returned to the room she shared with Aeolus, slamming the door shut behind her. With so much death everywhere they went, Nora couldn't believe how calm Aeolus was in sending another innocent to their death. Or how easily he could ignore his conscience, while Nora's, of all people's, screamed at her. "Maybe you didn't kill her father, but Charlie's death will sure as fuck be on your hands."

12

Evelyn

Heat enveloped Evelyn as she stepped into Sloane's apothecary in the same moment her eyes watered from the lavender-scented smoke in the air. The sound of Sloane swearing from somewhere within was the only thing pushing Evelyn forward through the fog.

"Sloane! Where are you?" Evelyn shouted, before covering her mouth and nose with the crook of her elbow and moving with careful steps. She scrunched her brow at the clanging sound from somewhere deep in the smoke, then jumped back to avoid being run into.

"Fucking stupid goose!" Sloane growled, appearing from the smoke like a phantom. Her lavender hair was more vibrant than ever and her blue eyes glowed bright like gems. "The thing had the audacity to bite me!"

Sloane marched passed Evelyn, her hands waving about to dispel the smoke as she moved around the apothecary, muttering angrily about the goose.

Evelyn hurried after Sloane, eager to be out of the smoky apothecary and back outside. "A goose bit you?"

"You'd think it'd heard the rule of not biting the hand that feeds you, but apparently not," Sloane huffed, blowing a strand of hair from her face and holding out her hand, blood dripping from one of the fingers.

Kylan's words echoed in her mind. *You are a Lys Alv.*

Evelyn breathed deeply then forced herself to push away her doubts and reached for Sloane's hand. Closing her eyes, she waited. After a few seconds of nothing, uncertainty again filled her mind. Was she supposed to do something? Feel something?

"What are you doing?" Sloane asked and Evelyn cracked open her eyes, locking down to where their hands joined. Blood spilled from between where Evelyn's hand met Sloane's tattooed one, the latter very much still injured. "Well?"

Evelyn dropped Sloane's hand with a frown, disappointment sagging her shoulders. What had she been waiting for and why had she thought what Kylan had said was true? "Sorry, ah, it looks deep. We should get you a bandage."

"Only a flesh wound," Sloane replied, looking suspiciously at Evelyn. "What I need is to get back in there and put that cauldron out before the whole manor stinks like smoke."

And with that, the woman took a few deep breaths and stormed back inside, the smoke parting as though loyal servants bowing to their queen. A few moments later, Evelyn worked up the courage to step inside the apothecary once more and found the place completely smoke-free. The air was clear, almost clearer than that of outside. A goose honked from the corner where it sat on a checkered blanket and made no move to get up. Evelyn prayed to the Goddess Nyssa … no wait, her God was Frode, that the goose stayed where it was.

"What happened?"

"Tonic got out of control," Sloane shrugged. "Is there a reason for this unplanned visit other than holding my hand? How have your memories been?"

"Still distant," Evelyn said, fidgeting with the sleeve of her dress. "But the other day, someone, not Phillip this time, was familiar. The familiarity came with headaches."

"Is that so? Who was it?"

A dull thud beat at the front of Evelyn's head, which she did her best to ignore. "He said his name was Kylan."

"How did you meet him?" Sloane asked with a raised brow, hands on her hips.

"I was asked to take him his meal down to the dungeon. He seemed to believe I knew him before."

"He's the son of King Dominic," Sloane said. "Prince Kylan would say anything to get what he wants. His father is killing innocents and passing terrible laws to justify more death and control."

"I saw letters from Royal Bay the other day," Evelyn said then quickly added. "I didn't read them, just saw them."

"King Dominic has ordered an army to march on the rebellion."

"Will Sorby join him?"

"Lord Maker remains out of *that* conflict."

"Yet he holds the king's son prisoner?"

"Everything is a thread in a larger tapestry. Moves in a game. Plans on a ruler's table."

"That's not an answer."

"It is, though not the one you want."

Evelyn frowned, rubbing her fingers in circles at her temple. "Prince Kylan. Did I know him?"

"Unfortunately, you do. He was here as a representative for his father," Sloane began, her voice softening. "He seduced you and then hurt you. That's how you became unconscious. He was the one who pushed you down the stairs. I know I said you fell but I wanted to protect you. He is only here as leverage, but he will be on his way soon."

Evelyn felt sick to her stomach when Verida's warning came into her mind. Could she trust Sloane's warnings about Prince Kylan?

"He is as sick as his father," Sloane added, and her lip curled in distaste. "Playing games with the lives of those he should be protecting. Don't worry. You will never have to lay eyes on him again. I promise."

She didn't understand why, but Evelyn's gut clenched at Sloane's words.

Stepping back, Evelyn positioned herself between Maggie and Verida, hands clasped behind her back with her shoulders straight. The plate of biscuits she'd been holding had been placed on the table in the centre of the pavilion. Circling the table were iron-framed seats filled with both fluffy cushions and the bottoms of the lords and ladies Lord Maker had invited to visit.

It had been three days since they'd arrived and Evelyn eagerly awaited their departure. She was exhausted from being at their constant beck and call. There was always someone who needed something; more pillows, less pillows, a fresh pot of ink, a minstrel, sweets, wine, cheese, hot water, fresh sheets … if it could be named, it was called for. Her feet ached and her mind was beyond tired; she'd barely had time to think beyond her tasks, not that she wanted to delve into her mind.

When it wasn't giving her headaches every time she tried to access a memory, it was leaving her in a confused mess over who she was. Everyone she spoke to had a different idea of her life before she woke up and the kind of person she was. No story was consistent with another, and nothing made sense.

Sloane said she was a common maid.

Kylan said she was a princess to be.

Verida said no one could be trusted.

Other than calling her new girl, Maggie was too busy gossiping to give her thoughts on the matter, though Evelyn was kind of happy about that.

"I've always wanted to live in a forest," one of the lords was saying to his companion between a mouthful of cake. He wiped his mouth with a napkin, smearing bright red jam all around his thin lips instead of removing it. "My estate is currently on the seaside so a tree change will be a happy contrast."

"So you're wanting Forest's Edge, then?" a lady asked, tilting her round head to one side. She was dressed in a finely made lemon-yellow dress, embroidered with beaded flowers trimming the edges of the sleeves and hem of the skirt. "I guess I can go along with that if I am given Ferieton."

"Are we allocating cities now, rather than when it's over?" a bearded lord asked, his facial hair hanging to his chest. "I assume we all have our preferences already."

"Yes," said the thin-lipped lord with a decisive nod. "And mine is Forest's Edge."

The woman sitting beside him with light brown hair that fell in curls tapped him on the arm and looked pointedly towards Evelyn with hazel eyes. Evelyn felt her cheeks heat and glanced away, hoping the sudden attention directed at her was just an enquiry for a refill. But they continued their conversation without calling her over. Evelyn wondered why they should look at her during their discussion.

Forest's Edge.

Kylan said that was where she was from, where her sister ruled.

"The woodsy city is nice, I am sure, but Giland is where I'd like to make my mark," another woman said, her posture as stiff as a stone pillar. "Giland is the true gem in this country."

"Then why do you think you'll be the one taking it?" the bearded lord asked gruffly, sitting back in his chair. "What makes you entitled to it?"

"My skill in running a prosperous city, perhaps? A city that size needs someone who understands commerce," the woman replied, lifting her chin. "Or perhaps it will be the size of my forces currently sailing here as we speak."

"There are plenty of cities to go around," Lord Maker said with a broad smile. "We are all allies here. This country is ripe for the picking and we will all enjoy its fruits."

"And when will we be doing so?" the thin lipped lord asked. "I am growing impatient."

"Soon," Lord Maker promised. "Valmenessia must first be brought to the brink. Once it is on the edge, it will reach out a willing hand to whoever offers to be its saviour, that is where we will be ready and waiting."

Evelyn clenched her fists at her sides, trying her best to keep any sign of the sudden anger rising within from showing. She didn't need memories to understand what they were implying or be angered by the nonchalant way they discussed the decimation of an entire country.

Between those gathered here, their combined forces could help end the war against King Dominic, and yet they were sitting in wait ready to claim whatever remained as a prize, exploiting the vulnerable who would be left when it was all over.

It made Evelyn sick to her stomach.

A hand gripped her wrist and Evelyn let herself be tugged away by Verida. She followed the maid from the room, her shoulders tense, and only once they were out of earshot did Verida speak.

"The others can handle the afternoon tea for now," Verida said, striding along the path. "By the looks of you, if you remained in there any longer, I worry you'd strangle one of the lords."

"Doesn't their inaction anger you?"

"Would yelling at them help? Do you think they'd listen to me?"

Evelyn pouted, folding her arms over her chest.

"There are other ways to act."

"What's that supposed to mean?"

Verida shook her head. "Come, we need to start preparations for the Feast of Frode."

"The dinner is days away," Evelyn replied with a groan as she trailed dutifully along back inside the main house. "And I want answers."

"It's a special event," Verida said, ignoring Evelyn's demand for information. "Even more so this year as Lord Maker is making an important announcement and wants everything to be perfect."

"An announcement?" Evelyn paused. "What kind of announcement? I can't imagine there's anything more significant to these nobles than divvying up Valmenessia right now?"

Verida looked back at Evelyn, the edges of her lips tugging down. "Haven't you been paying attention? What did I tell you about them?"

"No one can be trusted."

"And they are all greedy for more power."

August

Faint black lines covered his hand, branching out from a black spot on his palm. There was no doubt in August's mind what it was or that he'd caught the Makers' Curse. He was going to die.

How much time he had was unknown. The progress of the curse was slower than he'd seen. A promising sign that perhaps he had a little longer than most. It might have had something to do with being a Mors Alv. But death was still inevitable.

August put his glove back on and shoved thoughts of death away. He had too many things to do to dwell on it. Since discovering his infection he'd kept his distance, not touching anyone who bore magic with his bare skin. So far he'd managed not to infect anyone.

He doubted his luck would last. He told Omari and Tyler, apologising to the latter for not telling him sooner. Tyler made a joke out of it in true Tyler fashion, and then both he and Omari deemed August safe as long as he kept his hand covered. The curse was growing slowly, so far it was isolated to his hand, and had little to no effect on him. This and the fact Tyler wasn't sick meant it wasn't air-born, which was good enough for Omari. He set precautions, but other than that, August was free to behave normally among the others. It was more than August deserved.

August quickly finished writing the letter, popping the folded paper into his satchel. Another note to Nora. She would think it cheesy, but he hoped that if she ever received them she would appreciate the thought nonetheless.

August stepped outside of the tent he and Tyler were given to share and stretched his arms above his head. His sleep had been more comfortable than any they'd had since leaving Fellbun, thanks to the extra blankets and the Elementum keeping the cold at bay. Tyler was still fast asleep, so August decided to get breakfast with the hope his friend would be awake and ready to leave when he returned.

He'd thought long and hard about whether he should stay or not, and he'd come to the conclusion that he needed to continue south above all else. Time was no longer his friend and the idea of lingering any longer didn't sit well with August. Nora was in Midskopas and he was desperate to see her again. He didn't want to die without talking to her one last time. Not only that, King Dominic had to be killed before August himself took his last breath. He refused to die before he saw that happen.

August strolled through the camp, smiling politely at those nearby but ultimately keeping his distance. There were still those who feared him, muttering to their companions whilst glaring in his direction. Others simply ran away. He tried not to let it bother him as he wove through the tents, finding the one serving food and lining up for a portion. He got his meal and headed over to Omari's tent to notify the man of his imminent departure.

"August," Omari said in greeting as August entered. "What are you doing here so early?

"I'm leaving today."

"Are you sure? Jasmine is only a day's travel away." Omari rubbed at the back of his neck.

"I've thought about it and, you know I'm a dead man walking, what's left of my time would be better spent taking the king's life. Everyone knows it's a suicide mission, so it makes the most sense that I do this."

"Perhaps, though there is something you should know, something I should have told you when you told me you have the curse," Omari replied. "Sage is travelling with Jasmine and she is working to reconstruct the research she'd done with Phillip. She thinks she may have found a cure for the curse. Something to halt it from stealing magic."

"A cure?" August asked, dark eyes wide.

Omari nodded. "Before Phillip had run away with their work, Sage was finding a way to take magic from magical objects, she thinks if she can apply it to the curse then it could take away its power. She's still testing it, but she has high hopes, as we all do."

A cure. The possibility was beyond anything August could have hoped for. He'd already surrendered to the idea of his impending death.

"I'm sorry I didn't tell you before," Omari said. "I didn't want to get your hopes up, I still don't, however, I don't want you to leave without first speaking to Sage. Find out how far along she is with her work, then decide whether you want to still leave. What is one more day?"

August felt a smile tug at his lips. Time was short, but Omari was right. What was another day if there was a chance he could be cured?

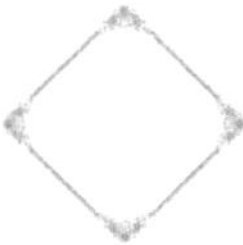

Right on schedule, the Northern Alliance descended upon the camp and the atmosphere among them changed instantly.

Everyone was eager to see loved ones and word of a possible cure had spirits even higher.

August and Tyler were called to Omari's tent and as soon as they stepped in, August came face to face with Jasmine. He was instantly reminded of Evelyn. But he pushed those thoughts aside and saw the clear wear on Jasmine's face. She looked tired; her long black hair was tied to one side, not in some pretty style like he'd only ever known her to wear. Her face appeared thinner too, either from lack of food or the overwhelming stress of the last few months, he guessed it was the latter. Jasmine had had so much put on her shoulders since August met her. First, her father had died, passing the ruling of Forest's Edge onto her, then Evelyn's kidnapping and the rebellion against King Dominic. Now the Makers' Curse had displaced many of the citizens of Forest's Edge and killed her mother. It was more than anyone should have had to bear.

"Lady Royd," August said, bowing his head in respect. "It's good to see you."

"You don't need to call me by my title," Jasmine smiled warmly. "I'm glad you're safe and back with us."

"This is Tyler," August added.

Tyler stepped from behind August and gave Jasmine one of his winning smiles. "August knows a lot of powerful people, but you are by far the most beautiful," Tyler said.

A faint blush crept onto her cheeks. "Does he?" Jasmine asked, quirking a brow at August.

Omari shot Tyler a look that said to watch himself.

"Yeah," Tyler replied, stuffing his hands into his pockets. "A few lords, ladies, and some royals too." He pointed to Omari. "A soon-to-be lord … just regular friends for old August."

"Sounds like you've had quite the journey," Jasmine said, turning her attention back to August. She ran her gaze over him, though not in the assessing way he felt others did, more as though she were checking to see if he was okay. "How were the

Periculum Mountains? Many Mors Alvs or is he it?"

August's dark eyes widened at how Jasmine had known where he'd gone and to whom he was seeing.

"Felix told us," Jasmine explained, noting August's expression.

"There is a whole community of Mors Alvs up there," August said, thinking back on his time in the mountains. "Living peacefully amongst themselves with the occasional aid from Lord Havilor."

"It's like a hidden city," Tyler added. "We all have our role to play to keep it running and thanks to Jord we are safe and able to live without fear of King Dominic."

"Our Gods and Goddesses watch over us all," Jasmine replied with a solemn nod. "Though I wish they would do more at the moment."

"Actually, it turns out, Jord is alive and well. Not answering prayers, but leading the Mors Alvs," August said, scratching his head. "The Gods and Goddesses are all among us. Felix, I assume he didn't tell you who he is judging by which name you use for him … well he's Aren, the Anima God."

Tyler nodded. "It's true."

"The Gods and Goddesses are here? Among us?" Omari said, shaking his head in disbelief. "Are you sure? And you say Felix is … Felix is just a normal guy."

"I've watched him shift into his eagle form a few times," August said. "He is Aren. I have no doubt the others are alive as well."

"Don't forget to tell them about the snow monsters in the mountains," Tyler added. "The giant beasts from our legends are real too. They're appearing all over the place."

Omari raised his brows at Tyler. "Those too?"

August shrugged. "A curse is consuming everything and everyone with magic and our deities roam the land disguised as our friends. Why wouldn't there be monsters on top of that?"

"Do you think the Mors Alvs will join us?" Jasmine asked August, hope filling her brown eyes.

"Unlikely," he said, drawing out the word. "Jord is very protective and Lord Havilor has lost all contact with them. His last messenger returned with news that everyone was gone. Who knows where Jord has hidden them."

"Whilst I understand her wish to protect the Mors Alvs, I do wish they would join us. The more we have on our side the better our chance at defeating the king. This affects everyone after all," Jasmine said. Then, as if the thought suddenly popped into her head, she changed topics to a more positive one. "Did Omari tell you of Sage's research? She's working tirelessly to find a cure."

"He mentioned it," August said, chest fluttering with hope. "I'd like to see her. Will too, if he's here."

"I'll find out where they've settled and ask someone to take you to them," Omari offered. He kissed Jasmine before disappearing from the tent.

"Have you heard from Evelyn?" August asked, his voice low as he carefully broached the subject.

Jasmine shook her head. "Nothing. All I know is the castle is preventing anyone from entering so my hope is she is safe behind its walls. Have you heard anything in your travels?"

"No," August replied. "But I'm on my way to Royal Bay now. I will get Evelyn back and kill that bastard of a king."

"Thank you." Jasmine wiped a stray tear from beneath her eye. "I sent guards after her, but none returned. They disappeared and I can't sacrifice any more lives for hers, as much as I want to, I have to take care of my people too."

"You've done the right thing," he told her. "I'll bring her home to you."

"We'll bring her home," Tyler corrected, and August smiled at his friend.

A few moments later, Omari stepped into the tent, closely tailed by none other than Ashe. The man looked straight at

Jasmine, his attention solely on the lady of Forest's Edge, and ignored August and Tyler completely. Odd considering the man had loved to tease August at every chance he got the last time they were together.

"You remember August," Jasmine said to Ashe, gesturing to where August stood. "I'd like you to take him and his friend Tyler here to see Sage and Will."

"No problem." Ashe nodded, then turned to face August. He didn't make eye contact, looking to the ground instead. August was curious about what happened to change Ashe's personality so drastically since last he saw him. "Follow me."

"Now that Jasmine and her forces have arrived, we'll only remain here for another day before continuing south," Omari said. "Meet with Sage and Will but don't get comfortable now your friends are here."

"Wasn't planning on it," August chuckled before he left.

They stepped out of the tent and Tyler shot August a quizzical look, angling his head towards Ashe. "What's his problem?"

"No idea," August replied as they followed Ashe outside. "His entire personality has shifted since I last saw him."

The man didn't speak to them, which was unusual because the last time August had seen Ashe, he wouldn't shut up. Always saying stupid shit.

"Possession?" Tyler raised a brow, mischief dancing in his eyes.

"Anything is possible these days." August laughed as they wove through the tents. "Hey Ashe, cat got your tongue?"

A moment passed and August thought he wouldn't respond before he said, "I've got nothing to say."

"That's unusual."

"Times change," Ashe replied with a shrug. "I'm not who I was when you left."

"I guess none of us are," August replied.

August didn't press any more on the subject, instead taking

to observe those who had recently joined them. Fighters stood in groups, practising their techniques while cooks worked around large pots with assistants preparing produce and meat beside them. Tents had been erected and members of the Northern Alliance milled about, patching clothing or repairing other essential items. Everyone was working as a team. They all had a purpose.

As they walked along, one area in particular drew August's interest. A workspace sat just beyond the tents where the blacksmith was moulding and hammering. The smoke from his magical fire that burned eternally hot and the sound of hammer on metal broke through the noise of the rest of the camp. Weapons sat in a wagon beside the work area, from swords and daggers to axes and arrow tips, an impressive collection was being prepared.

"Supplies to defend against the king?" August asked, stopping to observe the blacksmith at work. A stocky older man with a bald head beat a piece of metal with a hammer.

"And the curse," Ashe replied, coming to stand beside him. "That's Erik. He's a conjurer. Can make some pretty powerful weapons that we're hoping will help us on both fronts."

August thought of the name Erik. He'd heard his name before, but where, he couldn't remember.

"How are his weapons going to help against the curse?" Tyler asked, folding his arms over his chest. "Wouldn't it be better to create some sort of protection amulet?"

Ashe shook his head. "Sage is working on a cure. Erik is trying to create a weapon that can physically fight the curse. So far it's impervious to physical attacks, and magical attacks only make it stronger. But he's confident he can make something new that will at least cut through the vines."

August stepped from the path and strode over to where Erik was working. He stopped by the wagon inspecting the pile of weapons before him. There were many swords, axes and other weapons too, but he'd only really liked one weapon in particular.

He picked up a sword, testing its weight before moving it through the air, inspecting the exquisite craftsmanship.

"I've heard your name before," August said to the blacksmith. "You worked in Royal Bay."

"I did, under Bo," Erik said, stopping his hammer to look up at August. "How'd you know?"

"I have—had—one of his swords," August replied, holding up the one he had chosen from the pile. "Your weapons look very similar to Bo's style."

"I spent a year in Royal Bay during my youth learning his techniques."

"And now you're crafting weapons to fight a curse."

"Hopefully."

August placed the sword back in the wagon.

"What happened to your sword?" the blacksmith asked.

"Lost it."

"Some might say you're not worthy of another," Erik mused, scratching his moustache.

August shoved his gloved hands into his pockets and shrugged. "They're probably right."

"Maybe we'll see if we can piss those cynics off," Erik chuckled. "You're travelling with us?"

"For now," August said. "I have somewhere else to be."

"Don't we all," Erik replied with a wry smile. "I like you. Come back and assist me whenever we stop for camp, and I'll make you a sword in return."

August scratched his chin then held out his gloved hand. "Deal."

He left the blacksmith after promising to return the next time the Alliance made camp, and followed Ashe once again to find Sage and Will. It wasn't a long walk before they arrived at a row of tents marked with yellow suns. Healer's tents.

"Sage and Will are in here," Ashe said, lifting the flap of the larger tent. "Don't touch anything."

August nodded before entering, finding Sage and Will within. She stood over a large wooden table, vials and paper sprawled out all over, along with crystals and a variety of plants that Will was tending to.

"Omari said we leave in a day," he began, looking around the tent. "But you look settled in for the rest of Frost Season."

"August," Sage said with a grin, her brown eyes sparkling behind her gold-rimmed glasses as soon as she saw him. "You're here?"

She strode over, her arms wide to hug him and he let her. It was the first contact he'd had in a long time and knowing she couldn't catch the curse from him meant he could relax and let himself be comforted.

"I know we aren't really friends," Sage began as she squeezed him. "But seeing you made me think of Nora and I just—"

"Needed a hug?"

"Yeah," Sage replied, drawing back. "It's good to see you."

"It is a welcome sight to see the both of you, too," he said with a warm grin.

"You can go now," Will snapped at Ashe. He ran his hand through his dark mop of hair before going back to his work.

August frowned at Nora's old boss. The man was usually so nice, August couldn't help but wonder what Ashe had done to piss him off. Ashe scowled at Will but did what he was told and stormed out of the tent.

Tyler whistled one long note, watching Ashe go. "You don't like him much."

"He set up a friend and is an all-round awful person," Will replied, glancing at Tyler. "I'm Will, by the way."

"Tyler," Tyler replied with a grin. He strode further into the tent, glancing around at the space. "Nice place you have here."

"It does its job," Sage said, stuffing her hands into her coat pocket. "I'm glad you're here. How were the mountains? Cold?"

"Very," August chuckled. "We were on our way south when

we met up with Omari and he convinced us to join, at least for a little while."

"Any news of Florence and Nora?" Will asked, stepping away from his work.

"Nora is in Midskopas as far as I know," August said.

Sage looked up at him. "That's what we heard too. Do you think she is okay?"

"Omari said she was when I asked." He pulled Sage into another hug at seeing her eyes fill with tears. It was nice to be able to be close to someone without fear of infecting them. "I didn't ask about Florence, sorry."

"It's okay," Sage said, pulling away. She lifted her glasses to wipe her eyes with the back of her hand. "We would have been told if they weren't okay." She looked between August and Tyler. "So, what brings you here?"

"I'm nosey," Tyler stated with a grin, earning a chuckle from Will.

"And I wanted to check in on you both," August replied. "See how you're doing? How's your work going? Jasmine said you're working on a cure, Sage."

"It's going frustratingly," she replied with a heavy sigh. "So far, the dust is having no effects on the curse. I thought because the one I was working on with Phillip had the ability to absorb magic that I could replicate it to a degree and use it on the curse. Unfortunately, it hasn't turned out that way. Every sample I've made has done nothing. Others are helping me, but we have all found the same results. We sprinkle it on the curse and there's no effect."

"On the actual curse or the sick?"

"The curse," Sage said. "Jasmine has volunteers who take it out to the nearest location and test it, same as the weapons Erik is making. It's a lot of time and resources, but everyone is hopeful. As for testing on the sick, I can't force volunteers and the few sick we've had tend to leave to avoid getting anyone else sick."

"You can test it on me," August said.

Sage's eyes opened wide.

"You're infected?" Will asked, coming to his side.

"I … I haven't passed it on to anyone," August said quickly. "I keep my hand gloved and it's growing very slowly."

"I've been with him the whole time and he hasn't passed it to me," Tyler added.

"Interesting," Sage nodded. "Can I see?"

August slowly took off his glove and showed her his hand. It looked the same as it had that morning. Faint grey lines across his pale skin.

"Shit," Will breathed, squeezing August's shoulder. "I'm sorry."

Sage frowned at his cursed skin. "How long have you had it?"

"A few weeks, give or take."

"And this is all there is?"

"Yes."

She looked up at him, concern and a working hypothesis in her eyes. "I'll find the cure. We'll do it together. There must be something in your blood that's fighting the curse. Otherwise, you'd have died days ago. This is promising. Thank you for coming to me. I won't let you die, August. I promise."

Nora

In the dark of the inn's room, Nora made her decision. The usual grief-filled dreams that had her tossing and turning on the road had been replaced by indecision that night at the inn. Old habits and her newly developing emotions fought in her mind, but she'd finally come to a decision.

Charlie could take care of herself. The woman's stupid actions were not Nora's problem.

"You're awake," Aeolus said, his voice thick.

"How long have you been watching me in the dark like a creeper?" Nora asked, slowly rising to her feet. She stretched out her arms and legs, her body full of aches.

"You have been more restless tonight," Aeolus replied. She couldn't see his face but could feel his eyes on her. "It's hard to sleep with you tossing and turning."

"Well, it's your lucky day then because my mind is settled and I'm ready to get moving again."

She summoned a small ball of flame and the crackling orb

illuminated the room enough to see as she put on her boots. Her gaze ran over the now-illuminated space, searching for her pack, though her heartbeat began to rise at her inability to spot her belongings.

"Where's my pack?" Nora stormed around the room, lifting the bed sheets to look under the bed. "Where did you put it?"

"I haven't touched your bag."

"Where's your pack?"

"Here." He pointed to his bag next to the bed.

Nora raced towards it, searching in the area for hers. She had to find it. The necklace Aren had given her was in her pack. There was no way it could have grown legs and walked out of the room and if Aeolus hadn't touched it, then there was only one other person who'd been in there.

"That little bitch," Nora growled, hands on her hips. "She stole my bag."

"Why would she have done that?"

"I have no fucking clue, but she did." Nora reached into Aeolus' pack, taking out his coin purse and a blade. He had so many, she doubted he'd miss one.

"What do you think you're doing?" Aeolus glared from where he sat on the bed, his expression all that more unpleasant thanks to the shadows cast by the flickering firelight.

"Getting supplies and leaving."

"Where?"

"Off to find Charlie," Nora snapped, then strapped her dagger to her side.

"We don't have time for this, Nora," Aeolus stated, disgruntled. "Let her make her own mistakes. You and I don't have time for this."

"I don't care about her mistakes. She stole from me," she hissed. "I'm going to get my stuff back."

"Don't waste your time," he argued. "We need to stay on track."

Nora crossed her arms over her chest, staring him down. "Aren's necklace was in there."

"So?" He raised a brow.

Nora hated the condescending tone of his voice. "It's important to me."

"Are you sure this is not some hero complex playing out? Don't worry about Charlie. The King's Guild might welcome her with open arms," Aeolus suggested. "If her father is there, they could be happy to see her."

Nora glared at him. "They are a conspiratorial, king-loving group at the best of times and these are far from the best times. You think they'll welcome any outsider who happens to find them. Even if her father is with them, do you think they'll care? Do you have any idea what men do to lone women during war? Killing her would be the best outcome once they got their hands on her." Nora huffed. "But that's beside the point. She stole my necklace and I need to get it back."

"A million good deeds won't make you feel better for all the bad things you've done," he said, ignoring what Nora said about the necklace. "Trust me. I know better than most. Good deeds don't replace the ones that keep you up at night. Before long you won't even remember the good you've done. But the guilt won't ever let you forget. You will hold those regrets against yourself forever, no matter the good you do."

"Don't act like you can relate to me," she hissed. "You have no idea what it's like to be in my position."

"Nora."

"I don't have time for this," Nora snapped. She could be there for days discussing morals with him and wasting precious time that she should use searching for Charlie and her necklace. She'd already lost too much. "Coming with me or not?"

Aeolus pressed his lips together.

"You're so stubborn, but not in a good way," Nora seethed, turning her back to him. "Not to mention you're being stupid, you know that?

"*She* may not die by their hands, but if we go marching into a guild's camp, they will most certainly kill *us*. Is that what you want? You would sacrifice a chance at killing King Dominic, ending this war and his reign, and punishing him for all he has done to you for *her* life? You really want to throw your life away at the hands of the guild for a stranger?" He threw his hands in the air. "Sorry, not a stranger, a meaningless necklace."

"It means something to me."

With that, Nora strode from the room, extinguishing her fireball with the snap of her fingers. Her indecision had cost her time, but Nora was sure she could make it up and catch Charlie before she reached wherever the closest King's Guild hideout was. She had a few ideas of where to go. Being in the Alta, she'd had a couple of run-ins with guild members over time and knew a few who would talk, with the right motivation of course. Nora could be very motivating when she needed to be. Though she hoped she wouldn't have to resort to that. She doubted she'd feel good about it afterwards regardless of how vile the person was. Stupid emotions and all.

The inn was quiet, with dim candlelight providing minimal light at this early hour. As far as Nora could tell, she and Aeolus were the only ones up. She strode through the dining room, weaving through the chairs resting upside down on the tables and made her way outside.

The cool breeze caressed her face in welcome.

"Wait!" Aeolus called after Nora. He caught up, grabbing her arm as he strode to her side. "You can't go."

"I can," Nora said, whirling on the man. "And I will. So let me go, Aeolus. You're starting to get on my fucking nerves."

"If she's already with them, you'll never get out alive once you go in after her," he said, his hand still holding her. "You think you understand the guild, but you don't. You're making a mistake."

Nora tugged her arm from Aeolus' grip and summoned a ball of flame to her hand. "I can't lose this necklace." Her voice broke on the last word.

"I'll buy you another one," Aeolus said, speaking through his teeth with obvious forced restraint.

"I don't want you to buy one. I want the one Aren gave me."

"We have a job to do. Don't abandon it."

"I'm not, this is simply a detour." She walked away from him, but he strode with her, staying at her side. "If you aren't going to help me, then at least stop trying to get in my way."

"You'll die and for what?"

"Then increase my odds of survival and come with me," Nora said, hating that she actually hoped he'd join her. "Think of it as protecting me rather than helping me get my necklace back. Once we get it we can resume our king-killing mission."

Aeolus frowned. "Your necklace isn't enough for you to go to all this trouble. Not when it could mean jeopardising our original mission. It's just a piece of jewellery."

Nora's hope crumpled within her. It was amazing how brief the feeling was and how easily it was replaced with being pissed off. Aeolus was so good at getting her to feel that particular emotion.

"It is more than that." Nora halted, turning on him, anger sparking in her eyes like the magic she summoned so easily. "No one ever came for me, okay? No one fought for me. My so-called father abandoned me, too, but then I met August and Sage, Florence and Will and Aren, and you know what? They all fight for me and I refuse to not fight for them. Aren gave me that necklace and I'll be damned if I lose that piece of him."

"Nora…" he said, his voice softer than usual. She could see the pity on his face and fucking hated it.

"I'm going after Charlie. You can stay here; I don't care, Aeolus. But you won't stop me." Nora turned her back on him. "I don't need you to help me anyway."

Nora wasn't sure exactly where she would find the guild, but she was sure that if she kept moving she'd run into some cocky guild member soon enough, especially so close to Giland. The King's Guild were always so proud of themselves, determined to make their whole personality about how they followed the king. It would have been sad if Nora didn't have an immense dislike for them.

She left Aeolus in the street looking pissed off with the world and doubled back to the inn's stable. The inn hadn't been busy when they'd arrived in the late afternoon and she'd noted that only a few patrons had headed down the hallway towards the bedrooms once if had gotten later into the night. Luckily, she didn't need there to be many customers at the inn. All she needed was at least one horse.

A beautiful mare stood in a darkened stall and Nora was quick to get acquainted with the horse. She asked the animal a few questions before deciding the mare wasn't an Anima. After putting on the saddle, Nora offered a thank you to whoever was watching over her and made the mare so friendly.

She took Aeolus' coin purse from her pocket and left it in the stall before slowly leading the horse outside. Aeolus had packed coins for essential purchases and the horse was undoubtedly that.

In the cool tight air, Nora looked down the street from where she sat atop the mare. She knew of a few haunts where the King's Guild dwelled and would go to each one if she had to.

By the time she reached the third guild hideout days later, Nora was in a foul mood. The hideout was a lone stone cottage that sat atop a hill with a handful of trees surrounding it. There was no way to sneak up on those inside, so Nora simply tied her horse to one of the trees and strode towards the front door.

The first guild location she went to had been abandoned, and the second had been home to two mouthy guild members who'd swiftly lost their tongues, and then their lives. Nora was starting to think she'd never find Charlie. The possibility of which was very real; Charlie could have gone anywhere. Valmenessia was a big place after all.

The sun beamed down on the quaint scene and on any other occasion she may have thought the cottage was pretty. Vibrant yellow flowers grew beneath the windows and tiny green bushes lined the front path. The sight was almost picturesque. Almost. She knew who dwelled within and that ruined the whole scene.

Nora had been here once before with August. It hadn't ended well. For the man who lived there, that is.

Straightening her back, she took a deep breath and brought back Alta Nora. The woman without a care in the world. The woman who would do anything. Hurt anyone. She wasn't that person anymore, but right now, she needed to at least pretend to be.

She knocked hard on the door, the timber rattling on its hinges. Murmurs sounded from the other side and the door swung open, revealing a man with cropped brown hair, dazzling blue eyes and a stubbled chin. He was handsome; it was a shame what Nora and August had done to him.

A shame, but warranted.

The man's jaw dropped open, revealing a toothless mouth, and he took a swift step back.

"I don't know anything," he stuttered, hands raised before him, a few missing fingers on each. "I've nothing for you."

"Are you sure?" Nora purred, stepping inside.

"Where's your friend?" he asked, his nervous gaze moving behind Nora.

She kicked the door shut. "It's just you and me, August isn't here, and I want to have a little chat."

The man shook his head. "I still don't know anything about

nothing."

"I don't know about that," Nora replied smoothly. "Last I saw you; you had plenty to say. All you needed was a little encouragement."

"What do you want?" he asked, face paling.

"I'm looking for a woman named Charlie. She's looking for someone in the guild," she said. "So, which guild hideouts is she mostly likely to stumble upon if she was travelling around the south of Giland?

"I don't know who you're talking about," he said, lip trembling where he stood.

"She's looking for her father. Man who faked his death years back to run off with the guild," Nora replied. She recited a description of Charlie she'd been mentally recording as she pulled out a seat, blocking his path to the door.

"I don't know. She could be related to anyone."

Nora sat, sitting back in the chair with exaggerated casualness. "That's a bit of an exaggeration. Can't imagine you have *that* many Lys Alv among your lot."

"I need more information about the man or I'm guessing, just like you."

"Her father's name is..." Nora pretended to try and recall Charlie's father's name. Feigning confusion so the man would willingly provide the correct information. "Edward Walt. No, Edmin Wa—"

The man scratched his chin. "Edmund Wallis?"

"That's him," Nora snapped her fingers, sitting up straighter in her seat. "You're much more helpful than the others I visited. Where can I find him?"

The man swallowed. "Can't say."

"What's that supposed to mean?"

The man lowered his gaze. "Sworn to secrecy."

"Everything you say to me is supposed to be a secret," Nora drawled.

"Ahhh…." He swallowed hard. "They'll kill me."

"I'll kill you," she said casually. "And it will be much more fucking painful, let me tell you."

The silence was thick as tension filled the space between them. Nora waited, watching him and wondering whether he would fold. She hoped he would, the idea of inflicting pain upon him now made her feel sick. Everything she'd said had been a bluff and she prayed his fear meant he believed her.

"He's not someone I associate with."

"Are you telling me that guild members aren't all best friends?" Nora asked in mock surprise. "How can that be? Surely you all bond over your bigotry and hate?"

"Everyone is entitled to their beliefs."

"Maybe, but I tend to be of the opinion that we shouldn't force our beliefs on others," she replied, reaching for her dagger. She placed it on the table before glancing back up at him. "Now, as much as I'd love to stay and catch up. I have somewhere to be, so tell me, where is Edmund Wallis?"

"There's a base south of Giland by the lake," he told her, his gaze fixed on the blade. "I'm not telling you anything else."

Nora stood, relief filling her and making her smile come easily. "That's all I need to know."

August

Travel was slower than August would have liked now he and Tyler were with such a large group. He tried to help as best he could, carrying supplies and assisting where needed. Still, they moved at a snail's pace. It was to be expected and if it weren't for the letters he wrote to Nora and the nights in which he spent helping the blacksmith, Erik he would have gone crazy with restlessness.

The sun was setting and the camp began settling down for the night. August arrived at the blacksmith's work area and was faced with a cloud of steam as hot metal met water with a hiss. August was always impressed with the efficiency Erik got to work within minutes of Jasmine's forces making camp, setting up his conjured forge immediately so the eternal fire was instantly ready for use as August approached. The man stopped to stand with his arms folded over the leather apron covering his chest and glared at the sword he was making.

"I'm not happy with this one," Erik said in way of greeting

as August approached. He pulled the sword from the water, brandishing the cooled steel before August. "Thoughts?"

"It looks alright to me," August replied, gazing at the magnificent sword. It was beautifully made, a piece anyone would normally pay a lot of coin for.

"Ugh," Erik groaned, dropping the sword to the ground. "I knew you'd be useless."

"Then why did you ask me to come?" August asked, huffing a laugh.

"Curiosity," Erik replied. "I've never met a Mors Alv before."

"So what? I answer some of your curiosities and then you make me a replacement sword?"

Erik shook his bald head, the skin speckled with freckles and white spots. "Nah, I need assistance. Figured you look strong enough to help and as a bonus, your presence alone might keep the handsy opportunists looking to swipe a new weapon at bay. Despite what they preach, the common folk are still fearful of you and your race. Old habits and all"

"Some things never change."

"A lot of the time things do, it's just the pace of change that's the frustrating part. Some people are quicker," he clicked his fingers. "They receive new information and adjust accordingly. Others need a little more work. The change is harder to accept. But even hopeless cases can be used to your advantage, you just have to be smart about it," Erik chuckled. "Now, how are those arm muscles of yours?"

"I have the curse."

The words rushed from August on an exhale. Why at that moment? August had no idea. He'd been meaning to tell Erik. He'd come to enjoy working with the blacksmith but was afraid he would send him away if he found out. August's heart beat rapidly in his chest as he waited for the imminent reaction.

Erik looked up at him, expression serious as he gazed over

August. "You don't look sick."

"It's spreading slower than usual," August replied. "I've had it for weeks and it hasn't travelled beyond my hand. I feel fine and as long as I'm wearing my gloves, I haven't infected anyone."

"I take it you're not announcing it to everyone. Who else knows?"

"Tyler, Jasmine, Sage, Will and Omari," August said, a sense of guilt rising in him. Despite the reassurance of those few he'd told; he couldn't help but feel as though he was putting others in danger just by being in their proximity. His actions were selfish, he knew that.

"Don't tell anyone else," Erik said. "People are already afraid and if aren't going around infecting others then there's no need to add to that fear."

August nodded stiffly, the discussion apparently over. Soon after, he was put to task, beating metal on an anvil until the folded layers had formed a stronger piece for the blacksmith to manipulate further. It was tiring work, the conjured magical fire, burning hot the entire time as Erik barked orders. By the time August was finishing up, the camp was quiet, everyone in their beds, resting before the journey continued in the morning.

August was exhausted; exactly how he wished to be feeling. His limbs ached, his skin wet with sweat and his head pounded, much like the hammer had on the steel. He was ready to collapse straight into bed.

"Hey!" Ashe called, jogging over to where August was packing up for the night. "I hear you're planning to assassinate King Dominic."

"Who told you that?" August asked as he stacked tools away into a wagon.

"Tyler," Ashe replied. "I want to come with you."

"Oh? And why would you want to do that?"

"I want him dead too."

"I imagine there are a lot who do," August said, "Why now?"

"I owe Nora," Ashe replied. "I figure murdering the man who enslaved her is a good way to make things right."

That got August's attention. He put down the tools and folded his arms over his chest, giving Ashe his full attention. He couldn't help but think whatever happened with Nora may be linked to Sage and Will's obvious distaste for the man. It might also have something to do with why Ashe seemed like a totally different person. "This have anything to do with why Sage and Will are pissed with you?"

Ashe averted his gaze and said, "They have every right to be. But to be fair, I did what I did for good reason. I only had the best intentions."

"I'm sure."

He scratched his head. "Sage hasn't told you, then?"

"Nope. So, you can tell me your side first."

"After you left. I made a bad call. It's complicated, but at the end of the day, I set Nora up and almost got her killed. I told your Alta friends where to find her and arranged for Nora to be there at the agreed time. Needless to say, it didn't go as planned," Ashe admitted. There was no hint of holding anything back or attempts at justifying his actions. "I thought I was doing right by the faction and, honestly, I was jealous she was with Sage—"

August's gloved fist collided with Ashe's jaw, sending him stumbling back and almost falling to the ground.

"I deserve that," Ashe said, Checking his jaw wasn't broken.

"You pulled that kind of shit with Nora because you were *jealous* and think I'm just going to let you, what, tag along into the Alta den? What's to stop you from pulling the same stunt on me over something I said that hurt your feelings?" August barked, his body tensing. His magic rose to the surface, and it took all his willpower not to set it loose on Ashe. Luckily for Ashe, Erik was nearby. "You have some balls coming to me to ask for anything after that. Do you have any idea what we went through to get our freedom?"

"I know," Ashe held up his hands. "I know. I realise what I did can't be forgiven. I won't try to justify my mistakes, but you guys got a clean slate. A second chance to do the right thing. That's all I'm asking. You know I'm dedicated to the cause and how protective I am of it and the Alliance."

August sucked in a breath. Ashe had a point, as much as August hated to admit it. The guy had hurt Nora, but he seemed to be genuine if not remorseful. August had wanted to prove he was a good guy after all the bad he'd done. What kind of person would he be if he didn't give Ashe the benefit of the doubt?

"No," August grumbled. Turned out he was a petty guy. Good, but petty, too. He took a step closer to Ashe and lowered his voice. "Now, fuck off."

Ashe paled, but he didn't seem surprised. "Got it."

August watched the man disappear into the dark and felt another stride up silently behind him.

"You did well working the steel tonight," Erik said. His green-eyed gaze looked to where Ashe had disappeared but said nothing. August appreciated it. "If your shoulder isn't completely useless after that, I'll see you tomorrow night to do it all again."

"Great," August sighed heavily. His body may have ached, but he was glad for something to do outside of the painfully slow travel.

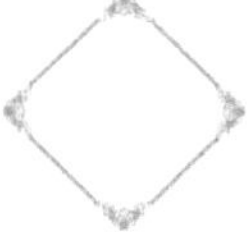

Each day August rode beside Tyler and at night he worked with the blacksmith, helping to create whatever weapons to fight not only the curse but the king's army. He'd visited Sage a few times, checking in to see how her cure was going and donating some of his blood for her to test what could be slowly the spread of the curse down. That's how he learned of Florence's death. She'd died while taking back Midskopas—with Nora.

Both Sage and Will continued to work hard, despite the news, yet at the same time, they were grieving. On the afternoons he popped his head into her tent, August found Sage red eyed. He'd been around a lot of death in his life, but he had never experienced the kind of loss that Sage and Will were feeling.

The only person close enough to him who could have that effect on him was Nora, and the idea of her no longer being alive was something he didn't want to contemplate.

So he didn't push Sage to talk or for results. It wasn't only the dust occupying her mind now. But he'd visit before working with the blacksmith and made sure to just be there if she needed. It was the least he could do.

"August," Sage greeted him as he stepped into the tent. She was sitting on her floor bed, scrawling in a notebook by the light of a lantern.

He held out a piece of freshly baked bread to her. "I got this for you," he said. It was still warm and smelled delicious. He'd already eaten his serving earlier, wolfing it down in a matter of seconds.

Sage looked up and glanced at his hands. A smile grew on her face at the sight of the bread. "Thanks. I'm starving. I'd forgotten all about eating today." She took the bread, tearing off a piece and stuffing it into her mouth with a happy little noise. "I'm also glad you're here—for more than just bringing me food. I think today is the day."

"Really?" His face lit up. "You're ready for live tests of the cure?"

She shook her head, finishing her mouthful and rising to her feet. "I know you volunteered yourself, but I do have other samples I'd like to test the dust on first."

"Samples?" August asked. "You mean the roots? I thought that form of the curse couldn't be cut."

"It can't," she replied with a grimace. "I have samples of

infection from dead carriers. The curse is like a parasite and it cannot be severed, these samples were taken by cutting around the afflicted area."

"Oh, are you sure you can't test on me?"

"Not yet," Sage replied. "I need to see if the dust has any effect on a sample of human flesh with the curse in a more controlled test first. There are too many variables I'm not confident factoring in yet, like the general physical fitness and health of a living test subject. We want to make sure we *know* it works on the curse before we introduce it to a living carrier. Biology and medicine isn't exactly my area of expertise, so we need to be careful how we do this."

He was slightly disappointed but didn't argue as he watched Sage gather a tray and another lantern. August lit the lantern while she put the tray on the ground and as the space illuminated further. He could see what she had been carrying. Several vials containing varying shades of purple powder sat on the tray and intrigued him, however, what quickly caught his eye after this were the jars of grey flesh with tiny black veins like webs on the skin.

"Alright, so I'll sprinkle the dust on the affected area and wait, keeping time of each one," she scrunched her brow as she thought through the process. "I'll use a different formulation of the dust in each jar and hopefully, we'll see something happen."

"Sounds good to me," August replied, reaching for a jar.

Sage quickly tapped his hand away. "You can just watch. I'm not brave enough to tell Nora that I accidentally gave you a premature death by exposing you to an experimental cure that did the exact opposite of what we wanted."

"Fair enough," he smirked. "Watching it is."

Sage opened the first jar and then picked up a vial filled with dust. She unstopped it and held it mid-air, pausing. Sage looked up at August, her brown eyes searching his from behind her golden-rimmed glasses. "Is it normal to be nervous? What if none of them work?"

August nodded. "Then we try again."

Sage smiled and hope swirled in August's chest. She tipped her hand and the dust fell into the jar like snow falling on a Frost Season day. Then she used a metal spoon to roll the flesh in the dust, coating it completely. The powder shimmered against the greying cursed skin.

"Okay," Sage said, putting the lid back on the jar and popping the vial away. "One down, four to go."

Sage repeated the process for the remaining jars and vials of dust, each one having no instant effect. August wasn't dissuaded, however. The dust would work. He had to believe it would. Once Sage finished, she picked up her notebook and pencil and sat beside him on the bed. "Now we wait and observe. The cursed samples are from a recently dead. If the results don't work on the dead flesh, it might be too late and we'll try samples from a live subject next. Or, if the results are good on this batch of recently infected, then we can start thinking about live trials."

They sat in silence for a few minutes, watching the jars with neither speaking as they focused on the dust with anticipation. If one of these formulas worked, it could be a cure for all Valmenessia. They were on the precipice of something huge. At least August hoped they were. As time passed and nothing appeared to change, August felt his excitement drift from him to be replaced by boredom.

"How do you keep yourself from falling asleep?" August asked, his shoulders drooping.

Sage looked up from the dust, dropping her pen onto the notebook. "It can be hard, but you get used to it. A lot of this kind of testing is waiting for results, but I think that's what makes the excitement all that much better when something does work. Like I've really earned it."

"I don't think I could do it."

"That's what Nora said too," Sage laughed. "Though it came

out with a little more sarcasm."

"Sounds about right," he chuckled. "So, you and Nora … you two made up then?"

"Yeah," Sage replied, shooting him a sidelong look. "I'm surprised it's taken you this long to ask."

August shrugged with a grin on his face, then sighed, running his hand through his hair. "You have a lot on your plate right now and, unlike my best friend, I try not to annoy those around me by getting in their business."

"But you are secretly nosey?" Sage teased.

"Only when it comes to Nora."

"Is this going to be some overprotective conversation about how I'm not allowed to hurt her, or you'll hurt me?" Sage quirked a brow with a challenge in her gaze. She could stand on her own two feet; August gave her that. She wasn't some meek girl with a crush who used Nora for protection. She clearly cared about Nora almost as much as he did. Giving her the overprotective talk would be a waste of breath.

"Nope," August laughed, and Sage's demeanour relaxed. "Nora is capable of taking care of herself anyway. This is me satiating my curiosity. I wasn't in the city when everything happened."

"You're a gossip then?" Sage smirked. "Who would have thought."

"So, are you going to fill me in about how you two fixed things?"

Sage chuckled. "Alright, alright. We tried being friends first."

"But it didn't work," August stated.

"I can't be friends with Nora," replied Sage with a sigh. "It's impossible."

"Trust me. You're not the only one who feels that way," said August. "Though, those who feel that don't want to date her so much as the opposite."

"I do," Sage smiled, eyes sparkling. "There's something about her. She's like a toxin they sell in a side alley."

"Bad for you?"

Sage shook her head. "Addictive."

August laughed. "I don't think I've ever heard someone describe her that way, but I'm happy you think that. I think you're good for her."

"You haven't been around when we are together."

"No, but over these last few days, I've gotten to know you more and I think you're just what she needs. I imagine you balance out her reckless impulsive behaviour with your logic and reason."

"Maybe," Sage looked off into the distance, then she shook her head and playfully slapped a hand on August's arm. "Enough about me and Nora. What was going on between you and Evelyn before she was taken to Royal Bay?"

August looked away from Sage. "Can I tell you something and you promise not to judge me?"

"Yes."

"I care about her and I'd do anything to get her back. When I left Jord, I was determined to go straight to Royal Bay to kill King Dominic and rescue Evelyn," he began, his shoulders sagging at the thoughts in his head coming to the surface. The truth that he had come to realise when the curse had struck. "But since being infected by the curse … it's made me think about how much time I have left. My mind is constantly filled with different end scenarios, one being if I would have had to choose between going to Nora or Evelyn."

"And you think you'd choose Nora," Sage said, voicing his thoughts.

He nodded. "She's my best friend, my family. It doesn't mean I don't care about Evelyn because I do, it's just that…"

August dropped his head. He didn't finish the sentence because he didn't want to voice the truth, the realisation that had come to him since becoming a host to the parasitic curse. He liked Evelyn, but he didn't love her. They had shared so much in their fleeting time of knowing each other and it had felt intense back then, but so had so many of his feelings. Maybe if they had had more time he'd feel different right now. Perhaps when they saw each other again, the intense feelings would return.

"You don't have to explain your feelings," Sage said, drawing August from his thoughts. "You feel what you feel and that's okay."

"I still plan on freeing Evelyn when I get to Royal Bay," he added. "If I live that long. She's still my friend, even if I don't think of her romantically now."

"You never know how you'll feel when you see her again. There's a lot going on and you've been through so much. Things might change once this is all over and who knows, perhaps you'll be overcome with love when you see her again."

"Maybe. Relationships are hard," August grumbled.

"Yep," she said, popping the 'p.' "I think they get easier with the right person, but that's just my experience."

"It's easy with Nora?"

Sage nodded and when August gave her a sceptical look she burst into laughter. "Okay, okay, it's not always *easy*. But we were opening up to one another more before we were separated, which helps the annoying things slide."

"You understand each other."

"Exactly."

August smiled at her. He was glad Nora had found Sage and hoped he'd find someone who could understand him. Whether it was Evelyn or someone else, he didn't know, but he wanted to find out what that was like.

After an hour passed, the two sat by the jars frowning at the dust.

"Nothing," Sage said with a heavy sigh, turning a jar this way and that. "No visible change. Can you see anything?"

August shook his head. "No."

"Damn," Sage sighed and took a few notes. "Maybe overnight they'll show some kind of reaction. Natural medicines can take days to work. I'd hoped this would be faster because it's based on magic. But the first pancake is never perfect so we'll move on to the next trial and hopefully that'll be the one."

"Hopefully."

"Wouldn't it have been great, if I found a cure so quickly?"

"Yeah," August smiled. "Unfortunately, life doesn't work like that."

16

Evelyn

"Any idea what the big announcement is?" Evelyn asked Maggie while they waited by the kitchen. The smell of roasted meats floated out into the hallway, causing Evelyn's stomach to grumble.

"No clue," Maggie replied. Then she lowered her voice and she looked around to make sure no one important overheard. "I did see Lord Maker visit Sloane though."

"The Healer?"

"That woman is definitely not a Healer, Evelyn," a waiter chimed in with a smirk on his handsome face.

"Do you know why he was visiting her?" Evelyn asked, brows raised at Maggie.

Maggie shook her head. "But hear this. So, I was walking past after…" She bit her lip, cheeks reddening.

"Collecting vegetables from the garden," the waiter quickly added, though Evelyn instantly saw through the lie, a smile growing on her face. The kitchen gardens were nowhere near the apothecary.

"Yes, that," Maggie replied hastily. "Anyway, we saw Lord Maker going to Sloane and you won't believe what he called her."

"What?"

"Grandmother," Maggie said with a giggle. "Maybe it's some weird kink they're into, I don't know, nor do I want to find out."

"Grandmother?" Evelyn tilted her head to one side.

"I mean, they do have the same cheekbones," the waiter shrugged.

"Do they?" Maggie tilted her head to one side as well.

"Sloane is younger than him," Evelyn stated. "Not to mention she looks about our age to begin with."

"Mmm, but as I said, she's no Healer. So what is she brewing in that apothecary of hers all day? An anti-aging potion?" Maggie asked. "There is definitely something odd going on. Ever since she turned up a few weeks ago, Lord Maker has been going to her for advice and his actual advisor, Mr Walker, is nowhere to be seen."

"I miss the guy," the waiter added, and Maggie patted him on the arm.

"I thought she'd always lived in Sorby, at least as long as she's been in Valmenessia," Evelyn said.

"Nope," Maggie replied. "Arrived around the same time as you."

"Me?"

"Yeah, why did you think I've been calling you new girl?"

"Shhh, you've said too much," the waiter hissed and Maggie's laugh was cut to an abrupt halt.

Evelyn missed their hushed conversation as Verida appeared, announcing that dinner was ready to be served. Evelyn's questions died on her lips as she took up her position and tray and headed to the dining room.

The festivities were in full swing. Lord Maker and his guests were again dressed in their finery and sat around a long table that had been decorated with golden candelabras, blooming yellow and red flowers, and glossy white plates bordered by shiny silver wear. Laughter filled the room along with triumphant chatter.

Not only were they celebrating the Feast of Frode, the smaller of the two celebrations of the night, but they were also revelling in the outcomes of their business dealings. It seemed certain alliances had proved profitable in securing future land in Valmenessia. From what she overheard, each lord and lady were posed to obtain a portion of the country, though Evelyn was unsure how exactly. The party gathered were only human, no match for the magical citizens of Valmenessia in a physical confrontation. Yet perhaps Evelyn underestimated the strength of commerce. After all, they were so confident in their futures. So sure they would obtain what they desired.

Lord Maker stood, his eyes shining brightly as he fiddled with a golden button on his jacket. His guests quietened and turned their heads as the man began to speak. "My friends, thank you for joining me tonight to celebrate the Feast of Frode, who has made all this possible for us."

Each of Lord Maker's guests held a crystal glass filled with expensive wine, toasting to Frode, the Human God, for their good fortune. To Evelyn's surprise, Mr Walker and Sloane were not among those celebrating.

Were the lord's advisor and Healer not invited?

Evelyn was about to whisper her question to Maggie when Lord Maker spoke once again.

"I must say, I have an ulterior motive for tonight as well," he continued, with a wry smile. His lips tugged up at one side. "I know you all have your hearts set on land to claim, I will not come between you and your desires. I will not claim land beyond Sorby. This is my home and the population here is mine, however, I do have one claim I shall make clear."

His gaze moved around the room, taking in each and every one of his guests, making sure to linger to make his acknowledgment of each clear.

"I propose that I shall be the new king of Valmenessia."

Mutters filled the room, yet Lord Maker didn't let it stop him. He simply spoke over the noise, his voice firm and commanding.

"I hear your concerns; however you are new to Valmenessia. You need a king to unite the lands, to maintain this allyship we have created over the years. I will be king in name; however, we will continue to work together to build the country we desire."

The room was silent and the air was thick with Lord Maker's proposition. The man did not waver, his shoulders remained high and his face a fixed mask of confidence. Evelyn's heart thudded in her chest. Her hands felt clammy as they waited to see what those gathered had to say. She hoped they would deny him. He didn't deserve to be king of Valmenessia. None of these nobles deserved to take any piece of the country. They didn't care about it. All they wanted was power.

One of the lords stood, his chair scraping on the floor as it was pushed back and he raised his wine glass once more. "To the king of Valmenessia. Long may he reign."

Others quickly followed suit, toasting to their new king before bowing in his direction. Lord Maker's mask slipped and a broad grin stretched across his face. He had claimed his title, now all he had to do was wait for the country to fall to ruin and he would claim that too.

Evelyn stepped back, one hand pressed to her chest and eyes wide. She was walking back to her room when she suddenly stopped outside the open door. It was after midnight and everyone else was already asleep or settling in for the night. Almost everyone.

Her heart thumped beneath her hand as she stared at the man in her room. She didn't get a chance to run before he grasped her wrist and tugged her inside, slamming the bedroom door shut. He swiftly locked it before he pressed his back against the wood, breathing hard as he ran a hand through his dark hair.

"How did you get out of your cell?"

"An opportunity presented itself," he said, flexing his hand. Her eyes fell to the blood on his knuckles and her heart skipped a beat. "Then all I had to do was find the maid's quarters."

Despite the fear that filled her, Evelyn couldn't help the temptation that rose in her to match his movements. To run her fingers through his hair and…

"I know how this looks," he said with pleading eyes, snapping her attention back to the present. "But I needed to see you." Evelyn shook her head, backing away and wiping all gentle thoughts she had towards him from her mind. At least those went easily, the mixed feelings she had towards him remained.

Had he really seduced her or was that a lie Sloane had told her?

Either way, she needed to be prepared to defend herself. Evelyn swept her hand over the bedside table for a weapon and ignored the part of her that felt drawn to him. Could she not trust herself either?

"Sloane confirmed who you are," she said. "Prince Kylan, son of that evil man who sits on the throne. You're a prisoner here."

"She finally told you the truth," he replied, his surprise clear in his eyes. "Evelyn—"

"She also told me what you did to me."

Kylan, the prince of Valmenessia, scrunched his brow. "What I did do to you?"

"You're the reason I've lost my memories.," Evelyn replied. She pointed a finger at him. "You lured me in, made me trust you and then did this to me."

"I'd never hurt you."

"I can't trust you," she snapped, her head already throbbing. Just being around him caused her mind to ache. "Get out, please. Just leave."

"No," he replied, stepping closer. His eyes filled with concern as she clasped her head. "I would never hurt you. I love you and you love me, whether you remember or not, that's the truth. Sloane and the others are the liars. They are the reason you can't remember. Not me."

"Please stop!" she begged, wincing as pain shot through her. "Please."

She banged a fist on the wall, hoping that someone, anyone would hear and she would be relieved from the torture in her head. It was too much. His being so close and everything he was saying…

It was all too much.

"Please." Her voice was strained. Commotion sounded from the other side of the door and Kylan must have heard them too. He flicked his wrists and then cried out, anguish shifting his features as he clutched the collar around his neck, and then stumbled towards her. He wrapped an arm around her possessively and pulled her close.

Despite the need for a shave and a bath, this close, there was no mistaking how handsome the prince was. Her body leaned into his, closing the gap between them as though her very being was desperate to feel more of him and didn't care about the pain threatening to tear her head apart. She shivered at his closeness, not from fear or disgust but something else. Perhaps a remnant of the seduction she could not recall, her body reacting on muscle memory. Sloane had said had all been a cruel lie, one that her body still believed it seemed.

"I'm sorry," he whispered, his eyes falling to her mouth. He wiped a finger over her upper lip. His gaze became one of horror at seeing the blood there. He released her as though hit with a jolt of wind magic. She instantly missed his closeness. "Evelyn. I didn't … I … I'll fix this. We will fix this."

Evelyn shook her head. "Please. You need to go."

"I don't want to hurt you but I need to talk to you. Please, Evelyn, think about it. What do your instincts tell you?"

His blue eyes watched her carefully as his hand reached forward, stopping short of her as though holding himself back.

"I don't know anymore," Evelyn admitted.

"It's because I know who you really are. Evelyn Royd, daughter of the Lord and Lady Royd, sister to Jasmine, the new lady of Forest's Edge. You're a Healer, a brilliant one too and your best friend Poppy was as well. Do you remember her? Poppy's death almost broke you. But you are too strong to break."

Evelyn closed her eyes, taking in a deep breath as she fought against passing out. She pressed her back further into the wall. She wished he would stop. It was all too much at once.

"You like to knit and read, though getting a new dress always seems to bring a bigger smile to your face than anything else. You don't consider many your friends, so when you do get close to someone you love them fiercely. You're caring beyond measure and have empathy for all those you meet. It's what makes you a great Healer. It was never the fact that you were a Lys Alv-"

"I'm human!" she declared, her eyes snapping open, tears filling them instantly.

"You're not," he rebuked, looking at her sadly. "I don't know what the fuck they did to you, but Evelyn, you weren't born human."

"The other things could be true, but that," she groaned, sliding down the wall until she sat with her hands in her lap. "That is impossible."

Her head dropped as she closed her eyes once more. Blood continued to spill from her nose, no doubt staining her skirts as it dripped onto her dress. She felt his hand on her cheek and she moved on instinct, leaning into his touch.

"Please, Evelyn. Please don't let these liars keep the truth from you," he said softly. "You know, deep down, that something isn't right. This isn't you; this isn't your home."

Beyond the door, urgent shouts echoed, becoming louder with each second and she focused on that sound, praying the pain in her mind would go away.

"Promise me," Kylan begged, his grip falling to her chin and tightening tenderly. "Promise me you won't blindly trust them."

A loud bang filled the room and Evelyn looked up to see the door open. Guards rushed in, charging towards Kylan. They pulled him roughly away from her and Kylan would have fallen to the ground if it weren't for them holding him up and securing his arms.

Kylan didn't put up a fight. He just let them shove him from the room. The entire time his eyes stayed fixed on Evelyn, and she couldn't help but hold his gaze as a knot formed in her stomach.

Once he was gone, Evelyn hugged her trembling shoulders. The pain receded almost instantly, leaving her with a dull bearable thud in her head.

Verida's words rang in her mind.

Don't trust anyone.

Yet, every time she'd seen Kylan her head had hurt. A kernel of uncertainty lingered within her. The pain was the only sure way of telling truth from fiction when it came to her memories. Sure she could trust that.

"Evelyn?" Verida asked hesitantly, stepping into the room. "Are you okay? I saw the guards take him away."

Evelyn nodded stiffly. "I'm fine."

"You don't look fine," Verida said, stepping closer. "You're bleeding."

"It's stopped," Evelyn replied, wiping her hand under her nose. Her arm dropped limply before her. She was so tired and perhaps that was why she voiced her thoughts to Verida. "Sloane is saying one thing and Kylan another. Which should I believe?"

Verida moved to her side, helping Evelyn to her feet and guiding her towards a bed. Evelyn's feet stumbled along; her body drained.

"I don't know you well enough to make that decision for you," Verida said softly, helping Evelyn to crawl beneath the blankets.

"Haven't we worked together for a while?" Evelyn asked through a yawn, curling onto her side.

"I told you not to trust anyone," Verida replied, as Evelyn closed her eyes.

She was ready to fall asleep, to submit to exhaustion now that her head no longer hurt. With another yawn, Evelyn curled her legs up and sighed into her pillow. The darkness called to her and she was desperate to follow.

"If you want answers, Evelyn, you need to find them for yourself," Verida whispered, keeping Evelyn conscious for a moment longer. "Until then, why don't you try getting your memories back with a tour of the estate? A more thorough tour that is. It hurts anytime something familiar crosses your path, right? Maybe something on the grounds will stand out to you? The crypt would be a nice place to begin."

Crypt? Evelyn thought. Though, she didn't think any more about it as she drifted into a deep sleep.

Nora

Nora was mentally kicking herself. The couple who had shared their cake with her had said the Kings' Guild had gone to the lake near Giland. Why she hadn't recalled that little tidbit until after traipsing around after guild hideouts was beyond infuriating. She was losing her touch. Nora hoped she'd catch up to Charlie before the woman reached the guild's camp.

The lake beside Giland was vast, beginning at the base of the mountains that cut Valmenessia in half and travelled the length of the mines towards the south. It was the size of the Grenblad Woods and according to the cake-sharing couple was home to a recently awoken legendary beast.

After passing Giland, keeping her distance and doing her best not to fall into a crumpled crying heap at the memory of Aren's death, she reached the water's edge and sighed. Why hadn't she just worn the necklace? She wouldn't be in this situation if she'd put it on in the first place. But she knew why.

"I don't think I've ever been so happy to see a lake before," she said to herself. She put her hands on her hips as she looked out over the pristine water.

The midday sun shone brightly, illuminating the calm blue waters that were a happy change in scenery after her travels passed the root-smothered Giland. Nora was tempted to take off her boots and dipped her feet into the water of the lake. Her rational mind prevailed, however. Even though it didn't get nearly as cold this far south at this time of year, the runoff from the mountains would be icy, making the lake freezing cold.

She hadn't had a single run-in with anything sinister on her way and she expected that her luck was due to run out. She couldn't shake the feeling of something horrible on the horizon. There was no way she could be that lucky to have everything go to plan.

Continuing south, she walked along the water's edge. She'd kept moving the entire time, never lingering for too long to rest. She was determined to find Charlie as soon as possible. There was so much time she had to make up, but at least the travel was giving her plenty of time to think and plan.

She needed to find out whether Charlie was already in the King's Guild camp. If she was, Nora was obliged to rescue her. Strolling into enemy territory to rescue someone was far from ideal. Discovering that the person you were intending to rescue wasn't there in the first place? Nora didn't want to be in that position if she could avoid it.

It wasn't difficult to track down the base, the hard part was avoiding scouts and patrols that might see her. She ditched the horse once she'd spotted the camp and then laid low, planning her next move. As far as she could tell, what looked like the majority of the King's Guild now resided at this base. She'd known there were a lot of members, but seeing them all now, there was enough for a small army.

Nora stiffened; her ears straining as she swore she heard

someone exhale nearby. Whirling around, she scanned the vicinity, expecting to see a guild scout.

There was no one that she could see, but she was certain someone was close by. She remained low and kept her senses alert.

An abrupt cry sliced through the quiet and Nora was on her feet only to burst out laughing as Charlie lay on the hillside after having fallen over. Her hair was a dishevelled mess, her eyes wide and dirt smudged on her cheek.

"Serves you right for spying on me," Nora smirked, folding her arms over her chest. "You better hope no one else heard you scream."

Charlie stumbled to her feet, wiping the dirt from her clothing and blowing the loose strands of her hair out of her face.

"Where's my bag?" Nora demanded, reaching out her hand. "Give it back."

"Your bag?" Charlie asked, eyebrows drawing together. Nora didn't buy the confusion, especially as her bag was currently hooked over Charlie's shoulder.

"Yes," Nora said, throwing her hands in the air. "I came to get back what you stole, now hand it over."

"I thought it was his," Charlie replied, a blush creeping over her cheeks. She slowly offered the bag up. "Sorry."

"You should be." Nora hurriedly reached into the bag, her hands rummaging until her fingers touched the necklace. She grinned, drawing it out and dropping her pack at the same moment. Nora quickly put the necklace on and sighed once it was around her neck. The pendant sat against her chest, peace filling her deep into her bones.

"Please don't tell me you're still thinking of going in there," Nora said, finally focusing back on Charlie.

"I was going to," Charlie chewed her lip. "For so long I thought he was dead and then Aeolus said he was alive. At first, I was hopeful that I'd get to see him again. But when I got here I remembered Aeolus can't be trusted. I'd already done something stupid by believing him and coming here in the first place. But then, what if it wasn't a lie and my father had been alive all this time and never once tried to contact me? But why would he do that? Aeolus had to have been lying."

"Aeolus wouldn't have lied," Nora said, then shook her head. "But that doesn't matter anyway. Time for us both to go."

"He's in there."

"Who? Your father?"

Charlie looked at her feet. "Aeolus."

Nora pressed her fingers to either side of her head, massaging her temples. "What the fuck is happening?"

"They, ah, took Aeolus," Charlie said, lifting her gaze and taking a step back. "He was lurking around much like you and they captured him. But he deserves it. He needs to be punished for what he did. He killed my father and then lied about it to me."

"Didn't you hear him?" Nora hissed. "He didn't murder your father. Aeolus doesn't lie about shit like that."

"How do you know? And why would my father fake his death? You don't even seem to like him so how can you possibly know if he's truly lying or not?"

"I know," Nora insisted despite the seed of uncertainty settling in her gut. "I just know."

"He lied to get rid of me. I should have killed him when I had the chance."

Nora huffed loudly. "*I'm* about to get rid of you. And not with lies but with methods that involve burying you deep in the ground."

Nora moved to a better position between some boulders and looked out on the guild's camp again. She didn't know where Aeolus would be; there were so many places he could have been kept. One possibility was the makeshift cages she could see clustered to the right of the camp. Except that she doubted Aeolus would be there by the time she reached it. There were only a few who guarded the area, meaning those prisoners weren't expected to make trouble. Which is something Aeolus would do.

No, it was more likely they knew he was a more valuable prisoner than the miners they were used to.

"You can't save him," Charlie said, coming to Nora's side.

"Aeolus is part of the Northern Alliance," Nora replied. "And I know you think he is awful for what you think he did, but just for a second, remove the murder of your father from the equation. Do that and you get a man who is fighting for a free world. Is that really someone you want to just hand over to the enemy? We are already low on numbers and power compared to the king. Aeolus is tough, but there's no telling what they might do to get information from him. That could jeopardise everything we've been working for. Is revenge worth how much we will lose?"

Charlie's shoulders sagged. "I can't forget what he's done."

"Fine, don't," Nora replied. "But stay out of my fucking way or I'll make you hurt worse than anything you've ever felt before in your life."

"You're really brutal." Charlie stared at Nora with uncertain fear in her eyes. Nora didn't let it affect her. She needed Charlie to cooperate and if that meant spinning a little white lie then that's what Nora would do.

"It's part of my charm." Nora offered Charlie a tight smile. "So what's it going to be?"

"I'm coming in with you." Charlie pursed her lips.

Nora groaned. "Oh for fuck's sake."

They waited until dusk when the guild was settling down for the night, when they would be eating their meals and letting their guard down, before the two women entered the camp. Nora and

Charlie moved closer, crawling on their stomachs in the long grass and waiting for the right moment to move.

Nora felt an excitement course through her. She may have been on a rescue mission but the prospect of hurting the King's Guild was a gift from whatever deity actually existed, if any did. Not to mention it would annoy King Dominic. He didn't outwardly side with them but would see an attack on them as a wound for him also. It may not have been a physical wound, but sabotaging his psychotic followers would piss him off. He'd done so much to her, taken so much, and any chance at making him hurt had her grinning from ear to ear. Soon he wouldn't just be pissed, he'd be dead. Soon Nora would return to Royal Bay and end his rein with her own hands. He had stolen her life; it was only fitting she would return the favour.

Nora and Charlie waited, watching until the sky turned dark until all they could see were those that gathered around fires or carried torches as they walked through the base. Everything else was covered in complete darkness. The lack of visibility did nothing to quell Nora's confidence. She didn't need to see to enact their plan. When she'd been an Alta, Rana had trained her to know how to rely on her other senses too.

"Are you sure about this?" Charlie whispered from beside Nora.

"Yep," Nora said with certainty. "You should stay behind while I go in, get Aeolus and get out. Easy."

"We are going to get caught."

"Again, you should stay here."

Charlie shook her head.

"Fine, then just act like you belong. Confidence is better than any disguise," Nora said and rose to her feet. "Let's go."

Nora ran towards the base, confident that Charlie would follow. The other woman couldn't help herself. She soon heard the pounding of feet as Charlie appeared at Nora's side. A grin spread on Nora's face. So predictable.

Nora and Charlie made their way to where the meals were prepped and served. As they drew closer, they slowed, moving into a stride as they avoided the larger groups of guild members and anywhere there was a source of light. All Nora could hear was the sound of her heartbeat and the commotion of the guild members who were so preoccupied with their conversations that they were none the wiser to the enemy in their midst.

They stuck to the shadows as they crept into the guild's base, heading towards a wagon. Nora pressed her side against the wood whilst Charlie took up her own position at Nora's back. She looked around, her eyes running over the area in search of a tent that had more than typical guards out front.

"See anything?" Nora asked in a whispered voice.

"Yeah, I think so," Charlie replied, her voice just as soft, and Nora turned to where Charlie was looking. A tent with two heavily armed guards was not far off from their position.

"Let's check it out," Nora said. They took off again, weaving through the tents with ease, sticking to the shadow and walking tall to prevent suspicion if anyone saw them from a distance.

Nora ducked down behind a wagon once they were next to the tent, dragging Charlie with her. "You wait here while I get a closer look."

Nora made to rise but Charlie gripped her arm, tugging her back down. "No point, he's not in there."

"How could you know that?" Nora asked in a faint voice.

The woman pointed to her pointed ears.

Right. Obviously, Nora thought.

"I was beginning to forget how handy it is to have an Alv around," Nora mused, thinking of August.

"One of the men around that fire is bragging about taking him to see the lord."

Nora raised a brow. "Wait, the guild doesn't have lords."

"Well, they apparently do now."

"They could mean Lord Gudrid," Nora suggested, thinking

of the lord of the Elementum city. "But I assumed he'd died in the Giland."

"He did. Every account from the survivors of Giland have said as much."

Nora chewed her lip. "If there's a lord here then they'll have the fanciest tent. I guess we better look for that one."

Talking drew their attention to the left and Nora placed a finger on her lips as they both froze. Shadows passed over the path, the light from a nearby fire flickering with each movement of the shadows. Nora waited until whoever it was passed before waving a hand at Charlie and continuing their search for Aeolus.

Turns out there were quite a few important people within the guild's ranks. At least there were a few who believed they were important enough for luxury tents.

Thanks to Charlie's Lys Alv hearing, the duo managed to check out each of the fancy tents without getting caught. So far, everything was going smoothly, yet as they continued deeper into the base Nora couldn't help that feeling of her luck running out.

Aeolus wasn't in any of the tents. But Nora wouldn't give up hope of finding him. What she was giving up on was the hope she could rescue him without getting into a fight.

Charlie stayed close by as they moved. Had it been daytime, the guild members may have noticed the two women who didn't belong, yet under the cover of darkness and thanks to the ale that was so free flowing amongst the supping guild members, Nora and Charlie were like shadows.

They passed a particularly rowdy group sitting around a fire who were singing, or more like slurring, some song that Nora couldn't decipher the words to. Charlie reached for Nora's arm and squeezed.

"I hear something," Charlie said in a hushed voice.

"Me too," Nora replied, scrunching her nose. "And it's awful."

"Not the song," Charlie replied. "I think I hear someone in pain. A man. It could be him."

"Are you sure?"

Charlie nodded. "If it's one thing a Lys Alv knows the sound of, it's cries of pain."

Nora frowned at that.

"It is what it is."

"Mmmhhmmm," Nora replied. "So where is it coming from?"

"Follow me."

Nora did just that, following Charlie as she passed the rowdy singers to a darkened area of the base. No fires were lit here, and they saw only a handful of members as if they all avoided the area. Nora heard the screams now, and her gut churned, recognising the voice.

"You wait here. I'll take out those two," Nora said once they found the tent in question. Guards stood outside the entrance, appearing as statues in the night. "Then I'll go in."

"There are others inside."

"Of course. I'll have to think quick once I'm in there, won't I?"

"You're going to get yourself killed."

"Nope," Nora replied, tapping her daggers at her hips, one she stole from Aeolus, the other her own which she'd just gotten back. "That's not part of the plan."

Leaving Charlie, she took off, moving with speed thanks to her wind. She rounded the tent and lunged, sinking her first dagger into the throat of the nearest guard before quickly slicing the second guard's throat. She caught them both with her wind, lowering them softly before they could thud to the ground. She listened for those beyond the fabric of the tent. The screaming had ceased, replaced instead by low voices.

"I wasn't sure I'd be alive to see the day," a female voice said.

"Luck is on our side, fate too," a man replied. "The righteous always win."

"Damn true," another man said, his voice gravelly. "Though isn't it about time he started spilling his secrets and begging for mercy?"

"I agree," said the woman. "Isn't there something more you can do, lord?"

Nora gave a thumbs up in the direction she left Charlie before stepping into the tent. She let her magic flow to the surface, readying herself for a fight.

"I hope I haven't missed too much of this little meeting of yours," Nora said, glancing around the tent and taking stock of everything and everyone in it. "I was delayed, but luckily I think I caught up just in time."

Inside was a woman and three men, one of whom had no shirt on, revealing numerous guild tattoos that covered his skin. Each had a mix of anger and surprise on their candlelit faces, their expressions almost menacing in the minimal light. They stood around a central table where Aeolus lay strapped to it, his skin slashed and bleeding. The smell of blood filled the tent.

"What are you doing here?" demanded the fully clothed man with the voice of a heavy cigar smoker.

"I've come for him," Nora replied cooly, pointing a dagger at Aeolus. "So if you could kindly give back my friend, I'll be on my way."

"Not going to happen," the woman snarled. "Grab her."

The presumed cigar smoker lunged for Nora, but she was too fast for him. Nora darted to the side and threw a gust of wind at him, throwing the man through the air. He collided with the tattooed man and the two hit the tent wall, dragging the support poles with them. One of which knocked Smoky out cold.

The woman roared, shooting jets of water at Nora as the rest of the tent collapsed around them. Nora ducked and dodged as best she could as she rushed towards Aeolus, desperate to get him free. The woman's water blasted frantically, tearing holes into the fabric of the falling tent. Nora twirled her wrist, summoning her wind to hold the tent above her as she moved.

Aeolus lay with his upper half exposed on the table, his eyes closed and tanned chest rising and falling uneasily. Dried blood coated him, with fresh blood spilling from the numerous new wounds. At the head of the table, the tattooed man stood with a blade to Aeolus's throat.

"Lord, I presume," Nora replied, her voice as smooth as silk despite the chaos around her. The other woman was still fighting though now it was with the fallen tent. Outside Nora heard the sound of guild members coming to see what was happening.

Aeolus' eyes snapped open, surprise and something else in them. Relief?

"Who are you?" the lord asked.

"I'm Nora," she replied simply, before summoning her water magic and throwing a ball at the man.

"Stupid bitch," he growled as he flew backwards, but not before cutting Aeolus' neck. The man disappeared among the layers of the tent.

"Shit," she panted and rushed to Aeolus' side. "What are you doing here?"

Thankfully, the wound to his neck hadn't been deep. "I came after you," he groaned. "Couldn't let you die over a trinket."

"Aren't you sweet," she smirked as she went about untying his legs.

"Not at all. Help me out here," Aeolus groaned. His throat was bright red, but the bleeding had already slowed. He'd survive.

"What did you think I was doing?" Nora said, undoing the leather straps on his arms now. "It's only a shallow cut by the way."

Free from the table, Aeolus slowly sat up and clutched his neck to inspect the wound whilst Nora was given a view of his bloodied chest. The cuts looked painful, the wounds so raw, but they were not what drew her attention. Under the blood was a familiar inky mark on his chest she'd never noticed before.

"You're a King's Guild," Nora stated, staring at his tattoo with wide eyes.

"Was."

"You gave me so much shit for being an Alta and you were a fucking King's Guild!"

"Nora, I can explain. Later."

"Explain? Explain how you did the king's fucked up bidding by choice and yet you treated me like an evil bitch when I'd had none?"

"Ah, Nora!" came Charlie's voice from outside the tent. "Now's not really the best time for an argument."

Nora huffed.

"How do you propose we get out of here?" Aeolus asked, aware that she was beyond pissed.

"I hadn't thought that far ahead," she snapped, using her wind magic to throw the fabric of the tent up and reveal the base outside.

King's Guild members stood with their weapons aimed in Nora and Aeolus' direction.

"Well, we're fucked," Aeolus breathed as Nora's gaze focused on Charlie standing before them with a blade pressed to her chest.

$$18$$

Nora

Nora hated deception. Hated seeing innocents being used. And most of all, hated her role in all the pain she inflicted while she was being deceived.

The fallen tent burst into flames around her. The intensity of the fire's light was almost blinding as the tent was engulfed. Aeolus cried out and threw an arm over his eyes, instinctively moving closer to Nora to avoid the flames. The guild members shouted and cursed, startled by the sudden burst of light. Crackling filled the air along with immense heat as the fire grew from embers jumping to the nearby tents. A clear path to Charlie remained untouched by the flames.

Forgetting Nora and her friends for the time being, frantic guild members rushed away from the circle of flame, shouting for water to be bought quickly and keeping their eyes on the fire licking its way closer to them. The man who held a knife to Charlie had been caught in the fire, burning up his back and causing his hand to drop from Charlie's throat. With one flick of her wrist, Nora launched him backward so that he was fully engulfed by the fire. His shrill screams promised to haunt her.

"Fuck," Aeolus gasped, looking at the fire that now protected them like the towering walls around a city. His brow was beaded with sweat and his eyes were red as they reflected the flames.

The remaining guild members shouted nearby, realising they couldn't bring enough water to douse the flames. Until another Elementum stepped into view beyond the flickering flames, her hands raised to summon water onto the nearest flames. Nora clenched her fists in retaliation. With each use of the woman's magic, Nora pushed her own to be stronger, bolder, and fiercer.

"Where are the other Elementum?" Charlie asked in a hushed voice as she moved closer to Nora. "She can't be the only one in camp to put this fire out."

"Who knows," Nora whispered, her words strained as she focused on not only the blaze that encircled them but those now spreading throughout the guild's base. She couldn't see the other fires, but she could feel them. Each one currently burning had a connection to her magic, lapping up the campfires and feeding off her power to burn hotter against the army's attempts to put them out. She gritted her teeth. "Not our problem."

Nora pushed her magic further than ever before, creating a path for them to move through. Her fire obliged, determined to devour everything it could until nothing but ash was left. Her breathing became laboured as sweat beaded on her forehead. But she wouldn't let up. Not until she'd done her job.

She walked, with Aeolus and Charlie following close behind. The fire closest grew hotter, wilder and the camp's Elementum stepped back, whipping an arm up to shield her face against flames that licked greedily towards her. The fire suddenly burst, throwing the woman back. Soldiers ran from the scene screaming as embers of the out-of-control fire jump onto nearby tents, setting them ablaze.

The orange flames filled Nora's vision, sending her mind

tumbling back to the fire that destroyed her home. As her memory surged so did her flames. Her magic was unstoppable now. Cries from the guild members mixed with that of her mother and brother, the two scenes blending into one.

Both fires were out of control, and she was helpless to stop either.

Her magic continued to draw from her, taking everything she had to give, willingly or not. Nora thought she heard her name being called, but it was so far away ... A distant voice that she wasn't sure if she was imagining or not. Was it her mother?

It didn't matter, they would all be ash soon.

"Nora!"

The camp slammed back into view around Nora. Her cheek stung and eyes watered as she became conscious of the destruction she was causing. Everything around her was alight, the screams of those caught in the fire's path filled the air along with the crackling of the fires. Aeolus gripped Nora's face, his hands on either side of her cheeks, and was physically trying to hold Nora's focus. His face was flushed and his eyes were wide as they moved left then right to each of hers. His dark eyes softened as he realised Nora had come to.

She trembled on her knees, clothing drenched and clinging to her skin. When had she knelt down?

"You have your shit together?" Aeolus asked, dropping his hands.

Nora nodded, unable to speak. She was so tired. Her magic was depleted, now only a whisper in her veins.

Aeolus wrapped an arm around Nora's waist, drawing her to her feet. "Too bad if you don't because we gotta go."

They ran, or more Charlie ran while Nora and Aeolus stumbled along, weaving through tents that were either still ablaze or had been consumed completely. Smouldering mounds littered the area, some large having been tents and others smaller with blackened bones resting among the ash.

Nora had burned more than she had intended; lit almost half the base on fire, yet she felt no regret, only a sudden intense satisfaction that she had caused so much damage. The king was sure to feel this. Maybe she was evil or just so broken by all the shit in her life that she was able to revel in the deaths of so many by her hand. Nora didn't care.

"HEY!"

Two guild members ran towards them, darting between the destruction with swords at the ready. Fury filled their features; their expressions were even more menacing thanks to the firelight.

Nora slowed, ready to take on the men. She had no magic and wasn't sure she could raise her dagger, but she wasn't one for backing down.

"Not happening," Aeolus hissed, pulling hard on Nora's arm. "We're playing this smart."

"I can take them," Nora replied, though she knew it was a partial lie. She wasn't sure what the outcome would be if she was honest with herself.

"No," Aeolus ordered. "You'll die here and then who will help me assassinate a tyrant?"

Aeolus' words were like a bucket of freezing water thrown over her. Nora could attack the body all she wanted, but nothing would change unless she cut off the head of the snake. She kept her dagger in hand but didn't move to attack.

They picked up their pace, and the relief was evident on Aeolus' face, but Nora wasn't able to move fast enough. The guild members caught up. The closer of the two launched himself at them and dragged Nora to the ashy ground, knocking her dagger from her hand before she could use it. She landed face-first in the dirt with a grunt, her body squished under the weight of the man. Her lungs struggled to draw in breath as he forced her further into the dirt.

She could hear fighting, but there was nothing she could

do. Nora squirmed, desperate for a burst of energy to power her movements when a scream filled the air. The man stilled atop her, clearly distracted by whatever had occurred and Nora took the opportunity to shove her elbows back into the man's ribs. He cried out but didn't release her, more surprised than hurt by her attack. He has the advantage and Nora was too weak. She was fucked.

A growl startled her, and the next thing Nora knew blood poured onto Nora, hot and sticky before the man grunted and fell still, pushing her further into the ground.

Nora made to push up in an effort to shove him off only for him to be dragged off. She raised her head and saw the man's throat had been chewed through by the wolf now dragging him away. She looked around and saw Charlie with more wolves. Arrows flew from Charlie's bow in quick succession, vaulting towards guild members and forcing them to the ground as the wolves launched themselves in the same direction with their teeth bared.

Nora stared at the scene in surprise. Where had all the Anima come from?

"We need to keep moving," Aeolus declared, reaching down and helping her to her feet. She quickly retrieved her dagger from the dirt as he signalled to Charlie. Taking the lead, Aeolus led them through the last few rows of tents.

Wolves, bears, lions, and other predators were taking down what remained of the guild around them. Roars mingled with their screams as the Anima fought. Exhilaration surged within Nora at the sight. Her fire had caused damage, but this new force was eliminating the threat entirely.

Charlie's eyes were wide as she ran beside Nora, clearly in shock. "I killed someone. Multiple someones," Charlie said, her voice high as her breath came in quick succession.

"Sure did!" Nora panted, no longer able to hold back her smile. The King's Guild deserved everything they'd gotten and more. "You did well!"

"I'm a Lys Alv!"

"Yahuh!"

"I heal people, not kill them!"

Nora's lungs were on fire, her muscles screaming at her to stop, but Nora kept going. Safety was within reach. "Now you do both! Wasn't that your plan though? I mean, you still want to kill Aeolus don't you?"

"I—" Charlie's mouth snapped shut and she didn't say another word as they ran.

Nora and Charlie chased after Aeolus, their exit almost in sight when bears darted in front of them. The three pulled to a halt as their path was blocked by the bears. So much for their escape.

Aeolus raised his hands and spoke calmly. "We are on the same side."

One of the bears growled deeply and it sounded like a rumble of thunder. He clearly didn't buy Aeolus' words and Nora had a feeling she knew why. Aeolus' chest was still exposed and that meant so was his King's Guild tattoo.

The bears stalked forward, and Nora reached deep inside herself for any drop of magic she could find at the same time as Charlie raised her bow. They would fight, but they'd most likely die.

Nora braced herself only for a wolf to dive between them and shift to reveal a tall man with the broadest shoulders Nora had ever seen. He was almost the size of the bears behind him.

"Not these three," he told the bears, who simply nodded and ran off to rejoin the fray. Stopping the bears had been as simple as that.

"Aeolus," the man said, turning to face them. "Long time no see."

"Lyle," Aeolus replied. "I thought the Southern Wolf Pack no longer existed?"

Lyle smirked. "You shouldn't believe everything you hear."

19

August

The Alliance travelled slowly south and August found himself unbothered about their unhurried pace. It was an unexpected change from the impatience he felt only a short time ago. Moving such a large group made up of mostly civilians who'd volunteered to join the few soldiers they had meant travelling only a short distance over an entire day before stopping to make camp for the night. And that was on the days they did travel.

Often they remained in the same place for a few consecutive days, letting everyone rest after travelling for so many days straight. It also gave time to those working on other tasks for the movement, like the blacksmiths forging weapons and armour or Sage who worked tirelessly on a cure.

At first, this annoyed August, but as time wore on and the full extent of his predicament settled within him, he found that his priorities somewhat shifted. He still wanted to remove King

Dominic and rescue Evelyn; however, the urgency had dwindled. His time was limited and it had him contemplating what he wanted to do with what was left of it.

Working with the blacksmith had allowed August to delve into his creativity. He had always loved to draw and, until recently, had carried around paper and charcoals to sketch images of what he'd seen in the world, as well as what he'd imagined.

Erik had August using those artistic inclinations. The blacksmith was frequently asking for his thoughts on new designs that would be more effective on the curse's roots, improving precision, speed, strength and even absorbing the impact of a blow. The hammering may have been arduous work, but the creative side made it all worthwhile. August found himself dreaming of weapon designs, of sword handles and arrow heads that would burrow deep and tear through the curse.

"Maybe you should be a blacksmith, Dark Prince," Tyler said. He leant against a barrel eating an apple while August worked. The man was no help at all, purely there to watch and talk. "It suits you."

"Don't you have somewhere to be? Someone you could be helping?" August groaned, letting the hammer hang loose in his gloved hand.

"I'm supervising you," Tyler replied. "It's an important job."

"I don't need a supervisor; I already have Erik."

Tyler shrugged. "Then I am your guard."

"My guard?"

"All royalty need a guard," Tyler said matter-of-factly, earning a disgruntled groan from August.

August did not need a guard nor was he royalty. He was an ordinary guy like everyone else travelling with the Alliance. "I'm not royal," August said, shooting Tyler a glare. He angled his head towards Erik who was thankfully preoccupied with his current project. "And you need to shut up about it."

"Okay, okay," Tyler raised his hands, the apple core perched between his thumb and finger. "My lips are sealed."

"Good."

"On that matter at least," Tyler grinned, throwing the apple core away. "When we reach Midskopas, are you planning for us to leave for Royal Bay straight away?"

August blew out a breath. "I haven't thought about it."

"Oh really?"

"Yes," August grumbled, narrowing his eyes at Tyler's knowing expression. "What?"

"I simply noticed that you're settling well into the Alliance, that's all."

"And?"

"I'm curious if your plans have changed?"

Had his plans changed? August shook his head; they hadn't, they had simply slowed down and somewhat shifted. If time permitted he would still go south to the king and Evelyn, however, there was less of a rush, and that was all.

"Once we reach Midskopas, I'll decide," he said. "Hopefully, we'll have a cure or a weapon to fight the curse by then. One of these swords has to work. I have to believe that it's only a matter of time before one comes back from a test successful. Sage also seems like she's making progress with her tests so that's a good sign too."

"Unless she's one of those always optimistic people? You know the unbearably positive type?"

"She's not," August said. "She's too logical to continue with something that isn't working. It's a process of elimination, she said. Finding out what doesn't work brings her closer to discovering what does, or something along those lines."

"Fair enough," Tyler nodded slowly. "We'll decide in Midskopas, then."

We. August felt a pang of guilt in his gut. Tyler continued to stand by his side, yet August hadn't thought about what his friend wanted in all this or whether he wanted to find where the

Mors Alvs went. He'd been selfish, only thinking of himself.

"Tyler?" August said, putting down his hammer and giving his friend his full attention.

"Mmm?"

"Why are you still here?"

"That's a rude way to ask me to leave," Tyler teased, slipping his hands into his pockets and shrugging his shoulders. "I thought you'd like a bit of company while you work."

"No, I didn't mean it like that," August replied with a sigh. "Why are you still with me? Why didn't you return to Jord, aren't you curious where they went?"

"You're not the only one with a reason to want the king dead." Tyler's features hardened. "King Dominic killed my family, August. The rest of the Mors Alvs might be happy to stay out of it, but I want my revenge. I want him to pay for what he did. I'm the last of my family line and it's all because of him."

August frowned. "I'm sorry."

"Why? It's not your fault. The blame lies with the evil bastard sitting on the throne," Tyler said. "I know it comes across as though I don't take life too seriously, but the king has taken so much from me, I won't let him take what good I still have left from my life. I cling to it, to every bit of joy because we only get one chance to live and he will not steal that from me, too. When the time comes, August, don't think I won't act. I will be by your side, whether I'm a part of killing him or fighting against his army. I want to be a part of this."

"We'll make him pay," August said, his jaw set. Tyler's words filled him with determination, not only to kill the king, but survive the curse and take on his friend's attitude. Tyler was right, the king had stolen so much from them and he wouldn't let King Dominic take what happiness he could still find.

"It disgusts me how the Mors Alvs we left with scurried away the moment the curse arrived. They didn't fight, simply fled and abandoned us. Is that why we lost so many Mors Alvs all those years ago? Are our kin cowards?"

"They're not," August replied. "They've just lost so much and are afraid to lose more. We can't blame them for not wanting to risk the lives they rebuilt after all that happened."

Tyler dragged a hand over his face. "You're right, shit I feel terrible having just said that."

"Don't apologise. Use your anger in the fight against the king. He's the one that deserves our wrath."

"And more," Tyler smirked.

"As for our next move," August said. "When we reach Midskopas, we'll find Nora and then we'll decide together."

Tyler rocked on his heels, offering August a grin. "Now, if you're done with all the serious talk, I'll be off. People to see, places to visit."

August smiled in return. "I thought you said you were my guard?"

Tyler shrugged. "I lied."

"Of course you did."

"I'm not the only one around here doing so."

"What's that supposed to mean?" August asked, brows raised.

"You said this blacksmith was interested in Mors Alvs. But I'm a Mors Alv who grew up with Jord and what's left of our race, and he has shown zero interest in me. Which is odd because I am by far the more interesting one of us. Also, I'm more approachable and chattier, among other things."

August glanced back at Erik again. The blacksmith had been busy this afternoon, but Tyler was right, he'd rarely spoken to Tyler since meeting him, if at all.

"Maybe he can tell that you're annoying and once you start talking you won't stop?"

"Or there's that," Tyler laughed. "Anywho, I'm off to see Will."

"Will?"

"Yes. I'm helping him train and we're going to meet with someone about making more of his little weapon things. Reckon they'll be useful."

"What?" August scrunched his brows.

"I believe he called it a gun."

"A what?"

Tyler breathed an exaggerated sigh. "You're lucky I'm around, Dark Prince. You'd make a terrible ruler with how slow you are at understanding things."

"Geez, thanks," August scoffed.

"Any time," Tyler grinned and with that, he strolled away, leaving August to resume working and not only wonder what this gun might be but whether he had a good point about Erik.

Unlike regular blacksmiths, Erik was a Conjurer, too which meant he could not only imbue his weapons with magic but he could forge them faster. Moulding and setting took significantly less time, and with August doing the bulk of the hammering and grunt work, Erik was producing weapons at an even quicker pace.

They worked in a rhythm, Erik barking orders whilst August did as he was told. It would have been somewhat peaceful, the routine of it all, if it hadn't been for what Tyler had said. Had Erik lied about why he asked August to help him? If not because he was a Mors Alv, then what?

"Why did you ask me to come work with you?" August asked, dropping his hammer to the dirt. He wiped the sweat from his brow and looked at Erik.

"I told you; I'm interested—"

"I don't think that's the real reason," August said, cutting him off. He folded his arms over his chest and sent the other man a grin.

Erik huffed, glancing up from his work at August. He muttered to himself and then went back to his task.

"You're not going to tell me."

Erik continued to work, his tool clanging against the metal of the sword before him. August waited patiently watching the blacksmith work.

"Fine," Erik grumbled eventually. "I lied when I told you I had never met a Mors Alv before."

"I figured as much seeing as you look old enough to have been an adult before I was born."

Erik blew out an exasperated breath. "Do you want to know, or do you want to insult me further?"

"Sorry," August replied, raising his hands. "Tell me."

"I knew your father," Erik replied, surprising August. "Those around us may have never seen General Natsky in person to know that you share many of his features, but I have. I knew the instant I saw you."

That caught August off-guard. He'd never mentioned his lineage to anyone here outside of Tyler. Unless he had overheard them talking just now. But that would only implicate his mother, not his father who was only a general, not a royal. "You didn't consider perhaps we were simply distant relatives? Cousins?"

Erik grinned. "Your lack of denial right now only solidifies my assumption. Besides, you share more than a simple likeness."

"How well did you know him?" August asked. His heart raced in his chest at the prospect of learning more about his father.

"He was friends with Bo," Erik replied and August recalled the man's mentor from Royal Bay. "We would make weapons for your father and his men. Bo always had us deliver them to him personally. He was a good man."

"Have you told anyone?" August asked, stepping closer to Erik. "Who I am?"

"No," Erik replied. "It's not my secret to tell."

August often found the man hard to read, but he detected no lie. "Thank you."

"You can thank me by getting back to work. We only have

so many hours in the night to work.”

August laughed as he picked up his hammer and then continued to work on the axe blade before him, all the while thinking about what Erik had said.

He was a good man.

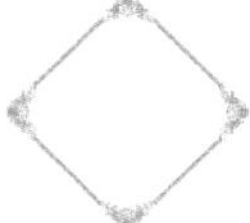

After finishing up working with Erik for the night, August popped in to see that Sage was still up. The woman stood over a small table, deep in concentration as she looked over vials and scribbled notes on the papers before her. She was still monitoring her samples, testing more combinations and adjusting her dust.

“Hi, how—”

Sage held up a finger, halting his words. She kept her back to him, writing with her other hand and grumbling under her breath. August snapped his mouth closed and waited, his hands behind his back. He could tell by the colourful language she said under her breath and the tension in her shoulders that it hadn’t been a good day. Maybe she was losing faith in her work after all. At least Tyler wouldn’t have to worry about Sage being always so optimistic, as he’d put it.

“Sorry,” Sage said, eventually turning to face him. She offered a sheepish smile. “Today hasn’t been great and I’m tired from all the travel.”

“It’s okay,” he replied. “We’re all entitled to be pissed off now and again.”

“This curse makes no sense,” she complained. “My research points to one solution and yet it’s not working. All these adjustments to the dust formulation don’t feel right but I’m starting to run out of ideas.”

“You’ll find the answer.”

“When?” She looked up and frowned. “When it’s too late?”

August shook his head. "Don't think like that. You will figure it out. I'm sure of it."

"And if I don't?" Sage asked. "What do I tell Nora?"

"That you did your best and that my death was not your fault," he replied. "Though I'm hoping I won't die any time soon and can tell her that myself."

The curse was progressing slowly, which gave him hope. His impending death would eventually greet him if Sage didn't find a cure, but until then he would use it to help him put some perspective into his life. Really think about what it was that he wanted. Seeing Nora again was a certainty. That he knew for sure.

"The curse is still progressing slowly. It's still only on my hand. We have time."

Sage nodded, biting a single fingernail before turning back to her work. "One of these has to work," she insisted, frustration coating her voice. "What about this one? Maybe this is the one?" She held up a powder that looked almost red.

"Haven't seen that colour before," he said, trying to sound hopeful.

"Then let's test it," she replied, determination clear in her tone.

The ritual was the same as before. She poured the dust over the flesh on a jar, stirred it around and they watched as nothing happened. At first, it was the same outcome; nothing happened. But then all of a sudden the flesh began to smoke before it burst into flames.

"Shit!" Sage gasped; eyes alight with fright.

August made to get his water skin, but she halted his hand, instead watching as the tiny fire attempted to consumed the cursed flesh in the jar. Despite its determination it was unsuccessful.

"I think I've had enough for today," she said, her shoulders sagging as the fire went out.

"You deserve a break," August told her. He rose to his feet, reaching a hand out to her. "Maybe take a day or two, then come back to it fresh."

"August … the Alliance is relying on me. You are relying on me."

"It's too much for one person to shoulder," he replied. "You need time to rest. Think about it this way, if you tire yourself out too much your brain won't function properly and then you'll be no help to anyone."

Sage chewed her lip. "You have a point."

"I know," he grinned. "I'm brilliant, what can I say?"

"Has anyone ever told you that you and Nora are very alike?"

"No one would be so cruel," he chuckled, a hand placed over his heart.

Sage grinned brightly. "Well then let me tell you. If I didn't know better, I'd have thought you were twins."

20

Nora

"We were almost gone," Lyle said, sitting by the fire. It burned in the centre of the group, though it was nothing like the blaze they could see still in the distance.

The King's Guild had fallen and all that was left was being consumed by the fire Nora started. She sat amongst the Southern Wolf Pack now and took note that, unlike their northern kin, there were more than just wolves among them.

The sun was rising, waking the world to a new day where the guild was no longer a threat. At least a large portion of it. It would have been a good day if it weren't for Aeolus' lies leaving a bitter taste in Nora's mouth. He had once been part of the King's Guild, a willing devotee of King Dominic.

"But we weren't about to go down that easily," Lyle continued. He was the leader of the Southern Wolf Pack and an old friend of Aeolus, as Nora recently discovered. "So we set our sights on the mines and recruited any we could rescue to join us."

"That's where you're all from?" Nora asked, looking at the Anima around her. That explained why they all had predatory shifts. King Dominic had been sending the Anima he feared most to the mines purely for existing. She smirked, that had come back to bite him in the ass.

Their new allies were spread out around them, mingling around numerous fires, receiving healing treatment or simply catching some shuteye after such a big fight. The impromptu camp was nestled between a cluster of hills, providing a clear view of anyone who might approach, while also providing plenty of places to hide. Not that they needed to worry about hiding for a while. There were few threats out here anymore.

"We rescued as many as we could and the others who managed to escape eventually found us," Lyle replied, as he, too looked around at those who followed him. His blue-eyed gaze softened and a smile ghosted his thin lips.

"Why didn't you tell the Alliance?" Aeolus asked, wincing as he pressed his hand to his side. "We had no idea you were still alive, let alone attempting rescues. We could have sent help."

His injuries had been bad when she'd found him and the escape had only made them worse. Charlie had made the surprising offer to heal him, but he'd refused. Instead, Aeolus decided to rely on bandages and his body to heal the old-fashioned way, unlike everyone else. Charlie was working her way through the Southern Wolf Pack, healing anyone who would accept her help.

"It was an unfortunate lie, but a necessary one. We couldn't risk anyone knowing we were still alive. These are strange times and we have heard of more than one tale of spies and traitors even among our friends. I regret the need for secrecy from the Northern Alliance, especially to Carl. I have worked closely with him ever since he came into power of the Northern Pack, but the king had to believe we were gone. All our efforts were prioritised on rescuing Anima from the mines, we couldn't jeopardise that."

"I get it. Sometimes it's more important to keep a secret," Aeolus replied, and Nora rolled her eyes with a huff. "Your pack could have really been wiped out if word had been leaked."

"Exactly," Lyle nodded. "Since the closure of the mines, we have focused on the King's Guild. We were already planning an attack … when we heard word of a great fire in their camp, where you lot had gotten there first."

"It wasn't intentional," Nora said. "*Someone* needed rescuing."

"Rescue or not," Lyle chuckled. "You did a lot of damage before we arrived."

Nora couldn't help but grin. She may not have planned it, but she'd struck a blow against the king and got away with it.

"Nora has more powerful magic than I thought," Aeolus said. His hazel gaze was usually filled with disdain when he looked at her, yet now there was something else there. Pride? Guilt? A mixture of both? "I'd say burning down an entire enemy camp on a straightforward rescue mission was a bit more than necessary to get the job done. Overachiever."

"Flattery will get you nowhere," Nora replied, her tone cold. She looked away, closing her eyes and tried to mask the resentment rushing to the forefront of her mind. He couldn't buy her forgiveness with kind words. He'd lied.

"Nora—"

She opened her eyes only to glare at him. Furious was too mild a word for what she felt at that moment. Aeolus' face held a pained expression when he saw her mask fail. She had no sympathy for the asshole. "Don't."

Lyle looked between them, his face no longer holding the humour it had a moment ago. "Whatever the reason you were there, it was the opening we needed and now the guild is nothing but ash."

"Here here!" A woman called, approaching Lyle and holding out a piece of fruit. Others joined in the cheer and the mood of the camp became one that was opposite of the tension between Aeolus and Nora.

"I better help them hand out what supplies they've found," Lyle said, rising.

Nora couldn't help but think he was leaving purely to get away from the discomfort between her and Aeolus. He took a bite of the pear in his hand then reached into the woman's bag and pulled out another two. After passing them to Nora and Aeolus, he left them alone to assist with food distribution. Nora looked at the fruit in her hands. They must have stumbled upon a pear orchard nearby.

"I didn't lie," Aeolus said with a sigh, breaking the silence between them. He was tired, but she didn't care. He deserved to suffer for all the shit he put her through. "I just didn't tell you everything. I don't need to tell you my life's story."

"I never asked you to," Nora growled. She shuffled in her seat, turning her back to him. "Like how I'm not asking you to explain now."

Nora spotted Charlie strolling towards them, rolling a pear in her hands. Charlie may have been a Lys Alv, but she'd used a lot of her magic on those around them, so she couldn't hide how tired she was. Her shoulders were slumped and bags had settled beneath her golden eyes.

"Other than you, I think that's everyone who needs my help," Charlie said to Aeolus and sat next to Nora. She took a bite of the fruit with a sigh.

"Where will you go now?" Nora asked. "Once you're rested will you go home?"

"I have no home," Charlie replied, looking between Nora and Aeolus.

"I assume you're no longer set on killing Aeolus," Nora said, though she would have liked to see him in pain right now. It might make her feel better.

Charlie bit her bottom lip. "I saw my father."

"You did?" Aeolus asked and Nora reluctantly turned to see his expression. Surprise had lifted his brows.

"You were right," Charlie continued. "He was alive."

"When did you see him?" Nora asked, her curiosity dulling her anger for the time being.

"He was one of the men fighting as we were escaping. He looked right at me," Charlie said, looking at Aeolus with sorrow in her eyes. "I'm sorry. This is all my fault."

"Don't," Aeolus said stiffy. "Don't apologise."

Charlie shook her head. "I should never have gone to the guild. I was wrong to not believe you. I can admit it."

"I'm glad someone can admit when they are wrong," Nora mumbled. She was beyond tired, not only her body was fatigued but her mind too. She rubbed her temple with the tips of her fingers and sighed. "I'm sorry you had to see your father like that. To learn, without a doubt, that he was alive would have been hard at any time, let alone when he was doing something awful."

Charlie wiped away a single tear and shuffled closer to Nora. "I just wish I knew why. Why did he choose the guild over me?"

"I understand. Knowing the reason might help bring some closure." Nora looked pointedly at Aeolus, who conveniently remained silent, before adding. "But the guild requires its members to be in 100 per cent. They don't tolerate anything that takes priority over the king's will. I doubt it was anything you did or didn't do."

"You're right. Maybe I'm better off not knowing anyway."

"What are you going to do now?" Aeolus asked Charlie, changing the subject.

"Find a home," Charlie said, looking down at the half-eaten pear in her hands. "You two have your plans and I won't bother you anymore. I have already taken too much of your time."

"Why don't you stay with the Southern Wolf Pack?" he suggested. "Lyle would be happy to have you. A Healer, and a

Lys Alv one that, would always be an asset. You'd be helping a good cause against people like your father. Plus you are getting better with your bow."

"You think so?"

"Yeah," Nora agreed, patting Charlie on the back. "I think you'd fit in perfectly."

The idea seemed to lift Charlie's spirits, the woman's golden eyes lighting up despite her magical exhaustion. The wolf pack would be a good home for Charlie. They would become her new family and she'd have a place amongst them, a sense of belonging. Like how the Northern Alliance had become for Nora. That was all anyone could really hope for in life.

The thought made Nora think of Sage and August. She needed to hurry up and kill the king so she could get back to them. She missed them more than anything in the world, and once she had them back, she was never going to let them go.

"Did you stage her father's death before or after you left the King's Guild?" Nora asked, sitting opposite Aeolus a few days later. They were in a small clearing a little far off from the road, watching the few travellers that went by.

Charlie had stayed with the wolf pack and Nora hoped she'd see the woman again one day. She hoped to find out whether she was happy there like she deserved to be.

Nora cut another piece of apple with her dagger. It was one of the now very limited possessions Nora had, thanks to her pack being burnt up during the attack on the camp. Nora took a bite of her apple slice, pursing her lips and squinting at the sour taste. Green apples were her least favourite, but they had limited coin now, and she was hungry so she couldn't exactly be fussy.

"Before I left," Aeolus replied curtly. He sat stiffly, at least more so than usual. This conversation was clearly one he didn't want to have. It also didn't help that he was still healing from his injuries and certain positions caused him more pain. Charlie had offered again to heal him before they left but he'd declined. Some stupid pride thing. Nora found herself smiling every time he winced from the pain and discomfort. "I'm not giving you details. I'm sure you can figure it out by yourself. You need to get over it."

"If you think I care that you killed, fake or not, or had a different belief system in the past then you're completely mistaken. I couldn't care less if you were a mass murderer," Nora said, her jaw clenching. "I'm pissed that you treated me like such shit when you met me, even though you came from a similar position once upon a time."

"And that's exactly why I was suspicious of you. I know how they draw the lost and abandoned in, those looking for guidance and a community," he said with a heavy sigh. "I know how easily you could have gone back to him. I was—am—protecting my home and those in it."

"You're a real hero," Nora deadpanned. He may have had his reasons, but she didn't care for them. Aeolus' attitude towards her still irritated her.

"And what, you are? Swapping sides and pretending to be some shining knight, chasing after pretty girls like you do is a joke. You're no hero either."

"Excuse me?" Nora snapped, throwing her apple core away and rounding on him. "I didn't go after Charlie because she was pretty, I did so because she stole something important to me."

"Admit it. You couldn't resist helping the damsel. That's what you did in Forest's Edge and that's why you helped that girl."

"See this is why I never see you with friends," Nora hissed, narrowing her gaze at him. "You automatically think everyone needs to be romantically driven. Just because I find girls, and guys might I add, attractive doesn't mean I want to be in a relationship with every single one." She rolled her eyes. "Sage is my girlfriend. I love her. No one else."

Aeolus stared at her for a moment, his head tilted to one side. "You love Sage?"

Nora paused, realising what she'd said. It had come out without her even thinking about it. But now that she'd said it, she knew it was true. She did love Sage and the moment she saw her girlfriend again; Nora would tell her exactly that.

"Yeah," Nora smiled. "I do."

Aeolus clicked his tongue, looking away. "Maybe you have changed, then."

"You think?" Nora raised a brow. "I can't believe you've been on the fence this entire time, despite asking me to come on this little quest of yours. I trained others in Forest's Edge, helped take back Midskopas, saved you from those guild assholes *and* lit the guild camp up like a bonfire, among a bunch of other things. And only now are you starting to see that I'm not the Nora you first met. I'm not an Alta anymore."

"You'd fooled us at first," he said. "There was no reason you wouldn't do it again."

"Except that I was freed from the king and left to make my own choices," she turned her body to face him. "I'm presuming this is why Gemma hated you so much when you first met. Did she give you as much shit as you have been giving me?"

"Yeah she did," he replied. "Gemma was a real bitch about the whole thing, and rightfully so."

Nora felt her annoyance flare. He may have treated her badly because he thought there was the possibility of her returning to King Dominic, but he also knew what it felt like to want to change and to have your intentions questioned all the time. He could have been suspicious and had compassion too, yet he had chosen not to.

Asshole.

"And now she trusts you enough to be her second," Nora stated flatly and clutched the pendant around her neck. "Stop being a cagey asshole who thinks the worst of me all the time. I know you don't think I'm all bad, you wouldn't have asked me to come with you if you did."

Aeolus chuckled. "Fine. Are you still mad at me? Even after I came to help you?"

"I am. I am really fucking pissed, but that doesn't mean we can't be friends," Nora replied with a grin. "I haven't forgiven you for lying so if you fuck up again I will stab you, despite you trying and failing to do the right thing by coming after me. If we'd have worked as a team we would have never been in this mess."

"Friends, but there's still a chance you'll stab me," Aeolus said, getting to his feet. "Noted."

It was only mid-afternoon. There was plenty of daylight left to make up some of the distance to Royal Bay. They'd lost a few days, but they'd still been spent moving south toward the guild. If they kept up a decent pace they'd be in Royal Bay within. But Nora could feel her body hadn't completely recovered after expelling so much magic.

"You know," she began, grumbling as she stood. "A little longer rest won't kill us; it actually might do us the opposite."

Aeolus shook his head. "At the risk of getting a blade to the back, the longer we take, the longer King Dominic sits on his throne and spews hate."

Nora looked up into the sky. It was bright blue and white fluffy clouds floated on by. If she could paint then it would have been a scene she'd like to recreate. She frowned. August would have drawn it for her, maybe not in the exact colours, but he would have drawn something beautiful. He was so talented.

Her heart ached. She missed him so much, and not just him, Sage and Will, too.

"I want to end this," Aeolus said. "I want us to go home to

our friends."

Nora released a breath. "Me too."

21

Evelyn

Evelyn had slept for a whole day after the prince had broken into the room she shared with the other maids and locked her in there with him. The idea should have scared her, yet there wasn't an ounce of fear inside her.

The only thing she felt was frustration.

The pain in her head had her torn between wishing to be nowhere near him so as not to feel it and wanting to seek him out. There had to be a reason her head hurt in his presence. Just thinking his name brought on pain.

So Evelyn had decided to test a theory. Her theory was to begin with small amounts of time in his presence and work her way up to longer meetings. Get her used to him; condition her mind. She'd been practising the theory by repeating his name and found that after a while the pain wasn't as bad as it had been initially. She just needed to figure out whether this was because the theory was working or if she was getting used to the pain.

Evelyn strode past the guards, carrying a tray of food down

the stairs to the cold dark dungeon. She kept her chin high with her resolve. She would get answers, even if it took years. She had nothing to lose. She'd already lost her memories after all.

"Hi," she said, her voice soft as she approached Kylan's cell. As expected, there was a dull thud behind her forehead, but she did her best to ignore it. It was manageable and what she wanted to know was far more important.

He made to rise from where he sat on the floor, but she raised a hand, halting his steps. "Please don't. If this is to work, then we need to build up to it."

"Okay," he replied, sitting back down. "I might need a bit of an explanation, though."

"I think we should work gradually towards a closer proximity and longer visits," she said. "I'm hoping then I won't get such debilitating headaches when I'm around you."

"I'm sorry I caused you pain," he said, though a smile stretched over his face. "I know I don't look sorry. But I can't hide my happiness, knowing you intend to visit regularly."

Her stomach fluttered and she dropped her gaze. She was there for a reason, not to feel flattered or anything else by the way he spoke to her, or looked at her for that matter. Taking a deep breath, she looked back at him.

"I need answers," she said. "And the only way I'll find the truth is to listen to all the lies from those who are trying to tell me who I am and figure out the truths amongst them using my headaches."

"I haven't been lying to you."

"Everyone else disagrees," she rebuked.

Kylan sighed. "What would you like to know?"

Evelyn chewed her cheek, thinking about it for a moment. There was so much she wanted to understand, yet perhaps she needed to start with something that wasn't too personal, something that wouldn't make her head hurt and shorten their first meeting.

"Tell me everything you know about Sorby and Lord Maker."

"Who?"

"Lord Maker. He is the lord of this city and the one who's imprisoned you."

"The lord of Sorby is Lord Holmgren. His family has ruled for centuries and he wasn't the one to put me down here. Elliot Maker, Sloane's grandson, locked me in this cell."

Evelyn tapped her chin. Kylan was the second person to tell her that Sloane and Lord Maker were related.

"How can they be related when they are so close in age?"

"She is a Conjurer and she's kept herself young for who knows how long."

"Say I believe you. Those with magic can't live in Sorby. It's a human only city."

"Correct," he agreed. "At least under the rule of Lord Holmgren."

"If you're implying they did something to the original rulers, then wouldn't the staff have said something? Surely a change of ruler wouldn't be beyond gossip."

"Sloane is powerful. She's taken your memories. Who knows how many others she's manipulated?"

"It doesn't make any sense. Why go to so much trouble? Nothing makes any sense." She rubbed her forehead, a frown creasing her features.

"I don't know. But this isn't something that happened overnight. Sloane must have been planning it for a long time. It must be linked to the Maker's Murders somehow."

"The what? Ugh, I think I should go," she said. Her head suddenly felt very heavy and a sharp pain started behind her eyes. "You're probably hungry and I don't want to push myself too hard."

"You'll come back?"

Evelyn nodded. "Yes."

He smiled, the sight sending fresh sparks of pain to scatter across her head. "Sorry."

"No, it's okay," she said, her eyes falling to the black band around his neck. "Before I go..."

"Yeah?"

She pressed her fingers to her own neck, the skin there bare. "Does that block your magic?"

"It hurts me if I attempt it."

"You're an Elementum, like your father."

He nodded.

"Why didn't you fight them? You'd surely be strong enough and if they're humans, or at least everyone but Sloane, you would have been able to fight them off."

"They threatened me with something I couldn't risk."

"Oh." She tilted her head to one side. "With what?"

Kylan looked at her intently, his gaze holding hers. "Your life."

If there was a crypt on the estate it was playing a very good game of hide and seek because Evelyn couldn't find it. Yes, she had limited time to look due to the extra workload the guests caused, but when she did get time, she searched. Boy, did she search.

Evelyn let out a deep breath and lifted her skirts once more as she trekked through the rocky path that wove through the trees. The small wood sat to the west of the estate and it was there Evelyn had been trekking in search of Sloane.

Sloane had left a note in her apothecary, stating where she would be, and Evelyn had followed the directions in the hope of clearing some of the questions in her mind. She had many. Curiosities about her past, things that Kylan had said, that Verida had hinted at, and of course the declarations of Lord Maker and his guests.

Or should she say, *King* Elliot Maker.

Taking another breath, Evelyn let the fresh air settle her nerves and tried to focus instead on the scent of the pine trees and the sounds of nature around her. The scurrying of tiny animals and calls of birds high up in the trees. She felt strangely at home in the woods.

She couldn't help but wonder if any were Anima. There would be no way of knowing if they chose not to reveal themselves, though it was highly unlikely they were Anima. Sorby wasn't exactly known for its hospitality towards races other than humans. The city, whilst part of Valmenessia, functioned much like the rest of the world beyond the waters, at least that's what she had come to understand.

Evelyn spotted Sloane through the trees and slowed at the sight before her. Sloane's hair was standing on end, an erratic mess of lavender strands that stuck out at all angles. Her clothing was torn and the colour was faded in patches whilst stains marred others. Yet that wasn't what had Evelyn slowing. There was a jagged glow, like small sparks of lightning dancing along Sloane's skin and when the woman turned at the sound of her footsteps, Evelyn was given a view of Sloane's eyes shining bright, the blue so pale they were now silver.

"I wasn't expecting you," Sloane stated, the words vibrating on the air.

"I know," Evelyn replied, keeping her distance, fear pooling in her stomach. "But I saw your note with the directions, and I need to talk to you."

"It wasn't for you."

"I'm sorry, it's just—"

"Never mind. I'm glad you're here. I have a story to tell you," Sloane interrupted. "My father used to tell it to me before bed when I was a little girl and I'd like to share it with you."

"Oh. Do you miss him?" Evelyn stammered.

"Very much, but he has been gone for a very long time. I

barely remember his face," Sloane replied.

Evelyn looked closely at the woman standing amongst the trees. Sloane looked as old as Evelyn, her skin smooth and youthful, yet her now silver eyes showed that she was not as young as she seemed. Their depths were filled with knowledge and experience that studied everything and everyone.

"I only really recall the timber of his voice, and even then it only comes to me sometimes," Sloane continued. "When you've been alive as long as I have, almost everything fades. Though some things do defy even the passing of time."

Sloane looked off into the distance. A single tear fell down her cheek, sparked with light, before falling to the dirt. Had she confirmed what Kylan believed? What Evelyn herself had started to think?

"Sloane, I hope you don't think me rude," Evelyn began. "But how old are you?"

"Old enough to know not to ask someone their age," Sloane replied with a sniff. "Now, are you ready for the story?"

Evelyn nodded, her curiosity growing inside her.

"Come. I will tell you the story. Once there were five little stars in the night sky that twinkled more brightly than all others."

"Actual stars?"

"It's a metaphor," Sloane said. "Their glow drew admirers from all over, and these stars loved being looked up to. As each day passed, they sought to grow brighter and together they wanted to shine their light upon the world and recreate it in their own way.

"Even the moon soon bowed to their light, unable to deny their glow. From then on, the nights sparkled, a wonder, yet it still had to cede to the day. The stars were not happy about the cycle and soon they began to believe they were the only ones worthy of being adored way up high in the sky."

"These stars don't sound very nice," Evelyn remarked, leaning her side against a nearby tree. "Greedy."

"Indeed." Sloane huffed a genuine laugh that surprised Evelyn. "Alone they were strong, but together they were a blinding force. The stars did not belong in the day, yet they continued to shine. Working together to outdo even the sun. Eventually, it too gave in to them. When the sun withdrew its light, they were ecstatic. They ruled the sky.

"The problem was, with no other competitors their bond began unwinding. They fought for the right to shine brightest of all. Destruction, death and chaos spread across the land, the people were afraid of the stars and all the power they held. It was time to take a stand, and so the Makers rose up—"

"As in the creators of the Gods and Goddesses?" Evelyn asked and then she couldn't help her curiosities spilling from her. "Or Lord Maker and yourself? His grandmother?"

"The Makers were not the parents of the Gods and Goddesses. Makers were what you call Conjurers in Valmenessia."

"So you and Lord Maker are Conjurers because you are related, aren't you?"

Sloane gave her a stern look before continuing with her story. "The Makers cursed the stars, banishing them from the sky to the earth. There they tore their light and sent them across the seas to a far-off land. Where the stars remain even now, unable to die, far from where they were once held up high. It is the only place where magic dwells."

"Valmenessia," Evelyn breathed, a chill running down her spine. "And the stars are the Gods and Goddesses."

"If you are to believe the story then yes, they are," Sloane said. "However, it was a story my father told me when I was a child, most likely to frighten me about the magical land across the sea. Who knows how much of it I actually remember correctly and how much this old brain has twisted and filled in with nonsense."

"If the part about the Makers being Conjurers is true, do you think the rest might be, too?" Evelyn asked. "The Gods and

Goddesses being immortals trapped here by the Makers?"

Sloane looked passed Evelyn, her gaze narrowing. "Over the years, I have found most stories have at least a grain of truth."

"Why do you keep either lying or telling me half-truths? It is beyond—"

Sloane wasn't listening and Evelyn looked behind her to see Phillip stumbling towards them as he not so gracefully made his way through the uneven terrain.

"This better be good, Sloane," he grumbled once he got closer. "Summoning me out here like some commoner after all I have done for you."

"You have done a great deal," Sloane replied. "Though I have no use for you anymore."

"Excuse me?"

"I asked you here so we would have privacy. It is time for you to leave and live out the rest of your days while you still have a chance."

Phillip's cheeks reddened. "How dare you! I will leave. I will go straight to Royal Bay and tell the king what you have done. What you are planning to do."

"Oh," Sloane glared at him and the man trembled as magic glowed brightly around her. "You are threatening me? What is it you think your king will do against me? He is weak, a bug that can so easily be squashed. Not only that but have you forgotten he knows you are part of the rebellion his army fights against even now." She smirked, the sight sending shivers down Evelyn's spine. "Go ahead, see if he will listen to you."

Phillip gulped, turning back the way he came only for Sloane to slice her hand through the air before her. A crack echoed through the trees as a spark split the air between them and hit Phillip in the back. Like lightning hitting the ground, Sloane's magic struck Phillip with a force that sent him slamming into a tree.

Evelyn gasped. The scent of burning filled the air as she ran towards Phillip. His crumpled body lay on the ground. She tried to find a heartbeat only to be met with nothing.

"You killed him! Why?" Evelyn exclaimed, looking to where Sloane stood unbothered. She hadn't moved, just watched calmly, her body sparking only a little less than before.

"He was rude and threatened to betray me."

"So you killed him?"

Sloane raised a brow. "Keep questioning me and I might feel inclined to do the same to you."

"Why don't you?" Evelyn asked, surprising herself by the firmness of her tone.

"Stay any longer and I will," Sloane hissed, shooting a spark of light towards the ground at Evelyn's feet.

Evelyn's confidence disappeared as her self-preservation kicked in. She jumped up and ran as fast as she could back towards the main house, fear propelling her.

Phillip's murder flashed through her mind over and over again. Not only had the sight been traumatic, but the reason for it chilled her to the bone. He died because Sloane had decided he was no longer of use to her. One day Sloane would feel the same towards Evelyn, though she was unsure why the Conjurer hadn't killed her already. Evelyn had gone to Sloane wanting answers and had left with more questions than before. What was her worth in the eyes of Sloane?

And, if the story Sloane had told her was true, then the Makers had trapped the Gods and Goddesses in the Valmenessia for doing something awful. Which only left Evelyn wondering why. If the Makers saved everyone from their tyranny, were the Makers not worshipped elsewhere? Why weren't Sloane and Elliot worshipped deities? Why hide amongst mortals? And where were the Gods and Goddesses now?

Evelyn sat on the ground with her back pressed against the cool stone wall and looked into the cell. Kylan watched her from where he stood close to the bars, his blue eyes never wavering from her. He didn't speak, waiting patiently for her to initiate conversation when she was ready.

"I feel so stupid for trusting Sloane," she began, clasping her hands before her. "I never expected her to do something like this."

"What did she do?"

"She killed someone. A man who had known my parents. She said she no longer had use for him and when he threatened to go to your father, she killed him."

Phillip's death from the day before filled her mind again and the lightning strike that had thrown him through the air.

"I'm sorry you had to see that," Kylan said, his voice soft.

"Will she kill me when she no longer sees a need in me?"

"I won't let that happen."

"How could you possibly stop it?" Evelyn asked. "I just wish I knew what she wanted from me and that I had my memories back so I could know who I am." She shook her head. "Maybe coming here was a mistake."

"It wasn't," he said, clasping the bars. "You came here for a reason."

"And what is it? To add more pain to my already messed up head?"

"For understanding. To find out who you are. When I first met you, I was rude to you," he said, the ghost of a smile gracing his lips. "I saw you as another way for my father to control me, use me for his gain. I remember sitting in the carriage with my book, determined to ignore you but then I saw you and it was beyond difficult to do so. I tried reading my book, I really did, but nothing made sense. I was too aware of you."

"You disliked me that much?"

Kylan shook his head. "I've never not liked you. Instead

of ignoring you, I settled on being your ally, maybe even your friend but that didn't last long. It was inevitable that I was going to fall for you."

Evelyn looked at her hands, his words sent a fluttering in her stomach. She was so confused. He was very convincing but then again, he could have been a fantastic performer. She had no idea how to tell if he was lying or not. Her head began to ache and she rubbed her temple.

"Evelyn, are you okay? Should I stop?" Kylan asked, voice laced with concern.

"Tell me more about you," she said, purposely not answering his question. "Every day I feel like I'm told something about myself and most of those things do not fit. Do not feel right. So, tell me about you instead. If we were as close as you say we were, then perhaps I could learn something about myself. What kind of person I am from the company I kept."

"Hmm, should I start with the basics?" he replied, scratching his chin. "My name is Kylan and I'm the second son of King Dominic. My mother was Queen Helen and she died when I was young. I feel her absence every single day. You never get over the loss of a parent. In some ways, it's like being homeless." He coughed, quickly continuing before Evelyn could say anything. "I have a brother and I had thought we were close, but it turns out he is too much like my father and doesn't truly care about what I think. Sorry, this is sounding sad and self-pitying."

"It's not," Evelyn said, the pain in her head growing. "Okay, maybe a little sad."

"How about, I like to read? I'm also interested in improving the country and you were helping me to see how I could go beyond what I've seen in Royal Bay. You taught me that, despite what I believed, I had my eyes closed to much of what was going on and that I needed to act. I'd thought my only power was through my father and brother, you taught me that I had my own."

"You are supposed to be talking about yourself," Evelyn

breathed, trying to ignore the headache that was pounding away.

"Not my fault that so much of who I am now is thanks to you."

"I think I should go," she said, rising to her feet. Her head spun and she braced her hand against the cool stone wall.

"Are you alright?"

"I will be. I think this may have been too much for now."

"Please visit me again. We don't have to talk about the past," he said. "We can sit in silence if you prefer. I just need to see you, to know that you are okay."

She looked into his eyes, seeing hope and something else, and the pain in her head grew stronger. She winced and he reached for her, his shoulder hitting the bars and halting his arm. They stared at each other, eyes locked and her heart raced in her chest.

"I'll come back," she said, dropping her gaze and turning away. "I promise."

Evelyn left, climbing the stairs out of the darkness and away from the prince who dwelled within it.

August

"When I went to the castle with Bo, your father was always surrounded," Erik said. He sat beside August on his wagon, recalling what he knew of his father. "Guards, servants, nobles… your father was an honourable man, trusted, and respected by all who met him. None who knew him ever said a word against him."

Erik held the reins tight as the horses pulled the wagon along. Anticipation grew in August's stomach as they drew closer to the city. "Except for the king," August said, glancing at the Alliance around them. Many travelled on foot between the horses and wagons, each eager to arrive at their destination.

"Maybe near the end," Erik said. "It may be hard for you to hear, but the king and your father were friends once. Looking back, I believe that is largely why King Dominic's influence over the country grew so quickly and strongly once he was crowned. All kings have power, yet the solidity of the court and all who served in Royal Bay gave a sense of stability. King Dominic was loved in the beginning. That's part of the reason his laws went unopposed for so long. We thought he cared about his subjects. We trusted him, the same as we trusted your father to guide him."

"It is strange to think of him in that way."

"I understand. Many previous rulers had infighting in their courts, King Dominic did not."

"Until he killed my parents." August's heart clenched.

Erik swallowed hard, his broad shoulders sagging slightly. "It was a shock. I am sorry to say when I first heard of what happened, I was angry at your father. I felt betrayed, so many of us did. We trusted him and to hear how he'd murdered our queen. Well, it was hard to find anyone who wasn't livid."

"He didn't kill her," August said, his voice low.

"I know that now," Erik glanced at him, his green eyes running over August. "But at the time, we trusted King Dominic's word."

"Even when he declared the eradication of the Mors Alvs?"

"I'd like to say that I opposed him from the beginning but I didn't. It wasn't until I had a sword in hand and a scared Mors Alv before me did I realise it was wrong. It took almost killing someone to see the horror of what was happening."

"What happened after that? What did you do?"

"Something I will regret until the day I die," the blacksmith grimaced. "I fled Royal Bay and left the Mors Alvs to their fate. I was a coward, but I refuse to be any longer. I will forge a weapon to fight this curse and give the Alliance its chance at defeating the king. His reign will end and I will play a part in it."

They travelled in silence for the rest of the journey and Erik's story went around in circles in August's mind. It was hard to hear what happened to his parents, especially when so many believed the king's lies back then. However, it did open his eyes to the mindset at the time and how they could so easily turn on the Mors Alvs. It just proved, yet again, how easily it was to manipulate the masses with fear.

The sun was setting when they reached the Midskopas settlement. It sat to the east of the city, which was now wrapped in the curse's embrace. The toll of the Makers' Curse on the land was more than death, but the displacement of so many as well. Homes and businesses were lost. Entire communities had to start over again.

August had never experienced that kind of loss. He'd never really had a home to begin with, nor had he owned anything beyond what was in his pack. The only thing close he had to a home was Nora. Nora was his best friend and the only family he had left.

August left Erik after helping to unpack the heavier items he had from his wagon in search of his friend. He was eager to see Nora and was somewhat surprised she hadn't sought him out yet.

Tyler jogged to catch up to him, slowing as his feet fell into step with August's. He made a point of looking around them. "I'd have thought your Nora would have sensed you near and crushed you in a hug by now. Maybe she's already forgotten about you?"

"Unlikely," August huffed a laugh. "The woman is always up to mischief and thrives on teasing me, she's probably making me wait on purpose."

"I feel like she and I are going to get on really well, Dark Prince," Tyler said with a broad grin. "We might even fall in love and spend our days tormenting you."

August rolled his eyes. "Nora and Sage are together. I think you're out of luck."

"Pity," Tyler pouted. "Just my luck. I'm destined to be alone."

"You're being a little dramatic."

"Me?" Tyler placed a hand on his chest. "Never."

August stabled his horse and left Tyler to his dramatics, looking for Sage. He wove through the Alliance's tents as they unpacked and set up their dwellings for the foreseeable future. The Alliance had plans to meet the king's army, but they would stay here to rest and plan first.

He finally found Sage's tent and stepped inside, coming face to face with Will.

"Hey," Will said, taking a step back. "We were about to come look for you." He turned to the man behind him. "Chester, this is August."

"Ahh, good. Lady Royd, Gemma and Carl have asked for you, too," Chester said, stuffing his hands into his pockets. "This saves us time. Ready, Sage?"

"Uh huh," she said, adjusting her coat. "Let's go."

August silently followed as Chester led the way deeper into the settlement where makeshift buildings had been erected and others were in the process of being built. Around these, tents had been set up in an orderly fashion. The paths were narrow and the population seemed beyond capacity, overflowing into every liveable space they could find without spreading the settlement out too far.

Chester offered greetings as they moved through the crowded paths and chatted with Will the entire time.

"Any idea what this is about?" August asked Sage as they walked. "I was hoping to find Nora."

"I assume Jasmine wants me to provide an update on my work to Gemma and Carl," she replied with a shrug. "And most likely Nora's with Jasmine right now. So that's probably why we are also being summoned."

"Or maybe we are being led somewhere for Nora to jump out at us," he suggested with a slanted grin.

Sage laughed. "That's too obvious, she would have something more devious planned."

"That's true." He grinned as their pace slowed to a stop.

"In here," Chester said, stopping before a wooden building, and pushed open a set of double doors. He waved for them to enter before he returned to his conversation with Will.

Inside, one long table bordered by benches sat in the centre of the room, filling most of the space of the room. A huge hearth had a fire burning on the far side. The table was full of people eating, talking and appearing to have an enjoyable time, the horrific events beyond the building's walls seem to not exist inside.

"This way," Chester said, leading them passed the tables to a door to the right.

August stepped through the threshold to find Jasmine, Gemma and another man sitting behind a table piled high with papers. A large window filled the room with light and gave a view of the settlement. On the other walls maps and large landscapes hung, looking almost like they too were windows to the world outside. Chester shut the door, leaving with Will.

"Thanks for coming," Jasmine said, clasping her hands before her. She looked at the man at her side. "Carl, this is August, Sage and Will."

"I've heard a lot about you," Carl said to August, leaning back in his chair.

"I hope only good things," August replied with a grin.

"Now, before you ask, she's not here," Gemma said simply, looking up at them.

August's heart dropped, his excitement twisting into a cold disappointment. "Where is she?"

"Nora wanted to make amends for her past actions. In my mind, she has done that with everything she did for Midskopas and the Alliance. But it seems it wasn't enough," Gemma explained, clasping her hands behind her back.

"So why isn't she with you?" His heart raced at the terrifying thought that filled his mind and chilled him to the bone. Fuck, he didn't think he would cope if she were no longer alive.

"She went south with Aeolus after Carl and I established the city here. Aeolus plans to assassinate the king and requested her aid in reaching him," Gemma replied, her words easing his racing heart but not washing away his worry completely. "As you can imagine, Nora agreed."

Of course, she did. When Nora was posed with a task she wouldn't turn it down, and a chance to get revenge on someone who caused her pain? He'd expect nothing less.

"When did they leave Midskopas?" Sage asked.

August had almost forgotten that she too would have been interested in where Nora was. He'd been so caught up in his own feelings.

"A few weeks ago," Carl said, then paused briefly before adding. "Though they were not travelling by foot."

"Aren was with them?" August asked.

Gemma's analysing gaze looked deep into his eyes. "You know about the God?"

"He does," Jasmine nodded. "Jord is alive, too."

Carl whistled. "Gods and Goddesses everywhere."

"Was he taking them all the way to Royal Bay?" August asked. If Aren were flying them straight to King Dominic's castle then they would be there by now; the king might even be dead already.

"No," the man shook his head. "The plan was to fly as far as Giland and travel by foot the rest of the way to avoid suspicion."

"If you choose to," Jasmine said. "I still hope that you and Tyler will stay. The king's army is still marching towards us. We need all the numbers we can get."

"And with your training," Gemma added. "You'd be an asset."

August had planned on making that decision once he'd arrived at Midskopas and seen Nora. He needed to re-evaluate that now. "I'll stay for the time being," August replied, surprising the leaders. "I'll continue working with Sage and Erik until I decide what to do."

Jasmine turned to Sage; brows raised. "In what capacity?"

"He's been helping with finding a cure," Sage replied. "So far the dust I have tested hasn't been successful on the samples so far. But I think I know why that could be. I want to begin testing on a different test subject. With your permission, that is."

"What kind of subject do you mean?"

"Living carriers of the curse."

Silence filled the room as everyone took in Sage's words. August hoped the leaders would accept Sage's proposal. It was the most logical way forward and he had faith in her. Those inflicted would die anyway. At least this way they were helping instead of waiting around to die.

"If August has given permission then I consent as well," Jasmine said finally.

"You're sick?" Gemma snapped, rearing back. "And you're here, with everyone. Are you trying to get us all sick, too? Jasmine, you knew about this?"

"I did," Jasmine replied, "And I have no reason to fear him spreading it."

"The thing is," Sage added quickly. "The curse doesn't spread as fast as it has on others. He hasn't transmitted it to anyone and I'm beginning to think he won't. I believe it has something to do with him being a Mors Alv."

"How can you be so sure?" Carl asked, leaning forward.

"I only have a theory. Mors Alv's magic works differently from anyone else's. My theory is that his magic not only slows the curse but stops it from spreading through the host. The Makers' Curse absorbs magic and his magic works similarly. Mors Alvs have the ability to transfer the health and magic from others to themselves, much like the curse does. So, whilst the curse is attempting to feed on him, for want of a better word, his magic is doing the same to it."

"You're saying they are in competition with each other."

"Yes, fighting over the magic," Sage replied.

They waited as the leaders contemplated Sage's words. August had a similar theory, though Sage had kept hers close without revealing it to him until now. She never even allowed him to see what she'd done with his blood samples, likely not wanting to give premature or false hope. Her words gave him a strange sort of relief. He may be sick, but his magic wasn't letting him die without putting up one hell of one.

"I'm fine with you testing the cure on August," Carl said. "And I am not worried about him living amongst us, granted he continues to keep wherever his infection is covered, just in case."

"Of course," August replied with a nod.

"We want this cure as much as anyone," Jasmine said. "But you must be one hundred per cent sure you can replicate it on the others who do not share his Mors Alv gifts. You must also do this as humanely as possible. I will not allow us to become monsters in the process of trying to free us."

"I'll do whatever it takes," August said. "I've nothing to lose."

Jasmine frowned.

"I know the limits and I won't cross them," Sage said. "I'm going to do this the right way and with August's help, I'm going to find this cure."

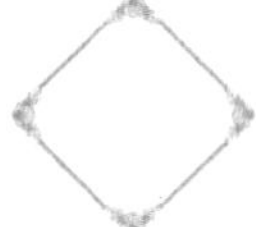

"So Nora, she's a feisty little thing," Carl said as he approached. He had a broad grin on his face as he came to stand before August. "Doesn't like authority much."

"When you've spent your life being used as a pawn in a game you were forced to play, it's hard to let someone tell you what to do once you've gotten your freedom back," August replied, stoking the fire.

After the meeting with the leaders of the Northern Alliance, August went back to help Erik. The tasks the blacksmith gave allowed him time to think and sort through all the new information he'd been given.

"Understandable," Carl nodded, watching August as he worked. Erik's hammering echoed August's and their combined movements had the clanging of metal filling the air.

"Though, even when she was an Alta she found it hard to do as she was told. Except of course if King Dominic gave an order," August said, thinking back on his time with Nora as part of the Alta. He dropped his hammer and started gathering scraps of metal. "Nora is strong-willed."

"That she is," Carl agreed. "What about you? Are you like her?"

"In some ways," he replied, picking up a jagged piece of metal Erik had discarded. "I guess our similar upbringing has moulded us to be alike in many ways."

"Except that she never had to hide her race," Carl said, following August. "The Mors Alvs were persecuted just for existing. You have lived with a threat looming over you your entire life. That is something a lot of people will never understand."

"I guess," August said, dropping bits of metal into a bucket and then scratching the back of his neck. He felt uncomfortable speaking so frankly with the leader of the Northern Wolf Pack. He'd only just met the man. "Is there a point to this? Can I help you with something?"

"You said you were planning to stay with us, I assume as long as it takes for Sage to cure you or Erik to forge a successful weapon? Or both?"

August said nothing, folding his arms over his chest and waiting for Carl to elaborate on why he was there.

"Gemma and Jasmine know what is facing us. The king's army is heading our way, and we have one chance to put a stop to it," Carl said. "The thing is the stakes are not as high for them. Gemma is a Lys Alv and Jasmine is human, they empathise with the cause, but they have not lived its consequences as we do."

"And what do you want me to do about it?"

"Stay permanently, be part of our rebellion," Carl replied.

"Let the Alliance see that, despite the king's actions, he cannot win. The Mors Alvs are still here, he did not eliminate you and he will not eliminate the Anima. Be proof and give hope to those here. Show them they are not fighting in vain."

"And what about what I want?"

"The king dead? Nora is already on her way to fulfill that wish and you are unlikely to catch up. I doubt she will fail, and this task you've set will be complete before you have a chance to reach her."

"So, I should stay and help despite those who still look at me with fear and trepidation?"

"Yes," Carl nodded. "Prove their fear wrong. Be a symbol of resistance *and* resilience."

August sighed heavily.

"If you want to chat go elsewhere," Erik barked, coming over to retrieve a tool from a wooden box. "You're distracting me."

Carl chuckled, raising his palms and backing up. "Sorry, Erik, I'm going."

August watched as Carl strode away, disappearing further into the settlement. The man's words played on his mind. What he was asking of August was a lot. To be some sort of symbol to those who never saw him as a person to begin with.

And then there was Nora.

Sure, she'd probably kill King Dominic before he was cured and got a chance to help out, but the thing was, going to Royal Bay would lead him to her regardless. They had been separated for far too long. He didn't want to die without seeing her again.

"You're staying," Erik stated without looking up from his work, hammering the weapon he had before him.

"Is that an order?"

"An observation."

August chuckled, shaking his head. "I need to talk to Tyler first."

The blacksmith said nothing, once again absorbed in her work, and August did the same.

Later that night, August wrote his longest letter to Nora. He filled the pages with all his thoughts from the last few days, the words spilling from him faster than his hand could keep up with. There was so much to say, and he grew frustrated with his writing. It was slow and some of his thoughts weren't transferring to paper as he wished they would.

His hand ached as he signed his name, then folded the letter in half and tucked it away with the rest he'd written. He sat on his bed and sighed, thinking about all that was being asked of him. No request seemed more demanding or less important than the rest. August just needed to figure out what he wanted to do with the time he had left.

Nora

It was official. Aeolus was by far the grumpiest person Nora had ever met. He grumbled the entire way south, always about one thing or another, as he recovered from his injuries.

His complaints only got worse once the rain started. The man had water magic, yet he hated the rain. Nora felt no pity towards him, not even when she used her magic to divert the rain away from herself to keep somewhat dry. She thought maybe the rain would wash away his shitty attitude.

It continued to fall as they reached a small cluster of buildings just off the main road, amongst them was a tavern they decided to stop at. After walking in the rain for the last few hours Nora's stomach growled at the sight of the tavern and the prospect of a hot meal and stretching out comfortably by a warm fire. Nora definitely felt she had well and truly earned the warm meal awaiting her after so long using her magic. She was more than a little tired and hungry.

Inside, the tavern was warm and Nora moaned in delight as Aeolus slid a tankard of ale across the wooden table to her. She curled her fingers around it and sat back on her side of the booth so that her back was against the wall and she could stretch her legs over the wooden bench seat, giving her a view of the patrons in the tavern as well as forcing Aeolus to look at the nude painting of a rather hairy man on the wall.

Aeolus muttered under his breath as Nora's head no longer obstructed his view of the man's detailed bear-like features. His clear unhappiness made it all the more entertaining for Nora. She had needed something to brighten her day, and whilst the ale was good and she was sure the warm meal would be too, watching Aeolus be annoyed would be the highlight.

"Lyle told me before we left that the curse took over Giland in a matter of days," Aeolus told Nora. "Apparently Lord Gudrid told his citizens it was nothing to worry about, so they went on, business as usual."

"Majority of its citizens were Elementum. When you believe you're the king's chosen people and are better than everyone else, it makes sense to think you're above a curse blamed on the Anima," she said. Nora looked bitterly at her ale before swallowing a mouthful. "There would have been so much magic for the curse to feed on, and if they were doing nothing to prevent the spread, well..."

Aeolus nodded. "Eventually the entire city was abandoned. They either joined the king's forces, or fled south to Royal Bay and the other Elementum cities. Regardless, they all seem to blame us for the curse."

"Wonderful," Nora groaned. "Just another thing we've apparently done. The ignorance is mind boggling."

"The Northern Alliance was already a villain in their eyes," he replied. "And once established as a villain, it is easier to believe we are capable of all horrors rather than to believe there are other factors at play."

"Interesting advice. Hypocritical as fuck considering how you treated me."

Aeolus pursed his lips. "Thought you were getting over it."

"I would if you'd stop being a duplicitous ass."

"Here," he slid his dagger along the table towards her. "Stab me like you promised."

Nora scowled at him. "You're not worth my time."

"Drink up then," he said, taking the dagger back. A small smile crept onto his lips, seemingly satisfied to have called her bluff. "Our food will be here soon and then we can rest in the room I got us. We're only staying the night."

"Fine," she snapped, hating that he'd gotten under her skin. What had she become? Aeolus was now her friend?

Nora ignored his now smug presence, glancing around at the other patrons in the tavern while the rain pattered rhythmically on the windows. Bowls and mugs floated between the tables and bar on Elementum wind, whilst a fire crackled in the hearth without any logs of wood. Conversation filled the air, yet there was a sullen mood lingering around the patrons. The Makers' Curse was like a depressing fog that hung over the entire country. She sipped her drink as she continued to observe those around her, almost choking on the liquid when her eyes landed on a familiar face nestled at a table in the corner.

He'd aged so his hair was streaked with silver now, but she'd never forget those brown eyes, his straight nose or the way he held his shoulders as though he was so self-assured, so confident in who he was no matter anyone else's opinion.

What were the odds of him being in the tavern?

August had once thought her apprehension toward Giland had been due to the man sitting across the room. It had never been the case. Money wasn't made in his line of work by remaining in one spot. She shot to her feet and ignored Aeolus' call as she stormed towards the man. Her heart hammered, its pace increasing the moment he spotted her, a knowing look in his eyes as she drew closer.

He recognised her. Of course, he did.

Nora reached his table and pointed to the door, her tone firm and deadly. "Either you come outside with me now, or I'm going to put on a show for everyone here."

Patrons shot weary glances their way, but Nora didn't give a shit. This man deserved what was coming to him, whether his punishment had an audience or not.

"Outside," he replied.

The sound of his voice made her flinch. She had once hung on his every word when his voice had been something that comforted her; made her feel loved. Now it was like a blade that cut her deeply.

"Let's not ruin the guests of this fine establishment's evenings with our little family squabble."

"We are *not* family," Nora spat, leading him towards the door. She glanced back to her table to see Aeolus watching intently. He raised his brow in question, and she shook her head. This was between her and the man she had thought had been her father.

Nora stopped once they were a few feet outside from the tavern, keeping her back to him and taking a deep breath. Rain fell on them and the distant sun was almost set, the last bursts of its light like a smouldering ember before it would be extinguished by the night.

"It is good to see you again," he said to her back. "I'd hoped that day many years ago in the king's castle wouldn't be the last time I saw your face."

"You could have seen me every day," she spat, spinning around to face him. "And yet you sold me to the king and left me there to be tortured and enslaved."

He looked at her sadly, though his voice held no emotion as the rain soaked his shirt. They were both Elementum yet neither conjured any sort of protection from the weather. "It was just business."

Nora scoffed. "Business? Like selling fruit at a market?" She shook her head. "Are you too much of a coward to admit that you exploited me for your own gain?"

"I know what I did and I don't shy away from it. Rather, I have a differing definition to yours," he explained. There was no sadness in his voice, no sign of regret for his actions or the harm they had caused. "I am an opportunist. You're powerful; strong in all three elements and therefore worth a lot of coin. As I said it was purely business."

"You manipulated me," she hissed through gritted teeth.

"At first," he nodded, stepping closer to her. "I did care for you by the end. I still do. You are my greatest achievement." He smiled broadly at her, his gaze looking her over, not as a person looks at another, but as a salesman looks at his wares. She was still just a possession to him.

"What I am has nothing to do with you. You ruined my life."

"Your life was already ruined," he said. "You and your brother were bastards, children of affairs. I could see that your mother was running out of money. Your home was falling apart, and she could barely afford to feed you. When I monitored the house, I heard you crying at night. You were so hungry."

"Liar. My mother took care of me and my brother. I remember."

That was why her memories of her mother and brother were so painful because she had been happy and loved. He was trying to twist the past, turn it into some story where he was the hero.

"Your memories are those of a child. Unreliable," he replied with a dismissive wave of his hand. "I offered to pay her for you, yet she declined and so I took you anyway. She could have given both you and your brother the lives you deserved, but she was selfish. You grew up in a castle, and the coin would have set your brother up for a prosperous future. She couldn't see past her own selfishness to do what was right."

"That's ironic coming from you," Nora spat, rain dripping down her face. "And I didn't grow up in a castle, I grew up beneath one. There is a vast difference."

"Perhaps."

"Perhaps? Perhaps, you should have left us alone! Perhaps, you aren't entitled to everything you want! Perhaps, you had zero reason to kill them!"

His face remained composed, despite her yelling, which only infuriated her more. She clenched her fists at her sides, doing her best to hold back her fire magic and stop herself from lighting him on fire right there.

"She denied me what I wanted. Your brother was collateral."

"You're disgusting," Nora sneered, her stomach twisting at his words.

"I prefer opportunistic," he replied with a smirk. "I remember the day I first saw you. You were playing in the field by your house, and you were so powerful. You didn't know how to wield your elements properly, yet I saw your strength. I was shocked at first to see that you had control of all three elements. That's rare. I couldn't miss the opportunity before me. A powerful child with no ties to anyone of worth. Your parents were nothing, no one. Your magical ability was a product of pure chance. One that I nurtured and ripened. There was no one left to come after you, you were the perfect sale. A clean sale.

"If you had stayed with your mother you would have never known the true potential of the power you wield or how to use it. I did you a favour and now you look at me with such hate. I am the best thing to ever happen to you, as you are to me. You may not have been born my daughter, but the fleeting time we spent together made you more mine than your own parents."

Nora shook her head. "I am nothing like you."

"I disagree. Rana sent me regular updates," he said.

Nora froze.

Rana had kept in contact with him? This whole time she had

been updating the man who sold her? The betrayal was hard to swallow, like a toxin swirling in her belly. Nora hadn't realised she'd expected Rana to have some loyalty towards her until it had been taken away.

"You are exactly like me. Ruthless. Cunning—"

"She may be all those things."

Nora turned to see Aeolus moving to stand behind her. He folded his arms over his chest and glared at the man she had once thought was her father. His presence strengthened her, and she found herself standing taller, her unchecked anger cooling. Maybe having him as a friend wasn't so bad after all.

"But she is far more," Aeolus continued. "She is loyal, brave, and hardworking, among other things. All traits you have proven you don't have."

A tear fell down Nora's cheek, mixing with the raindrops, as she raised her chin. Aeolus was right. She may share similar traits, but she wasn't him. She was her own person, and she was finally beginning to like who that was.

"Any final words before I end you and then go kill the king you love so much?" Nora asked as she stepped forward, closing the distance between them and unsheathing the dagger from her hip. She didn't wait for an answer before slamming it into his stomach in one smooth motion, angling it up. She'd planned to torture him, make him feel all the pain she had felt over the years as an Alta. Every single injury that was inflicted on her as part of her training or as pure entertainment from the older Alta. But now that she was here she just wanted to end it.

He gasped, leaning forward as he looked down at her, his brown eyes almost glowing. He didn't try to fight back or summon his Elementum magic, letting her kill him like he had already accepted his fate. "King Dominic is already dead, daughter, and Lady Elizabeth marches with his army. You are too late."

"Dead?"

"Yes," he breathed. "You killing him wouldn't have given

you meaning."

"No. It would have given me satisfaction."

"True, perhaps this will help instead. You were my best discovery, Nora. I knew the moment I saw you that you would make me rich. You gave me life."

"And now I'm giving you death," Nora said, twisting the blade.

"Better you than the curse," he gasped, then dropped to the ground.

Nora stepped back, knocking into Aeolus' chest. "We need to leave, now!"

"Why? What—?" Aeolus tried to grab her, but she was already darting out of his reach.

"He was infected with the curse," she said, opening the tavern door wide. "We need to warn everyone."

The sound of buttons popping caused them to turn in time to see her false father's coat burst open as the curse pushed out the dagger lodged in his gut. The blackened roots possessively crept over his body, feeding on his magic and turning his flesh grey. His head tilted back at an unnatural angle and his jaw opened wide as the curse pushed out of his mouth to wrap itself around his neck. The Makers' Curse throbbed, pulsing as it drained him.

"Run!" Nora shouted, rushing into the tavern and leaving the terrifying scene behind. "Run!"

Nora called for an evacuation as the sounds of Aeolus' shouts for everyone to leave and warn others, joined hers.

"The curse?" someone asked. "Say it isn't so."

Nora nodded, frustrated at the lack of urgency. She grabbed the fabric of the person's coat and dragged them out of their seat. "Hurry."

At first, no one moved, but once a few looked through the windows and witnessed for themselves the curse's roots outside, chaos ensued. Patrons shoved each other in their desperation to get out through the narrow corridor at the back of the tavern. No one used magic, too afraid to draw the curse to them.

Nora shoved a few people as they tried to push her out of the way while she and Aeolus hurried with the rest of them. They passed into the small kitchen and then were out the back door. Patrons ran in every direction in their haste to get away.

"We need to get as far away from here as possible," Aeolus said at her side.

Nora didn't need to be told twice. They headed in the opposite direction of the tavern, moving swiftly. Shouts echoed as word spread. The duo didn't stop to watch the town's reaction.

Guilt tried to force its way into Nora's mind. But she pushed it back. She told herself that killing her false father could have accelerated the curse's effects, but he was the one who went to a populated area and hid his affliction. It wasn't her fault. He put this town at risk.

He was the selfish one. Even in death.

24

Evelyn

"You were the one who gave me the courage to stand up for my beliefs," Kylan said, sitting with the cell's bars against his side.

Evelyn had returned, true to her promise, and now sat with her legs crossed and her back against the wall. She found herself looking forward to these nighttime visits where she'd bring down his dinner and they would talk for a time. The headaches didn't even deter her anymore. She wanted to be there.

"I always thought I could wait out my father's reign and work with my brother to fix all the damage my father had done," Kylan continued. "I'd been such a fool and you were the one who showed me that. It took time to get through my own stubbornness, but I saw it in the end. That's why I left Royal Bay. I was following you, hoping to do something good with the power I had."

"Then, you don't agree with your father's laws?"

"No," Kylan replied, shaking his head. His dark hair fell

into his eyes and he brushed it away. "We had planned to return to your home, to Forest's Edge, and help your sister and the other rebels stop him." He glanced around his cell. "As you can see, it didn't work out that way."

"What happened?" Evelyn asked, bracing herself for the bad news that was sure to come.

"Your maid, Louise, in her ignorance, had believed a lie. We trusted her and didn't see the truth until it was too late. I was imprisoned and your memories and magic were stolen."

"It's not possible to steal magic."

"You still don't believe that part? Is it really that hard to accept after everything you've learned about Sloane?"

"I don't understand why she would have taken it. Mind you, I have no idea why she has any interest in me at all."

The ache in her head simmered, but she was learning to embrace it as a confirmation of something or someone she knew in her past. Kylan brought out the strongest headaches by far, though uncertainty still lingered in her chest.

Sloane may have lied about some things, but there were also truths in her words. She could also have been telling the truth about Kylan, so Evelyn wouldn't let her guard down.

"What do you know about the Gods and Goddesses?" Evelyn asked.

"I know that they are not some beings in the sky who listen to our prayers," Kylan replied.

Evelyn's brows rose at that. "Sloane told me a story. In it, the Gods and Goddesses are just power-hungry magic users imprisoned in Valmenessia by the Makers."

Kylan thought for a moment, tapping his finger on one of the bars. "It could be true."

"You think she was telling the truth?"

"Frode and Thyra are alive, I have seen both. And their magic is like any others only more powerful," Kylan said. "What's to say the others aren't also walking around Valmenessia? As for the Makers, I don't know. Sloane is powerful, but I'm not sure about the rest of her bloodline."

"She said Makers are what we now call Conjurers."

"Hmm, well then maybe they do have the power. I wonder what the Gods and Goddesses did to end up trapped here."

Evelyn bit her lip. "She didn't say."

"Maybe we'll never know."

"If the Gods and Goddesses are alive, why aren't they stopping the king?" Evelyn asked. Surely, even if they weren't deities they still had the power to stop a terrible man and all the pain he was causing.

"Thyra encourages my father. They are working together," Kylan replied bitterly. "The Gods and Goddesses aren't *good*. If Sloane is to be believed, they were imprisoned for doing something awful and, even with all the time that has passed, it seems they haven't all learnt their lesson."

"Then, we are just playthings to them."

Kylan nodded. "We will all die and they will live on to continuously entertain themselves by pitting the people against each other. We are just a blink in their existence."

"There has to be something we can do."

It felt like she was fighting against a strong gust of wind with no way of defending herself. She had no memories, no knowledge of who to trust or how to decipher truth from lies other than a headache, and then there was King Dominic, King Elliot Maker and now, the Gods and Goddesses all trying to fit inside her head. Yet, despite all that, she couldn't let herself give up. She would get her memories back and then she would do whatever she could to fight for a world that the population of Valmenessia deserved. A world that she deserved.

"Kylan?"

"Yes?"

Evelyn took a deep breath, her words rushing out of her on the exhale. "Did I love you?"

He looked at her, his features softening. "I think we were heading down that path and I think you still want to. That's why you keep coming back because, deep down, you know what was between us. And even though you don't have your memories, you can still feel it."

A sharp pain filled her head, crackling through her mind like lightning through the sky. She clutched her head between her hands and a moment after she felt blood trickle from her nose as she gasped for breath.

"Evelyn!" Kylan exclaimed, his voice close though she couldn't see him, her eyes clamped shut as she braced herself against the pain. "Evelyn!"

She tried to shut him out, ignoring his calls as her mind whirled. Why had she asked? It had been a mistake, one that she was now paying the price for. Urging her mind to go blank or at least focus elsewhere, Evelyn attempted to ignore Kylan entirely, pretending as though she were alone.

"There is no one here but me," she whispered to herself. "There's no one here but me."

She was alone.

All alone.

The pain eased and she didn't look back at the prince as she sprinted from the dungeons, all the while chanting to herself.

"I am all alone."

Maggie sat beside Evelyn in the servant's communal area, polishing the plate before her. She was telling Evelyn all about her love of painting as the sun trickled in through the windows and a light breeze blew through their hair. The other workers went about their business around them, all content with their duties. Apparently in her free time, the little they were given,

Maggie spent it creating small artworks.

"They're not much, but I do my best with what I have available to me," she said, holding up a plate and admiring her work. "Colours may be limited but creativity is not."

Evelyn smiled, though she found it hard to fully invest herself in the conversation. As much as she wanted to hear of the maid's passion, her mind kept returning to Sloane in the woods. The flash of lightning and Phillip's lifeless body. She hadn't told a soul other than Kylan about what had happened that day. If Sloane was Elliot's grandmother, then telling anyone about Phillip's death would only get her into trouble.

"Evelyn, are you okay?" Maggie asked, a frown creasing her brow as she looked at Evelyn with worry in her eyes.

"Fine," she replied with trembling hands, placing the cutlery she'd been polishing on the table. "I mean, I think I'm not well. I'm going to have a lie-down."

Dismissing herself and leaving with wishes for a speedy recovery, along with instructions to care for herself, Evelyn hurried through the hallways towards her room.

Everything felt all too much.

She was a tree in the wind, bracing herself against a storm, except that she had no roots to hold her to the ground, to stabilise her and ground her. Instead, she was doing her best to weather the winds with no support and hoped she didn't get blown over.

Evelyn pushed open the bedroom door and moved to sit on her bed, only to get up immediately and pace the room. She couldn't sit still. Her body shook as she tried to process her thoughts.

"What's wrong?" Verida asked as she entered the room, shutting the door. Her brows creased as she looked at Evelyn with worry.

The woman had an uncanny ability to find Evelyn when she was distraught. Was that another thing for Evelyn to worry about? Or was she being paranoid?

"I'm sick," Evelyn stated, waving her hand dismissively towards the other woman.

"No, you're not," Verida replied, folding her arms over her chest. Her eyes were filled with concern and Evelyn felt she was being suspicious for no reason. Verida was a good, caring person. "What happened? Did you find—"

"Sloane killed Phillip," Evelyn blurted. Then the rest spilled from her lips in a torrent. She couldn't have held it all back even if she'd tried, though she'd have to brace herself for the consequences.

Verida simply listened without interruption and once Evelyn breathed a heavy sigh and wiped the tears from her brown eyes, Verida finally spoke. "Have you been to the crypt?"

Evelyn gaped at her. Okay, maybe Verida wasn't as caring as she'd thought. "That's your response to what I just told you?"

"Well, have you?" Verida pressed.

"No," Evelyn shook her head. "Are you going to tell the guards about what I said?"

"Lord Maker won't act against Sloane."

"I thought as much, but won't you tell them that I'm a traitor or something?"

Evelyn stared at Verida as the maid simply laughed.

"What?" she asked, confusion creasing her brow.

"Go to the crypt, Evelyn," Verida said, taking Evelyn's hand in hers. "Just go there."

Evelyn bit her lip. "I couldn't find it."

Verida rolled her eyes and then recited the exact directions for Evelyn.

"Why didn't you just tell me that in the first place?" Evelyn exclaimed. "I wasted so much time trying to find it."

"How much I share with you is a risk," Verida replied. "I know what happened to the last maid who assisted you."

Evelyn placed a hand on her chest and frowned. Kylan had mentioned another maid, Louise, but nothing else. "What happened to her?"

"She's dead and I'd rather not end up that way," Verida supplied matter-of-factly, though the tone didn't stop the chill that coursed through Evelyn, nor the guilt that filled her. "Sloane makes whoever gets between her and her plans go away."

Evelyn swallowed hard, thinking of Phillip. Was that what happened to her memories? They got in Sloane's way so she made them go away too?

"Go to the crypt, Evelyn."

The air was still and musty underground. The flickering light from the sconces along the mossy stone walls was all that moved, besides Evelyn, of course, who jolted forward rather than taking smooth assured steps on the dirt.

There was no other way Evelyn could describe the feeling of being down there other than creepy. The fine hairs on her arms stood on end and an incessant chill tickled her spine. She did her best to ignore her unease and pushed on, following the tunnel further into the depths.

As far as she could tell, the tunnel led in the opposite direction of the main house, and it wasn't long until she found herself facing multiple paths.

"Of course," Evelyn sighed to herself as she glanced at each path. She'd made excuses about her tasks, and traded jobs in order to explore the crypt; now she was worried she wouldn't have enough time. "Nothing is easy."

Chewing her lip, Evelyn chose the path to her left for no particular reason other than it was the first in the row and headed down the tunnel. The sound of dripping water echoed around her, getting louder as she continued further down. She travelled deeper and deeper into the depths of the earth, questioning her choice, when at last, she stepped from the tunnel to find the source of the dripping. Water trickled from stalactites into a round pool that looked like the night sky filled with stars. The air smelled of lavender.

Evelyn looked around at the beautiful place, a feeling of wonder made her want to linger and explore. Unfortunately, she had to ignore her curiosity; there was no sign of a crypt, and she didn't have time to explore for enjoyment. Heading back up the tunnel, Evelyn contemplated which path to take next, imagining what would await her at the end of each. Would there be more beauty or something else entirely?

Reaching the intersection once more, she continued with the same strategy, deciding on the middle route for no reason other than it was the next in line.

The middle path was shorter than the first, and soon the walls grew further apart until she stepped into an open space. Along the dark walls, stone coffins sat, each towered over by statues she didn't recognise but assumed bore the likeness of those who lay within the coffins.

At the centre of the room, another stone coffin sat on an altar, candles burning brightly around it like a wall, except for in a single spot. It was big enough for a person, like an invitation to stand there. Evelyn cautiously walked forward; her steps hesitant as she had to force her body to move. Her curiosity was her only driving force.

As she reached the altar. Evelyn closed her eyes and murmured pleas of safety, hoping she wouldn't regret her actions. Was she making a mistake? Had Verida sent her into some sort of trap? Was Sloane going to come out of the dark and strike her down like Phillip?

Evelyn could feel her resolve wavering, her curiosity was no longer strong enough to keep her searching for answers. Coming here had been a bad idea. She was out of her depth, out of her mind. It was time to leave.

"What are you doing here?"

Evelyn almost jumped out of her skin. Her eyes sprung open, and her gaze immediately dropped to where the stone slab of the coffin before her had been pushed to the side. A man was asleep within.

He was not dead; at least as far as Evelyn could tell. His chest rose ever so slightly, and his light brown skin had a blush to the cheeks. Her eyes snagged on the familiar necklace that sat on his chest, the pink pendant encased in gold, the stone appearing as though swirling within its hold.

"I asked you a question," the commanding tone said, scaring Evelyn once more. She spun around, heart pounding as she turned to see Mr Walker, Lord Maker's advisor. She hadn't seen him since the day she'd woken up.

"I—I—" she stammered.

"You do not belong here," he continued.

His tone sent a tremble through her bones as he strode assuredly towards her. Evelyn hastily stepped off the altar, the man passing her by with a huff. He looked down at the sleeping man within the coffin and his shoulders sagged, his expression forlorn.

"I'm sorry," she said, her voice soft. "I didn't mean to intrude, it's just—"

"You want answers."

"Please," she replied with a nod that he couldn't see. "I need to know who I am."

"I can't tell you that because I do not know you," Mr Walker grumbled irritably. "However I can tell you who I am."

That wasn't the answer she was looking for, but she'd take it. Verida had said to come to the crypts; what this man had to say had to be important.

"I am Frode. Or as many call me, God of Humans. Yet I'm sure you can tell by now, I am no God," he said. "I am merely a man who did terrible things and paid the price with the one I love.

Cursed with immortality, to rule over a people I outlive, over and over again all the while never being able to leave this wretched place. Worst of all, my love lies here, sleeping for eternity."

"Then, Sloane's story was true," Evelyn breathed. Kylan too, had said Frode was alive, but to hear the words from the God himself was another thing entirely.

"Ahh, Sloane," he shook his head. "I have invested so much in her."

Evelyn thought of the pendant around the sleeping man's neck. "She gave that to you. The pendant."

"Yes," he replied. "It will remove the magic that confines him to sleep … and right the wrongs of the past."

"It removes magic?" That's why she recognised it. She'd had it around her neck when she'd first awoken. Had Kylan been right about her magic too? Had she been a Lys Alv?

"I should never have let them do this to you, my love," Frode said, leaning over the sleeping man, ignoring Evelyn's question. "I'm sorry. It is all my fault, but I will fix it. I will make it right."

"Frode?"

"Leave me."

"But—"

"I said, leave me!"

Evelyn jumped back, her heart racing once more. She'd outstayed her welcome. Turning on her heel, Evelyn hurried back up the path. Both Sloane and Kylan had been right about the Gods and Goddesses, yet that was not what lingered with Evelyn.

The sleeping man had been wearing a pendant. The same one Sloane had taken from her when she'd woken up.

August

"Lord Havilor's forces are still trapped by the curse," Carl said. He stood before a large crowd, where almost all of the Northern Alliance was present. "Yet we shouldn't let that dampen our spirits. There are enough of us here to defend, not only the city, but our way of life."

"We're all going to die," a man in front of August grumbled as Carl addressed the gathering. "The king has more soldiers and better-trained ones too. By the time they are finished with us, this is going to be a mass burial site."

A few murmurs of agreement sided with the man and August clamped his mouth shut, trapping his words. He stood at the back of the crowd, maintaining enough distance just in case he hadn't properly covered his infection. Luckily, his Mors Alv hearing helped him pay attention to what was being said.

"It won't be an easy fight," Carl said. "Though that doesn't mean winning is impossible."

"Liar!" A woman shouted with her hands cupped around her

mouth. "You are leading us to our deaths!"

"Here, here!" others shouted.

August's dark eyes scanned the crowd for the ones who disagreed.

"We are leading you along the only cause of action that will give you freedom from a tyrannical king," Carl said. His tone was firm and August could see the man held back his frustration. His clenched fists at his sides were an obvious tell.

"The battle will be a massacre!" a man bellowed, his face bright red and gaze burning with rage. "Whoever survives will be left to the curse! You have doomed us all with your empty promises! We are not free. We are no better than cattle waiting for the slaughter!"

"I understand that many of you are afraid," Carl called over the crowd. "It isn't an easy task before us—"

"How dare you mark our concerns as fear! You lead us to death for your own glory and expect us to simply follow blindly!" another man yelled and August frowned at the number of people who nodded their heads at the man's outburst.

"And what do you propose is the alternative?" Jasmine asked, her voice calm and soft despite the vitriol in the air. She stepped forward, placing herself between Carl and the crowd. "What would you do in our position? Perhaps you have a way to defeat our enemies without any risk that we do not know about?"

The crowd went quiet and Jasmine looked out over them, her face a gentle mask. This was the first time Jasmine had spoken to the Northern Alliance since August had joined them. Usually, Gemma, Carl or even Omari were the ones who gave updates or directions.

"Well?" she said, clasping her hands in front of her and holding her shoulders back.

Where the others commanded attention by demanding it, Jasmine's very words were simply given it. The Alliance respected her and it was a sight to behold.

"I did not come into power lightly," Jasmine began. "There is not a day that goes by that I do not wish my aunt and father were still here, leading you. They knew what it took to be a leader. I am still learning. No decision that is brought before you has not been made on a whim, Carl, Gemma, Omari, me and many others in the Alliance discuss at length before bringing our proposition before you."

"You did not speak with us! You don't care what we think!" the first disgruntled man shouted before spitting on the ground.

"Then I invite you to come meet with us," she said, not flinching at his angry display. "But know this, you cannot come with only yourself in mind, not even thoughts of your family and friends. You must think of all those gathered here today and those who cannot be present. I challenge you to find a solution that makes every single person happy."

She held the man's stare and August couldn't help the smile that spread across his face. Jasmine may not have been overly vocal, but she was a true leader despite what she said before. She was smart, caring and, most of all, willing to see the viewpoints of even those who didn't agree with her.

"Thank you," the man said sheepishly. "I will attend."

"Good," Jasmine smiled. "Now, are there any more concerns before we end this meeting?"

The crowd disbanded not long after, but August remained, listening. He wasn't the only one impressed by Jasmine and he was starting to think that if Lady Royd wanted to be Queen Jasmine, then it wouldn't be difficult for her to claim the crown.

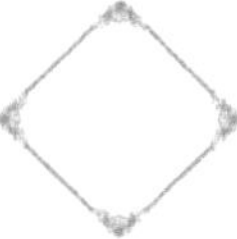

"How long have you been waiting for me?" Sage asked as she strode from Midskopas' tall walls.

The doors to the city were wide open, welcoming whoever

dared step foot inside. Mostly it was just the humans who'd been tasked with filling the holes that the beasts had crawled out of, sealing them so no more could surface. August hadn't seen them, but the descriptions alone were terrifying enough. They didn't sound like the creatures that had awoken in the Periculum Mountains, but there was no wonder what other creatures had awoken too.

August had been forbidden from going into Midskopas, the leaders had even warned him from getting this close, even being infected himself. But he wanted to see Sage. She'd made a few adjustments and now she was going to test her dust on him, he was sure a cure was within reach.

"Not long," August replied with a shrug. "How'd it go?"

"I found some ingredients in a few abandoned businesses marked on the map Carl had given me," she said, readjusting her satchel on her shoulder. "Are you ready to start?"

"I've never been more ready," he said, smiling and offering his hand.

She sighed, giving him her pack. As they walked, Sage filled him in on what she'd found in more detail and the ideas she had. By the time they were back at her room within the settlement, August was struggling to hide his eagerness. Her room was in a recently built dorm and had more space than she'd had in her tent on the road. He sat on the bed, one of his legs bouncing in anticipation as Sage organised herself. Nerves danced in his stomach and his palms were moist as his anticipation grew. The cure was so close he could almost taste it.

He removed his glove and rolled up his sleeve, only to find Sage staring at him.

"What happened?" she asked, her gaze analysing him. "It was contained to your hand only the other day?"

"I don't know," he replied. The curse had spread beyond his hand and was now licking at his wrist. Sage stepped closer and trailed a finger on his skin.

"I hope this works," she said, dropping her hand from him, her words like a prayer.

She collected what she needed, placing them on a table beside the bed, then pulled a stool close to August. She sat down and began to prepare. She was meticulous. Everything was neat and clearly labelled; her notebook and pen were ready for the results and her observations.

"Your room is nice," August commented as he waited.

"I think Jasmine has given me too much," Sage replied, unstoppering a vial. "Others are still in tents and sleeping on the floor. Here I am with not only a room but furniture, too."

"You need it more," he said. "You're working hard."

"Everyone is," she rebuked. "We are all doing our best. Now hold out your hand."

He did as he was told, and she sprinkled some blue dust on his pale skin. The granules were vibrant on his hand, a contrast to the grey lines of the curse. She slowly rubbed the dust into his hand with her fingers and then they waited.

At first, he felt nothing, but a moment later a cool sensation tickled his skin. It was pleasant, almost relieving if the cool sensation didn't continue to get colder. August didn't show it on his face. The dust was now so cold it was almost burning. He hoped that meant it was working. He wanted this to work so badly.

"August?" Sage asked, watching him carefully. "How do you feel? Everything okay?"

"Fine," he replied, the words hissing through his teeth.

Sage poured water over his hand, washing the dust away and instantly giving him relief. "I knew it wasn't. This isn't going to work if you don't tell me exactly what's happening."

"It was only a little bit of pain."

"Maybe, but I still need to know. Look at your hand." She pointed a finger at his cursed flesh. "The dust had no effect, why endure the pain for nothing?"

"It might have worked after a few more minutes," August said, sounding like a child, even to his own ears.

"Or it could have gotten excruciatingly painful for nothing," she replied with a sigh. "Are you sure you want to do this?"

"Yes," he nodded. "Sorry, I'll tell you exactly what is happening with the next one. I promise. I need to do this, Sage. The curse will eventually spread further. We don't have time to wait."

She left him to dry his hand before returning with another vial. This one was both pink and purple, the dust within not mixed entirely. Sitting back down, August held out his hand and she hesitated for only a second, giving him a stern look, before pouring it on his skin and rubbing it into his hand. Unlike the previous one, he felt nothing. His shoulders drooped. Even as minutes passed, not a single sensation prickled his skin.

"One of these has to work," Sage said, wiping off another failed test. "How is Erik going with his weapons? Any progress?"

"Not yet," he replied with a shake of his head. "They've tested everything he's made so far with no luck. It's handy having the curse so close but the daily failures hit hard."

"Tell me about it," Sage huffed.

"Why don't you combine your skills with Erik?" Tyler asked, stepping into the room. "Yes, I was eavesdropping as I was coming over here but you two talk so loudly, and these ears," he tapped his pointed ones, "are so good at their job."

August rolled his eyes.

"What do you mean by combine our skills?" Sage asked.

"Well, you're both getting so close but not succeeding," Tyler said, shrugging a shoulder. "Maybe your dust would work if a Conjurer made it."

"Sage is more than capable—"

"You've got a good point," Sage said, rising to her feet. "Why didn't I think of that?"

"Not everyone can be a genius like me," Tyler grinned.

"If Erik worked with me, we could not only make a cure but embed it into the weapons he's making," she said, halting her steps. She grabbed a satchel and began packing, dropping boxes and vials almost automatically without stopping to check which was which. "And I have just the method he could use, too."

"So you're going to try it? Right now?" Tyler asked, seemingly surprised at Sage acting on his idea.

"Yes," she replied, hoisting the bag over her shoulder and striding from the room. "Why wait?"

"I'll come with you," August said, following Sage.

"Unbelievable," Tyler shook his head as they walked off. "Wait! I'll come too."

Once they found him, Erik didn't take much convincing. As soon as Sage made the suggestion he cleared his workspace and began barking orders for August and Tyler to bring specific tools and supplies he would need.

"Okay," Sage said once everything was prepared. "Where do you want to begin?"

August watched with Tyler as Sage and Erik worked. She directed him through the motions of making the dust, the process more complicated than August had realised.

"This is the one that should have worked," Sage said as she watched Erik mix the dust. "All my calculations, trials and research notes point to it."

"Trust your gut," August said. "It will work."

"We'll test it on you first, then I'll use it all in forging a weapon," Erik said, pouring ground crystal into the bowl. "My conjuring works through forging, but it would be stupid not to test the dust."

"Good plan," Sage agreed before reading out the next step from her notebook.

Once the dust was created, Sage sprinkled it over August's exposed hand and waited. It glittered against his greying skin, but other than looking pretty, had no effect on the curse.

August's shoulders sank, though he wasn't completely hopeless. There was still a chance to fight the curse and even though he would not be cured others could be saved.

Erik set to work creating a weapon with it. August moved alongside him, stepping into the rhythm he'd grown used to since they began working together. Erik rarely had to ask for anything, putting out a hand with August knowing what was expected. They worked well into the afternoon and then late into the night as stars began filling the dark sky. Not that August could see much of them. Smoke billowed around the group, the sound of the hammer working against metal as Erik created a weapon they hoped would put an end to the curse.

At some point, Will came by with food and they stopped for the briefest of breaks to eat, determined to keep working. Anticipation floated around them, the possibility of what was being created driving them to work harder.

The night was still and the settlement was fast asleep when Erik stopped his work. He stood by the smouldering fire and held a polished sword before him. It was a fine weapon, beautifully crafted, and embedded with not only Sage's dust but intricate markings had formed along the blade as well. August stared at it in awe. New anticipation and hope coursed through him. He glanced up, noting Sage's expression and knowing that she would been feeling the same.

"It's done?" Will asked, rubbing his eyes and nudging Tyler who'd fallen asleep with his head on Will's shoulder.

Erik lifted the sword higher. "It's done."

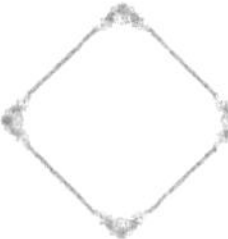

The sword did not affect the curse and the next day the group returned to help Erik and Sage forge another weapon. And then another. Swords, daggers, spears, axes … nothing worked. The weapons were not wasted, each one would be used to fight the king's army instead.

Day after day, they gathered, the new dust was tested on August and it failed. Then a weapon was forged, one they hoped would be the one. The one to fight the curse and save them all.

A human volunteer would take the weapon into Midskopas for testing and all they could do was wait. Confidence was dwindling, each time the man returned with bad news. The weapon didn't work, the curse was too strong.

Over a week later, August lay in bed staring up at the dark ceiling and wishing for Nora. She would have some sarcastic comment that would cheer him up and make him forget, even for a brief moment, the shit show he'd found himself in. Unfortunately, she was far away and all he had were memories of her.

All that would change. He'd wait to see one more weapon be forged and if it didn't work, he'd leave. He'd lingered too long, hoped for too long. Now it was time to face reality.

26

Nora

Aeolus hadn't spoken a word of what happened between Nora and her imposter father, and she had never been so grateful. She didn't want to talk about it because there was nothing to say. He'd wronged her and she finally punished him for it. Now she could move on with her life. Simple. Or at least it should have been.

Killing her imposter father should have closed that chapter in her life and helped her move on, yet it felt as though the page had been marked and put on a shelf. Not finished but not forgotten either.

It wasn't so much the man himself lived in her thoughts, more so the words he had spoken. The revelations of her family tainted the memories she had of them.

He had taken her life, and now he'd taken the only good memories of her family too. She questioned every thought about them that came into her head. Especially those of her mother.

Instead of prying questions and uncomfortable discussions,

Nora and Aeolus had drifted between discussing the curse and silence, at least now it was silent. Her fake father had brought news of King Dominic's death; however, they'd decided to continue south to Royal Bay. For all they knew it was a lie by a desperate man and until they saw or heard the words from a trustworthy source, they would stay true to their original plan.

They'd come this far, what was a little further?

Many from the small village had joined them on the main road, escaping south with whatever belongings they could carry before the curse took over. It had moved so quickly, growing and feeding on Nora's bastard of a fake father's magic, consuming the place. It hadn't taken long for the travellers to thin out, and as time wore on, more and more either stopped to rest or slowed. Their fear of the curse subsided as their concerns about where to go and what to do next took priority.

It was quiet now, the night still and dark as Nora and Aeolus pushed on alone. By the time a farmhouse came into view, Nora had had enough of walking. She was over having her feet split and ache. She was done.

"Where are you going?" Aeolus asked as Nora detoured from the main road towards the black shadow of the nearby building.

She strode passed the main building with purpose, careful to tread softly so as not to announce her presence to those inside and headed towards the barn. A grin spread wide on her face as she carefully pushed open the large wooden door, her gaze sweeping over the inhabitants within.

The animals were fast asleep; however, they were not the sort she was looking for. She stepped back outside and curled her fists as frustration coursed through her. Why was the world against her and her poor feet?

She stomped over to where Aeolus stood, spotting dark figures beyond the stable. She lit a ball of fire, slowly floating it over and hoping it didn't frighten them.

Two horses stood in the fenced-in paddock, and Nora would

have hugged Aeolus if she wasn't still pissed at him. Finding the horses was easing her anger, but only a little.

"They could be Anima," Aeolus said, following her as she made her way towards the wooden fence. "Not to mention this is theft."

"A risk I'm willing to take," she said, hoisting herself over the fence and landing on the grass.

"They don't have any saddles," he pointed out.

"Make yourself useful then," she said as she neared the closest horse, her fire letting her see the beautiful creature, pitch black like the night.

"Hello gorgeous," she said, offering her hand to the horse. It stepped back, unsure of her. But she waited patiently, cooing softly until the horse dropped its head and let her stroke its nose. "Do you want to come on an adventure with me?"

As if the horse could understand her, it stepped forward, pressing its head further into her hand.

"I'll take that as a yes."

She stayed with the horse, patting and offering compliments to the animal until she heard shouts from behind. She spun around, spotting a figure storming out of the cottage after Aeolus who ran like the wind in Nora's direction.

"Looks like we aren't getting a saddle," Nora said to the horse. "Think I can still have a ride?"

The horse whinnied and Nora used her wind magic to hoist herself onto the horse's back, extinguishing her fireball. Arrows shot in her direction, falling short as if only meant to intimidate lest they strike the horse by accident. Another person came running from the cottage sending balls of fire at Aeolus with less foresight. The fire landed on the grass, catching light, and left a blazing trail behind him.

Ushering the horse forward, she held its mane and summoned her wind magic to help Aeolus onto the other horse. He grunted and Nora took the sound to mean he was seated.

With a gust of wind, Nora blew part of the fence down and the horses bolted through the opening. Aeolus caught up quickly behind her and the two of them escaped. Nora waved goodbye to the farmers as they galloped past, the horse beneath her unbothered by the turn of events. Nora couldn't help the laugh that escaped her. She felt alive.

They galloped down the main road until she was sure they weren't being followed. Then she lit a fireball once more and grinned at Aeolus.

"We shouldn't have stolen the horses," he said. To say he was pissed would have been an understatement. His horse was a spotted grey mare that was only slightly shorter than her horse. His face was livid.

"So self-righteous," Nora said, rolling her eyes. "From one extreme to another."

"What's that supposed to mean?"

"First you were a guild member, now you are a stickler for rules," Nora said. "You know what they both have in common? There's no grey area. Live a little. Join me in the shades between black and white."

"We could have walked," he said. Rage simmered, evident in the set of his jaw and shoulders and the fire that burned in his eyes. "There was no reason to steal."

"Think of it as payment. They paid for their freedom from a tyrant king by funding my services."

"He may already be dead. Then how do you justify your theft?"

"If you want to believe a psychotic liar," Nora loosed a breath. "I'm not inclined to do so."

"Unbelievable."

"Look, my feet no longer hurt so I have zero regrets," Nora said, glancing at him. "And just think, with the horses we'll be in Royal Bay in no time."

They were close to Royal Bay and Nora felt a mix of emotions pool in her stomach. She was excited to be back and put an end King Dominic and his sadistic reign, if he was still alive that is. However, she would be stupid not to recognise the anxiety she felt as well. She was returning to the place where she'd never held power over her own actions, the place where she was a slave, where she had been tortured and trained to kill without remorse. A place where she had killed innocents.

She wished August was with her. They had been separated for too long and she hated it. She would have been more relaxed with him by her side, watching her back whilst she looked out for his. They were a team; no they were more than that.

They were family.

"Going to fill me in on the plan?" Aeolus asked, dismounting. He led the animal over to a nearby stream and Nora followed suit. "The curse will up the number of unknowns we're walking into. If something goes wrong in there, we'll be fucked."

"Royally," Nora grinned, enjoying her little joke. Aeolus rolled his eyes, but she caught the way his lips tugged at one side before he quickly hid it. "There's a hidden entry, so just follow me and don't lag behind. Once inside the walls of the city, I'll lead us to a passage that will take us to the castle. Your job is to watch our backs."

After the horses had a drink and a feed on the grass next to the stream, they set off again for Royal Bay. Aeolus continued to question her plan, asking for every single detail and she obliged him until she finally snapped, sick of his badgering.

When Royal Bay appeared in the distance a few hours later, Aeolus finally shut up. Nora anticipated a scene much like Giland or Midskopas; a city taken over by the curse. But it wasn't as horrific as Giland, but it was in no way untouched.

The curse spilled out from the gates and into the land beyond, the blackened roots pulsing as they clutched the sandstone walls, as though desperate to hold onto their latest possession. Chills ran through Nora at the sight.

"Think there will be anyone alive in there?" Aeolus asked.

"There are humans on the wall," Nora said, squinting where guards stood in the gaps between the curse on the ramparts.

"Between the curse and the guards, there's no getting in."

"You can be so negative, you know that?" Nora quipped before looking at the horses. "Time to send them home."

"If they remember the way," Aeolus grunted once he and Nora dismounted.

After freeing the horses, Nora led Aeolus closer to the city wall. They hurried away from the main gate towards a blind spot in the guards' view. Thick, rich green vines grew up the wall, alongside the curse, and Nora quickly slipped in behind them, careful to not come in contact with the blackened roots that reached out towards her. Walking between the plants and the stone and counting her steps Nora turned to face the wall and placed her hands where there was no sign of the curse. She pushed against the cool stone, using her wind magic to give her some extra strength. The curse must have sensed her magic use as it crept closer, snaking towards her from every angle. Luckily, the wall moved inwards before it could reach her, opening to reveal nothing but darkness on the other side.

"A hidden door," Aeolus said.

Nora rolled her eyes. "Exceptional observational skills."

She summoned a small ball of flame and strode forward, not waiting for the curse to follow or Aeolus for that matter. She knew they both would.

Nora led him through the long passage inside the wall as sunlight flickered in through small cracks in the stone, like stars in the night sky. Her heart hammered in her chest and her hands were clammy as she walked. She felt on edge, the feeling of dread filling her. It didn't take a genius to know the reasons why.

Only a fool strode willingly into a cursed city, within arm's length of something that hungered for their death, and then on top of that, there were the Alta that could appear at any moment, a vicious king and a merciless Elementum Goddess.

Apparently, Nora was a fool. A stubborn one at that because she pushed down the feelings of needing to flee and continued on. She focused on counting each step, then extinguished her flame when light filled the passage from the gaps around a door.

This was it.

The city she remembered flashed in her mind and her pulse quickened at what would greet her beyond the door. The walls surrounding the city may have been taken over by the curse, but had the city inside borne the same fate? Would there be more of the curse? A destroyed city? Stepping closer, she leaned in, listening to the sounds coming from outside.

Nothing but silence. Nora was about to find out the city's fate.

She held up her hand and Aeolus nodded. His shoulders were tense with his hands fisted at his side as she pushed open the door and stepped out onto the street. She instantly regretted it.

"Look who's come crawling back."

Zaim stood before her, sneering. Around him, the familiar faces of the human Alta stood atop crumbling buildings, the curse splitting the stone and embedding itself in the walls. There were no civilians in sight, only the Alta whom Nora wished painful deaths upon. Preferably by her hand.

Each was armed with weapons strapped to their Alta uniforms. To Nora's horror, they were also holding guns. The metal weapons were clutched in their fists and pointed towards her and Aeolus. How they'd gotten replicas of Florence's weapon was beyond her. The gun had been a secret; a new weapon to fight the king, not to be wielded by his devotees.

"King Dominic will be very pleased to see you."

"Rumour has it he's dead," Nora said as Aeolus stepped to stand beside her. She felt more confident to have him by her side.

Zaim scoffed. "No curse could kill him. King Dominic is a God amongst us."

Nora rolled her eyes and prepared to summon her magic, her fingers flexing at her side as it rose to the surface, readying to take out the Alta if they tried anything. She'd deal with the curse and the consequences her magic would incur later. "Spare me."

"That I can do," Zaim sneered and fired. Aa resounding bang echoed from his gun, filling the air.

Nora gasped, her heart hammering in her chest, as Aeolus dropped to his knees at her side, crying out as he clutched his stomach. Blood seeped through his fingers, bright red and in a rush to escape him. She threw her fire at Zaim, rage rising inside her. But the Alta dodged her attack and before she could summon more magic, arms wrapped around her from behind and cool metal was pressed to her temple.

Zaim laughed, firing another shot at Aeolus.

The Elementum crumpled to the ground, face falling into the dirt, his body stilled. A lump rose in Nora's throat and she fought the tears that stung her eyes. She would not let Zaim, or the other Alta see her cry.

Another friend lost.

Aeolus' death would not be in vain. Instead of launching another magical attack, she instead let her grief well inside her. She embraced it, letting it fuel her anger and drive to stay on the path she and Aeolus had set. The curse pulsed around them with a root slithering closer as it sought out Aeolus' form. Another magical meal for it to devour.

Nora simply stood there, staring Zaim down as he pointed his gun at her now. He wasn't the only one. Every gun was directed at her, though she knew all were empty threats. They may hurt her, but none would kill her. No, they wanted to take her to the king so they could be praised like good dogs.

She held Zaim's gaze even as the man who held Nora leaned in, his breath hot against her ear as he spoke. "Welcome home."

Gunshots cracked through the air and Zane's smile was maniacal as Nora cried out, falling to the ground beside Aeolus.

August

The four of them stood in a line with the sun slowly rising in the sky at the edge of Midskopas. August, Erik, Tyler and Will looked out at the city, waiting for the axe to return along with the news of whether it could cut through the curse's roots or not.

Erik had finished forging the axe in the middle of the night and they'd been too eager to wait. Like every weapon before it, they were impatient, despite the previous failures.

Sage had taken the axe into the city for testing and now all they could do was wait. August stood, looking at the curse and how it enveloped the city, much like it had his hand and forearm in the weeks since they'd started forging dust inlaid weapons. The last of his hopes were all on the axe. If he had still believed in the Gods and Goddesses, he would have prayed to one.

"Still refusing to go in?" August asked Will, breaking the silence. Will was human and could have seen the axe's test for himself.

"I'm too nervous," Will replied, bouncing on his toes. "It doesn't lessen each time we do this."

"Same," Tyler agreed, dropping an arm over Will's.

August's heartbeat picked up as Sage appeared in his line of sight. She was a small speck at first and August was unable to see the Sage's expression, despite how hard he tried to focus. When she drew closer, August could make out the axe in one hand … and a black stick in the other.

August couldn't believe his eyes. He jolted forward, disbelief etched on his features.

"What? What's going on?" Will asked, his human eyes unable to see what August could. Will slipped from Tyler's hold and grabbed August's arm, shaking it. "What can you see?"

"She's carrying the curse," August breathed as Tyler started laughing. "She cut it."

"It worked?" Erik asked, looking to August and then back at Sage walking towards them. "It actually worked!"

Sage was closer now and the others were finally able to see what August and Tyler could. She ran the rest of the way towards them, a smile filling her face.

"We did it," Sage exclaimed, her voice cracking and eyes welling with tears. Dropping the axe and curse, she pulled August into her arms, and he held her tight. "We did it."

"You did," August replied, squeezing her. "You and Erik did. You've done it."

He looked over her head to see Erik, tears spilling down his cheeks as he picked up his axe. August smiled at him, and the man nodded, wiping his eyes with his sleeve.

"We finally have a way to fight this thing," August said, relief evident in his tone.

"I knew it would work," Tyler said, his hands on his hips as he rocked on his heels. "Looks like you can all thank me for the idea and saving the world."

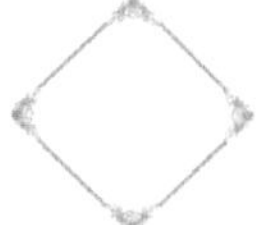

News of the axe spread like wildfire through the settlement and brought a newfound hope. Erik was busy working with Sage to create as many weapons as possible and August was doing his best to help out where needed.

Not only did the axe cut through the curse but once severed, the limb died almost immediately. Sage had spent tense hours looking over the piece the man had brought back and deemed it, for all intents and purposes, dead.

The axe was the hope the people needed.

Jasmine was quick to act, sending humans into Midskopas with newly forged weapons to cut back the curse as much as possible and free the city. It was a hard job, but there was no shortage of volunteers. Everyone was desperate to return to the safety behind the city walls, especially with the king's army drawing nearer each day. Everyone wanted the curse to become a distant memory. They wanted to rebuild. Move on with their lives. August wanted that too.

Unfortunately, the dust still didn't work on those infected. The curse refused to give up its claim on its hosts. Even after Erik had made it, there was still no effect on its own, those who were sick remained so. It worked with the weapons or not at all, Erik's conjuring only taking effect during the forging process and August had resigned himself to his fate. He would die soon and there was nothing anybody could do about it.

"Cheer up," Tyler said, sitting beside him in the room they shared. "There's still time. They're still working on a cure."

August ignored his friend. He wasn't in the mood to feign hope for something that wouldn't come to fruition. He didn't want to think about his impending death any longer. He'd waited around long enough and now it was time to act.

"I'm leaving."

Tyler startled. "What?"

"I'm going to Royal Bay," August replied, rising. He ran his hand through his hair. "Nora might have already killed King Dominic by the time I get there, but if I wait here I might never see her again."

"So we're leaving?"

"No, you need to stay here," August said. "You need to show the Alliance that the king's power only goes so far. You're the symbol of how he couldn't rid Valmenessia of the Mors Alvs. You can give them hope. They need to keep fighting. The king's army is only drawing nearer."

Tyler shook his head. "They don't need me, they need you. The son of the queen who broke free from the king's hold and now continues to fight. You are the inspiration they need, not me."

"They don't know who I am."

"Then tell them," Tyler said. "Let them see who you really are. Stop hiding. Nora isn't the only person who knows you anymore. I do, Sage, Will, Erik, all your super powerful friends you've accumulated," Tyler smirked. "We all know you and have stuck around. Nora isn't all you have any longer."

August stared at his friend. For someone who joked around a lot, he was insightful when he wanted to be.

"Stay," Tyler commanded.

"I can't," August's shoulders sagged. "I'm cursed."

"Stop making excuses to leave and start planning your next move in defeating the curse. Fuck the curse," Tyler growled. "Not literally of course but, you know what I mean."

'Tyler…"

"Look, are you attached to that hand?" Tyler asked, jumping to his feet, determination in his gaze.

"Literally." August's joke came out flat.

"You might hate me for this suggestion, but I have proven to be a man of brilliant ideas," Tyler wiggled his brows.

"I don't like that look."

Tyler grinned mischievously. "How would you feel about cutting it off?"

28

Evelyn

Frode had more to say and Evelyn knew as much. There was no way the Human God wasn't privy to secrets. However, getting the man to speak would be a difficult task when they'd ended their interaction so poorly. She would give him a few days before attempting to talk to him again.

Luckily, their first meeting hadn't been a loss. He'd given her some answers, or at least some information that led to more answers. Pieces to a puzzle, albeit a very big one. The pendant was one of those pieces. It gave weight to Kylan's words, that perhaps she had been born with magic. Frode said the pendant took magic away and she had been wearing it when she woke up. The possibility that Sloane may have taken away her race though was something too horrible to comprehend. What kind of person would do something like that? She clutched her stomach, nausea rolling through her.

She needed to speak to Kylan and hear his thoughts on what happened with Frode. Evelyn had wanted to see him straight after but had waited, wanting to sort her thoughts out before acting on her knee-jerk reaction. Doing so only made her realise he was most likely the only person she could trust right now other than Verida. Unfortunately, the woman never gave clear answers, so Evelyn made her way down through the dark towards his cell.

"Prince Kylan?" she called. It was cold in the depths, the air damp and the lingering scent of suffering all around.

There was no reply to her call, not even the shuffle of a mouse scurrying along the ground.

"Hello?" She stepped closer to the bars of Kylan's cell, straining her eyes to see whether he was curled up in a corner or asleep on the ground. She hadn't brought food with her and immediately felt bad. Her need to see him made her come prior to dinner time, but he may not realise and expect food. "Kylan?"

Something scuffed the stone floor behind her and Evelyn turned around, her heart racing to see Maggie walking towards her. Evelyn took a step back and Maggie offered her an apologetic smile, raising a hand as though to calm a wild animal. The girl's other hand was behind her back and Evelyn could only just make out she was holding something.

"I didn't mean to frighten you," Maggie said, her voice low. "When I saw you come down here, I followed."

"It's okay," Evelyn replied, her breaths slowing. "Did you need me for something?"

"I came to tell you that he's not down here anymore. They've taken him away."

"Oh, I was—"

"Not bringing him his meal," Maggie finished for her. "I know you don't just deliver his rations for the day. You're down here too long for that."

Evelyn bit her lip, watching the maid closely, unsure what Maggie was going to do with that information.

"I'm not going to tell anyone," Maggie said hurriedly, offering Evelyn a reassuring smile. "You're secret is safe with me.”

“Thank you,” Evelyn sighed in relief. “Do you know where they took him?”

Maggie shook her head. “Sorry.”

“No point lingering down here, then,” Evelyn sighed, taking a step. Despite Maggie’s promise not to speak of Evelyn’s visits with Kylan, she didn’t want to test fate.

“Wait,” Maggie said, holding up her hand again. “Lord Maker told us not to tell you anything, but I can no longer be silent. Did you know that my grandfather considered you a nuisance?” An amused smile gracing her lips. “I didn’t believe him, but he kept saying that you stick your nose where it doesn’t belong and think you’re above the rules.”

“Oh?” Evelyn tried her best not to show the anxiety that spiked in her. What was Maggie talking about? She tilted her head to one side. “I don’t think I know him.”

“Probably because you don’t remember any of your past. Just so you know, I don’t agree with him, at least not entirely,” Maggie said with a light laugh. “You do have a knack for getting yourself into trouble though.”

“It’s not intentional.”

“I know.”

“I don’t mean to be rude, but who is your grandfather?”

“*Was*,” Maggie corrected, shoulders sagging. “He died recently. I think you knew him as Phillip.”

The blood drained from Evelyn’s face, and she pictured the last time she’d seen the man before Sloane had murdered him. No one deserved that fate.

“I’m sorry for your loss,” Evelyn said and meant it. She may not have remembered the man, but she’d come to know Maggie and felt for the woman. “Were you close?”

“You probably knew him better than me, at least, if you could remember that is,” Maggie said with a shrug though there was sadness in her eyes. “But I had been learning more about him. He arrived not long before you did and had many stories to share. He knew you, Evelyn. You and your family."

"He knew my family?" Interesting. Sloane had told the truth about that at least.

Maggie nodded. "You have parents and a sister, but unfortunately your father passed away. Phillip said he was trying to save someone and lost his life in the process. Your sister is the lady of Forest's Edge now."

Evelyn took in Maggie's words, rolling them around in her mind and tried to think logically about what she was hearing rather than dwell on the news of her father's death.

This was all further confirmation of what Kylan had been telling her. Why hadn't she believed him? Trusted her headaches and the subconscious need to be near him? She'd been afraid and now it was too late.

Kylan was gone.

"You need to be careful," Maggie said, warning lacing her tone. "My grandfather said the reason he left Sorby was to go to Forest's Edge at Sloane's request. She wanted him to create a tool to remove magic and not to return without one."

"He succeeded. He must be the one who made the pendant," Evelyn said, voicing her thoughts aloud. His tool had taken her magic and was now being used by Frode.

"Pendant?" Maggie scrunched her brow making her look villainous in the light. "I don't know what it is that he made, only that he told me he didn't fully understand what she was asking of him until he returned to her."

Evelyn's mind whirled. "He didn't know what she was using it for."

"He thought he was helping her make magic accessible to everyone, but that wasn't the truth. She wanted the pendant to free someone named, Kai."

"Kai?" Images of the man in the crypt flooded Evelyn's mind. "Do you know who he is?"

"My grandfather said Kai is a Conjurer, an old one at that."

"She and Frode are using it to remove Kai's magic," Evelyn said.

"Frode?"

"He is posing as Mr Walker."

Maggie stared at Evelyn, eyes wide and mouth agape, and then she quickly snapped it shut and drew her hand from around her back. She held out an old book, offering it to Evelyn.

"My grandfather told me to give this to you," Maggie said. "If something ever happened to him."

"Thank you," Evelyn said, accepting the book. "What is it about?"

"I don't know," Maggie replied. "I haven't read it, but if he wanted you to have it then I think it's important."

Evelyn ran her hand over the front of the book where a faded Makers' Mark was inked into the cover. "Did he tell you anything else?"

"No, but listen, Evelyn. You need to be careful. If Frode is among us and he and Sloane can take magic, then this is bigger than your memory loss."

"You're right," Evelyn said, determination filling her. "It is bigger than me, but that only means that I need to stop them. To do that, I first need to find Prince Kylan."

Evelyn had no idea where Prince Kylan was.

Maggie had covered for her so she could search for him. She spent the rest of the day investigating the remaining cells, the many rooms of the estate, and even the other passages beneath the ground but she hadn't been able to find him.

After serving dinner and completing her late-night duties, Evelyn hurried back to her room where she retrieved the book

Maggie had given her from her bed before leaving to find somewhere private to read it.

Evelyn sat on the ground, nestled in the corner of one of the estate's many empty rooms with a candle burning at her side. She opened the book on her lap, dust spilling from the yellowing pages.

The Maker Family Tree

Evelyn ran her gaze over the page, though, unlike a family tree that had many branches, this one was a single line that ran to the bottom. Each generation had only one descendant.

She looked closely at the names and dates, her breath catching when she saw that the dates of each descendant born matched the death of their non-Maker parent.

Evelyn turned the page, the family tree continuing for a few more until she came to what looked like diary entries. Each one was written in a different hand, the entries filled the rest of the book.

To my family,

I am writing this in the hopes that you might understand why we must bear the burden of protecting the world. I know it feels unfair and to that, I say, it is. What we sacrifice is beyond anything anyone should have to endure, though it is what had to be done.

If we had not stood against the six, then many more would have died and the world would not be as it is for you. It would not be free.

They had to be stopped and it was our only choice.

Outside Valmenessia, I am the last of the Makers. It is my duty to continue the line as it is yours. Stay strong and remember that you are what stands between the world and the six.

Do not falter.

Evelyn frowned at the page. Six? At first, she thought the

writer had been referring to the Gods and Goddesses being trapped in Valmenessia, however, there were only five of them. Who was the sixth?

Evelyn continued reading the entries and as they went on, more and more heartache filled the pages. A similar story over and over again; growing up with only one parent and then the loss of the love of their life on the day their child was born.

Tears spilled from Evelyn's eyes as she read, her chest aching for the authors of the entries. It was cruel and she was yet to discover why such a horrible fate had to occur over and over again.

I find it difficult to comprehend the logic behind the decisions the Makers of the past made. Were the six so terrible that we had to sacrifice our loved ones to imprison them? And not only that but to take magic away from the world beyond Valmenessia? Was it truly the best course of action?

Evelyn reread the sentence, unsure if she was comprehending it correctly. Magic was taken away from the entire world?

They live, safe in their magical country, ruling there whilst beyond the seas we have no access to our magic and must suffer the deaths of our loved ones.

It doesn't make sense to me and I fear it never will, yet I will continue to endure and weep when my son grows older and feels the loss that I have felt.

Evelyn blew out a breath and wondered how the sudden loss of magic for all outside of Valmenessia had gone undocumented. Had the Gods and Goddesses been imprisoned so long that what occurred had been lost from all living memory?

Wood creaked and Evelyn froze, her gaze searching the room though she couldn't see much in the candlelight beyond her legs. The night was still as she waited for another sound that didn't come. Not wanting to get caught, Evelyn closed the book and hurried back up to her bed, the entire time feeling a deep sorrow for all the Makers.

August

August was pretty sure he was going to throw up.

He sat on a bed in one of the Healer's designated rooms with sweat covering every inch of him, making his shirt cling to his skin. He'd endured torture and subjected to horrible training, yet nothing had prepared him for what was about to happen.

"There's still time," Sage said, holding his healthy hand in hers. She sat beside him, her face pale. "You don't have to do this."

"If he waits any longer then we'll have to cut more off," Tyler said, making August grimace and his stomach whirl. Bloody Tyler.

Sage leaned in closer to August, her voice low. "You can change your mind. You don't have to go along with his crazy ideas. Tyler may have been right about forging the weapons with dust, but that doesn't mean he is right about this."

"I can hear you," Tyler sang. "And I have proven to be a

genius. They will write stories of me and my amazing mind. Ballads that will be passed down over the centuries."

"If you're so smart, how come you didn't come up with a better idea than cutting off my arm?" August grumbled, squeezing Sage's hand tighter.

Removing his arm from the elbow down wouldn't be like any other injury he'd had. He usually healed, either absorbing health from others or from a Lys Alv's magic, but neither of those two options would help him grow a limb back. Once they cut off his arm, it was gone forever. Bile rose in his throat and he swallowed hard.

"At least it's your left," Tyler replied nonchalantly. "So silver lining, hey buddy?"

August groaned, looking down at his infected hand. The skin was grey, the curse like a parasite holding the limb in its web that crept up halfway to his elbow. He flexed his fingers and frowned.

"Do we even know if this is going to work?" Jasmine asked from where she stood in the corner with Omari by her side.

August was the first person to try cutting the infection with one of the new weapons and everyone was interested in the result. If it worked, they could save so many lives if they acted quickly enough.

"Judging by the way the axe had severed the curse, there is a chance it will, though nothing is certain until tested," Sage said, offering August an apologetic look. "A high chance."

Jasmine stepped closer, looking down at August. "Are you sure this is what you want to do? There is no shame in changing your mind. It is a lot for us to ask of you."

"I'll do it."

"You have already done so much. Been through so much."

"What is a little more?" he said, and she frowned at him, sympathy filling her eyes. He looked away, not wanting to see her pity.

His life had been hard, but he wasn't the only one to endure difficulties, and losing his arm was not a selfless act. If it worked, he would no longer have the curse. He would be free and most importantly he would be alive.

"Very well," she said, stepping back and letting Omari wrap his arms around her middle. "Thank you, August."

"Any time," he replied sarcastically. He released Sage's hand and moved to kneel on the ground. "Can we just do this?"

Erik instructed him on how to position himself and August placed his arm on the chopping block as instructed. The rings on the wood stood out against the light brown bark, the fresh scent of pine filling August's nose.

If he could pretend hard enough, he could almost imagine being outside. They had chosen to do this inside, away from prying eyes and August was glad they did. He didn't want an audience beyond his friends. His pain was not a show.

Taking a few deep breaths, August prepared himself for the pain. It was going to hurt so fucking much, more than anything he'd ever experienced, but he kept telling himself that there was a Lys Alv in the room to help him heal as quickly as possible.

The pain would be fleeting, at least that's what he tried to remind himself.

"Are you ready?" Erik asked, and August looked up at the blacksmith standing before him with the axe in his hand. The first weapon to cut the curse.

The blade shone in the light, glowing like it was forged for a hero to wield in an epic battle. August guessed that severing his arm to save him from the Makers' Curse was a sort of fight.

August nodded stiffly and shut his eyes. Breathing in deeply, he sent his mind elsewhere. Eating cake with Nora, sitting on a rooftop with Evelyn, and joking with Tyler. Hiding in happy memories that he cherished above all else.

Blinding pain seared through him, and he could not stop the scream wrenched from his chest. Agony threatened to engulf him as he tumbled to his side; his eyes were still squeezed shut and every inch of him felt as if it were on fire as cloth was quickly brought to his left arm.

His mind screamed as it fought to understand what was happening, despite him knowing full well what had occurred. It was as though there was a disconnect inside him. Panic roared through him, interlacing with the pain and setting his heart racing faster than he'd ever felt and August was sure he'd have a heart attack.

Tight grips squeezed his shoulders and legs, the floor disappearing beneath him, and his panic soared higher, igniting his magic within him. It was desperate, a hungry beast, latching onto whatever it could.

August collided with the ground within seconds, his breath whooshing out of him as more pain twisted within. Though now it was slightly less than before and he could hear shouting as he slowly came back to reality. The hurt lessened, though it was still present. But it was enough for August to open his eyes and see Omari hunched over on his knees nearby, panting as he clutched his chest. Tyler was slouched against the wall, his features drawn. Guilt rammed into August's chest like a wild animal, fighting for dominance over the pain that still radiated from where his arm had been severed.

"Don't move," Sage said, coming into his line of sight and blocking out the others. She didn't touch him, keeping her distance in case she too would fall victim to his magic. It bubbled at the surface and he fought with all his might to keep it at bay. "They're fine, just stay still."

August attempted a nod, gritting his teeth and biting the inside of his cheek. Blood filled his mouth, the metallic taste coating his tongue. Despite the relief his magic had given him, it still wasn't enough. He held still as best he could as the Lys Alv Healer carefully moved over him. His eyes tracked her hand to his arm.

Or what was left of it.

Blood and bone filled his vision before the world blurred, and blackness stole the light.

August awoke in his bed, his body stiff but free from pain. He made to rub his eyes and sit up, only to have the reality of his new life crash down on him. It was a strange sensation to no longer have his left arm. His brain had not yet accepted that the limb was missing, and August was left wondering if he'd ever get used to not having it.

"Here." Tyler stepped to his side and leaned in, helping August to sit up. "It'll take some getting used to."

"I know," August replied, grunting as he adjusted himself until he was comfortable. He glanced to his left, inspecting the place where his arm should have been. Instead of the healed wound, his shirt sleeve had been folded and pinned to where his arm had been cut. Neat and tidy; nothing like how he felt about losing the limb.

"And it adds to your whole look, by the way." Tyler winked. "Fits the Dark Prince thing too."

August huffed, his lips tugging up at one side. "What I was aiming for."

"How are you feeling?" Sage asked, coming to sit on the bed. She ran her gaze over him as though he was one of her research projects. He guessed, in a way, he was.

"Tired, but fine," he told her. "No pain."

"Fantastic," she smiled brightly. "Good news is there's no sign of the curse on you anymore. I've been inspecting your wound and shoulder every time I visit and your skin is completely clear. I suspect the tiredness is from the healing, which is understandable. It is a lot for the body to endure. When the Healer came by earlier, she couldn't feel the curse in your body either.”

Relief swirled in August's chest and a grin spread on his face. He didn't try to hold it back, to hide what he felt inside. He was no longer cursed. He would live.

Tyler placed a bowl of cold porridge on August's lap and handed him a spoon, offering August an apologetic smile.

“How long have I been out?” August asked, looking down at his meal. He didn't have it in him to grimace at the food. It didn't matter what he had to eat because he had a long life ahead of him.

“Two days,” Sage replied. “You've been in and out but I don't expect you to remember. You were pretty delirious.”

“Said some interesting things that I'll have to tease you about when you're feeling better,” Tyler added, mischief glinting in his eyes.

“Of course,” August laughed. “I'd expect nothing less.”

“Jasmine and Omari just left,” Sage said. “They have also been checking in regularly to see you were okay. Will said he'd come by later, too.”

“Lady Royd and Omari would have stayed longer if they hadn't had to rush off,” Tyler said, gesturing for August to eat.

August tasted a mouthful. It was as bad as it looked but he didn't care. “Why? What happened?”

“As you know, the king's army is getting closer,” Sage replied. She chewed the inside of her cheek whilst fidgeting with her fingers.

“And?”

“Scouts returned this morning saying the soldiers are spreading word the Alliance started the curse.”

“What?” August gaped.

“Not only that,” Tyler said, sitting down on August's other side. “King Dominic is hiding out in Royal Bay like the coward he is. He's sent others to do his dirty work while he waits in his castle.”

"Fits his pattern. It's to be expected. He had the Alta, the guild, and even his sentries to enforce his will for years. So who is leading the army?"

"A Lady Elizabeth," Sage said. "I'm not sure who she is, but that's what the messengers say anyway."

"She's the king's advisor," August explained. "An Elementum who never leaves his side."

"Well she tore herself away and is heading towards us," Tyler said. "And here's the real punch to the gut."

August looked at Tyler. "There's more?"

Tyler nodded. "There's another army heading this way. From the west."

"Who?" August dropped his spoon, porridge splattering on his shirt.

"No idea," Sage said with a frown, worry dancing in her eyes. "They don't fly a banner. We don't know whether they are allies or enemies. We don't know whose side they are on."

"Fuck," August hissed. When was the bad news going to end?

"So, good news, you're going to live," Tyler said. "Bad news, we are being surrounded and there's nothing we can do about it but wait."

Nora

While drifting in and out of consciousness, Nora did her best to fight the despair that threatened to take over her. It was difficult to keep it at bay, especially alone in the dark. Her injuries caused her constant pain and made it hard to stay mentally strong.

She sat slumped in a cell deep beneath the palace in the Alta quarters. The stone was cold and moist and the single flicker of the sconce flame was a lonely sight in the all-consuming darkness. The lingering scent of blood and other bodily fluids filled the air, reminders of past prisoners, that were now mixed with her own. Nora knew the cells well; however, she'd only ever been on the other side of the bars before now.

The cells were usually reserved for special kinds of prisoners, ones that King Dominic wanted the Alta to play with. They were essentially waiting areas before an inevitable death.

Nora grimaced, thinking of the various forms of torture she'd seen inflicted behind these bars and how her hand had been forced to perform more than a few on those who had been brought to the cells. Many had deserved it, their crimes so heinous that torture and their subsequent death seemed too kind. At least in Nora's opinion.

There were, however, those who had purely made a mistake in the eyes of the king. And those whose mere existence had fault according to King Dominic.

The thought made Nora sick to her stomach. Not just the king's belief, but the role she had played in exacting those beliefs. It looked like the next part she would play in was her own death. As it drew closer she was slowly finding it hard to care.

Aeolus had died before her eyes, the man whom she only just started warming to the idea of calling a friend. She mostly liked to annoy him, but they had actually become friends in their own way.

It was for him that she didn't let herself succumb to her grief despite its attempts to tear at her chest. It clenched a tight fist around her heart, making each beat ache. Nora could deal with the pain if only to hold out long enough for a chance at ending King Dominic. She was determined to finish what she and Aeolus had set out to do. She would do it for him.

For all of those she'd lost.

Nora reached for Aren's necklace only to remember it had been taken. She'd gone through so much trouble to retrieve it from Charlie only to have it stolen again, this time by the Alta.

Her head lulled forward. Nora breathed through the throbbing pain that radiated from her thighs. Whilst the Alta couldn't disobey orders and kill her, they had still shot her. Twice in fact. Her legs had been bandaged to stop the bleeding but that was it. Infection would come for her soon enough. She just hoped it wouldn't kill her too quickly.

It had been tempting to unleash more of her magic on the Alta after Aeolus' murder, Zaim in particular, but she'd restrained herself. She needed to bide her time. They had come so far, and

Nora would finish what they started. Even if it meant enduring pain and sitting in a filthy cell underground where nothing but her grief and the Alta could find her. King Dominic would die by her hand. Nora rested her magic and her body so that, when the time came, she could use whatever she had left to complete the task. Including her life.

They had planned to kill the king and return to the Northern Alliance together, but plans never worked out the way you thought they would. Now she would have to find a way to do it alone. Nora refused to dwell on the reality that now lay before her in case the fear broke her resolve. The darkness and solitude did not help either. Death was coming for everyone, whether you were ready or not.

Nora looked beyond the bars to the darkened hallway, her eyes working hard to see the man walking arrogantly towards her cell, as though he were the king himself and not just a slave to the crown.

She closed her eyes. Out of sight, out of mind.

"Look at you," Zaim said, his tone full of bravado.

Nora kept her breathing calm, focusing instead on listing her favourite cakes. Chocolate cake, apple cake, carrot cake...

"I dreamed of this moment."

…Fruit cake, the classic sponge ... she chuckled to herself, thinking of August and the parade they'd invented to get free cake so long ago.

"Bitch!" Zaim shouted and Nora's eyes snapped open when his hands slammed against the bars. "I'm talking to you."

"No, you're talking *at* me," Nora calmly corrected.

Zaim's lip curled. "You never learnt any manners. Maybe I should teach you a lesson in how to speak to your superiors before the king sees you."

"You're not superior to me though, are you? King Dominic believes that the Elementum is the superior race, and seeing as you follow him and prescribe to his beliefs, doesn't that mean you agree?" She tilted her head to one side and slowly pointed at him. "Human." Then pointed to herself. "Elementum."

"Fuck you." He spat in her direction. "You'd think you'd be clever enough to quit the smart mouth now that your time is almost up."

"I'm unpredictable, what can I say?"

"Looks like your attitude remains unharmed, despite the state of your legs."

Nora smiled at his glare. "It's the strongest part of me."

"I have a few new methods of breaking a prisoner," Zaim said with a menacing glint in his eyes. "Shall we try them?"

"I'll pass."

"Now, now," he smirked. "Don't be shy."

He produced a key, unlocking the cell and stepping inside before locking it once more behind him. As he moved closer, Nora spotted a blade he withdrew from the sheath at his side.

Injured or not, Nora reminded herself that her magic wasn't the only weapon in her arsenal. She knew how to fight and if Zaim got any closer she would remind him of that too.

Zaim towered over her, toying with the dagger in his hands. Nora readied herself and as he crouched to her level, she lunged, shoving him backwards. She let a scream rip through her as her body burned from an invisible fire that radiated from her legs, protesting against the sudden movement. Panting, her vision blurred as she straddled him and grabbed his wrist, slamming his hand into the stone floor over and over again in an attempt to make him release the dagger.

Zaim snarled, punching her wounded thigh.

Blinding pain shot through her, and another cry ripped from her throat as he rolled them over so that he was atop her. Nora continued to fight through the hurt, punching him in the ribs, the only place she could reach. But it was useless. Zaim absorbed the blows as his training aided him in enduring her feeble attack. Her movements became sluggish and she struggled to catch her breath.

Zaim gripped her face in one hand and ran his dagger over her cheek with the other. Blood seeped from the wound and she shivered.

"Remember when we used to play like this," he said, his thighs tightening around her hips. "We used to have so much fun."

Memories of when she was younger flashed in her mind. Moments of him cornering her in the darkened hallways, blindfolding her before using her body to test out his blades. Back then, if she couldn't see, she couldn't aim her magic at him. But his twisted lessons had taught her one invaluable lesson; Nora didn't need all her senses to wield magic with precision.

"Was a real hoot," Nora hissed through gritted teeth. Her body felt heavy, her eyes fluttering closed.

Zaim didn't like that. He slapped her hard on the cheek, splitting her lip, and her eyes flashed open. Nora cried out as he lifted her head and slammed it into the ground. Then he grabbed her face again, forcing her to look at him.

Her magic was desperate to come out, to drown him until not a breath was left in his lungs, scorching him from the world. He deserved it, not just for what he'd done to her, but for taking Aeolus' life as well. Nora's heart stuttered at the thought of Aeolus and she fought her instincts to draw on her magic. She crushed her magic to the very depths of her being.

It wasn't time.

Soon, but not yet.

She could endure this.

Zaim's blade once again sliced through her skin, carving a line from her cheek to her ear. A deeper cut than the one he'd made before. Zaim dropped the dagger beside her ear, his hands like steel around her wrists as he held her there. He leaned forward, breathing her in, and the euphoria on his face sent chills down her spine. Zaim licked her cheek, tasting the blood from her wound. It made her gag.

She knew he was a psycho, but this was a whole new side of him she'd never seen. He tasted her, making sure to raise his head just enough for her to see him lick his lips.

"You're disgusting," Nora spat, no longer fighting him. All her effort was being used to restrain herself from unleashing her magic. If she did, she'd never leave the cell. The curse would surely come for her and she'd never get a chance to kill King Dominic.

"Everything is disgusting to someone," he replied, manoeuvring her wrists so that they were above her head. He held onto them with one hand, using his weight and strength to keep them in place. "And by the time I'm finished with you, I'm certain that more than one person will feel that way about you. This is just the beginning of our fun together."

"Oh, goodie. I was worried it was over already," Nora said in a deadpan voice.

He reached for his dagger and grinned menacingly. "Where shall I bleed you next?"

Evelyn

Evelyn stood in the crypt again with her hands on her hips as she glanced about the open space. She searched everywhere for Kylan and ventured below ground in the hope of finding him down there. It was a slim hope and one that was squashed pretty quickly.

Kylan was not in the crypt.

She wasn't going to waste her time, though. She stepped into the underground cavern and her gaze landed on Frode. He wasn't who she was looking for, but Evelyn would take the opportunity nonetheless. After what she'd read in the Makers' book the other night, she had many questions for the God of Humans.

"Before you try to send me away, I'll let you know now that I'm not leaving without answers," Evelyn said, hoping to appear brave despite the tremble in her voice.

"I have nothing to say to you," Frode replied curtly. "Now leave me."

"Actually, you have a lot you can say about what I want to

know. You also owe me."

"I don't owe you anything," he grumbled.

"I was a Lys Alv until Sloane put that pendant on me. She tested it on me before you used it on Kai," Evelyn said. When she thought back to when she'd woken up in Soby and the brief interest Frode had shown at the time, it had all clicked.

"I will not apologise for what happened to you," Frode said, turning to face her.

"I'm not asking you to," she said. "All I'm asking for is some answers." She watched as he eyed her, weighing her up to see if she was worthy or not. He was the God of Wisdom after all.

Finally, Frode dipped his chin. "Go on, then."

"I know Sloane and Lord Maker are related; that she's his grandmother and they are both Conjurers. Or what used to be known as Makers."

"Sloane is his grandmother, though not directly," he said. "I don't know how many generations are between them. She is a Conjurer but Elliot is not. They may have the blood but it still takes work to learn to conjure."

"How did Sloane learn conjuring if she is from outside Valmenessia?" Evelyn recalled that Sloane had said she was from a place called Devotion.

"She came to this country, seeking a way to learn how to conjure. I taught Sloane everything she knows by using Kai's diaries."

Evelyn recalled Maggie saying Kai was the name of the man sleeping in the crypt, Frode's lover, and that he was a Conjurer. "Why did she want to learn conjuring so badly? What does she want?"

"To free us from this prison and thus free her family line."

"And you helped because you want her to free you and the rest of the Gods and Goddesses?"

Frode shook his head. "I want her to keep Kai alive. He's

not just a Conjurer, but the lock binding all with magic to this wretched land, and keeps me from dying. The pendant will take his magic, free him and thus free every magical being from Valmenessia."

"So you can go back to the horrible things you were doing before? The deeds that got you trapped in here?"

"I made mistakes in my youth and have paid the price for them," Frode replied, sounding tired. "All I want now is to grow old with the one I love. I have waited long enough to hold Kai in my arms, I will wait no longer. I want to live out whatever life I have left and die like everyone else, with him by my side."

Evelyn searched his gaze. "You've been surprisingly honest."

"I no longer care to lie, lies are for a game I no longer wish to play."

"So you'll be free to leave Valmenessia?"

Frode nodded. "And grow old with the one I love."

Evelyn felt the sorrow mixed with longing radiate from Frode. Evelyn's thoughts went to Kylan, a headache joining soon after. She missed him. As soon as she left Frode, she'd go back to searching for him.

"Isn't this lovely?"

Sloane's words echoed through the crypt. Evelyn spun around to see the woman looking at them with wild eyes.

"What are you doing here?" Frode demanded, arms wide before the stone coffin as though protecting the man he loved from Sloane.

"Don't mind me, continue telling Evelyn all our secrets," Sloane said, stalking closer.

Frode glared at her and Sloane simply grinned in reply.

"Or would you like me to continue?" she asked. She didn't wait for a reply before turning to face Evelyn. "Did you know that Frode here was a very naughty boy when he was younger?"

"I know he did things that made him a prisoner here in

Valmenessia," Evelyn said. "That your family trapped him long ago."

"Yes, because he and his so-called brothers and sisters were determined to tear the world apart. The five Gods and Goddesses, and the sleeping Maker, moving from city to city to invade and kill all for power."

"I've made my peace with my past," Frode said through gritted teeth.

"Really? How does one rationalise killing thousands?" Sloane asked, raising a brow.

"What do you want Sloane?" Frode hissed. "Other than torment me with my past."

"I've come to the conclusion that Valmenessia cannot be free with you alive," Sloane said as tiny flashes of lightning danced at her fingertips. Her eyes glowed, no longer holding colour. It was like looking into the sun. "My family cannot be free with you still breathing."

Evelyn found herself trembling in the woman's presence, not from fear alone, but from the sheer power of her magic felt right to Evelyn's bones.

"Yes it can," Frode rebuked, unafraid of the woman before him. "You know how the conjuring works. You read it in his books. Rid the world of magic and it is over."

Rid the world of magic? Evelyn blanched at Frode's words.

"He could have been mistaken," Sloane snapped, glaring at the God. The crypt began to tremble as rocks and dust began falling from the ceiling. "I cannot take that chance."

She raised her hands in the air, lightning electrifying the rest of her just like when she killed Phillip in the woods. Terror shot through Evelyn, and she stumbled backwards, throwing an arm over her face. A loud bang echoed through the crypt at the same time a flash of light consumed her senses entirely.

The world went white and suddenly there was no sound other than a faint ringing in her ears.

And then there was nothing.

Evelyn curled onto her side and tugged the blankets over herself. Her head pounded as rubbed the heel of her palm against her temple, desperately trying to ease the pain. She couldn't remember what caused the headache, or how she'd gotten into her bed, let alone falling asleep. Yet here she was. Anxiety and dread swirled through her stomach, nausea rising at the missing information.

A scraping noise nearby had her slowly lowering the blanket and cracking her eyes open, wearying of the blinding sunlight. Sloane looked down on her, smiling as bright as the sun that filled the room.

Memories of what had happened in the crypt came flooding back to her. Frode. Kai. Sloane. The flashing light.

Then, in the blink of an eye, the rest of her memories came flooding in. Every last one.

Evelyn squeezed her eyes shut, the pain growing as she clutched her head between her hands. Agony ripped through her. Her entire body trembled as she braced herself against the onslaught of information. The pain consumed her. It was all that existed, all that would ever be. It coursed through her body and found its way into every crevice of her being. A scream broke from her lips, hoarse and desperate.

Then as suddenly as it all began, the pain disappeared.

With a shaking breath, Evelyn lay there, attempting to recover from what just happened. Sweat coated her skin, drenching her clothing, and her head stung from where she'd dug her nails into her scalp. No doubt she'd have little crescent moon-shaped scars hidden beneath her dark hair.

"Evelyn?" Sloane asked, sounding hesitant, which was so

unlike the Conjurer.

Conjurer. Evelyn knew for certain that that was what Sloane was. A Conjurer and a murderer. She refused to look at Sloane, not wanting to see the woman's face, to know whether it matched her cautious and caring tone.

"Why did you do this to me?" Evelyn accused through gritted teeth. "There were other ways to stop me from using my magic. You didn't have to take it!"

"I was facing two problems and needed to solve them quickly. Test the pendant and save your life," Sloane replied.

The latter reason subdued some of Evelyn's anger. Turning her head, Evelyn finally looked up at Sloane. The woman's hands were clasped before her as if she were harmless.

"The pendant works and you're a human now. But most importantly, safe. Both problems solved."

"So you can continue with your plan of ridding the world of magic?" Evelyn asked, her voice shaking as she slowly sat up, her fury rising once more. "How could you ever think that's okay?"

"It's what needs to be done and you should be thanking me. I made you safe."

"Safe like you made Louise? And the others Kylan and I arrived with?" Evelyn seethed. She clenched her fists at her sides. "I haven't seen them at all. Did you kill them, too?"

Sloane's gaze narrowed. "You remember."

"I remember everything," Evelyn hissed. "Every awful thing you have done."

"To others, but not to you." Sloane shook her head. "The conjuring I performed, when I took Louise's life, it is an undoing of magic. People are calling it a curse, but it's not. It's an undoing of the conjuring my family did long ago. A remedy to a curse that already exists here. It will rid Valmenessia of the true curse placed on the land all those years ago."

Chills ran over Evelyn's skin. Sloane was no longer just

planning; her plans were already in motion. "Your remedy is destroying magic," Evelyn said, the words tasting sour on her tongue. "All to free the Gods and Goddesses from their prison."

"You really need to stop calling them that. They are no deities and the price for their imprisonment has been paid. Overpaid," Sloane said, her chin set. "They will not survive the undoing."

"Frode?"

"He and Kai are dead. The others will fall soon, too. Their time on this land has come to an end."

"And everyone else with magic? Will any survive what you have done?"

"The undoing consumes magic. *All* magic."

Evelyn froze, her breath catching in her chest. "It takes their lives as well as their magic."

"It is currently consuming every magical person in its path as we speak. Every magical object. That is why I made you human."

"Why?" Evelyn looked up at Sloane. "Why are you doing this? Why did you choose me for this?"

"For Louise," Sloane stated, sorrow flickering across her face. "At first, I worried you and the prince would be a complication, but she brought you for a reason."

"Why would you care what she wanted? You killed her."

"She was my friend. She knew the sacrifice she was making," Sloane said. "As for you, at first I thought in saving you I would make amends for what I did to her. As time went on, I started to see myself in you. My life was stolen from me. Rian was stolen from me. I didn't want you to face the same fate."

"Yet you imprisoned Kylan," Evelyn hissed.

"Not all plans are perfect."

"I suppose that's your excuse for killing the entire magical population to free your family? Do you really think that's what Louise would have wanted?"

"She wanted to remake the world," Sloane snapped, her

demure persona gone. "I am remaking it."

"And committing mass murder in the process."

Sloane moved forward and gripped Evelyn by the chin, tugging her head up so their eyes met. A fire blazed within Sloane, her anger burning brightly as her nails dug into Evelyn's skin. "My family is the last of the true Maker line. Do you think my family should continue to suffer for you all? Is that it? You think your lives are worth more than my kin?"

"No, but—"

"This is the only way." She released Evelyn roughly. "Enough. We've paid enough."

"I don't understand." Evelyn shook her head. "You're condemning so many innocent people. What you're doing is worse than what Frode's family did."

"Sometimes you don't need to understand," Sloane said, clasping her hand in a fist. "Sometimes all you need is to trust those that know more than you."

"I can't do that. Unfortunately. You've told far too many lies."

Evelyn shoved Sloane to the ground and stuffed her hand beneath her pillow, retrieving the Makers' book before scrambling from the bed. Sloane swore as Evelyn ran from the room barefoot.

Sloane called after her, but Evelyn didn't slow. Sloane had sent a so-called undoing on the world. But it was a curse and one deserving of the namesake. Sloane had set it upon them all, and Evelyn couldn't sit back and do nothing.

If Sloane had her way, Valmenessia would no longer be a place of magic.

Countless were going to die.

Those she loved were going to be amongst the dead.

Now that she had her memories back, it was time to act.

Sloane had taken her magic, her race, who she was, but she wouldn't take anything else ever again.

But first, she had to find Kylan.

She ran barefoot through the hallways of the main house, searching desperately as she simultaneously avoided Sloane. Evelyn called for Kylan as she looked, ignoring the wary glances from the staff as she ran like a crazed woman through the manor.

Startled lords and ladies cried their alarm as she rushed past them. She didn't apologise or linger, instead, she rushed on to the next room.

Sloane was close on her tail as Evelyn ran through the front door, startling a few maids, and raced outside towards the woods. She needed to hide and plan her next move, and what better place than among trees where she felt so at home?

She would wait, bide her time, and then she would find Kylan and get as far away from Sorby as possible.

32

August

Preparations began for the inevitable battle. With an army coming from two sides, the Alliance needed to be able to defend themselves from both attacks. August worked overtime with Erik as a result, forging weapons both imbued with the cure and not. He couldn't complete all his usual tasks, but he did his best, making modifications where needed so he wouldn't let Erik down.

The clock was ticking and the enemy was almost on their doorstep. Both of them. Any plans of leaving were now dead and buried along with his hand and a good portion of his arm. August was still getting used to his new limitations, but at least he was alive. Daily tasks had become somewhat difficult, but he was learning new ways of doing things and tried not to let his frustration eat away at him. Others with the curse were now attempting to find similar success in removing the cursed parts of them or being test subjects for a modified version of the dust.

Apart from the two armies heading their way, things were

looking somewhat positive regarding the curse.

The rest of the Northern Alliance was just as busy as Erik and August. Everyone had a job to do and was busy from early morning to well into the night. The leaders were relocating those who wished to fight, positioning them in the southern part of the city now that the curse had been eradicated from much of it. Erik's weapons and the hardworking humans who spent tireless hours cutting the curse away had been freeing the city street by street, building by building. Not only had the curse been cut back, but each severing had weakened it. Magical people no longer had to give it a wide berth for fear of infection.

New fortifications were being erected and materials were brought from all over the city to rebuild and secure Midskopas' southern walls. Those unable to fight were moved to the northern part of the city where it was the safest from the fighting. It also provided them with a quick escape if needed. August hoped they wouldn't need it.

"I see you've stayed," Erik said, adding a newly finished sword to the pile. "Even after being cured."

"Your original observation was right, I guess," August replied, wiping his sweaty brow with the back of his wrist. His shirt clung to his chest, the heat from the fire and the nonstop work taking its toll.

"I know," Erik said simply. His face was tinged red, the only evidence of his work. He was affected less by the heat, the years making him immune to not only the fire but the physical labour. "I have something for you."

"Yeah?" August watched Erik closely as the blacksmith strode off to the side, picking something up near the wall.

"I promised you a replacement for your lost sword, but I think this is more fitting," he said, holding up an axe. The one that had cut off August's infected arm.

August stared at it, blinking at the sight.

Erik scratched the bottom of his chin with his free hand. "If you would prefer something else?"

"No," August said, stepping forward and accepting the weapon. "It's perfect."

He held the axe in his hand, flexing his fingers around the handle as he tested its weight and grip. It was perfect, that was no lie. It felt right in his grasp like it had always belonged there. Like it had been made for him.

"I also took the liberty of making you this," Erik said, holding a bundle in his arms. He placed it on his workbench and removed the blanket, revealing a shield. It was large, with spikes attached to the shiny metal at the front and an N engraved at the centre. "You strap it to your arm."

"Thank you," he said, admiring the shield, gaze snagging on the N for Natsky, his father. Erik picked it up and strapped it to August's arm without a word. It was lightweight and covered a good portion of his stomach and chest. He'd trained with a shield before, part of being an Alta was knowing how to wield a variety of weapons and the shield would be just that. Not only would it protect him, but he would be used as a weapon too. "I appreciate it."

"You more than earned it," Erik replied, watching August as he tried out the axe and shield together for a few minutes before barking new orders. "Enough dancing around. Get back to work. You'll be required to remain by the wall in a few hours and we have lots to do before then."

August chuckled, putting down his new axe and removing his shield. He fumbled with the first strap, but once he'd figured it out, the rest were easy enough to undo.

Running a finger along the edge of the shield, August thought about how much his plans had changed. They'd been completely derailed since leaving Fellbun, but he was no longer upset about it. The curse had scared him. Yet, he had been given another chance and he was determined not to waste it. He would make his time count, however long that now was.

August was part of the Northern Alliance; part of the community here. He would help them fight the incoming armies and defend the lives they held dear. The life they deserved. And after, whatever the outcome, he would seek out Nora.

Tyler had been right; it wasn't just August and Nora anymore. She was no longer all he had; all he could rely on. His circle had grown, and he couldn't leave his friends here knowing what they would face.

August would fight beside them.

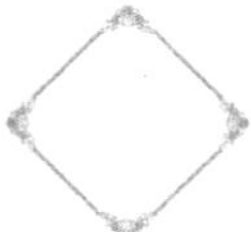

August had no idea why he'd been called beyond the city's southern walls until he saw her. He stood frozen at the entrance to Midskopas, the gates open as preparations were still under way for the impending battle. August's steps halted, and his heart almost did the same as he stared at the newcomer standing before Omari and Jasmine.

Jord.

She stood between two stone pillars, the big cats of the late Lord Akedale's family still sitting above it, though they had seen better days. Jord's long black hair swayed in the wind, the only hint of softness in her appearance. She was as solid as the stone pillars themselves, dressed in black armour perfectly moulded to the shape and movement of her body, accentuating every curve and muscle.

"Thought you weren't coming," he said, his feet remembering their purpose as he continued towards her.

Jasmine and Omari turned at his words and he schooled his features. They had called him here for a reason and August wasn't going to let his surprise distract him from that.

"Hello to you, too," Jord replied, her dark eyes sparkling. "I'm glad to see you again. I thought you'd feel the same."

"I am," he nodded. Uncertainty lingered in his chest. Jord had said she wasn't joining the cause so why was she here now? "Though, I am curious what brought you down here after you were so adamant not to come."

"Nyssa wrote me a letter." Jord turned her head to where the Lys Alv Goddess approached with Gemma and Carl by her side.

Like her sister, Nyssa was captivating. She wore full lips and high cheekbones on an endearing face. Nyssa's golden eyes sparkled beneath her long lashes and her hair framed her dark face before falling to her waist, tight curls cascading down her back. She wore similar armour, the same shade of black as Jord, the attire accentuating her form all the same. Where her sister came with no visible weapon, Nyssa had a sword, the golden hilt glistening in its scabbard.

Neither Jord nor Nyssa had come with any sort of guard. They were either confident in their magic's ability to take on any threat or they weren't here for trouble. August chose to believe the latter.

"It is time to act," Nyssa said, clasping her hands before her, a single golden band around one of her fingers. "We have been bystanders for far too long."

"Speak for yourself," Jord scolded her sister.

"Fine. I will," Nyssa said, her face turning solemn. "I have many regrets for what happened with the Mors Alvs and my inaction. For so long I let myself slumber as tragedies occurred. But I am awake now and I wish to do right this time. By you and Jord. I should never have abandoned her."

Jord glanced away, something in the distance apparently catching her eye, though her shoulders became less rigid, and her face softened. August too felt himself lowering his guard. Nyssa and Jord were here to help.

"Their armies wait to join ours," Jasmine told August, her gaze running over his features, trying to read his feelings on the matter. "We wanted to confirm that they are who they claim first."

"I have never met Nyssa before," August said and the Lys Alv smiled warmly at him, "but I am certain this is Jord. I trust her."

"Good," Jasmine replied, sounding relieved. "Because we need all the help we can get. Word from Lord Havilor is they've managed to find a way out but they are delayed. They are fending off attacks from humans wielding the cursed dead, slowing their progress and making it difficult for them to reach us."

Carl grimaced. "Despicable."

"Tyler and I encountered those fanatics on our way south as well. Speaking of Tyler," he said then turned to Jord, something suddenly occurring to him. "How'd you get here so fast? It took us weeks to arrive here, and we left before you."

"I have my ways," she said dismissively. "There are many tricks I've learnt over the years."

August quirked a brow. Alvs were known for their speed, but they couldn't move that quickly. There had to be more to it. "You could have shared these tricks instead of making us walk so far."

"It's character-building," Jord smiled. "And before you ask, the rest of our kin is here with us."

Nyssa huffed a laugh. It sounded pretty innocent though August doubted Nyssa was as harmless as she made herself seem. You didn't become a Goddess by being gentle and sweet all the time.

"Her tricks involve Conjurer's magic and swift travel on the Alv part. She'd have been doing her own character-building otherwise," Nyssa explained. "And the Lys Alvs are here also. Those who can and are willing to fight, as well as those offering their aid in healing the wounded, have come from Ferieton to put a stop to Thyra."

"Thyra?" Jasmine frowned. "She is here, too?"

"The extent of her involvement is yet to be seen," Nyssa replied. "Though we received word that a Lady Elizabeth leads the king's forces. I asked for a sketch of the woman to be made and I have no doubt this Lady Elizabeth is Thyra. I will never forget Thyra's face."

"She's always been power-hungry," Jord added with a sneer. There was no love between Thyra and Jord, though why would there be? If Thyra was Lady Elizabeth then the Goddess was responsible, along with King Dominic, for what had happened to the Mors Alvs.

"We all have been," Nyssa said with a heavy sigh. "It is time to prove it's never too late to change."

"Some of us matured long ago," Jord said, jutting out her chin. "Nevertheless, we will stop her and put an end to this once and for all."

The Alv armies descended upon Midskopas two days later, coming in from the west. August had thought there would be more weariness on the Northern Alliance's part, but the Alvs were welcomed with open arms. Spirits rose along with the number of those who were now poised to fight the king's army.

"Tyler found you, then," Will said as August approached. He picked another few bright green leaves from the plant before him, placing them into a box.

"Yeah, he said you wanted to see me," August replied, glancing around.

Will had found himself a small room above an old shop to tinker when he wasn't busy training or completing tasks Jasmine set out for him. Cuttings from plants August didn't know the names of were placed in jars with water on every available space, their stems growing roots visible in the water.

"I do," he said, putting away the box and rummaging through a collection of bottles. "I have something you might like."

"Oh?"

Will grinned, offering a round bottle to August, the glass a deep brown.

"What is it?" August asked, holding it up to the window in the hopes of getting a better idea of what it was in the sunlight. He gently swished the bottle, the liquid swirling within.

"Just a little something I have collected for a few friends," Will said. "It's extremely poisonous so don't open it yet. When the king's army is on our doorstep, just pour it on the blade of your axe and anything else you plan to stab through the soldiers with."

"It's always the quiet ones you should watch out for," August chuckled, glancing at Will. "Thanks."

"We all have our skill sets."

"We do," August agreed, pocketing the poison. "How is your gun training going? I'm dumbfounded at how Tyler is supposed to be any help."

"He's not," Will laughed. "He comes along and watches, makes a ridiculous joke every now and again."

"Sounds about right."

"But mostly," Will said, his tone softening. "I think he just wants something to keep his mind busy. When he's not with you, he's with me. I don't think he wants to be alone."

"He's not with either of us now," August pointed out, his playfulness half-hearted.

"The other Mors Alvs are keeping him company now they're here, but he'll be back, don't you worry," Will replied, slipping on his gloves and setting to work on pruning another plant. "Like us all, Tyler has a lot of scars and most aren't visible. The difference between us and him is that he refuses to face them."

"The king fucked us all up, didn't he?"

"Seems so."

"We have to win this," August said, clenching his fist. "We've all been through too much. It's time to stop surviving and start living."

33

Nora

"That's cheating," August exclaimed from where he lay on the ground with dirt smeared over his cheek.

Nora grinned down at him, pointing the wooden sword at his chest. "There are no rules when it comes to fighting out there."

"We're in the training rooms," August replied, slapping her sword away.

He rose to his feet, gathering his own weapon from the ground and holding it out before him. Nora watched him carefully, the way his feet moved, his hunched stance and the way he held his sword. She knew August's weaknesses like the back of her hand, could pick his tells within seconds.

The problem was, he could do the same for her.

Knowing each other so well often made it hard for either to win a fight. Except of course when there were rules. August was a stickler for rules.

Nora; not so much.

"No cheating this time," August warned her. "Or the next time I find us some cake, I won't share."

"You wouldn't dare."

"I would." He grinned and Nora lunged, her sword swiping through the air as he dodged her attack.

They moved through the dance they knew so well, trying to best the other. Nora loved training with August like this, when no other Alta were around to ruin it, and she could just enjoy it.

Nora let her mind wander to distraction so she stumbled, falling on her ass. August laughed as he knocked her sword away with his foot.

"You'd have cut yourself if that was a real blade," Nora said, rolling onto her side and springing to her feet. "You've only got one leg, Mr Rules."

"Fine," August grinned, moving to stand on one foot. He waved his sword at her, beckoning her closer. "Come and get me."

Nora didn't bother with her sword and ran toward him. The two laughed as she knocked his weapon away and they descended into hand-to-hand combat. Nora couldn't help but think of the families she'd seen on the street, the siblings playing with each other.

Being an Alta meant she had no family, yet she was lucky because having August was better than a family ever could be.

August tackled her to the ground and—

"Nora."

The memories faded. Nora squinted into the darkness, searching for the familiar voice. Rana drew forward, slowly coming into the light, and smiled sadly down at her. It may have been less than a year since Nora had seen Rana, but the leader of the Alta appeared as though she'd aged at least a decade. Her blonde hair was greying and flat, her face lined and drawn as though she hadn't eaten in a while. Rana's steps appeared difficult and she held no pride in her stance.

"What do you want?" Nora snapped, though it sounded more pained than the bite she'd been going for. She no longer had the strength to give anyone attitude. She was beginning to think she no longer had the strength for anything anymore.

"To see you."

Nora tried to spread her arms wide, groaning as her fingers dragged along the ground, and revealed every cut Zaim had sliced into her. He'd stayed for hours, savouring each drop of her blood as it spilled from her wounded skin. "You've seen me and now you can go."

"I want to help you."

"Let me out, then," Nora said. "Easy enough to do for someone of your ranking."

"I don't have a key and the locks have been changed," Rana said, coming closer. She gripped the bars and looked down at Nora. Her eyes went wide at the sight of the bloodied bandages around Nora's thighs and the cuts all over her face, though Rana quickly schooled her features. Rana had been privy to worse; a few injuries were nothing compared to the scenes she'd have witnessed. "Zaim visited you."

"He's a real treat, though you already know that about him," Nora replied with a heavy sigh. "Have you come to help me or watch me suffer at the hands of the Alta monster you trained?"

"I have many regrets, Nora," Rana said, frowning. "Standing aside and letting someone cause you pain being one of them. When I heard you were in the castle I wanted to see you desperately, but I wasn't permitted."

"The king let you come now or…" Dread filled Nora. Had she endured torture for nothing? The king would have never freed Rana, so the alternative had to be death. "Is the king dead?"

Rana shook her head. "No, he hasn't died. His eldest son and daughter-in-law, however, were victims of the Makers' Curse, yet they are the only royals who were. The king somehow survived, and Prince Kylan and Miss Evelyn disappeared hours before the outbreak.”

Relief filled Nora, spreading through her chest and easing some of the pain there. Evelyn was alive.

“Let me help you. This will heal any infection,’ Rana smiled though it held no joy. She knelt slowly, her knees trembling, then rolled a vial along the ground towards Nora. “I care for you even if you think I don’t. I did raise you and August, remember?”

“You did a shit job of it,” Nora said through gritted teeth as she moved to grab the vial. Unstoppering it, she sniffed it briefly then drank the clear amber liquid in one gulp, as though it were an elixir of life not just a simple tonic for infection. “We’re both killers. We’ve done terrible things and now I’m about to face my death after being tortured by a psycho with a penchant for lapping up his victim’s blood. I’m going to die here, Rana. I’m not sure raising kids is your calling. I’d suggest not taking any more children under your wing.”

“I did the best I could within the circumstances we live.” Rana’s chin jutted. The woman still held her pride after all despite everything.

“Why did you join him?” Nora asked. She’d never voiced the question before, never broached the topic of how Rana became not only an Alta but the leader of the group. “Why choose to be a part of this?”

“Because I loved him.”

Nora couldn’t believe what she just heard. “What?”

“I loved him. Back when I was a simple Elementum girl who came to Royal Bay with her family and the other elite families for a special Frost Season ball. The moment I saw him, it was instant and I’d thought he felt the same way, too. I stayed in Royal Bay for weeks and he told me his plans for the future, about what he wanted, and I’m ashamed to say I agreed.

“Then he started courting Queen Helen. I was devastated, but he asked me to keep seeing him in private, said his parents were forcing him and that he really wanted to be with me. I believed him. I was so young and naïve, so when he asked me to bind myself to him, I thought it was a mark of our love.

"As you know, it wasn't. I was the first Alta and for so long, more years than I would like to admit, I did everything he asked of me, tried to prove to him how much I loved him.

"A week after he married Helen, he faked my death and told everyone I killed myself because I was so heartbroken. My family didn't make a fuss, but why would they with the coin he gave them and the extra land back in Giland as compensation? I was made to hide for years until one day I was permitted to be seen, not one person who had known me acknowledged my presence. Not even my family.

"I couldn't even be angry or heartbroken, I was tied to him by the tattoos. I was made to feel whatever he wanted me to. I was the first in his collection. Most Alta he recruited were due to power or viciousness, but there were others like me. Those he kept purely because he didn't want anyone else to have them. Owen—"

"August?"

Rana nodded. "August he wanted to keep close, a reminder of the betrayal."

"August was made an Alta as a reminder and then what? Punished his whole life on behalf of all the Mors Alvs he never even met? That's fucked up."

"No, he was not being punished for all the Mors Alvs," Rana said. "Only one. His father. General Natsky. August was born of the general and Queen Helen."

Nora's mouth popped open, then she quickly snapped it shut. Rana knew. She'd known all along who August's parents were and knew the turmoil inside August for never knowing where he came from. Rana knew and hadn't said anything. She'd raised him, claimed to love him, and yet let him suffer.

"You knew who his parents were, and you never told him?"

"I wasn't allowed."

Nora glared at Rana. "And you can talk about it now? There's always a workaround. You could have made it known somehow. You just told me for fuck's sake. I could have told him."

"I can only tell you now. The king swore me to secrecy. It was more powerful than any other of his commands, but I am free to speak the truth now, as you can see. Everything I've said, I wouldn't normally have been able to say either. I have so much to tell you, but I fear I'll never get a chance. I'm dying."

Rana pulled up her sleeve to reveal her bare skin. No longer did she bear the stark inky black tattoos that usually wound around her wrists. Instead, the curse wrapped itself around her skin.

"I have the curse. Each day as it consumes more of my magic and the king's shackles I can see more clearly all that I have done. It is a strange feeling to have death creeping slowly towards you and with it a freedom that is like a breath of fresh air. I want to do right and make up for the wrongs I've committed, not just in the king's name but in the misguided beliefs I held when I was younger. I want to do right. For August."

Nora looked at Rana, really looked at the woman who raised her for so many years. She'd never been as warm to Nora as she had August, their personalities clashed more than anything, yet she'd looked out for Nora in her own way. Rana looked tired, yet there was a determination that still burned within her. Rana did not love Nora, not how she loved August. However, he linked them.

"And how do you plan on doing that?" Nora asked.

"I am going to help you. The king is alone here but for only Zaim and a handful of others. Everyone is dead or has fled, and Lady Elizabeth—"

"Thyra."

Rana tilted her head to one side. Now it was Nora's time to fill Rana in.

"Lady Elizabeth is Thyra. The Gods and Goddesses aren't real, well they are, but not what we thought they were. Aren, you knew him as Felix, he told me, but let's not get into that whole story right now. So Lady Elizabeth…"

"Is leading the army north."

Shit. "Ahh, I see why Zaim is even more unbearably cocky these days. He thinks his side is winning."

Rana smiled sadly. "Zaim leads what's left of the Alta now. They no longer have the tattoos that bind them to the king thanks to the curse, but they are as devoted as ever to him. Not to mention they have weapons that far outweigh anything I've ever seen. One is frighteningly dangerous. I'm told he learnt about it whilst North."

"The gun."

"Yes, they are all equipped with one and impatient to use them."

"I noticed," Nora replied, looking to her wounded legs and thinking of Aeolus and how quickly he'd been shot dead.

"The king will call for you later today," Rana went on. "You were right. You are going to die here, whether he executes you or you die from your injuries."

"Or I take matters into my own hands."

"Yes."

"How come he hasn't killed you?" Nora asked. "Why has he kept you even though you're sick?"

"Sentimental value? I couldn't tell you," Rana shrugged. "Let me help you, as you say, take matters into your own hands."

"I'm listening."

"Take this," Rana said, holding up a second vial with string wrapped around the glass and something that appeared to be a rock hanging from it. "They will come for you in a few hours, and it will stop the pain."

Nora reached forward, but Rana shook her head. Nora scrunched her brow.

"Before I give this to you, I want to know that you understand what you're doing. This will not heal you, only mask the hurt and give you a burst of strength. You will have one chance, if you don't take it, King Dominic will kill you and his reign will continue."

"Gotcha, piece of cake," Nora replied, her voice the steadiest it had been in a long time. "You did train me after all."

"You're braver than me," Rana said, her voice softening. "You've always been. Despite what the world throws your way, you always seem to find a way to make it seem like you were the one who came out on top."

"Seem is the imperative word there."

"Maybe, but it doesn't change the fact that you have strength far greater than many," Rana said. She rolled the vial towards Nora. "Take it when you hear them coming, not a moment before. Good luck, Nora."

"I don't need luck," Nora said as she held up the vial, finding Aren's necklace wrapped around it. Her heart skipped as she detangled the necklace and clasped it to her chest. "That bitch can stay out of it. She's never been on my side anyway."

34

Evelyn

Darkness fell and Evelyn continued to wait, watching the manor from where she hid amongst the trees. She managed to lose Sloane after an hour of chase, with the Conjurer eventually giving up and shouting about Evelyn starving out in the woods before storming away.

Evelyn sat up high in one of the trees with her legs dangling in the air and the night coming alive around her. It reminded her of home, and she wanted nothing more than to go back there. It felt like an eternity since she last set foot in Forest's Edge.

When the manor fell into a slumber, the lights within extinguishing, Evelyn made her move.

She climbed back down the tree and raced through the woods, careful where she tread as she clutched the Maker diary tightly in her hand. Her breaths were quick by the time she reached the manor, her nerves adding to the increasing panic within. As quietly as she could, Evelyn crept back into the manor determined to find Kylan.

She moved through the downstairs rooms, even venturing back into the dungeons to double-check check he hadn't been returned there. Evelyn made her way upstairs on silent feet. The second floor was the riskiest as it held the sleeping quarters of everyone residing in the manor.

Dread filled her as she looked around the empty hallway. She couldn't remember which rooms were occupied and which weren't. She stood silently chewing her lip as she tried to work out how to next proceed. Evelyn felt as though she'd never find Kylan.

She desperately wanted to leave Sorby, but she couldn't without Kylan. The thought of leaving him behind was something she refused to entertain.

Taking a single step forward, Evelyn's arm was gripped hard and she was suddenly tugged into the closest room where a hand clasped around her mouth to smother her scream. Thoughts of the attack in Forest's Edge filled her. The man with rotten teeth leaning over her. Her slit throat and the mark on her head.

Evelyn lashed out, thrusting her elbow into whoever had grabbed her. They released her and she spun around to see Elliot Maker standing there, palms raised. A candle flickered on a table nearby, casting the room in a low glow.

"Evelyn, it's me," Elliot gasped, his wide-eyed gaze running over her. "What's wrong?"

"Where's Kylan?" she demanded, trying to calm her breath.

"Hiding," Elliot replied at the same moment Sloane called her name from somewhere downstairs. The Conjurer must have kept an eye out for Evelyn leaving the woods and was now heading this way. Elliot looked towards the door. "She's gone mad. We can no longer trust her. After what she did to Phillip, I was afraid of what she'd do to the prince, so I offered to hide him. I'm glad I did because she killed Mr Walker today."

"You mean Frode?"

Elliot nodded. "Yes. I take it you know who we all really are then. She's my grandmother, but even I can see she's gone mad with power. Quickly. I'll hide you, too." He indicated to follow him.

Evelyn remained frozen on the spot. "Why should I trust you?"

"I may be of the same blood, but I prefer honesty to the theatrics of riddles. I thought she and I wanted the same thing. But I never knew the lengths she would go to make that happen. I want to be king, but not at the price of genocide. Look, I can't make you trust me, but what other option do you have? You'll be safe and with your prince."

Sloane called for Evelyn again, her voice closer this time. Fear trickled down Evelyn's spine and she made the rash decision to trust Elliot. Even if the only good to come from it was finding out where Kylan was. She followed as Elliot led her down the hall and into his study. He strode towards his large desk, reaching for something underneath. A click sounded and a metal pole dropped into his hand. It was long and thin, as tall as him with a hook on one end.

"No one ever checks the ceilings," he said with a wink.

Evelyn watched as he lifted the pole to the ceiling and hooked it onto something. With a tug, he drew the panel down and revealed a folded ladder. Elliot went about unfolding the ladder and then gestured for Evelyn to hurry.

"Quickly."

Evelyn hesitated. She was a chicken caught between two foxes. Either way, she was trapped. "I know this is a trap," she said, clutching the book to her chest. "But you protect me and Kylan from Sloane, and I will do everything in my power to help you become king."

"You'll convince Kylan as well?"

"Yes."

Elliot smiled, the sight reminding Evelyn of a fox yet again. "He is up there and you are both safe as long as you keep your word."

"I will," Evelyn said. She reached for the ladder with her free hand and climbed up.

It felt like an eternity passed when she was finally able to see inside the roof and relief filled her as she caught sight of Kylan. He sat in an armchair, one leg crossed over the other, a book on his lap and a candle on the table beside him, illuminating the attic. He was clean, his hair cut and combed, his face shaved and the blue eyes that looked up and held hers sparkled. Evelyn raced up the remaining ladder rungs into the attic. The creak and click of the ladder quickly being folded and closed away was a distant sound as she rushed towards Kylan. He sprung to his feet, his book dropping unceremoniously to the floor.

"I was looking for you everywhere," Evelyn said. She dropped her own book and threw her arms around his neck, drawing him to her as their lips collided. His arms wove around her, one hand on her lower back and the other gripping the back of her neck. The kiss was desperate, their lips moving with a need to be close. To make up for all the time they had been apart.

She'd known she'd missed him, but the extent had only become apparent upon seeing his face. The way his blue eyes had widened on his handsome face. She hadn't forgotten how handsome he was, but the sight of him had all thoughts disappearing from her mind.

There was only Kylan.

They broke apart, though she still felt his breath on her lips as she looked up at him. He didn't release her, holding her close as though he were afraid that if he let her go, he'd never see her again. His hand at her neck caressed her skin softly as it moved to cup her chin. He tilted her head, his gaze searching hers.

"You remember?" he asked, as tears began to fall down her cheeks.

"I searched for you, even before you I got my memories back," Evelyn said, her shoulders shivering. "I remember everything. I'm sorry I forgot and I'm sorry I haven't been able to rescue you. I made a deal with Elliot and we are safe as long as we work with him."

"Don't apologise," Kylan replied. She pressed her forehead to his chest, breathing him in as he stroked her back "You've done nothing wrong. Everything is going to be okay and if working with him is the price, then so be it."

"But it's not okay," she said, shaking her head against his chest. "It's worse than you can imagine and if we don't stop Sloane then everyone with magic is going to die."

"We won't let that happen," Kylan promised. He stepped back then gently placed a finger beneath her chin and lifted her eyes to him. "This is just a setback."

"A setback in a long list of setbacks," Evelyn sighed. "I feel like I'm constantly at the whim of the powerful, no matter how hard I try to escape I get sucked back in."

"It's not like I've ever been free either," Kylan said, tapping the collar around his neck. "It blocks my magic and not only that, something has been done to this room. I can't leave it, no matter how I try. But even with these obstacles before us, we shouldn't stop trying. If everyone gave up then those with terrible wishes to cause harm would get away with no consequence."

Tears began to fall again as she looked up at him, the determination in his gaze. "It might be too late," Evelyn said, then told him everything she'd learned.

Strong arms held Evelyn on the bed as her back was pressed to a hard chest. She'd never felt so safe, even if she were trapped in an attic by a power-hungry man and his crazed grandmother. Kylan had a way of making her feel as though the world could be crumbling around them and she'd be okay as long as they were together.

The night before, she'd felt overwhelmed when she saw him. Her guard had come down, feeling like she no longer had to be on alert and constantly watching for puzzle pieces or people trying to manipulate her.

With Kylan, she could just be.

Kylan must have sensed her waking as she was squeezed around the waist and tugged closer. "I've missed you," he mumbled, his breath caressing the back of her neck.

Evelyn's heart skipped a beat and she let herself melt into him, snuggling back into his warmth and embracing the way his touch made her feel.

They hadn't kissed again.

She'd always felt so nervous, her anxiety making her question everything she did or said. Somehow, with Kylan, it was different.

Evelyn turned in his arms, placing her hands on his chest as she looked into his sleepy eyes. "I missed you, too."

Kylan smiled, the sight making her stomach do flips. Evelyn didn't think she'd ever get over how handsome he was.

"You're staring," he said, opening his eyes and searching hers as though looking for the words she wasn't saying. In truth, there was something she'd been meaning to say.

Evelyn's cheeks flushed. "Would you prefer if I didn't?"

"Right now? Yes," he said in a gravelly voice that brought a smile to her lips and a flutter deep in her stomach.

She didn't get to reply as he pressed his lips to hers. This time, their kiss was slow and tender. Kylan's lips were soft against Evelyn's, his kiss gentle in an almost heartbreaking way. She leaned in closer, eager for more as he slid his hand along her jaw to grip the back of her head, his other hand pressed against her lower back.

There was no urgency, just a drawn-out passion as the kiss deepened.

Kylan had a way of kissing her like she'd never been kissed before, like every moment needed to be savoured. His tongue stroked Evelyn's as her heart pounded in her chest and he consumed her entirely, making her forget everything but the feel of his touch.

His hand slid caressingly down her neck towards her chest, where he tugged at her clothing and exposed her breast. A moan escaped Evelyn's lips as he squeezed, his thumb grazing over her hardened nipple. Her fingers dug into him as she tried to get closer, feeling him harden between them. She dropped a hand between them and dragged it down his chest toward the waistband of his undergarments. Evelyn wanted to feel him; to touch him, but Kylan shifted, grabbing her hand and breaking their kiss. She searched his eyes, fearing she had done something wrong.

"Evelyn," he said, his voice rough and causing the already building heat between her legs to spark further. "Are you sure?"

"Yes," she said, looking deep into his eyes. What she felt for him was overwhelming. "I need you."

"I need you, too," he replied, then leaned in and whispered against her neck. His hot breath sending welcome shivers down her spine. "You're all I want. Forever."

Kylan pressed his lips to hers, and she made to reach between them only for Kylan to beat her to it. His hand slipped up her skirt to the spot between her legs that was desperate to be touched. She gasped as he massaged his thumb against her, feeling her release building.

Evelyn breathed heavily against his mouth, grinding her hips into his hand. "Please."

"Always so polite," he replied huskily, biting her bottom lip.

Kylan helped Evelyn slide off her dress before he removed his own clothing and settled over her. His hands roamed over her body, exploring, his eyes dark and possessive. There was no hesitation in Kylan's touch, yet there was a thoughtfulness that spoke volumes.

"You're beautiful," he whispered, looking at Evelyn in a way that made her believe it.

She ran her fingers through his dark hair, resting her hands on the back of his neck and tugged him towards her. Kylan kissed her passionately as he entered her slowly, gently.

At first, it was like their kisses. There was no rush to their movements, savouring every moment of touch and building to a more desperate, quickened pace. Evelyn breathed heavily as she ran her hands over his chest, feeling his heart beating beneath. Each thrust dragged her closer and closer to the edge of oblivion. Their movements became more impatient, and needy. Evelyn held onto him; their eyes locked as her body revelled in the feel of him.

He was hers and she was his.

Evelyn's back arched as her pleasure shuddered through her and she clung to Kylan, crying out his name as he followed her over the edge.

Breathless, Kylan relaxed on top of her. His weight was comforting as he pressed his chest to hers, their hearts beating as one. She could have laid there forever with him.

And she would have, if not for the book she caught sight of still on the ground where she'd dropped it. Clutching the sheets to her chest, Evelyn manoeuvred out from under him and went to pick the book up.

"Where are you going?" Kylan grumbled, tugging the sheet to keep her close.

"I want to show you this," Evelyn said, returning to the bed with the book. She sat down and held it out to him. "It's a book about the Makers. The real ones."

Kylan took the book and carefully opened it, his gaze running over the pages.

"When the Maker has a child, their partner dies," Evelyn said, looking at the upside-down page. "It's part of the magic that keeps them here. The rest of the book is filled with diary entries, mostly talking about the pain of their lost loved ones. It's tragic."

"Does Sloane have an entry?" Kylan asked, turning the page.

"I, ah…" Evelyn frowned. "I didn't think to look. I read the first entries then merely flicked through the pages to find they were all much the same. I felt sad reading them and didn't think to check for Sloane's. But if she has a grandson, however many greats removed, means she must have had a child of her own, and a love who…."

Evelyn watched as Kylan moved through the pages, internally scolding herself for not looking for Sloane's entry. How could she have been so stupid?

"Listen to this," Kylan said, the book opened at random in the middle. *"Our ancestors may have imprisoned them, but now they call themselves deities. Magic has made the world forget them and their crimes, so they have created a new story for themselves. The five Gods and Goddesses of Valmenessia, children of the Makers. They laugh in the face of our sacrifice and revel in their new immortality."*

"So, that's why no one knew what happened," Evelyn said. "Magic made everyone forget."

Kylan nodded, looking at the page. "It seems only the single line of Makers was left to preserve the truth and the magic holding the Gods and Goddesses here."

"I read an entry that said magic once existed outside of Valmenessia, can you imagine what it would have been like to have all the races spread out all over the world?"

"Maybe one day we will see it happen again."

Evelyn smiled at the prospect, letting herself feel hope, even if for the briefest moment. She lay down beside Kylan and curled into him as he continued to read. As time wore on, she felt her eyes drift closed. She was exhausted, the events of the last few days and the safety she now felt being with Kylan, had her easily falling asleep.

Evelyn awoke to Kylan gently shaking her and she smiled up at him sleepily only for Elliot's voice to ruin the moment.

"Hope I'm not interrupting anything," Elliot said and she looked towards the opening in the floor to see him smirking at the two of them. "But we have somewhere to be."

"Where?" Evelyn asked, looking at the lord standing on the ladder. He was only visible from the chest up, but he looked every bit that of a future king in his embroidered coat and regal demeanour.

"Royal Bay, of course. It's time to stake my claim and the two of you are going to help me do just that."

After getting dressed, guards escorted Evelyn and Kylan outside to a carriage that stood in a long line of other impressively lavish looking carriages. Once the two took their seats the carriage door was closed behind them and they were locked inside. Evelyn looked out the window as Kylan's hand took hold of hers and she watched the lords and ladies climb into their own carriages.

"We stay put," Kylan said, shifting in his seat beside her and placing a book on his lap. She smiled, unsurprised that he thought to bring it with him. "Play nice until we reach Royal Bay and then we run. We'll have a better chance of escape somewhere familiar."

"You're right," Evelyn chewed her lip. "Though, it'll take weeks to get to Royal Bay from here. Longer with so many carriages."

"Just think, only a few weeks until we are free."

"What about this?" she asked, running a finger over the collar around his neck.

"We'll figure something out once we're safe," he replied,

leaning in and kissing her softly. "In the meantime, I found an entry you might want to read." Kylan offered her the Makers' book and flipped it to the very last entry.

"Is this Sloane's entry?" Evelyn asked, eagerly looking at the page.

"No. Her father."

I have studied our family history over the years and have come to terms with what is expected of me; however, my daughter is not of the same mind. She has never taken to my teachings and I believe I have failed not only her but our family.

Sloane is not content with the life destined for her and refuses to accept it. The pain from losing Rian has blinded her to any form of reason, so much so that she has left her daughter and fled to Valmenessia, determined to undo what our family did long ago.

All I can do is hope she will not succeed.

"She abandoned her daughter?" Evelyn looked up at Kylan. "How could she do that?"

"She must have been so caught up in her grief over the man she loved that she wasn't thinking clearly, perhaps she still isn't."

"Was there anything else you read of note?" she asked, closing the book.

"Only reiterations of what we already know," Kylan replied. "That the Gods and Goddesses are not deities but tyrants who tried to conquer the world and so the Makers used their magic to imprison them in Valmenessia. Thus confining magic to this country and erasing all memory of it, from what I can gather, everyone but the Makers and deities themselves."

The door of the carriage swung open and Sloane stepped inside, sitting on the seat opposite them.

"You two have been very nosey," Sloane said, looking between Kylan and Evelyn. Her purple hair was more vibrant than usual, standing out against the black of her dress. "But you are correct, to a degree. There are a few details you missed."

Evelyn's heart picked up its pace at the sight of the Conjurer. She gripped the book in her lap, skin paling around her knuckles.

"Care to fill us in?" Kylan asked calmly, though he'd edge closer to Evelyn, so that his side pressed against hers.

"Of course," Sloane nodded as the carriage rumbled forward. "Now, what can I add? Hmm, well first, how about the fact that the conjuring my ancestors did to trap this country's so-called deities requires the sacrifice of a loved one to keep its magic intact? That I, and those who came before me, fall desperately in love regardless of whether we want to or not, only to lose that love in order to maintain this prison. Do you think that is fair?"

Evelyn opened her mouth to speak but Sloane cut her off.

"And is it fair that I had to leave my daughter to be raised by my friend, to never know my child, so that I could attempt to free her and the rest of my family from this curse?"

"No," Evelyn breathed as Sloane's eye colour began to shift.

"Elliot is named after her father, not mine nor my husband. All because I wasn't there to teach my daughter, my family, our history. So when you tell everyone the true history of your country, perhaps you might like to include the injustices that my family have faced in order to protect the rest of the world. You may not agree with my actions now, but my family has given enough. It is time to set the Makers free."

She snapped her fingers and the carriage jerked to a halt. Evelyn fell forward, Kylan's arms swiftly grasped her and tugged her back into her seat. Sloane rose, unbothered by the sudden stop and stepped out before turning to face Evelyn and Kylan once more.

"I want you to live, Evelyn," Sloane said, gaze fixed on her. "I chose you. First as a way to repay Louise, but now because I have come to see who you are. You didn't let pain or uncertainty stop you from seeking out the prince. You fought, just like I am doing now. You may hate me, yet you can understand why what I am doing needs to be done.”

“But you’re killing everyone with magic.”

“I am freeing my family,” Sloane replied. “And if it came to choosing between the world and those you love, you would do the same.” The door slammed shut and Sloane strode from view.

Evelyn’s heart raced. Was Sloane right? She knew she would go to extraordinary lengths for those she cared about. But would Evelyn do horrible things to save the ones she loved?

“She’s lost her mind,” Kylan said, looking out the window in the direction Sloane had gone and drawing Evelyn from her thoughts.

“Do you think she’s right?” she asked as the carriage began to move once more.

“No,” he said instantly. “I think she is simply trying to justify her actions and feel less alone. If she believes you would do the same then it would mean what she is doing is validated.”

“Are you sure? She is right about me doing whatever I had to for the ones I love, for you.”

“Being right about that doesn’t make her right about everything else. You are the most selfless person I know. There is no way you’d act the same as her if the positions were reversed. She may claim to be doing all of this for the sake of her family, but her actions are because she is in pain and wants someone to pay for her husband’s life. You would never do that.” Kylan drew her close and she curled into his chest, sinking into his embrace.

“Thank you,” she said.

“For what?”

“For being you.” Evelyn smiled, looking up at Kylan.

“It’s easy to be me when I’m with you,” he replied. “I don’t have to hide who I am or be something I’m not. I can simply be.”

“I feel the same when I’m with you.”

Kylan leant down, kissing her gently. “Then we better stay together for the rest of our lives.”

"Good thing we are engaged to be married then," she said, earning a broad grin from Kylan.

"That is good, isn't it?"

Evelyn laughed, and the sound was swiftly smothered by another kiss.

The carriage made its way from the estate. When it made an unexpected turn, Kylan stiffened.

"What is it?" Evelyn asked, sitting up and running her gaze over him. What happened?"

"We're going south."

"South? But Royal Bay is west from here." Confusion creased her brow.

"I think we're going back to where we arrived," he said. "Back to where Sloane killed Louise."

Shivers ran through Evelyn and she shuddered. "Portal magic." Portal magic was very tricky. Sloane had said if it wasn't done properly then those attempting to travel wouldn't just die, they'd cease to exist. Evelyn's stomach did a flip. "But there's so many of us."

Kylan nodded; his lips pressed into a thin line. "She's much more powerful now. I'm not sure there is anything she can't do."

35

August

Walking into the Mors Alv camp in Midskopas, August was surprised by the warmth that filled his chest. For most of his life, he'd wondered about his kin; what it'd be like to be around those like him. He'd been made to believe that he was the only Mors Alv for so long, that he was all alone. It had been far from the truth. Seeing them now, revealing themselves and joining the Alliance filled him with pride.

This part of the city had been somewhat restored thanks to the Mors Alvs helping the Alliance to reinforce the buildings so they were safe and habitable. Shop fronts had been patched up, roofs mended, and walls repaired. Alliance members, Alvs and Midskopas' civilians moved about the newly fixed city, preparing for the oncoming battle. Anticipation was alive around him. The fight was more than defence for them; it was vengeance, too. Tearing down those who'd taken so much.

"I was wondering when you'd be coming by," someone said, and August turned to see a familiar face sitting on a set of steps. "Hiding from us again?"

"I'd been meaning to visit," August replied, sitting next to the older man, his grey hair now cut too short to be tied in a bun at the base of his neck.

"But you've been busy," the man chuckled. "It's good to see you. I heard you were going after the king, but I'm glad to have found you here instead. You are meant to be with us."

August rubbed the back of his neck. "Didn't feel right to leave."

"The king tried to take away your identity, yet you defied him by making a place for yourself. Not only with your kin but with the Alliance as well. Your parents would be proud of your resilience."

August didn't know what to say to that. His stomach hollowed at the man's words. Knowing that he'd never truly know how his parents might have felt about him caused his chest to ache. He hoped he made them proud, that they would be happy with the choices he'd made in life once he'd gotten control of it back from King Dominic.

"What are you two gossiping about?" Tyler asked as he approached. He leaned against the nearest wall and folded his arms over his chest. "Conspiring?"

"Against you?" August asked. "Always."

"I knew it," Tyler replied, clicking his fingers.

August should have expected Tyler to be there. Will had said he was avoiding being alone.

"I never thought you'd be one to stay true to your word," the older man said, looking at Tyler. "When the others returned not long after you all left the mountains, I expected to see you turn tail, too."

Tyler straightened. "Not everyone can be as brave as me."

"You joke, but you are indeed brave. Stupid, but brave. And loyal."

"Stop, you'll make me cry," Tyler feigned embarrassment,

waving the man away.

August rolled his eyes. "He's still insufferable."

"I can see that, and I also see you have a badge of honour like the rest of us," the man smiled. The gesture wrinkled the scar that cut through one of his dark eyes. The injury had completely blackened it, the coloured ring that should have been a bright circle was completely gone. "Now you truly fit in."

"The curse," August said, lifting his severed arm and twisting it left and right.

"Ahh," the man sighed. "Another thing trying to murder us."

"We're quite popular."

"Indeed. Well, I say let them all try. What's a few more scars."

August laughed, the sound filling his chest and shaking his shoulders. He would take any scars if it meant he'd get to keep living. He had so much to see and do, and he'd fight for as long as it took to make them a reality.

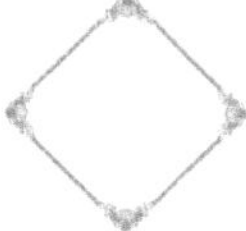

"I know Nyssa made it seem like she convinced me, but coming here was not an easy decision nor the change in my mind her doing," Jord said at August's side.

They looked south to where the king's army would be upon them soon, an attack as imminent as the coming Bloom Season. August turned away from where the Elementum filled a large ditch with water, creating a river that flowed before the city and would act as a moat to slow the oncoming attackers. He looked at the Mors Alv Goddess.

She was poised, elegant in her all back but also fierce. He wondered what she saw when she looked out in the distance. Did she see a threat or another bump along the road of her very long life?

"You still acted because she asked you to," August pointed out. "You denied me."

"Yes, but her words wouldn't have had the same effect if I had not met you prior. Nyssa's truths would not have meant anything to me. You changed that, reminded me that we are all one," Jord said. "I have lived a very long time and seen so many things. I let my fear lock me and the others up in the mountains. I came to believe we were separate from the rest. I wanted to keep us safe and, in doing so, I played right into King Dominic and Thyra's hands."

"They divided us."

Jord nodded. "Not anymore. We are one again and we will defeat them."

"And the curse? We have weapons to wound it. But I don't think they'll kill the curse. It's too vicious. Like it has a vendetta"

"I agree, this curse is looking for revenge," Jord said. "I fear it will not rest until it has what it wants."

August looked at Jord, but was unable to read the expression on her features. It was as though she were an artist's sketch before detail was added. "What do you think it wants?"

Jord turned to face him, her dark eyes filled with sadness. "Those of us that don't belong here."

August remained a short while after Jord had left him, contemplating her words. She was right. King Dominic had tried to divide them and as separate groups, they were easier to deal with. However, now they were united. They were a force that would no longer stand for his tyranny. They would make him afraid, make him tremble before them.

Turning back towards the city, August saw fighters move through drills in the bare land that sat between the new river and the city walls. Extra fortifications had been erected; a stakewall had been placed to defend against cavalry and two towers rose on either side of the ramparts with archers already taking their positions. Wolves, bears, tigers and other predators were armoured and already stalking along in fortification, whilst birds flew above, monitoring the enemies position and advancement.

Mors Alvs and Lys Alvs mingled with the other fighters, sharing valuable skills they knew and learning new ones. No longer did anyone falter at August's presence, especially since Jord had told everyone of his heritage. The news spread like Elementum fire and soon the entire camp knew who his parents were.

The leaders of the Northern Alliance now included his name in speeches, hoping to inspire. The king had not killed August. His army would not kill the Alliance either.

August ascended the nearest tower, contemplating all he'd seen. Their defences were formidable, the fighters strong and skilled. Yet, he'd been an Alta and witnessed the training of many of the king's soldiers. They were just as skilled, if not more so and they were merciless. The win would not be easy on either side, though the odds were stacked against the Alliance.

Nevertheless, they had a chance, even if it was small, and he clung to it like a rope keeping him from falling.

"Lord Havilor's forces are still days away," Jasmine said as August reached the top of the tower. "And Kaldom is as stubborn as ever. They continue to refuse to get involved."

The leaders were huddled together, looking out at the Alliance forces below and the country stretching to the south. Trees had been cleared, providing a clear view of when the army would appear on the horizon.

"Stubborn fool," Gemma grumbled. "How far off is the king's army now?"

"Scouts say within days," Carl replied.

"Will we be ready?" Jasmine asked, tugging her cloak around her shoulders.

Gemma's lips tugged to a thin line. "As we will ever be."

"The Alliance is strong and they're inspired by Jord's and Nyssa's armies joining us. They have something to fight for,"

Carl said, then glanced at August before adding. "And proof that winning is possible."

"What do Jord and Nyssa think?" Jasmine asked August. He'd been the middleman between the two armies, relaying messages from one leader to the other. "What do they believe our chances are?"

"They wouldn't be here if they thought we'd fail," he said, and she stood taller at that.

After relaying the information Jord had given him earlier, August looked to the distance as the leaders continued their assessments and went over their strategic plans. Nerves filled August and he felt a pang of loss at not having Nora beside him. It was strange not having her there, especially going into a fight. He wondered where she was and hoped she was okay.

Smoke rose in the distance, a single plume. Dozens more quickly followed it, billowing up to the sky and obstructing their view. Realisation dawned on him. "Shit," August swore, drawing the attention of the leaders who followed his line of sight.

"Fires?" Jasmine asked, an edge to her words.

Gemma slowly shook her head. "That smoke is too thick. They're burning greenery to make smoke, not fire. This must be their plan."

The smoke filled the horizon, and they watched as it blocked their southern view.

"They don't want us to know where they are," August said. "We need to be on high alert from now on. Keep an eye out for anyone slipping out from their ranks to try and flank us."

"Agreed," Carl replied, moving quickly. He headed to the stairs with Gemma at his side, both eager to adjust plans and ready their people. They didn't want to leave anything up to chance and August was relieved by it. "I'll ready the fighters. Gemma find as many of your Elementum with wind magic and see what they can do about the smoke. Any visibility is better than this."

The conversation faded as they dispersed, and August was left with Jasmine, staring out at the smoke that blocked their sight of the incoming army.

"So, they're finally here," Jasmine said, her voice soft as she turned to face him. "We cannot lose. This is it. If this stand doesn't hold, then, curse or no curse, Valmenessia is doomed."

That night, August sat down and wrote his last letter to Nora by the light of a single candle. The day had been busy, full of preparations and heightened emotions. The smoky sky only increased everyone's nerves. The king's army was close, now in sight, and the impending fight was no longer just words and plans.

Tomorrow he'd give the letter and the others he had tucked away in his satchel to Sage. He hoped Nora would never need to read them, but they were there, just in case. The letters weren't a goodbye. At least he hoped they weren't.

The Alliance stood a chance at defeating the king. They had trained hard to fight, but most of all, they had the knowledge that if they lost, the world they hoped for would vanish, spurring them on, too.

Nora

They'd come for her, just as Rana said they would. Nora's body ached as she was hauled through the dark dungeon, each jostling movement earning a hiss from her lips which were still wet from Rana's tonic. It hadn't come into effect yet, but it would soon if Rana could be trusted. Nora didn't let herself think of the alternative.

The Alta were not gentle with her, not that she had been expecting them to be, as they dragged her along. They snickered at every gasp and groan, revelling in her pain as they'd always done.

As they moved through the Alta quarters, she was reminded that this place had once been her home. Nora closed her eyes, not wanting to remember the life she had there. The cruelties that had taken place within its walls. So much of her time growing up had been some form of torture, whether it was the actual act or training that felt so much like it.

Her friendship with August had been the only good thing

amongst all the bad. He'd saved her from turning out like the sadists currently enjoying her pain. From becoming Zaim.

Today was the last time she'd step foot in the Alta quarters, in the castle, too.

Her final day.

Her final hours.

Maybe less.

She wasn't going to spend it reminiscing over the horrors of her past.

Nora cried out as her lax legs slammed against a step, then another as they ascended from the Alta quarters. There were so many steps and her legs hit each one, accompanied by a laugh from one Alta or another.

She felt them all, Rana's tonic hadn't taken effect. Luckily, the stairs ended, and Nora breathed a sigh of relief at the respite of being dragged along a smooth surface once more.

Opening her eyes, Nora took in the somewhat familiar castle hallway. The curse was present along the walls, clinging to the cracks and chips it had forged in the stone. Nora tried not to focus on it, instead looking out at the night sky that was visible through the windows. It was a beautiful night to kill a king.

The rest of the castle had not fared well from the curse either, the once exquisite place was now cracked and in disrepair. The curse had imbedded itself within the walls further down the hallway where it had woven through the stones, indifferent to the ancient paintings hanging on the walls. The blackened roots had pierced holes into the canvases, creating monstrous artworks, and knocked over artefacts. The once valuable pieces lay shattered on the cracked tiled floor.

Dirt covered nearly every surface.

This was not the place she'd once known any longer.

A chill crept over Nora. The lack of any sounds from living inhabitants filled her with more unease than the damage.

Dozens of people had once filled the place; the royal family, court members, staff and soldiers giving the castle life. Nora couldn't help but wonder what happened to them all. Had they escaped the curse or were their remains somewhere within these walls, waiting to be found? Now the castle was an empty shell. A void.

Or at least it would be very soon if everything went to plan.

She was going to kill King Dominic and the Alta. If she could have smiled, she would have. Instead, she settled for whatever expression her mouth decided it could move into thanks to the mess Zaim had made of her face.

They stopped and one of the Alta pushed open the door to the throne room and shoved her inside. Nora fell onto her front, her hands barely catching her before her chin hit the tiles with an audible crack. A hiss escaped her lips, but she looked up from where she lay, her hands trembling with the effort. The sight before her threatened to coax her old self to the surface. Turn her back into the woman who had worshipped the man in front of her.

King Dominic stood before his throne, his hands clasped behind his back and a cocky smirk on his pale face. Unlike the castle, the king was unchanged. Slick black hair styled to perfection, his clothing pressed and sitting perfectly on his broad frame. Gold buttons were polished to a shine and even his black shoes glinted in the light from the multitude of sconces along the walls. His hazel eyes glowed with satisfaction as he looked down upon her, his once lost Alta dragged back to him.

"Pathetic," the man said dismissively as though he hadn't been waiting for her to arrive.

"Funny, that's exactly how I describe you," Nora said, pushing herself up until she was kneeling. It was painful, but she refused to be prone before the king. Rana's tonic still wasn't working, and Nora was starting to think it had all been a lie. It was probably poison. The floor was hard against her wounded flesh, and she was sure she was bleeding again. The white tiles were tarnished by her dirty knees and the blood that seeped from them.

Unlike the hallways, the throne room had remained untouched by any disrepair, much like the king. There was no sign of the curse, no damage caused by its desire for magic or lack of staff to tend to it. King Dominic's red and gold banners hung from the ceiling, the fabric draping all the way to the polished tile floor. Portraits of past royals adorned the walls, the subjects posing proudly in their finery.

Arrogant bastards.

Behind the throne, large windows looked out towards the city, though she couldn't see it. Nora could only imagine the view. It was once a beautiful sight, now it would have brought nothing but sadness. A city fallen.

One of the Alta sneered at Nora's snide comment and took a step towards her with a raised hand. She braced herself only to have the king hold up his hand to halt them. Nora met King Dominic's gaze with a look of determination. He loved feeling superior, something that Nora hadn't cared to look into when she was an Alta but now that she wasn't tied to him, she was able to see what lay beneath the exterior he worked so hard to uphold.

The fear.

The king was a scared bigoted man. He feared what he couldn't control, what he couldn't understand. His inability to think beyond himself, to understand others, had twisted him into a hateful creature. Rather than let the world shape him, he chose instead to try and shape the world.

"Are you proud of what your little rebellion has done?" he asked, his upper lip tugging up at one side. "The curse they have subjected the world to?"

"The curse has nothing to do with us," Nora said, holding her head high. She expected pain but the movement held none. Relief sparked through her, and she suddenly felt light, capable of anything. Rana hadn't deceived her after all.

"Is that what they told you? How foolish you are."

"We're fighting it, just like everyone else."

"Yes, because they had no foresight of the destruction it would cause. I wanted to create a better world; one you would have prospered in if you'd only behaved. Instead, you have sided with rebels and destroyed Valmenessia."

"See, this comes back to what I said before," Nora said, her tone almost bored. "You're pathetic because you believe your own lies. You're delusional."

"The delusional one is you," an Alta behind her snarled, smacking her on the back of the head.

Nora fell forward, though this time she caught herself easily. Straightening again, she glared at King Dominic who was smiling, enjoying her pain.

"It is a tragedy how you stand in the way of your own race's greatness," the king sneered. "You say you want peace but do everything you can to perpetuate a world that is far from peaceful. The only way for peace is through equality. We can only be equal if we are the same. One race. Elementum."

"There are grains of dirt with more intelligence than you," Nora spat. "Even as Elementum we are all different. Your rationale is beyond delusional and you are using it as a way to push your real agenda. You don't want peace, you're just a bigot who hates the other races. Own it, don't try to hide behind some notion of peace."

"I do not hide."

Nora scoffed. "You literally created the Alta, an all but invisible group, to do your dirty work where no one could see."

"The Alta was made to right the wrongs of the land. Many are blind to what truly needs to be done."

"I count you among them."

Another blow landed to the back of her head and she couldn't contain the cry that escaped her lips. Though she was able to remain upright this time.

"To think you believed you could escape me," the king said smugly. "How mistaken you were. Now your time has come to learn your lesson. Today you will face your fate."

"I'm really looking forward to it," Nora said, plastering the widest smile she could on her face. "Trust me, I am. But I was wondering if I could have one last request before you do your thing?"

Zaim appeared beside her, gripping her hair tightly in his hand and holding a gun to her temple. "Enough with your smart mouth. Show some respect."

Her gaze snapped to him, challenging him. "Or what?"

"Or I won't hear your request," the king boomed, and Nora could have sworn the walls rattled. "I've had it with your nonsense. Punish her."

Zaim grinned and then slammed the gun hard against her head. Nora fell to the side, blood spilling from the spilt in her skin. Her ears rang and her vision blurred as she landed on the tiles. She fought back the urge to vomit. Bright side? The pain was short-lived. Rana's tonic was coming to the rescue and numbing it.

"Now," King Dominic said. Nora blinked, the Elementum king becoming clearer with time. "What do you want?"

"I'm too shy to say with everyone listening," Nora replied, getting to her knees once more.

"She's hardly shy," Zaim sneered, gripping her arm tightly and stopping her from shuffling forward. "I've never known someone to say every little thing that pops into their head like she does."

"Maybe," she said, reaching for her magic. "But this is different."

King Dominic took a few steps forward then pulled up short and laughed, the sound echoing off the walls. "You must think I'm an idiot. I've had enough."

Nora flexed her fingers at her side, feeling her magic rise.

She'd use it soon. Every last drop. She'd take out everyone in the room and unleash everything she had in one last effort to kill the king. She'd been afraid after Rana left her in the cell. The reality of her near end finally filled her and had her shaking, yet now she embraced the feeling. She let herself feel the fear, then twisted it, forging it into a weapon. Her fear was her strength. Not her fear of dying, but her fear of what would happen to those she loved for not acting. For letting King Dominic live.

King Dominic stared her down. "Kill—"

He never got to finish his sentence. Nora pushed to her feet, her legs wobbling from the movement. She may have had no pain, but her injuries were still very much present. Blood warmed her thighs as she dove for the king, unleashing all her magic. She let everything she had loose on the man, throwing all of it.

All her pain, her anger, her fear.

Nora unleashed it all.

Her magic burst through her. Fire, wind and water came together in a ferocious storm that shook the room and everything within.

The world turned bright, hot, and loud. Every one of her senses ignited. Water rushed in torrents as her fire combusted and her wind roared and tore the throne room apart. The walls shuddered and the ceiling cracked, the starry night sky now visible as the curse hurried in, eager to accept the invite and lap up the magic it was being gifted.

The entire castle trembled at Nora's wrath.

Nora fell onto the king, pushing him to the ground with her remaining strength. The man howled, his flesh burning as her flames ate at him with the eagerness of a starving animal. She focused solely on the king beneath her, her magic flowing out of her in a torrent.

This had to kill him.

There was no way he could come back from this.

Gritting her teeth, she let her magic consume everything,

pushing it to near breaking point. The Alta screamed, though their cries were short lived as her magic stole their lives. Nora's mind was a mess, her body exhausted beyond measure, but she would continue until there was nothing left; until she was dead, and she'd taken everyone in the room with her.

King Dominic's magic rose beneath her, but her will was stronger. Nora's magic claimed his and turned it against its master until the king's final scream rang in her ears. He was torn to pieces beneath her, his body ripped apart and burnt until there was nothing but ash that blew away on her wind. It was over.

Nora collapsed to the ashy tiles, exhausted beyond measure.

Her vision darkened, her breath like embers that burned her throat and tore at her chest. Visions of her life filled her mind. Her home with her mother and brother, growing up with August, her friends in Forest's Edge.

Sage.

Tears streamed from her eyes, her limbs spasming as the last of her magic, of her, was spent. Embers flickered in the air, a light breeze caressing her limbs as flecks of raindrops fell to the tiles.

And then, everything stopped.

The sound of her breathing was all she could hear beyond the ringing in her ears, her vision going completely dark.

She prayed, not to anyone in particular because that had all been one giant fucking lie, and begged for her actions to have been enough. He couldn't come back from what she'd done.

It had to be enough.

Laying there, Nora accepted her fate and waited for her time to come.

A voice called to her in the dark.

Death had come for her.

Evelyn

The carriage hadn't stopped since Sloane's abrupt departure the day before and their journey continued south. Evelyn had spent the entire journey staring out the window whilst Kylan read more of the Maker book, occasionally reading out loud to share something interesting with Evelyn.

There had been no new information within its pages, just more sad tales of love lost and sacrifices made. Her heart ached at the parts Kylan read to her and she'd found herself wishing she could go back in time and change it. Prevent all the loss from ever happening.

Eventually, the carriage began a climb upwards and dread pooled in Evelyn's stomach. The possibility of where they were going dawned on her and spiked fear deep within her.

Elliot and Sloane were taking them back to where they had first arrived in Sorby. To the garden in the mountains. Her hands trembled as they drew closer and no amount of holding them or sitting on them could stop the tremors.

Once they'd arrived, Evelyn hadn't been able to stop staring at the pit where she'd last seen Louise's lifeless body. Memories flashed through her mind of her friend's hopeful face and the blood that had spilled from her chest. It had felt like an eternity since that moment.

A lifetime.

Now, Louise's body was no longer there. Instead, the pit was filled with blackened limbs that squirmed, trying to escape the golden barrier Sloane had placed around it. The smell of rot filled the air, a contrast to the beautiful garden around them, and Evelyn shivered, watching as each limb twisted and turned.

"Now what?" One of the lords asked, his disgust clear as he glanced around with his upper lip raised. "Why have you brought us here?"

Every lord and lady Elliot had invited to Sorby was present, along with a handful of guards. The rest of their forces, she assumed having heard about them at one of the many dinners she'd served at, would be docking their boats in Royal Bay soon enough.

The people of Valmenessia were fighting amongst themselves, completely unaware of those who wished to take the country out from under them.

"Now we travel," Sloane replied, her voice like an upbeat song. "Make sure you're within the black circle or you'll either be left behind or killed. Portal magic is tricky work. If you don't complete the travel you are lost."

"Lost? As in transported somewhere else?"

"No, lost as in neither alive nor dead."

Faces blanched as they pushed closer together. Evelyn felt Kylan's arms wrap around her and draw her close. She leaned into him, seeking his comfort.

"How does this work?" another lord asked, directing his question to Elliot. The man's eyes were wide with panic.

But Elliot simply smiled, as calm as Sloane. "This is portal magic, though of a different kind to what Sloane has done before. The magic you see here," he waved a hand towards the pit and the tendrils thrashing around within. Evelyn grimaced at the larger ones which pulsed. "Is present throughout all Valmenessia, meaning Sloane can take us anywhere we like. As we wish to go to Royal Bay, that's where she will lead us."

"If she hasn't done it before, how do you know she won't kill us?" a lady asked, her hands clasped at her chest.

"Trust," Elliot replied. "I trust not only Sloane but her magic. I urge you to do the same."

Because that's easy. Evelyn thought, shutting her eyes and trying to ignore everyone else. She didn't want to hear any more talk of the portal. She was well aware of the risks she was once again being forced to take. Instead, she rested her head on Kylan's chest and listened to the beat of his heart. The sound was a comfort despite what was happening around her. All she had to do was get through this, and then when they arrived in Royal Bay, she and Kylan would run. They'd escape north, back to her family and friends and never look back.

"Here we go," Kylan whispered into her ear, his hold tightening as Sloane began to chant.

A breeze blew at Evelyn's skirts, though, unlike the first time she'd travelled by portal magic, there was no smoke, no feeling of being in the centre of a storm. This time she felt a tug in her belly and the strange sensation of being pressed in at all sides. She kept her eyes closed as the sensation of being squeezed surrounded her and hoped she wouldn't get lost along the way.

Her feet hit solid ground and Evelyn opened her eyes to the destruction around her. At the centre of it all, was Nora.

Evelyn's heart leapt into her throat at the sight of Nora. The Elementum was bruised and bloodied, and Evelyn feared she may no longer be alive. She rushed forward without another thought, holding her hands high, protectively. The roots of the curse froze in their path. She was under no delusion that she had any power over the wretched thing; Sloane, however, did and there was only so much longer the Conjurer would wait.

"Nora," Evelyn breathed. She stepped forward only to have Kylan place a hand on her shoulder, keeping her in place. "She's my friend." She looked to Sloane with pleading eyes, hoping the Conjurer would help in some way.

"And why should that concern us?" one of the lords asked, grimacing at Nora lying still on the tiles.

Nora was petite on a good day, but she seemed smaller than usual. Her dark hair was covered in ash, bloody seeping from wounds on her pale skin.

Around them, the throne room was a crumbling mess, a far cry from the room Evelyn had once been in. The walls had cracks zigzagged through them, the art that used to adorn them so proudly now lay broken on the floor. The throne was pitch black except for the embers that were still burning the once-wooden seat. All the glory that had filled the room was now dust.

"Because this girl has killed the king. She's clearly disposed of any opposition that might have concerned you as well," Sloane answered in a tone that made Evelyn surprised that she didn't finish the sentence with 'you idiot.'

"I rather doubt any opposition would have been much of a threat," the lord replied, clearly not taking note of Sloane's tone. "If this one woman could kill them all."

Sloane waved her hand and Nora gasped; her breath raspy. She curled into a ball as she coughed, her entire being convulsing. Kylan let go of Evelyn and she hurried to Nora's side, falling to her knees beside the Elementum.

"Evie," Nora gasped, gripping Evelyn's arm tightly.

"I'm here," Evelyn replied, helping Nora to sit. "It's going to be okay."

Nora looked around in a daze, her brown eyes taking in her

surroundings. She was covered in dirt and blood though, as far as Evelyn could see, there was no injury on her. Evelyn could have sworn there had been a few cuts before, if not more.

"I'm supposed to be dead," Nora said as though she too was surprised by her miraculous health.

"You were close," said Sloane, smiling smugly. "On the brink, in fact. But no, you live again. You're welcome."

Nora raised a brow at Evelyn.

"That's Sloane."

"Uh huh," Nora replied as if Evelyn's explanation made all the sense in the world. The lords and ladies continued to bicker with Sloane, but Nora seemed unbothered. More interested in Evelyn. "Your eyes?"

"Her magic was taken," Kylan said, coming to crouch beside Evelyn. "She is human."

"How'd they do that?" Nora asked, tilting her head to one side.

"Phillip, he gave Sloane—"

"Sage's pendant," Nora said, looking Evelyn over. "It absorbed your magic."

Kylan scrunched his brow. "How'd you know about that?"

"Sage is my girlfriend," Nora said with a broad grin.

"Where is the king and the rest of the royal family?" One of the lords demanded, face red as he interrupted the trio.

"The king is a little over there," Nora pointed to a pile of ash and then to her shirt. "A little here. Did you ever meet him? Clingiest bastard I'd ever met, even in death he can't seem to let me be without him. As for the royal family, I believe Prince Kylan is the last member alive."

Evelyn grimaced, glancing at Kylan beside her. He may not have liked his father, but he was still family. It couldn't have been easy hearing of his father's death like this, or his brother's. "Who were the others?" The lady who wanted to claim Forest's Edge asked, nudging one of the bodies with her polished shoe.

"A couple of idiots looking to gain power," Nora said. "Always knew they were delusional, told them as much, but some people refuse to listen."

"Do you always talk like this?" the woman asked, lips pursed. "Prattle on."

"You call it prattle, others call it insight," Nora shrugged.

"Where's Thyra?" Sloane asked, speaking over the woman who was left with her mouth open like she was trying to catch flies with it.

"I was told she went with the army north, though I was also told the king was dead before getting here, so interpret that as you will," Nora said with a wave of her hand. "The Alliance have their own forces rallying in Midskopas for the army's arrival so whether she's with the army or not, she'll come out of the woodwork soon, I would think."

"Midskopas," Sloane nodded. "I'd heard as much." She turned to Evelyn. "Gather your friend, I assume she wants to come, too."

"What?" Elliot's eyes widened. "You're leaving? We only just arrived."

"Yes, I brought you here to help you take the throne. Well, there it is and now I must leave to finish what I've started," she said, stepping closer to him. "You have the strength to do the rest on your own."

She reached into her pocket offering a necklace to him. It was the pendant, the one that had stolen Evelyn's magic as well as her race.

"This pendant contains magic," Sloane told him. "Take it and soon you will be the only one in Valmenessia, in the entire world, to have magic."

Elliot carefully took the necklace, staring at the pink gem. "Only I will have magic?"

Sloane nodded and Evelyn's gut clenched as gasps echoed around them. Elliot would be the only one to have magic? Sloane was still determined to kill all races other than humans. Chills skittered down her spine.

"The Maker blood runs through you," Sloane said. "Our family books, as well as Kai's notes, have been left somewhere safe for you to access when you are ready. You will be king of this country and a true Maker. I may be leaving you now but I have not forgotten you. You will be the most powerful person in the world, I do hope you use it wisely."

"Thank you," Elliot breathed, embracing Sloane. "I will make you proud."

"You already do," Sloane smiled then snapped her fingers, and Evelyn hurried to her side with Nora and Kylan. Sloane looked at the prince, her gaze dropping to the colar around his neck, and grimaced. Dark whisps of smoke suddenly appeared around it then the collar fell, hitting the floor with a clang that echoed through the throne room. "Now, where was I?" Evelyn shared a wide eyed look with Kylan as Sloane faced her grandson once more. "Goodbye Elliot. Remember, everything I have done is for you and all who follow you in our family. The future is in your hands, don't squander it."

Sloane clasped her hand around the blackened vine closest to her and the next thing Evelyn knew, she and her friends were no longer in Royal Bay.

38

August

The king's army appeared like something from a nightmare. Emerging through the smoke at the break of dawn, the king's red and gold banners appeared foreboding amongst the sea of grey.

Despite their best efforts to clear the ruse with Elementum wind, the Northern Alliance and the Alv army were still caught by surprise.

August stood atop the southern walls, his axe in one hand, shield strapped to his arm, and watched the oncoming attack. They had planned for this, yet the king's army had still found a way to surprise them.

Orders filled the air as everyone moved into their positions.

The fight was upon them.

The time had come.

Anima shifted and their bird forms launched into the sky, soaring towards enemy lines. They gripped fiery packages in their talons, which exploded once dropped on the enemy. Archers shot flaming arrows at the incoming army from above. The assault was designed to delay the army, perhaps make them consider their assault, if the Alliance was lucky.

It wasn't.

The Elementums in the king's ranks blocked most of the arrows and unleashed return fire at the birds overhead. One of the birds managed to drop their package before it could be returned to it, causing an explosion to erupt in the army's ranks.

Cheers sounded around August, but he didn't celebrate. This was only the beginning. The army was larger than they were and overall more skilled. The enemy pushed forward, their lines reforming around the fallen. August stared at the force heading their way, at the brutality and disregard they showed for their fellow soldiers.

"Are you coming?" Tyler shouted from the top of the stairs.

August took one last look at the king's army before following his friend down the stone steps. They raced to where the ground assault was organising. The city gates remained closed, but soon they would be breached, and the fight would truly begin.

"How rude," Tyler said as they moved through the crowd. So many faces were set in sheer determination, yet there was also an equal number of fearful and blank expressions. "I was hoping for a bit of a sleep-in. Couldn't they wait another hour or two?"

August rolled his eyes. "Go out there and let them know you're unhappy about the time and see if they'll retreat."

They made it near the frontline, where Gemma and Carl stood on wine barrels looking out over the fighters. Humans, Alvs, Elementum and Anima, some already in their shifts, wore mismatched armour and held weapons of varying degrees. This part of the city had been cleared, the space like a fighting ring only bigger. If the army got through the front gate then they would be herded where they would face the next line of defence. Above, the archers, Elementum and a small group armed with guns were stationed and launching their attacks on the approaching force.

August caught sight of Will with a helmet on, leaning on the wall, his arms braced and his gun in his hands. The enemy was close and Will was ready for them. Florence had left the gun in his care and now he was putting all the practice he'd been doing with Tyler to use.

"Today is our victory!" Gemma shouted to those gathered. Her usual attire was replaced with visibly dented armour, yet her sword shone in the morning light where she held it towards the sky. "Today we show them that we will not be broken! We will not fall to the tyrant king's legacy and their bigotry! Today we fight and take back the lives they have stolen from us!"

"We have trained for this," Carl yelled, his voice filling the air. "But not only that, we have to live for this. To fight for what is ours. To defend what is ours!"

Now, August cheered, raising his axe and shouting his fury to the sky. Around him, the other fighters did the same. King Dominic had tried to divide them, but he hadn't succeeded. They were united, they were strong, and they were going to fight for what was right.

The ground force dispersed into the side streets, awaiting the signal from either Gemma or Carl. The thundering of the incoming army's marching grew louder, the cries of those falling to the arrows filled the air.

Anticipation grew and August readied himself for what was to come.

He'd learnt to prepare his mind for an attack growing up and push aside any emotions that would cloud his judgement. To win, he needed to be smart, remember his lessons as an Alta and find his opponents' weaknesses. Be confident and assured. To dismiss his fears and most of all, his compassion. Now was not the time to feel the connection he had to all people.

He caught sight of Jasmine and Omari, embracing before the former rushed away from where the fighting to somewhere safe. Jasmine had wanted to be a part of the battle, but the leaders had all disagreed with her. Someone had to rebuild after this was over, no matter the outcome.

The front gates burst open, a torrent of water throwing the wooden doors off their hinges and into the city, flooding the ground. August braced himself as water circled his ankles. It appeared their moat had only given them more ammunition. Shouting from the army storming into the city rang loud and the clang of metal on metal made the fight real.

It was time.

August ran towards the oncoming army. The flood slowed the Alliance and the stream of soldiers, but it didn't stop the latter from pushing forward. Arrows and bullets rained from above along with fireballs, jets of water and targeted gusts of wind that added to the chaos.

August was in the battle of his life.

Swords clashed, teeth tore flesh and magic whirled around him. Wolves lunged at soldiers, tearing out throats and ripping off limbs, blood leaking into the water at their feet. Whilst Mors Alvs sliced with their blades and unleashed their magic which was just as potent as they stole health and left crumpled bodies in their wake. Despite their power, the sheer number of attacking soldiers was making it difficult for the Mors Alvs to turn the tide, especially when they were targeted with attacks that were designed to incinerate or were directed at the heart—Precision blows that insured instant death. The Lys Alvs were much the same, healing themselves and Alliance fighters as they went with their own light magic. The Alvs were the closest things to immortals as they pushed through the onslaught of soldiers.

The Northern Alliance was not going to make the battle easy for the king's army. They had something to fight for beyond greed and misguided beliefs. It was either to kill or allow their families and friends to be wiped from the land. There was no in-between.

August fought beside Tyler, the duo moving in unison as they cut down their opponents. August swung his axe, slicing through flesh and bone. The fight felt manageable, like for a second they might win, but the enemies soldiers continued to pour in a never-ending stream.

It wasn't long before he lost sight of Tyler to the fray as his friend disappeared amongst the madness. Axe in hand, August pushed on, striking the soldiers around him and embedding his blade in more than one foe. He used his shield to knock away attackers, impaling them on the spikes that Erik had embedded in the metal.

He may have been felling soldiers in his path, but the familiar faces around him were also dropping to the ground. August tried to remember each person who fell, using each death to aid in his attacks. The fuel behind his axe that would avenge them.

Blood splattered in every direction as the massacre continued. The army was strong, ripping into the Alliance as much as the Alliance held them back. No one was safe.

The Elementum in the Alliance worked to counter the army's magical attacks, and August caught sight of Omari wielding his water magic with a vengeance. His water twirled and lashed out at the soldiers, throwing them to the ground before crushing them within their metal armour. Omari was a force to be reckoned with, his water leaving nothing but destruction in its wake.

August summoned his magic too, lashing out at the soldiers closest to him and taking their health in one quick swoop. They fell to the ground like sacks of flour, their vitality now powering August's blows.

Using his magic was a thrill and the health he received each time he killed had the temptation of an addiction if he gave into it. It was easy to get caught up in the moment of battle, however, August knew that post-fight, he'd feel the weight of his actions. Each life he took was a mark against his very being.

Now was not the time to dwell on it.

A soldier swung his sword at August, the brawny man moving faster than expected. His sword slashed through the air, narrowly missing August again and again as he dodged the attacks. August raised his shield, not able to dodge the next strike, and the sword came down hard. His arm shook with the force, his knees tempted to buckle, yet August grit his teeth and pushed back. The soldier stumbled backwards but quickly regained his footing and charged for August once more.

Bright blue eyes narrowed in on August as the man howled as he ran, sword raised. August didn't wait for the attack to arrive, throwing his axe. The blade landed true. The soldier pulled up short, sword falling to the ground as his gaze went cross-eyed, staring at the axe embedded between his brows.

The man collapsed to the ground and August moved quickly to pull his weapon from the man's flesh before moving on to another attacker.

The ground rumbled. Around him, king's soldiers and Alliance members struggling to fight as they all fell to their knees. August shoved his shield into an attacker and then braced himself. The dirt beneath his feet trembled and then something erupted nearby. Bodies went flying as dirt filled the air and all August could do was look on in horror as monsters tore themselves from the ground and joined the commotion.

A slate grey body slithered through the destruction. Its tale whipped around, throwing people in every direction. Screams echoed through the air as the fight resumed, though now a new enemy was in the mix, one who did not care for the king's army or the Alliance.

Magic flew. Water and fire were hurled by the king's Elementum at the monster but it continued unbothered, ignoring the attacks and launching its own.

August sliced and stabbed, dropping soldiers as quickly as he could, all the while keeping an eye on the beast drawing nearer. Its big black eyes glistened, its fanged teeth dripping with the blood of those it had killed.

Fear spiked through him as the monster's head snapped towards him. Its teeth latched around the Alliance member that stood in front of August and the woman cried as she was snatched away. Her screams silenced when it clenched its jaw. Blood rained down on those below.

"Fuck," August hissed, fighting to get away from its path.

He wasn't the only one, others were shoving and stabbing frantically, all desperate to get away whilst still trying to land a blow against their enemy. August stumbled, falling into the mud and cried out. Pain burst through his knee from the impact and he gritted his teeth, breathing in quick rasps. He tried to stand but couldn't put pressure on his knee, his leg wobbling and falling beneath him.

A soldier tried to take advantage of his predicament, but he didn't let them get the upper hand. August let his magic rise, stealing the soldier's life and healing his knee in the process. The soldier collapsed, his lifeless eyes rolling to the back of his head and August was already on the move, defending an attack on his left side.

August spun, cutting through soldiers with his axe before shoving them backwards with his shield. He moved with a rhythm of sorts, taking down enemies all around him

Shrieks sounded from behind and August's focus went back to the beast. He watched as Mors Alvs attacked the monster, drawing blood and wounding it with their blades. The beast snarled, whipping around in an attempt to throw the Mors Alvs off, but they held strong. They moved as one and it was unable to fight them all off as they pulled it to the ground and ended its life. Pride filled August at the sight. His kin taking on a beast and saving those around them.

But his distraction cost him. Sharp pain sliced through the back of his shoulder and he spun, growling at his attacker and embedding his axe into their chest. Reaching out with his magic,

August stole health from a soldier nearby, the man's weapon dropping to the ground, and provided an opening for an Alliance member to stab him with a sword.

August's shoulder knitted itself back together and he dove back into the fighting. With every soldier he killed more replaced them and August was starting to think the fight would never end.

He moved on to the next king's soldier.

And the next.

And the next.

Until all that there was, was the swing of his axe, the block with his shield, the rise of his magic and death.

So much death.

Nora

Nora's knees buckled as she hit the dark stone. She stifled the urge to gag and slowly rose to her feet, the familiar surroundings of Midskopas coming into view. When she'd left, the city had almost been overrun by the curse, its blackened roots taking hold of every aspect of the place and holding it tight within its grasp. Now, as she took a few steps forward and looked out from the balcony on which they'd arrived, she could see how the city had changed once more.

No longer did the curse consume it.

The walls were bare of its hold, albeit still having seen better days, and signs of repair had Nora filled with hope. How the Alliance had managed such a feat was beyond anything she could have ever imagined. They had done it; rescued the city from the curse.

Sloane apparently didn't feel the same about the curse. The woman shrieked at the sight, sparks dancing over her skin.

"No," she gasped, clutching her chest. "NO!"

Sloane began chanting at a feverish pace, her words racing from her lips as she clutched the curse's roots in her hand. One moment she was there and the next Sloane disappeared to Nora had no idea where.

"I know she healed me, but I'm not gonna say I'll miss her," Nora said. "She really freaked me out."

Kylan barked a laugh and Nora grinned at the prince she'd known at a distance for so long, though her good mood was short-lived as she got a glimpse of the south of the city.

Chaos had erupted in Midskopas. In the distance, the battle had begun. The king's army was storming through the front gate as magic and arrows filled the air.

"We need to get down there," Nora exclaimed, rushing to the nearest doorway.

"Wait!" Evelyn called and Nora paused only to have arms thrown around her. Evelyn held her close, squeezing her tight.

"Good to see you too, Evie," Nora said, patting Evelyn on the back.

"You have no idea how good it is to see your face," Evelyn said, drawing back to let her eyes run over Nora. Nora let a grin slip onto her face, the other woman's relief was contagious. "I was so scared when I saw you in the throne room. I thought I'd lost you."

"Okay, now you're trying to make me cry," Nora replied, pursing her lips then she clapped her hands and turned away. "And we don't have time for that so let's get a wriggle on, shall we?"

Nora raced off the balcony and through the building, hurrying to get to the fight. She didn't have any weapons After playing prisoner, but she still had her magic, and with the curse mostly gone from the city she could unleash it at will. She took multiple stairs at a time and Evelyn and Kylan remained close on her heels. Nora vowed to make sure Evelyn stayed nearby until they knew more about the situation. She'd lost too many friends;

she wouldn't be losing Evelyn too.

"So that woman, what's her deal?" Nora asked as they ran down the street.

"She created the curse and wants to destroy all magic," Kylan replied.

Nora noted he held Evelyn's hand in his.

"Figured she was a bit loopy," Nora said. She turned a corner, leading them down another street, then another, as they made their way south. "Valuable in a bind if she's on your side, though. She seems to like you, Evie."

An explosion echoed through the air, shaking the buildings and causing dust to fall over them as they all dropped into a crouch. Kylan draped his body over Evelyn's protectively.

"What was that?"

"Nothing good," Nora hissed, jumping to her feet and taking off again. She didn't bother summoning her magic, needing it for when she reached the battle. "Wars are the fucking worst."

"I'm glad he's dead. This is all his fault," Kylan said, running just behind Nora. "Mine too, I should have done something when I had the chance."

"Kylan…" Evelyn began.

"It is your father's fault," Nora said, glancing back at the prince. She could tell he was beating himself up about it, taking the blame on. It wasn't his though. His father's actions were not his. "But it's not yours, don't hold that over yourself."

"She's right," Evelyn agreed. "Don't blame yourself."

"Easier said than done," Kylan replied. "I've learnt my lesson. I'm done sitting on the side, accepting what's happening."

"That's the spirit!" Nora exclaimed, pumping her fist in the air. "So, back to the woman. Why does she like you so much, Evie?"

"She thinks we're the same," Evelyn said breathily.

Nora barked a laugh. "You're as similar as chocolate cake and sponge cake."

"They're both cake."

"Yes, but other than that they are very different," Nora said, looking back to see the prince clasping Evelyn's hand and smiling down at the woman, his eyes softening. "You're the sponge cake, I like it more. Though it depends on whether it has fresh strawberries or jam…"

"Jam?"

"Couldn't agree more."

"Nora," Evelyn began, releasing Kylan and picking up her pace to run beside Nora instead. "About…"

Nora raised her hands before her chest. "None of my business. I'm not getting involved."

"But August is your best friend."

"Yeah? What's your point?"

"Well, if you thought I did wrong by him…"

"You haven't seen each other in months and even if you had, you don't owe him anything," Nora said. "It's your life, it's got nothing to do with me."

"So—"

"Evie," Nora said, grabbing Evelyn's arm and pulling her to a stop. "He's a big boy. Plus you can't force someone to love you. It's given freely or it's not true."

"That's wise of you."

"You've been gone too long," Nora grinned, holding her arms wide. "This is the new me, full of wisdom, care for others—"

"Hey!" a voice called, and Nora looked to see Ashe striding towards them. A small group lingered behind him, looking around cautiously. "What are you three doing here?"

"Holidaying," Nora replied then pointed in the direction of the battle. "Though by the sounds coming from over there, the place has been overbooked."

"The king's army is here," Ashe said, ignoring her joking. "Where are Aeolus and Aren?"

Nora's expression grew serious and an emptiness filled her

chest. She swallowed hard. "Aren was killed by the curse and Aeolus was murdered by Alta."

"Shit," Ashe cussed.

"You believe my word all of a sudden?" Nora raised a brow, surprised by Ashe's reaction.

Ashe nodded. "I know you can be trusted now. I'm sorry for what I did. We better hurry."

They followed Ashe as he led them closer to the battle and Nora did her best not to tease him over the apology. It was difficult but she managed it … just.

"We were on patrol," Ashe explained, glancing around the streets, his eyes alert and looking for any threats. "It's our job to make sure the army doesn't come through the back."

Nora nodded. "Put the ass at the rear. Gotcha."

"Nora," Evelyn groaned but the impact was lessened by the chuckle that came from Kylan.

"What?" Kylan asked, looking at Evelyn.

"Don't encourage her."

Nora's smirk fell as she saw the panic evident on the faces they started passing, citizens huddled in doorways and peeping out of windows.

Fear filled Nora at the sight of all the children.

They turned, heading south of Midskopas where the streets were filled with chaos. The injured were being carried and rushed into a building with a yellow flag hung at the front. Cries of pain filled the air, mingling with the terror of it all.

"I can help," Evelyn declared, her gaze running over those around them.

Kylan grasped her wrist before she could rush off, twirling her around and kissing her. Nora felt a tug at her heart, the sight making her think of Sage and how much she wished to see her girlfriend.

"I'm no use here," he said. "I'll go with Nora. If my father's army can see me fighting with the Northern Alliance, then maybe they'll rethink what they're doing. They're not all zealots. It's not a sure bet, but it's something."

"If they're devoted to the crown, it should at least give them pause," Nora said. "It won't hurt to try."

Kylan gave Nora a tight-lipped smile before turning back to Evelyn. "Be safe,"

"You too," Evelyn replied, she made to step away but stopped, her gaze on Ashe. "Find my sister and bring her to me. I have information she needs."

Ashe nodded and Evelyn quickly kissed Kylan once more before hurrying towards the wounded.

"We need to get to the battle," Nora said to Ashe. "Which way?"

"I'll take you," Ashe began, but Nora stopped listening.

Nora thought she was going to die in Royal Bay, but it turned out her heart was destined to stop in the streets of Midskopas. She was about to run off with Ashe but froze and stared ahead at a face that stole her breath and had her heart pounding with a new lease on life.

Nora took off running towards Sage.

Nora reached her girlfriend and wrapped her arms around her, holding Sage tight. She breathed her in and wanted more than anything to experience every inch that was Sage and commit them to memory, but now was not the time. Pulling back briefly, she placed her hands on either side of Sage's face and pulled her in for a kiss. Her lips were soft, their kiss tender and full of longing.

"I missed you," Sage said, drawing back as tears welled in her eyes. "I'm not letting you out of my sight ever again."

"Are you sure? I mean would it ruin the romance if you saw me relieving myself?"

Sage rolled her eyes. "You're unbelievable."

"Thank you," Nora grinned. "You're pretty amazing, too."

A cough drew their attention and Nora looked at Ashe over

Sage's shoulder. She narrowed her gaze, and he dropped his immediately.

"We're kind of in the middle of a war," Kylan said moving to Ashe's side. "Evelyn has told me so much about the famous Nora, now I want to see what you can do for myself."

Nora nodded, reluctantly stepping back from Sage. "Can't keep my fans waiting any longer."

"Of course not," Sage chuckled through tears. "Go. I love you."

"I love you, too."

"You better come back."

"I promise."

And with that, Nora turned and left.

As she raced towards the battle, Nora felt her old self trying to take hold. She let it slip in, though this time, her Alta training wasn't all she had. She wasn't running towards a fight because King Dominic commanded it. She had something to fight for now.

Nora could feel it in her gut as she drew closer to the chaos.

The end was near. Everything that had happened culminated to this point.

It was time to see who would make it out alive.

40

Evelyn

Inside the healing quarters, the noise of the clash between the king's army and the Northern Alliance was still deafening. The cries of agony only added to the horror of the whole event. Evelyn looked around, searching for where she should begin, for who required her help most. The instinct to summon her healing magic rose to the surface, but she stifled it and kept a cool head. She may not have her Lys Alv power anymore, but she still held all her medicinal knowledge and could still be of use. There would be time to continue mourning the loss of her magic, right now the injured here needed her.

"Patient over by the window," Margot ordered. Evelyn's old mentor marched to her side with a basket of vials and handed it to Evelyn. "Use them sparingly and when this is all over you will sit down to tea with me and tell me everything that has happened since you left Forest's Edge, including why you look … human."

Margot never missed a single detail.

"Of course," Evelyn replied, taking the basket.

Margot gave her a tight-lipped smile. "I've missed you."

"I've missed you too," Evelyn said though Margot had already hurried away to tend to a patient.

Evelyn quickly sought out the patient Margot had directed her to, finding the woman sitting against the wall beneath the window, her hand pressed to her stomach and blood seeping between her fingers from the wound. Her face was covered in dirt and blood. A few cuts still bled freely down her cheeks.

"Lay down," Evelyn instructed, putting on her Healer training like an old coat. "Let me have a look at this wound."

The woman did as she was told and soon Evelyn was stitching the cut closed. It wasn't a deep one, though it bled more than Evelyn liked. She went through the motions, grateful for the extensive training she'd once thought was excessive when she'd first started learning. Her father had insisted she learn everything about the body and how to heal it. Her Lys Alv magic worked on instinct and simply healed what was needed, but her father had been adamant she understood what and how it was healing an injury or ailment and how others without Lys Alv abilities would treat them. Had he been preparing her for something like this all along?

After the final stitch, she applied a salve to the woman's injuries and moved on to the next patient.

And so it went.

Over and over again.

Stitch, bandage, ointment, salve or tonic.

Evelyn moved through the motions, the number of wounded needing care never decreasing despite her continuous work. The injuries became worse and worse too, and she couldn't fathom the carnage that was going on beyond the city walls. The brutalities that were being inflicted.

Fear prickled her inside, but she didn't let it take hold. She would not turn into a trembling mess over her loved ones when there were those who needed her. She needed to keep her wits.

So, she refused to think of Kylan and the others fighting.

They are going to be fine, she told herself.

"Help me with this one," one of the Healers said, and Evelyn hurried to his side to help him lift a patient onto the makeshift bed.

The patient was going in and out of consciousness as he bled from a wound on his head, his ear having been cut clean off.

"A Lys Alv Healer?" The Healer asked, worry in their eyes.

Evelyn shook her head. "They cannot grow ears back and would be needed for more severe injuries at this point. We can fix this. We need to slow the bleeding and cauterise it."

The Healer's eyes widened, and they shook their head, backing up a few steps. "I've never done it before."

"That's okay," Evelyn said, hoping she sounded reassuring. "I'll show you."

Evelyn set to work, guiding the other Healer through the steps that her father had taught her. She felt alive despite the trauma all around her. She was where she should be.

For months she'd felt like she'd had no purpose. Constantly at the whims of others, yet here she was in charge of her life. She knew what she had to do and was able to solve the problems before her. People looked to her for help and healing. They trusted her without question.

Evelyn had thought she didn't want this life. Had thought it was simply the one mapped out before her rather than a choice she had made. It had been her father's passion. But now, with each person she cared for, she realised it was hers, too. It was what she wanted and, not only that, it made her feel closer to her father.

Teaching someone as he taught her filled her with pride as his advice came instantly to mind with each injury she was presented. His voice was clear and calm, guiding her as she did as instructed. He was with her every step of the way.

Evelyn had chosen to be here in this room, tending to

patients. She had chosen it and the choice felt good.

This is where she belonged.

They finished tending to the patient, wrapping his head in bandages after applying an ointment, and Evelyn moved on to the next person in need, feeling that although the world was in chaos around her, she'd finally realised her calling.

Hours later, Evelyn's knees buckled and she grasped the nearest bed, stopping herself from falling to the ground. Her eyes filled with tears causing the sight of Jasmine to blur as she wept.

"When did you get here?" Jasmine asked as she wrapped her arms around Evelyn and held her tight. "How are you here?"

Evelyn tried to speak but all that came from her lips were sobs. Jasmine was here and it felt like coming home. Everything was going to be alright.

"I'm so sorry," her sister said, rubbing circles on Evelyn's back. "I should have done more to rescue you."

Evelyn drew back, looking at her sister. It was so good to see her familiar face. Jasmine's eyes widened in shock and she placed a hand on Evelyn's cheek. "What happened to your eyes?"

"My magic was stolen," Evelyn said with a sniff. She wiped her eyes with the back of her hand. "I'm human now."

Jasmine's fingers drifted upwards, moving Evelyn's hair and revealing rounded ears. "It's impossible."

Evelyn shook her head. "I thought so too once, Phillip brought a pendant to Sorby, to a Conjurer named Sloane. She is the one who started the curse."

"Why?"

Evelyn delved into an explanation, albeit a short version of all Sloane had done, of the Gods and Goddesses being imprisoned in Valmenessia and the Makers' sacrifice, and finally of Elliot in

Royal Bay.

"That's a lot to take in," Jasmine said, placing her hands behind her back as she considered all Evelyn had said. "Is there a way to stop her?"

"Other than give her what she wants?" Evelyn shook her head. "I don't think we can."

"There has to be a way."

A thunderous boom filled the air as the room shook and debris fell from the ceiling. Healers and injured inside cried out in panic, terror ripping through the already fearful room. Evelyn gripped the bed and braced herself, whispering under her breath that everything was going to be okay.

It wasn't the first time the room trembled, nor did she think it would be the last. The battle was not only hurting the Northern Alliance but the city was feeling the brunt of the attack as well.

"Where's mother?" Evelyn asked, her stomach dropping at the sorrow that filled Jasmine's eyes.

"I have to go." Jasmine declared, ignoring the question. She hugged Evelyn once more, then drew back, her hands on either side of Evelyn's arms as she smiled tightly. "I have much to share with you, too. But now is not the time. There are people who need to hear what you've said. I will be back, I promise."

"Go," Evelyn said, kissing her sister's cheek. "I'll be waiting for you to return."

Jasmine left and Evelyn breathed in deeply, calming her heart. The injured needed her, crying wouldn't let her help any of them.

"What was that?" The patient closest to her asked, eyes wide and darting around.

"I don't know," Evelyn replied, her lips pressed into a thin line. "But it can't be good."

The ground settled and Evelyn went back to her duties, treating the injured as quickly as she could while the stream of wounded continued. They were at capacity, even with those able to be moved taken further into the city to make space for others.

"Wounded incoming!" a man shouted, covered in dirt as he carried in wounded on his wind magic.

"How many?" Margot asked, directing the man where to deposit the injured.

"I don't know but sections of the wall are crumbling to the ground and fighters are buried beneath the rubble. You'll need to make more space."

Evelyn finished up with her patient and hurried to help the newcomers as more injured were being brought in.

"I've got this one," a Lys Alv said, darting in front of Evelyn. They placed their hands over a woman's bloodied chest and shut their eyes.

Evelyn felt another pang of loss for her magic as she moved out of the way. She walked quickly down the line of beds when someone grabbed her skirt, tugging her to a halt.

"My leg," the man groaned from where he lay, his head lolling from side to side.

She looked down only to see the man's legs ended at his knees. Blood already soaked the bed linens, his legs looking as though they'd been torn off. Evelyn had never seen anything like it. Hiding her shock, she set to work, tending to his wounds as best she could. He'd need a Lys Alv, but they were all busy.

"Everything is going to be okay," she reassured the man as she worked.

"We are losing."

"It's not over yet, there's still time," she replied, attempting a smile. He didn't notice, his eyelids fluttering as they closed.

"Dead," he continued, licking his lips. "We're all going to be dead."

Evelyn's gut churned. How bad was it out there? Were they really losing?

"Volunteers!" Margot called with an urgency in her voice. "I need Healer volunteers!"

"We're all dead," the man repeated as a Lys Alv appeared at Evelyn's side. "Dead. Dead. Dead."

Evelyn quickly explained what she'd been doing to her fellow Healer then grabbed a few supplies before racing towards Margot.

"I volunteer," Evelyn said, somewhat breathlessly. She'd promised Jasmine that she'd wait here, but there were injured who needed her. She'd just have to survive and find Jasmine later.

"You'll be going onto the battle grounds," Margot replied, softly.

"I volunteer," Evelyn said again.

"Very well," Margot nodded, pointing to a small group walking out the door. "Follow them."

Evelyn didn't hesitate, her heart racing as fast as her legs as she ran after the group. Together they made their way towards the south of Midskopas, the sounds of the fight deafening as they drew closer. Her mouth dropped open as she took in the sight.

Chaos.

Fires burned with a vengeance as winds whirled through the air, throwing anything in their path. Soldiers and Northern Alliance members clashed in a frenzy, desperation powering their strikes as they tried to tear the other down. Howls filled the air as Anima lunged, sharp teeth bared.

Evelyn stood frozen to the spot, her feet submerged in muddy water, and watched it all unfold.

She'd known battles were horrible, yet she hadn't expected this. There was no structure to the fighting, just a mess of people determined to survive.

"Come on," one of the Healers said, waking Evelyn from her shock. "This way."

They ran towards the crumbled wall, where the injured bled upon the stone, at least those she could see. How many were beneath the rubble was unknown.

An arrow shot by, and Evelyn yelped, clasping a hand to

her upper arm. Blood was warm against her fingers, though she knew it was only a graze.

She'd survive.

She couldn't say as much for everyone else.

Hurrying to the collapsed wall, she began her Healer duties. She still had time to save some.

41

August

The world was falling apart and all that was left was death. Weapons and magic flew through the air, clashing as the battle wore on. More lives were taken with each passing second. The screams of the dying rang in his ears. Their horrific melody was something that would haunt him for the rest of his days, along with every face he'd seen. Those he'd killed and the ones he simply watched die; all would be etched permanently into his mind.

The trauma didn't halt him though. August kept going. Not when blades sliced and drew blood or when fire burned his flesh. He ignored his injuries for now, using the health he stole from others to give him strength to push on instead. To continue when many grew sluggish from fatigue.

August would heal later; first, they needed to defeat the king's army.

At least there was a silver lining, a sliver of hope. Many of the Anima in the army had switched sides, joining the Alliance and attacking the king's soldiers.

He swung his axe, slicing through the woman in front of him before she could attempt another attack. Her fire magic burnt off most of his shirt and singed his chest in retaliation. Her final words were a gargled sound, the flames in her hand extinguishing before she fell to be with the other dead in the ankle-deep water. August watched for only a second as her pale face sank into the water, blood and mud tainting its colour.

Another life taken. Another face to add to the others.

He lifted his shield to block an arrow and caught sight of Gemma, her sword at the ready and features fierce. She barked orders as she moved as one with a group of Alliance fighters. Like a bull moving through a field, the soldiers around them fell like blades of grass.

Seeing Gemma made August think of the others, and he scanned the fighting in search of their faces, hoping they were alive. He spotted Omari swirling his hands before him and launching giant balls of water at clusters of soldiers, knocking them to the ground.

Omari was completely drenched, working with those around him to push the attack back. The king's army had knocked down part of the southern wall, their forces streaming in faster. The Alliance wouldn't be able to keep up with the onslaught much longer. Omari threw another giant water ball, throwing more soldiers back the way they came. It wouldn't have caused more than a few bruises and they would return, but Omari's attack was slowing the ambush and giving the Alliance a chance to fight it.

August thrust his shield at an oncoming soldier, slamming the spike into their face with a sickening crunch. He ignored the way his gut churned, dragging the spike from the soldier's eyeball and turning to face the soldier coming from his other side.

This time he swung his axe, but the soldier dodged the blow. And the next one. August grit his teeth, pushing his attack.

The soldier could only be so lucky. Finally, his axe landed true, wedging itself between the soldier's neck and shoulder. It was August's turn to dodge as they came for him, blade slashing through the air. August moved swiftly, avoiding the attacks that grew sloppy as the soldier drained of blood. On his knees, the soldier attempted to lift their blade only to fall forward. If the blow didn't kill him, then drowning certainly would.

A sudden pain pierced August's side and he spun, his axe hand rising. Instead of using the weapon, he summoned his magic to the surface. His power reached forward, pulling the life right out of the soldier and filling August, healing his wounded side.

The soldier collapsed and August's gaze fell on Will, shooting soldiers from atop a section of the wall that was still standing. Soldiers threw magic his way, fireballs flying at him as fast as arrows whilst others attempted to scale the stone.

August knocked an attacker to the side, using their momentum to propel them and raced towards Will.

Tyler got their first, running at those climbing towards Will with his hands raised before him. The soldiers froze on the spot and then fell to the ground after Tyler's magic reached them, drawing away their lives in seconds. Tyler didn't stop once the climbers had fallen, immediately entering into a sword fight with other soldiers on the ground around the ladder.

August joined Tyler, together dropping soldiers and taking lives around them. Too many to count.

Soldiers continued to invade Midskopas as though there was a never-ending supply, fresh and ready to draw blood. Thyra was throwing the king's entirety of the army at them, attempting to break them purely through brute force.

The strategy may have worked if it were only the Alliance fighting her, but the Alvs had come, healing themselves with the strength of the enemy soldiers. Thyra's army might win, though her victory would not come as easy as she may have expected.

Jord and Nyssa were in the fray, fighting soldiers with a precision that showed a lifetime of skills ... many lifetimes in their cases.

Nyssa fought with her sword in hand, slicing through her opponents as though they were nothing but fruit. She took on multiple attackers, cutting them down as she twirled her blade. Rana had said fighting was like a dance As August watched Nyssa he truly understood that sentiment. The Goddess moved with grace, each thrust or swing of her sword an elegant manoeuvre.

Jord remained by her side, though weaponless, the Mors Alv Goddess relied solely on her magic. Her hands moved gracefully as her magic snatched life from the soldiers in her wake. Multiple at a time fell, often mid-strike, their blades tumbling to the ground with their lifeless bodies.

The Goddesses were a force to be reckoned with.

Yet Thyra had yet to enter Midskopas.

Was she afraid? Or was she simply biding her time? Waiting for the perfect moment to strike?

A soldier pushed through the battle towards the Goddesses and the next thing August knew, the two women abandoned their positions and followed the man away from the fight.

Were they fleeing, abandoning the Alvs and the Alliance to be slaughtered by the king's army?

His gut twisted, anger rising in him. How dare they?

August used the anger in each swing of his axe. If they wouldn't fight for the Alliance, then he would fight harder. He would not abandon the cause or the people within the city.

He thought of all those who couldn't fight, of all the children who were hiding in the northern part of Midskopas, waiting and hoping for victory.

He would not let them down.

Nora

Nora ran past the wounded, hurrying towards the commotion before her. Arrows flew overhead as water and fire filled the sky, racing towards their marks. Swords clashed and cries of pain echoed around her. There was so much agony, so much death.

None of it deterred her.

August was out there somewhere and that was all that mattered.

Another loud rumble shook the ground, the air filling with dust as more of the southern wall crumbled. Alliance members fell from their stations, some buried beneath the stone as the screams pierced the air before they were suddenly cut short.

Nora tried not to think of all those losing their lives, of the faces she knew and how many of them she'd never speak to again. Like Florence, Aren, Aeolus…

How many more would she lose?

Leaping into the fray, Nora slashed with the sword she'd

been given. Her blade went through one of the king's soldiers before she kicked out at another and launched a fireball at a third. She didn't pause in her attacks, shoving through the chaos and taking down as many enemy soldiers as she went.

Her sword and magic tore through those around her, blood splattering her face, yet Nora wasn't paying them her full attention, her gaze searching for August.

He was her best friend.

Her family.

She would find him if it were the last thing she'd do.

Her magic swirled within her, rising to her call as she shoved out a pulse of her wind, throwing the soldiers drawing nearer off their feet before storming on.

"You're a little scary," Kylan shouted from behind her as she pierced a soldier through the chest.

"You have no idea," Nora said with a grin, sliding the blade from the lifeless chest. Blood trickled down the metal, dripping to the water around her ankles.

The prince's skill with his sword left much to be desired, but his magic was strong. Centuries of selective breeding to produce powerful royals meant his magic was a force to be reckoned with.

Kylan kept pace and they worked together, fighting off the soldiers as she continued to look for her friend. Nora was so caught up in her search that it wasn't long before she lost sight of Kylan.

Guilt ran through her for losing him. Evelyn loved the prince and Nora was no longer able to protect him. Once she'd found August, she'd go back and look for Kylan. From what she'd seen already, he could take of himself.

Soldiers dropped around her. Her fire and water magic was as deadly as the sword she wielded. All her years as an Alta had trained her for this; the fighting, the gore. None of it bothered her as she slashed and stabbed, summoned magic and took lives without remorse.

Madness reigned, death was in the air and yet Nora pushed forward.

She spotted August to her right, moving with proficiency as he fought soldiers on multiple fronts. Each strike and defence was like an elegant move, his skills honed the same as Nora's after so many years of being an Alta. None could reach him, his attackers falling around him.

His axe cut through the air, landing true whilst his magic, though invisible, was at work in succession, his enemies collapsing as he stole their health. August had always been strong, but now he was an unstoppable weapon.

Nora couldn't help but feel proud of him. Yes, he was killing, but he was so fucking good at it.

She hurried to his side, lunging with her sword and taking position at his back. It was just like old times. Nora and August against the world.

"Took your time," he shouted at her. His teasing was evident despite the situation they were in.

"I had a king to kill,' Nora called back. "Minor task compared to watching your ass."

Nora ducked as August's axe sliced over her head and landed in the chest of the man opposite her. At the same time, her water magic shot a jet of water that hit another soldier, sending him flying backwards and taking out another four in his wake.

She grabbed August's axe from the dead man and flipped it back towards him. She flicked her wrist, blocking shots of fireballs with her wind magic as the enemy converged on the two former Alta. Summoning more wind, Nora created a barrier, shielding them in a tight circle. Taking advantage of the brief respite, Nora raced towards August and enveloped him in a quick hug.

"Show off," he laughed, looking around at her win barrier. The battle continued around them as magic was launched at Nora's wind. "I have so much to tell you."

"Like how you're doing fancy tricks with your magic, too?"

"That and this," he replied, holding up his shield arm.

"You know when I told you scars were hot, I meant small ones," she drawled. "You were always an overachiever."

August barked a laugh as Nora dropped the wind barrier and the two of them braced for the onslaught. Soldiers stormed towards them, but August had them dropping to the ground before they could get within striking distance, his magic stealing their health faster than a blink of an eye.

"Now who's the show-off," Nora called.

"Jord taught me to target it," August yelled back at her. "She also taught me about my parents."

"Rana told me about them," Nora shouted, dodging a sword. She jumped back and then summoned her fire magic. The soldier before her went up in flames, his screams filling the air as he flailed around, running away. "Your mother was the queen. I always knew you were a royal pain in the ass."

August chuckled, his back pressed to hers. "General Natsky was my father. I'm going to take his name and I want you to as well."

"Umm, awkward time to propose," Nora teased, turning a jet of water directed at her into steam and directing it towards another attacker. The soldier clutched their face, skin blistering as they screamed in agony, and fell to their knees.

"Don't be gross," August shouted, leaving her back to take on more soldiers. "To think I missed you."

Nora moved left and right, dropping more and more soldiers to the mud at her feet. She could hear August fighting behind her, no doubt doing the same.

"I missed you, too," she called, slicing through a soldier's throat. She turned her head from the spray of blood and caught sight of August fighting with determination. Multiple soldiers attacked him from all sides. But August's axe drew blood and his magic dropped those around him.

Suddenly the world moved in slow motion.

Nora raised a hand to summon her magic, sending her fire toward the soldier behind August. Her aim was true as a scream wrenched from her throat.

It was too late, the soldier's sword pierced through August, the blade sliding through his back and out his chest.

Nora's magic exploded out of her, soldiers and allies launching away from her in every direction until it was only her and August. She reached him as he fell to his knees, catching him before the rest of his body hit the ground.

"Fuck," she hissed, shaking August's shoulders. "Take my health. Heal yourself enough so I can get you to a Healer."

She shook him again, his silence sending her heart racing in her chest.

"August?" Panic filled her as she lay him on his side and then looked down at him. His dark eyes stared ahead; his face expressionless as blood pooled around the wound in his chest. Dread coursed through her, the sight breaking something deep within her very soul. "No, no, no! August!"

Fire shot passed her head, and the world came back to her in a rush. Nora rose to her feet, her loss becoming a powerful weapon. She summoned her wind magic, shielding August's body from the battle then let herself loose.

Soldiers fell around her as her grief and her wrath turned the mud to blood. She killed as if she were merely taking a stroll in the park. The only thing on her mind; they had taken August from her.

He was her only family.

Now he was gone.

Like a demon of the night, a true angel of death, Nora killed without hesitation.

Nora sliced through flesh with her sword, burned bodies with her fire and crushed bones with jets of water. King Dominic had wanted her because she had been a powerful Elementum, now she would show the world just how strong she was.

Kylan appeared at her side, his own magic joining hers and making quick work of the king's army. They worked together, to take out a rather aggressive group before Nora's attention was caught elsewhere.

Her eyes found flaming red hair drawing closer to Midskopas. Thyra.

She'd stoked the flames of Elementum superiority. Schemed and supported King Dominic's reign. Now she'd pay for it.

"Take August to the Healers. To Evelyn," Nora shouted at Kylan, pointing to where he lay. "Take him straight to her and don't let anything happen to him. He's your brother."

She didn't wait for a response as she took off.

The thought that it was too late only further fuelled Nora. The pain powering her on.

Fighting her way through the mass of people, Nora was determined to reach Thyra. It was her fault; all of this was the fucking Elementum Goddess' fault.

Nora wasn't the only one who'd spotted Thyra. Two women who looked just like the pictures she'd seen of Jord and Nyssa were headed towards the Elementum Goddess.

But Nora wanted to get to her first.

As she sprinted through the soldiers, Nora met Thyra's gaze as the Elementum strode through what was left of the city's gates. Nora's eyes narrowed and a cry left her throat as she launched her attack. Fire fell from her hands, forming into giant lions that roared with embers flying from their mouths. Soldiers balked in terror as the beasts leapt at Thyra.

The Goddess didn't wait for the attack to reach her as her own magic morphed into a legendary beast that towered over even Nora's giant lions. The dragon hissed, water spraying and drenching Nora to the bone.

Nora wiped the water from her eyes as her lions collided with the dragon, sending hissing steam rising into the sky. Nora's attack was strong, more than any other she'd ever unleashed. She couldn't help but wonder whether Sloane had done something to her power when she'd brought her back from the brink of death.

This close to the city gate, there were only soldiers of the king's army around them. The Northern Alliance had fallen back further into the city, the press of the soldiers forcing them to use the layout of the city to break the numbers up.

Nora took advantage of this and summoned her wind magic. She didn't need to worry about friendly fire here, so she created massive whirlwinds that were indiscriminate in who they whipped about. Soldiers were flung through the air, screaming as their bodies were lifted only to come crashing down again. Thyra mimicked Nora's attack, her own whirlwinds joining Nora's, not caring for the lives of those on her side.

The winds picked up and Nora braced herself against the onslaught. Her dark hair flew into her face, her clothing lifting at the edges. Nora gritted her teeth, throwing more magic into her fiery lions. They continued to battle the water dragon, teeth dragging into each other's elemental flesh. The dragon had the upper hand, dowsing the fire of Nora's lions. Nora may have been strong, but she was no immortal Goddess.

Blood dripped from her nose, and she gritted her teeth again, forcing all power into her lions. Her winds ceased, though Thyra's continued on as the dragon roared, clamping its teeth around one of the lions and lifting it into the sky. Nora's legs trembled as the lion was extinguished.

The dragon charged for the other lion only to stumble. Nora's eyes widened, looking to Thyra who glared to Nora's right. Nora followed the line of sight to see the Alv Goddesses had joined the fight.

Jord stood with hands raised, her fingers moving as though gripping an invisible sheet and dragging it towards her. Thyra's winds died out just as Nora's lion bit through its leg and severed the limb. The dragon roared as Thyra let out a shriek.

Nora watched as Nyssa launched her own attack. The woman thrust her sword at Thyra, drawing the Elementum's attention to the more immediate threat. The two Goddesses began to battle, Thyra swiftly drawing her own blade to block Nyssa's onslaught.

Thyra fought Nyssa, Jord and Nora on all fronts, but Nora could see the woman was tiring. Even she was not strong enough to go up against all three of them. Nora continued to push all her magic into her remaining lion even as the ground trembled beneath her.

Cracks formed and the land shifted as the curse suddenly shot through it, the blackened roots twisting and lashing out as they launched from the soil. Soldiers and those in the Northern Alliance were snapped up and flung around. The Makers' Curse was indiscriminate to either side. It wanted magic and cared not for politics.

The roots whipped around, one diving for Nora only for it to freeze mid-air. The curse stilled and then, standing atop the largest of the blackened roots was Sloane. Her purple hair was wild, her eyes glowing like stars in the night sky. The curse slowly lowered her to the ground as everyone ceased fighting and stared, eyes fixed on the Conjurer.

"Enough," Sloane declared, her voice otherworldly. "This ends now."

43

Evelyn

Evelyn had been standing atop the wall, watching the fight unfold. Terror and worry for Nora had her heart race so fast that her chest pained.

She'd come to the wall to help only to be forced to flee as an Elementum in the king's army had launched an attack, blowing up another section of the wall and killing many, Healers included. Evelyn had tried to scramble up the stone wall in her escape, only making it thanks to Will's outstretched hand. She hugged him once at the top, squeezing him tight and then set to helping those who needed it whilst he shot at the enemy below.

The guns were loud, making it hard for her to hear much else. She tended to wounds, crouching low so as not to draw an attack. By the time she'd run out of her limited supplies, she'd peeked out over the battle only to see Nora and instantly felt sick to her stomach.

The fighting around them had all but stilled, every soldier and Alliance member transfixed on the battle between Nora and

Thyra. Giant fire lions and a water dragon fought, the beasts terrifying beyond measure.

Evelyn found Will again and clung to his side as she watched the creatures fight. The magic used was like nothing Evelyn could have ever imagined. It was as though they were conscious beings made of fire and water.

They roared and hissed as they met, like they were as enraged as the Elementum who wielded them. Nora was strong, but Evelyn was amazed by the extent to which Nora could wield her power. Going up against a Goddess and holding her own. The skill she had in manipulating her magic. It had been awe-inspiring and yet, even as Nora's attacks met Thyra's blow for blow, Thyra was winning.

Then Jord and Nyssa joined the fight and turned the tide. Together the three pushed back. Hope swelled in Evelyn's chest, and she reached out to squeeze Will's hand.

Unfortunately, Thyra wasn't the only threat they should have been looking out for.

The curse erupted from below, the blackened roots targeting anyone left in close range. Evelyn's face fell at the sight of Sloane. The Conjurer had been at the centre of the curse, looking more like a god than those who had been fighting moments before.

Sloane was unlike any deity. The image of her was terrifying as she was lowered to the ground. The air crackled around her, the lightning at her fingertips sparking, and her eyes glowed in that eerie way Evelyn had seen before.

Power rippled from Sloane, tearing through the sky as though it were paper. More lightning flickered around her, snapping and cracking, foreboding what was to come.

"Enough," Sloane declared, her voice otherworldly. "This ends now."

Evelyn stared, trembling at the sight before her. Sloane had disappeared when they'd arrived in Midskopas and Evelyn had gotten so caught up in the battle she'd forgotten about the

Conjurer.

A mistake she regretted.

"No!" Thyra shouted, her voice a battle cry. Her water dragon shifted into a cord of wind and fire twisting together into a rope and lashing out at Sloane.

The curse intervened, entwining itself around her power. Thyra ran at Sloane, sword raised as the curse crushed her magical attack, absorbing it and growing in strength. That didn't stop Thyra from launching another attack.

Wind so powerful it threatened to tear the curse from the ground suddenly tore through the air. On the ground, soldiers and Alliance members raced to escape its path of destruction as it hit a stone building, shooting through it like an arrow through an apple.

Evelyn swore, unsure of which she wanted to succeed. They were both as evil as each other, determined to sacrifice others for their own desires.

Thyra's dragon returned; this time made of smouldering embers. It roared, rattling the world as fire spilled from its mouth and covered the curse.

Time stood still as the dragon burned, heat berating Evelyn's skin. Eyes watering, she refused to take her eyes off the scene before her. Would Thyra be able to do it? Defeat the curse and Sloane as well?

The fire was suddenly extinguished and the dragon disappeared in a puff of smoke. Evelyn's heart sank. Sloane stood there, unharmed and smiling wickedly, the curse still very present around her.

"Is that all you have?" Sloane's lightning crashed into the ground before Thyra.

But the Goddess wasn't deterred, leaping around it and continuing on towards the Conjurer. "I'm just getting started," she growled, the muddy water rising. A giant wave built as every drop of water from the battlefield joined it until the wave towered over the city walls, casting a shadow over everything.

"Nora," Will breathed and Evelyn spotted their friend being dragged away by Kylan. Evelyn's heart filled; Kylan was saving her.

Thyra let out her rage, sending the wave crashing down onto Sloane. Evelyn held her breath, watching intently as the water receded to see whether it had been enough. Much to her dismay, Sloane was alive, well and completely dry.

"If you're finished," Sloane said as though speaking to a child. Sloane flicked her wrist and Thyra was thrown backwards.

The Goddess tumbled, rolling over herself. She glowered at Sloane, rising to her feet, her teeth bared. "Are you going to stand by and let her kill us?" Thyra demanded, looking at Nyssa and Jord. "Kill everyone with magic? That bitch's little curse is going to devour everything magical until there are only humans left. Not even your precious Alvs will survive."

Jord glanced at Nyssa, her expression calm, resolute. "Yes."

"What?" Thyra balked. "You can't be serious. Didn't you just hear what I said?"

"We did," Nyssa said, stepping towards Sloane and turning her attention to the Conjurer. "We know what you are trying to do and we surrender."

Silence filled the battlefield.

Evelyn glanced at Will with eyes wide. "Is she giving us over to Sloane?"

"We will fight even if she does," Will replied.

Around them, Alliance members and the king's soldiers drew closer. Anger hardened their gazes, their weapons drawn towards the Conjurer.

The curse lashed out in Sloane's defence but curled back as it was cut through by an Alliance sword. Sloane growled at the sight, throwing lightning at those who wished to harm her and the curse. They retreated quickly, aware of being completely out of their depth.

"I do not surrender," Thyra shouted, glaring at the three powerful women before her. "And neither do the people."

"It's time that you shut up and accept what is happening," Jord hissed. "After everything you have done. It is time to do what is right. We have lived for far too long. Our time is over."

"The conjuring the Makers did to imprison us here is tied to us and us alone," Nyssa said to Sloane, sheathing her sword. "Aren has already passed, but Frode and Kai are not here. You will still need to find them."

"Frode and Kai are dead," Sloane stated, striding towards the three Goddesses. "And now I will take you three. They should have killed you all that time ago for what you did. Trapping you here was a mistake; one I will rectify."

"Your family fucked up and we are to blame?" Thyra shouted. She opened her arms wide. "You would condemn *all* magic? Punish them for *your* family's stupidity?"

Sloane narrowed her gaze, lightning snapping erratically along her skin. "I blame you, as should we all. It is your fault. You are the reason it has come to this."

"Nyssa! Jord!" Thyra hissed, looking to the Alv Goddesses. "We can't let her do this."

"It is our fault," Jord stated, looking around at those huddled around the edges of the scene unfolding. "It was never meant to be like this. It is unnatural"

"Nothing is ever as planned. That's how nature works. If it was so unnatural, why does our magic exist in the first place?" Thyra argued with her fists clenched at her sides. Flames burst into life around her legs, burning brightly atop the water.

"Perhaps," Jord replied, reaching out a hand to Nyssa. "But it is time to accept our fate."

"I'm not ready for it to end!" Thyra shouted, alarm in her eyes as lightning danced along Sloane's body.

Nyssa grasped Jord's outstretched hand and the Goddesses closed their eyes.

"No!" Thyra screamed, though it went unheard. Her fire rose in furious flames, lashing out in her anger.

The twins ignored it, Jord's free hand reaching towards Thyra and though Evelyn could not see Jord's Mors Alv magic, the effects were clear. Nyssa's skin paled as she fed her light into her twin whilst Jord used their combined magic to attack Thyra. The flames extinguished in a puff of smoke as Thyra's eyes bulged. The Elementum Goddess was no match to the strength of the Alv Goddesses, especially as Nyssa was evidently prepared to sacrifice her life.

Thyra raced towards the Goddesses, stumbling as her magic was being stolen from her. Nyssa gifted her entire self to Jord, the Lys Alv Goddess falling to the ground at the same time as Thyra finally succumbed. Both lay lifeless, though for how long? Evelyn was unsure how their immortality worked. Would Nyssa heal? Would Thyra?

"It's time," Jord said, holding her arms out wide. "I cannot do it myself."

Lightning slammed down from the sky, the bright light hitting where Jord stood. Evelyn gasped at the sight, the entire world trembling as the Mors Alv Goddess was wiped from the land.

The air thickened, sound became dull.

Sloane's entire being fractured, like cracks in a marble statue. Light shone from each break, splitting her until she exploded, both light and darkness burst from her. The power was stronger than any conjured wind as it threw everyone to the ground.

Pain laced through Evelyn, more excruciating than anything she'd ever suffered in her life.

Her entire existence felt like it was being shredded, ripped and pulled from her.

Evelyn cried out, yet no sound escaped her lips. Tears were desperate to fall yet her eyes remained completely dry. She felt as though she were falling and lying down at the same time.

Convulsing and remaining perfectly still.

Everything was a contradiction; her senses were overwhelmed.

Then as fast as it had begun, it was all over, and Evelyn was left lying on her back and staring at the sky above. A brilliant blue with fluffy white clouds drifting along, unaware of what was happening below them.

She was both fine and utterly not at the same time.

Nora

Nora staggered to her feet with a groan, her head was still spinning and her eyes watered from Sloane's magic as it ripped through the world. Others moved groggily around her and she imagined they felt much the same. Rubbing her eyes, her vision cleared to see those who were standing had frozen, looking up into the sky.

Nora followed their gaze, seeing the millions of tiny stars that rained down upon them. The last remains of Sloane and her curse. It was ironic that something so horrible had turned into a beautiful sight. The glittering stars slowly faded and Nora became overly aware of the battle that was still very much present.

But something had changed.

Thyra, Jord and Nyssa, the three Goddesses, all lay motionless on the ground at the centre of the battlefield.

Nora looked to Kylan; his eyes wide. "They're gone," he stated. His words were a whisper as though afraid if he spoke too loudly the Goddesses would simply wake up. "They're dead."

"Thank fuck for that," Nora replied, each word coming out around heavy breathing. She lit a ball of fire in her hand, her magic coming to her quickly and she grinned up at him. "Sloane didn't take our magic."

Kylan shook his head, a relieved smile gracing his lips as he too lit his own ball of flame.

She turned to look around, at the others that were testing their magic, seeing the relief on their faces at finding it had remained. Sloane's curse had died with her. The blackened roots were now gone, having exploded into stars just like their maker.

"Gods or not! Magic or not! We came for one thing! To cleanse the land of your rebellion in the name of the king!"

Nora's elation sank into her gut and fluttered out at the shout that came from one of the generals in the king's army.

Roars of agreement rose and a sword was sliced through an Alliance member near Nora, the man toppling to the ground as blood spilled from his chest. Her magic rose to the surface and she threw a gust of wind at the king's soldier, launching him in the air. The man collided with more soldiers, knocking them all over into a pile.

Nora snickered.

"Stop!"

Kylan stepped forward; hands raised as he strode into the space Sloane had left. The soldiers halted at his presence, wide eyes and raised brows showing their shock at seeing their prince among them.

"If you don't know me," Kylan began, his voice echoing around the destruction. "I am Kylan, the second son of the late King Dominic and now true king of Valmenessia."

Murmurs erupted around Nora, the king's death fuelling the whispers.

"And my first order as king is to put an end this conflict," he continued, his voice carrying over all those gathered. "I call for a retreat of the army to outside the city walls until further notice."

"Traitor!" A soldier barked, storming forward and spitting on the ground. "The true king isn't dead! You are a traitor to his name!"

"My father is dead," Kylan replied calmly. "And if you follow the crown then you will do as I command or show yourself to be the true traitor."

That halted the man's tirade. Soldiers glanced at each other, uncertain of what to do. They had no leader beyond their generals. King Dominic and Lady Elizabeth were dead and if they were truly loyal to the country, they would do as their king commanded.

The general who had shouted for the battle to recommence stepped forward and Nora braced herself for a fight. Kylan straightened his back, watching as the man drew closer. The general dropped to one knee, placing his sword on the ground and Nora almost choked on her surprise.

Other soldiers followed, some Alliance members too, and then the air was filled with a single chant.

"All hail, King Kylan."

The army retreated as Kylan had commanded and there was an uncertain peace, but peace nonetheless. Nora snuck away from the celebrations filling the streets. Some of those remaining were hesitant about what had occurred, but others had seen it as a victory, the start of a new country.

She didn't want to participate. Not when there was only one place her heart wanted to be. After speaking with one of the Healers, Nora made her way towards the northern part of the city. Each step pulled a shaky breath from her lungs.

She stuffed her trembling hands into her pockets and pushed on.

August's body was right where she'd been told he'd be. Nora slowly entered the room. For some reason, she was scared of making a sound as she sat on the floor beside him.

It felt like taking Midskopas all over again, except this time, the loss she felt was not only August but a part of herself, too.

Nora stared at her best friend, her brother, and wished that there was some way to bring him back, even if only for a moment. They had been together for so long, only to be torn apart moments after reuniting. It felt worse than cruel.

Torturous.

Nora was afraid that she would never come to terms with his loss. He'd been the only constant in her life, the one person she knew had her back no matter what and now he was gone.

She ran her gaze over him. She took in his hair that was shorter than the last time she'd seen him, no longer sitting below his chin, having grown down to his shoulders which also appeared broader. Then her eyes moved to where his left arm had once been. August had changed since they'd parted, both in appearance and in himself. She longed to know of his time with the Mors Alvs, of his travels since leaving the mountains and the man he was becoming.

It was the part of him, the only part, that she would never know.

And then there were the changes in her that he had missed out on. All the feelings she was sure he would have loved to tease her about, but would have secretly been happy about. Would he have liked the person she was becoming, the woman without the tattoos that bound her to King Dominic?

Again, Nora would never know. There was so much they couldn't share with each other now. Nora's throat swelled as she realised there would be a lifetime's worth more that she could never share with him the way they always had. Her best friend was gone.

"Hey," Sage said, coming to sit beside her and wrapped an

arm around Nora, pulling her close. Nora rested her head on Sage's shoulder and let the tears finally fall, spilling down her cheeks.

Sage didn't say anything else, just held Nora as she cried. Nora didn't think she could love someone more, but Sage kept teaching her that it was possible. That love was infinite if it was with the right person.

Soon Will and someone named Tyler joined them, and they all sat together on the floor in their grief.

"He would be giving me so much shit if he knew I was sitting here, crying my eyes out," Nora said with a sniff, breaking the silence. "Of course, I'd have the better sarcastic comment."

"Of course," Sage chuckled.

"It feels wrong. He should be here. He'd been through so much. He should have been able to finally live his life."

"Unfortunately, this is how life works," Tyler said, his black eyes were rimmed red, his features drawn. "It's unpredictable and unfair. It doesn't care what you deserve or what is right. You just live it and hope that during the time you're given, you get to experience as many of the good things it has to offer as you can. August may have gone through some terrible shit, but he knew what it was like to love and be loved. I would like to think that I had something to do with that, but the truth is he experienced that through you, Nora, and that's something you should hold onto."

Sobs escaped Nora and she turned into Sage's chest, her grief and Tyler's words overwhelming her. Will shuffled closer and Nora clutched at his shirt, drawing him even closer still.

They stayed that way for a while, mourning not only August but all those they'd lost. The lives that had been stolen all because of a greedy king, imprisoned deities and a Conjurer set on freeing her family.

EPILOGUE

Nora

"What am I supposed to do with that?"

"Feed him," Sage called from the next room.

"He's always eating," Nora groaned. "And he kept me up all night, little gremlin."

"I told you before we took this big step that there would be sleepless nights," Sage said. She appeared in the doorway, leaning her side against the frame. "If you want to raise him right, you have to devote time to his upbringing."

"I didn't know it would be this much work," Nora replied. He was cute, she wasn't blind. But she'd always been of the opinion that anything that adorable was probably evil. That's why so many got lured in so easily. Can't deny a cute face. She sighed heavily, resigned to her fate. "I'm a slave again."

"Don't be so dramatic," Sage laughed. She strode towards the mat before the fire and as soon as she sat down the puppy hopped into her lap.

"I thought a dog would be easy," Nora said, retrieving a treat from a box. "I didn't think it would be bordering on having a people baby."

"People baby?" Sage chuckled. "Trust me, a puppy is a lot easier than that. Come sit, you'll see, all the hard work will be worth it."

"Nope," Nora said. She handed the treat to Sage and quickly stepped back, "That's how he will manipulate me. He'll do the eye thing and nuzzle his little nose into me and then I'm going to be stuck there. Unable to move without feeling guilty. Unless my movement involves doing something for him that it is."

Nora left Sage and the puppy, heading up the stairs of their home that was nestled in the trees, and went into the study, closing the door softly behind her. The walls were covered in charcoal drawings, all sketches August had in his satchel. The bag itself hung on a hook by the window that looked out at Forest's Edge.

The city was still being rebuilt after the Maker's Curse tore through it. Jasmine and Omari employed countless people to aid in the reconstruction of homes and workplaces, as well as artists to engrave the wooden panels of said buildings. The curse had inflicted so much damage on the city, but it had disappeared completely along with Sloane a year ago.

The Conjurer had exploded in a beam of light, taking the three Goddesses with her and ending the imprisonment of the magical races in Valmenessia. The Goddesses' sacrifice had managed to save those with magic in the process, Jord and Nyssa's last act to protect all the people of Valmenessia.

Nora sat in her chair at the desk and took out a sheet of paper. She stared at the blank page, unsure where to begin whilst she toyed with Aren's necklace around her neck. August had written her letters, detailing his time between leaving Fellbun and the war at Midskopas. She'd read them countless times, but only now had worked up the courage to reply.

He wouldn't receive it, though Sage had suggested writing one to help with closure. Nora doubted anything would help heal the hole August's death had left in her heart.

But she picked up her pencil and began.

Dear August,

If you were here, you'd most likely be questioning my mental state because writing a letter, especially one about my feelings, is definitely not something you'd ever believe I would do. You might even think I'm doing this under duress, but surprise, I am writing this to you of my own free will.

To think you believed I'd never surprise you.

I'm not sure what I should tell you, so I'll just start with something easy.

Sage brought home a puppy the other day. Apparently, he's supposed to help us with our trauma. (She's been researching a LOT about it, but that's just typical Sage). She also has me speaking to someone about my feelings after everything. The whole country has been through some shit, and I feel completely ridiculous talking about my problems. I still do.

I go to my meetings though ... the things I do for Sage, huh? What else...

At first, Kylan refused to take any part in ruling the country after his father died but somehow Jasmine and the others convinced him to take it on. Elliot Maker tried to rule too, but that didn't last long, nor did his friend's dreams of taking over the cities.

They all scurried away to their homes across the seas, which by the way, we can go to now.

Magic still exists despite what Evelyn was made to believe. She told me about Sloane's plan after the fight finally ended. I would have been seriously pissed to not be able to summon my fire magic during Frost Season.

Interestingly though, magical races have been appearing outside of Valmenessia. Babies are being born with magic, meaning it was always there, just dormant.

Evelyn still doesn't have her magic, though she seems okay with it. She's too busy being a queen to have time to heal anyone anyway. She and Kylan are currently overseas, meeting with the other rulers and making friends for the first time since, well ever. Evelyn was pretty excited about going to a town called Devotion, though I have no idea why.

Kylan didn't seem too keen on the idea either, but whatever, he does whatever she wants. Kylan is a sucker because he's in love. Easily manipulated.

Kind of reminds me of a certain blond-haired half-brother of his.

Sometimes I find it so weird to think of him like that, but he does remind me of you in some ways, I wasn't lying about that. When he's around I feel like you're still here with me too.

I miss you.

The feeling never goes away. After everything we'd been through, it's so cruel that you're not experiencing this new world by my side. But just know that I carry you with me everywhere I go.

Not literally, because that would be weird and Sage would probably think I'd lost the plot, but you know what I mean.

I did what you asked me the last time we spoke, the whole last name thing, and I hope that in time Sage will, too.

Ugh, I can just imagine you grinning like a madman at that.

Even in death, you make me cringe.

See this is why I've delayed writing this letter for so long. I'm not good at talking about this stuff. You were always the more emotionally attuned one of us.

Anyway, I just wanted to say that for so long I had no idea who I was. I spent years being told to be something and I think if I hadn't had you by my side I would have been truly lost.

It's nice after all these years to finally be able to know who I am.

A daughter.
A sister.
A girlfriend.
A friend.
Most importantly, I am me.
And I exist.
Nora Natsky.

ACKNOWLEDGEMENTS

Since I was a child, it has always been a dream of mine to write a novel and sitting here today, I am proud of not only fulfilling that wish, but going beyond it.

The Valmenessian Chronicles has come so far from what I'd imagined in the early days and that is largely due to the people around me who have given me so much support and advice.

First and foremost, thank you to Mitch. I would never have been able to even begin this endeavour without you. Your encouragement and eternal belief in me has helped make my dreams come true.

Thank you to Liam and Zoe for just being the wonderful people you are. I love you so much.

Thank you to Jess for reading all the versions of my stories, for chatting about ideas and for making me feel like my story was worth telling.

Thank you to my mum and Zia Rita for your never ending love and support.

Thank you to Emily for always going above and beyond. Thanks for all your advice and for working through ideas with me. I appreciate all you do for me.

Thank you to Chloe for being there on the days I thought I'd never finish this book.

Thank you to Jodie for not only Beta reading Vice and Verity but for helping to share my books with the world.

Thank you to K.D. Ritchie at Story Wrappers for another stunning cover. It has been a pleasure working with you.

And finally, thank you to all of you readers for giving this series a chance and for going on this journey with my characters.

If you enjoyed Vice and Verity, please consider leaving a review on Amazon and Goodreads. It would mean the world to me!

About The Author

Rebecca Camm was raised in Melbourne by a single mother who encouraged her passion for reading and all things magical. She has been writing stories since she was a child to help manage her anxiety and make sense of the world.

Rebecca strongly believes in the power stories have in changing lives. Just like her, Rebecca's characters are flawed, yet they are continually learning. Unlike her, they are confident, witty, and just generally more exciting.

Rebecca lives with her husband and two children. When her children allow her free time, she is either writing or attempting to conquer her ever-growing tbr pile.

Stay in touch!

Website rebeccacamm.com

Newsletter rebeccacamm.com/contact

Instagram @readingwritingdaydreaming

TikTok @readingwritingdaydream

Facebook @readingwritingdaydreaming

Facebook Group facebook.com/groups/
rebeccacammsreadergroup

THE FIVE RACES OF VALMENESSIA

HUMANS

- BORN WITHOUT MAGIC OR SPECIAL ABILITIES
- CAN LEARN BE A CONJURER AND WIELD MAGIC THROUGH SPELLS AND RITUALS

ANIMA

- LOOK LIKE HUMANS BUT CAN SHIFT INTO AN ANIMAL FORM
- FAMILIAL ANIMALS ARE COMMON BUT NOT A RULE, ESPECIALLY FOR THOSE WITH MIXED HERITAGE

ELEMENTUM

- LOOK LIKE HUMANS
- CAN WIELD FIRE, WATER AND WIND
- THE STRENGTH OF MAGIC AND THE USE OF INDIVIDUAL ELEMENTS DIFFERS BETWEEN INDIVIDUALS
- MOST CAN ONLY WIELD ONE ELEMENT

Lys Alvs

- Look like humans except for their pointed ears and golden eyes
- Speed healing of themselves and others
- When healing others, they take on the injury and then heal themselves
- Can sense the degree of an injury
- Their healing magic is more powerful during the day
- Some have sharper senses and movements

Mors Alvs

- Look like humans except for their pointed ears and black eyes
- Absorb magic and health from others and some objects
- Can sense a person's race, magical degree and health
- Their magic is more powerful during the night
- Some have sharper senses and movements

NOTABLE CHARACTERS

Nora - Elementum
Evelyn - Lys Alv
August - Mors Alv

NORTHERN ALLIANCE
(Forest's Edge, Midskopas & Fellbun)

Sage - Human
Tyler - Mors Alv
Will - Human
Aeolus - Elementum
Lady Jasmine Royd - Human (Conjurer)
Omari - Elementum
Gemma - Lys Alv
Carl - Anima (Wolf)
Chester - Anima (Fox)
Erik - Human (Conjurer)

SORBY

Prince Kylan - Elementum
Sloane - Human (Conjurer)
Lord Elliot Maker - Human
Verida - Human
Maggie - Human
Phillip - Human
Kai - Human (Conjurer)

ROYAL BAY

KING DOMINIC - ELEMENTUM
ZAIM - HUMAN
RANA - ELEMENTUM
PRINCE XANDER - ELEMENTUM
PRINCESS HARLEY - ELEMENTUM

GODS & GODDESSES

AREN - ANIMA (EAGLE)
THYRA - ELEMENTUM
JORD - MORS ALV
NYSSA - LYS ALV
FRODE - HUMAN

www.ingramcontent.com/pod-product-compliance
Lightning Source LLC
Chambersburg PA
CBHW031434200726
48289CB00001BA/77

* 9 7 8 1 7 6 3 5 2 7 7 2 0 *